THE DANDELION TREE, PART ONE

A.S.R. GELPI

SILVER RIVER
PUBLISHING

Book cover design by germancreative
Cover images: DepositPhotos
Other images: Canva
Map by Cartographybird Maps
Fan Art Illustrations by @colouranomaly, @saramirza_art, @jemeny69, and Sam Balgruuf

Silver River Publishing
P.O. Box 1272
Santa Maria, CA 93456

E-book ISBN: 979-8-9895382-4-9
Paperback ISBN: 979-8-9895382-5-6
Hardcover ISBN: 979-8-9895382-6-3

First Edition: May 2025

To every sister who is as devoted as Saya was to Kharis.
To every woman mentor who is as fierce and courageous as
Yuna was.
To every woman out there who, like Kharis, is stubborn enough to
pave her own road despite the odds.

PART ONE

THE DANDELION TREE

AUTHOR'S NOTE

This is the **second installment** in *The Dandelion Chronicles* epic fantasy series that delves into the story of Kharis, a woman bound by a curse that enslaves her and her sister.

To enhance your reading experience, a brief pronunciation guide is included, along with a comprehensive glossary of terms and detailed explanations at the end of the book.

The Empire of Zahar is depicted as an inclusive society where same-sex couples are an integral and normalized part of the world.

This story addresses a variety of adult themes and situations that may be sensitive for some readers, including:

- The death of a parent, including loss of a pregnancy mid-term;
- Alcohol consumption;
- Violence in a fantasy context, using magic and medieval-inspired weaponry;
- Themes of abuse, assault, suggested stalking, and verbal harassment;
- Medical conditions, some potentially graphic;
- A terrifying fire that burns forests and villages;
- Closed-door, fade-to-black depictions of sexual content and references to sexual awakening;

- Mental health struggles such as compulsive obsession, panic attacks, depression, suicidal thoughts, and PTSD;
- The protagonist experiences vivid nightmares and night terrors.
- There is in-world cursing. No modern cursing is used in this book.

I value you as a reader and encourage you to consider these elements before embarking on this journey through Zahar.

Thank you for choosing to read *The Dandelion Tree, Part One*. I hope this fantastical tale captivates and inspires you as you accompany Kharis on her quest for truth.

A.S.R. Gelpi

GLOSSARY OF PRONUNCIATION

A more thorough list of terms used in this book is available at the end of the book. However, here's an initial list of words to get you started. How you sound the letters in your head will be close enough, so don't sweat it. Go forth and confidently read this book. Welcome to Zahar.

- Adatari Haguru - a-da-TA-ree ha-goo-ROO
- Akumi - A-koo-mee
- Aghet Mendi - A-ghet MEN-dee
- Agham - A-gam
- Akumi - A-koo-mee
- aljaicin - al-ha-ee-SEEN
- Almarim - al-ma-REEM
- Andaheimur - an-HAEE-moor
- Arjun Ghan - AR-joon ghan
- Arisûn - a-REE-soon
- Asurûn - a-SOO-roon
- Barhan - BAR-han
- bhiksun, bhiksunim - BEEK-soon, beek-soo-NEEM
- Chul - chool
- dangu - dan-GOO
- denek - DE-nek

GLOSSARY OF PRONUNCIATION

- Djinnshirukh - GEEN-shee-rook
- Duri - DOO-ree
- Götrid - GHO-0-treed
- Gutxi - GHOOT-chee
- Hala - HA-la
- Haize-Ibiltaria - ha-EE-se ee-beel—TAR-ree-a
- harrizkoetxea - har-rees-kot-CHE-a
- Herisvalen - he-REES-ba-len
- Hesharat - he-SHA-rat
- Hillal - HEE-lal
- Hröld - RO-old
- Ibaia - ee-BA-ee-a
- Jordha - JOR-da
- Kahurang - ka-hoo-RAN
- Kharis - ka-REES
- leagh - LE-ach
- Mahabhal - ma-ha-BAL
- Marya Levandran - ma-REE-a le-VAN-dran
- mavah - MEE-ba
- Mizha - MEE-sa
- Orlen Dëtka - OR-len de-ET-ka
- Rawiri - ra-WEE-ree
- Regia-Zenka - re-jee-a-SEN-ka
- Reza Zhegur - RE-sa ZHE-goor
- Saya - SA-eea
- Sendatorsum - sen-da-TOR-soom
- Sorukhipa - so-roo-KEE-pa
- Taika - ta-EE-ka
- tavah - TA-ba
- Teppe - tep-pe
- Tung - toong
- txakurra/txakurri - cha-KOOR-ra, cha-KOOR-ree
- Urrun - oor-ROON
- Välissa - BA—a-lees-sa
- xakea - cha-KE-a
- Xia Dhan - CHEE-a dan
- Velathari - be-la-TA-ree
- v'leta - BLE-ta

- Yuna Chantarasang - YOO-na chan-ta-ra-SANG
- Zahar - sa-HAR
- Zahar-Ghak - sa-har-GHAK
- Zahar-Homa - sa-har-HO-ma
- Zahari - sa-HA-ree
- Zahar-Eliza - sa-har-e-LEE-sa
- Zahar-Katea - sa-har-ka-TE-a
- Zahar-Regia - sa-har-RE-jee-a
- zaldun - sal-DOON (singular)
- zaldunak - sal-DOO-NAK (plural)
- zenka - SEN-ka

Quick Explanations:

- **The Zahar-Regia** is the imperial walled enclave within Zahar-Ghak, the capital of Zahar. It consists of an inner, middle, and outer ring.
- **The Sendatorsum** is the royal compound at the heart of the inner ring, encompassing the imperial palace and royal residences. The term may appear in its shortened form, the Senda.
- **The Ghak** is the shortened name locals give to the imperial capital.
- **Bhiksun/bhiksunim** - Singular/plural genderless term that refers to monks, nuns, priests, and their acolytes.
- **Expletives** - The most sedate are "blasted" and "fires burn me." Then come "txakurra" and "txakurri." The worst is "spear me and gut me, too," often shortened to "spear me." This book does not use modern expletives.
- **Tavah/Mavah** - informal terms for father and mother used in the private/familiar sphere.
- **Asurûn / Arisûn** - formal terms for father and mother used in the public/court sphere.
- **The Hesharat** is the escort of the imperial king, comprising highly trained White Guard officers.

- **The Velathari** is the escort imposed on the Djinnshirukh, consisting of twelve highly-trained White Guard officers.

THE COMMONWEALTH OF NATIONS

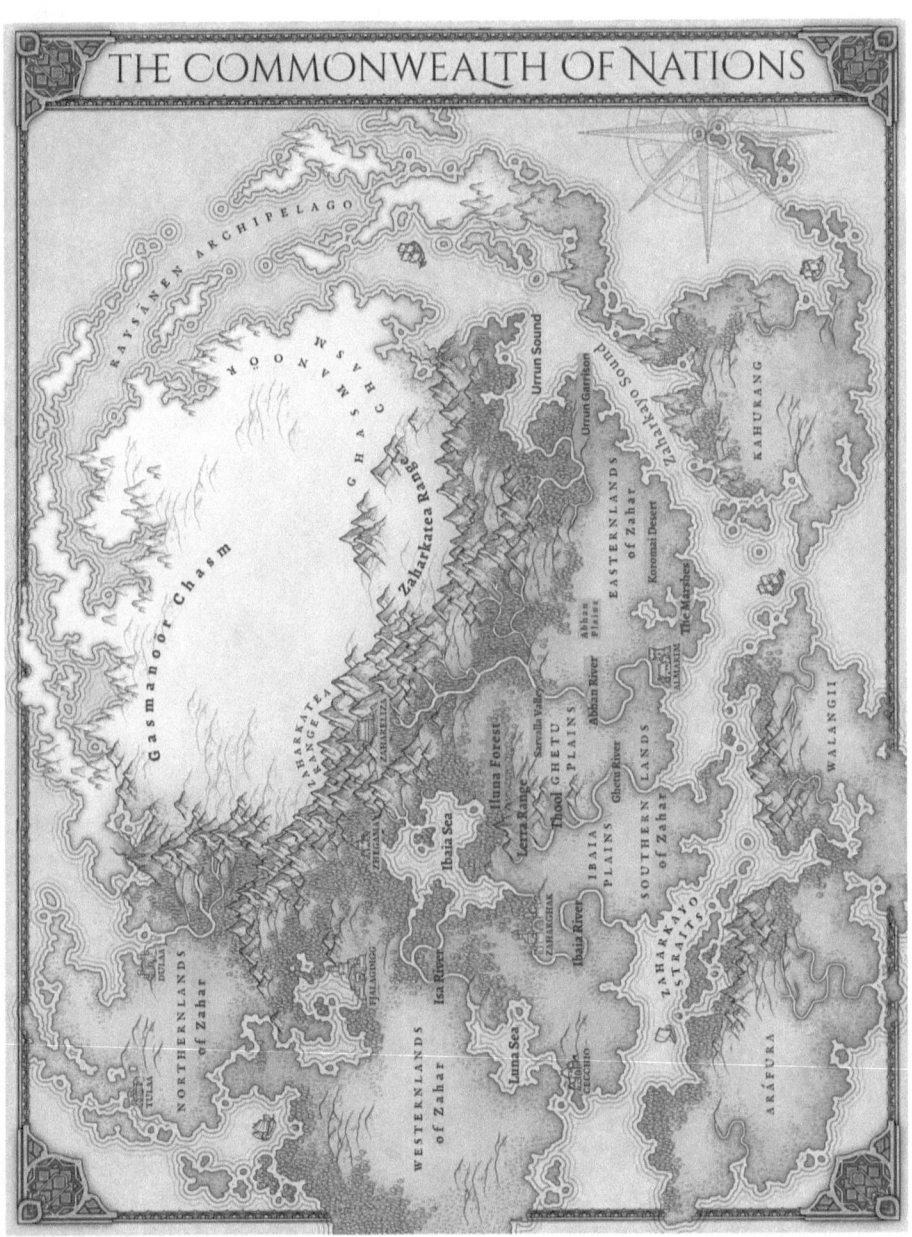

PART ONE
THE SHADOWS LURK

CHAPTER I

KHARIS, THE DJINNSHIRUKH

Release your worries and let them scatter like dandelion seeds in the wind. – Poliormos

Kharis Ghan ground her molars until they ached, biting back the urge to set the world on fire, because, ironically, she possessed the magic to do so. To burn it all. Probably shatter it, too. How easy it would be to surrender to her anger...

Whispers slithered through the crowd, vile murmurs she'd long stopped trying to silence. She strode forward through the Zahar-Regia with her Velathari, her White Guard escort—six ahead, six behind, their armor gleaming, their expressions carved from stone.

The people parted for her, not in deference, but in loathing. Not a single head bowed, defying the respect her title demanded.

A rotten apple core struck the ground near her boots.

"Doombearer," someone muttered. The slur crept like smoke, quietly, menacingly. Another voice echoed it, then another, until it coiled through the crowd in a hushed chant.

"Doombearer. Doombearer."

It rolled like a curse passed in secret. Like a prayer for her undoing.

The Velathari officers neither acknowledged the insults nor intervened to stop them. Her escort wasn't for her protection. It was to protect everyone from her.

The memory of the massacre would cling to her forever. No matter how fiercely she fought to prove otherwise, it shadowed her every step. The insult was damning, but the truth was worse: the power to incinerate the world did reside within her.

Her exhale was slow and measured. Some days, it took everything she had to keep her anger from boiling over and not to drown beneath the resentment swelling inside her chest.

Her day had started with a fight, needled, as ever, by fools who thought her silence was submission. Idiots who believed they stood outside the reach of the proverbial chains holding her back. She could take the jabs; she usually did. But not this. Not when they dragged her sister's name through the dirt. General Salazar had intervened, punishing Officer Duarte—a rare victory. The broken nose she'd dealt Duarte would cost her. She knew that. But this price was worth paying.

Let them mock me, call me a demon and a monster. She'd heard it all before.

But Saya?

No one—*absolutely no one*—touched her sister with cruelty.

That was the line, the only one that mattered.

Ahead, an imposing three-story building rose from the sun-bleached stone.

The second lecture of the day was about to begin.

The Royal Academy of the Healing Arts—hospital and school—housed Zahar's finest healers, all blue-robed bhiksunim. A gilded doorway stood tall, adorned with intricate floral patterns and flanked by fluted columns gracefully supporting a richly decorated entablature.

Humble purpose veiled in opulence.

Waiting in the vestibule stood two women she loved.

Light streamed from a large arched stained glass window, casting dappled colors across the mosaic-tiled floor. Yuna's silver hair, cropped close to the scalp, glinted in that light. The woman was intelligent and cunning, shaped by her indomitable courage. Her memory was as sharp as a blade, forgetting nothing of her sixty-eight years on this good earth. Kharis loved her aunt fiercely, the closest thing to a mother she'd ever known.

Ner nana.

Saya stood beside her, chestnut curls tied back in a simple bun, her golden eyes radiant—gods-touched and unearthly. The Sorukhipa was always a gorgeous mortal, and her sister wasn't an exception. Her beauty was otherworldly, her skin luminous. Even the air around her shimmered with her power.

"Blessed be the earth and sun," Kharis greeted them with a formal bow.

"May they sustain us," came their reply.

Before the last syllable faded, Kharis was already in Saya's arms. The scent of jasmine and orange blossoms flooded Kharis's senses. She clung to Saya for a moment longer, wishing for it to become eternal. Saya was everything to her— sister, tether, truth—and she couldn't imagine a world without her.

Yuna pulled her into a quick, firm embrace, pulled away, and patted her cheek with a knowing smile that made Kharis gulp. "Let's head to my study." She waved off the Velathari with a flick of her hand.

The women walked silently, sunlight filtering through stained-glass windows, painting patterns on the winding staircase. Each step tightened the knot in Kharis's stomach. The lecture was coming—of course it was.

Hoping to delay the impossible, Kharis entered and drifted past the polished mahogany desk to push open the balcony doors. A gust of warm summer air greeted her.

From three stories up, the imperial city sprawled beneath them—plazas, market stalls, buildings, and streets. Bhiksunim queued for roasted chicken skewers; vendors hawked tea and fruit, and children chased one another through the fountains.

What would it feel like to belong to that world?

"To stand in line. To walk free. To die when the Blessed Mother decides it," she said aloud. "Is that too much to ask?"

Yuna's voice tightened. "Gutxi—"

"No, Nana." Her voice trembled with the same ache that whispered how her life would never be hers. "I'm done pretending."

"You're the Djinnshirukh," Saya said.

"Do you think I don't know this?" Kharis shot back, turning around. "That I somehow forgot? Because not a blasted day goes by when I'm not facing sneers, glares, and insults. I'm so tired of it."

Saya gently placed herself between Kharis and Yuna, as if shielding Nana from her. "Please calm down." Her palms rose in a soothing gesture. "You mustn't get angry."

That refrain again.

And the fear behind it—because six years ago, when fury unshackled her will, twenty-seven souls were lost to her magic.

Kharis ground her teeth, jaw tight against the memory.

"I *am* angry, Saya. It doesn't mean I'll burn the world." No matter how tempting it would be to explode and send it all to the Netherworlds of Ifran.

"How can I help?" Yuna asked softly.

"Advocate for me," Kharis replied. "If I can't be free, have the restrictions lifted."

Yuna's brow creased. "Do you think I don't do this?" The hurt in her voice stirred Kharis's guilt. "That I don't beg Hröld, Hala, or the Regia-Zenka ministers?"

Saya reached for Kharis, but she pulled away, facing the balcony. The urge to leap—if only to feel the air on her face before the ground met her—throbbed like a pulse behind her ribs. If she couldn't be free—truly free—was death the only escape left?

"I've done everything I can to show I'm not a monster ever since that blasted, *spear-me-forever* day—"

"Khiri," Saya scolded. "Language."

Language was the least of her concerns. Kharis pressed the heel of her hands against her eyes. "It's been useless. Nothing has changed."

"We're different," Saya insisted.

"How, exactly?" Kharis spun around, badly curtailing her sarcasm. "Go ahead. Tell me."

Saya's lips thinned, her gaze pleading for the conversation to end. Kharis held fast, unwilling to yield.

"It wasn't always this way," she said. "Former Djinnshirukh danced, traveled, and fell in love. Lord Athon had lovers by the dozen. Lord Larek sailed during wartime. Our mavah bore five children. Why am I forbidden from enjoying the same?"

"Former Djinnshirukh were adults who chose these roles," Yuna said. "You were born into them."

"Fine. But why the restrictions? We're no longer children."

The heat crept beneath her skin, magic pulsing hotter with each heartbeat.

"I've done the work," she said. "Countless hours scouring through the Royal Archives, reading every account I've found —a thousand years of history, biographies, and lore. Former Djinnshirukh were denied *nothing* because of the sacrifice they made on behalf of the Empire. A few Sorukhipas were married when the gods called upon them, their eyes turning gold overnight." She turned to Saya. "Should we ignore our dreams when they didn't?"

"I'm not saying that." Saya's voice wavered.

"Why must we live like this?" Her gaze bore into Saya's, searching for her answer.

Saya said nothing.

"Well?" Kharis pushed. "Wouldn't you want to choose how your day will go, not chained to an immortal's curse?"

Saya's brow furrowed, rubbing the skin between her eyes as if she could smooth all the other wrinkles in their lives.

"Of course, I would," she huffed. "Why would I deny myself such an option?"

Kharis sank into the nearest chair, all heat drained from her bones. "Then let me find a way out of this curse."

Fear made Saya's eyes glow. "Khiri, it's dangerous."

"Everything I do is dangerous," Kharis said dryly. "But I will find a way to undo this curse before the Akumi king corrupts my mind and the unraveling begins."

Her gaze found Saya's again.

"And before you, my dear sister," she said quietly, "become my executioner."

CHAPTER 2
THE BURDEN OF MEMORIES

In the darkest moments, courage guides us through, unwavering and strong. Only the fearful are blinded by its light. - Poliormos

Kharis jolted awake, a gasp escaping her lips. The remnants of her nightmare lingered in her mind like a ghostly echo. Slowly, she blinked into wakefulness. Shadows clung to their corners, still and familiar. Only the distant rumble of thunder stirred the night.

She closed her eyes, hoping to fall asleep again, but after a long pause, she groaned silently and sat up.

It was a sweltering summer night. Soon, the monsoon rains would arrive, making the air muggier while filling it with the aroma of petrichor.

Saya slumbered peacefully, the heat never affecting her—an essential condition to deal with an incendiary Djinnshirukh.

Kharis perched on her bed, the marble flooring cool against her bare feet. Her linen shift had stuck to her sweaty skin, and she pulled on the collar, hoping for relief from the oppressive heat. She lifted her braid over her head and fanned her neck. Spotting her water glass, she sipped first, then gulped the rest. Large, cool drops slid down her neck, sending a pleasant shiver across her skin.

She pushed on the latticed doors and stepped outside onto the terrace.

The scent of midnight jasmine clung to the air.

Sharan, the ivory moon, had already sunk behind the western horizon, leaving Tung's red glow to stain the sky. As the lore went, Tung chased after Sharan. When it did, it gave Sharan a red eye for three nights. On this night, the Silver River, an imposing swath of millions of stars, commandeered the night. Kharis got lost in it, perpetually awed by its beauty.

Familiar sounds filled the villa's courtyard. Crickets chirped. Frogs croaked. An owl hiding in the palm fronds hooted a few times. One of the Sendatorsum's mastiffs barked in the distance.

The expected hum from a large city drifted in the air as a bead of sweat rolled down her back, making her shudder.

Leaning on the marble balustrade, she replayed how her day had gone. A morning fight. An afternoon argument with her nana and sister. And then—

Everything tilted.

"Prince Taika has welcomed a son," her father had announced at dinner, his voice steeped in statecraft. *"Kahurang rejoices."*

Once, the prospect of a marriage with him had played with her hopes for the future. She was thirteen, he fifteen—perfect ages for the two nations to enter betrothal agreements and strengthen political ties. Better yet, they'd liked each other. It was an ideal situation, except for one little challenge: Kharis was Zahar's Djinnshirukh.

Had the world been different, she would have married Taika and lived in Kahurang. She would have learned to sail beside Prince Rawiri, and Taika's firstborn son would have been hers.

If only things had been different...

Would she ever break this curse and be free? She begged the Silver River for an answer. None came.

Was this how it would be—where hope dissolved into a whimper, a tumble of broken sounds and dreams?

At twenty years of age, she saw no path forward. No dreams. No life.

The massacre had branded her, and the weight of her chains had increased.

She didn't need the Akumi king's magic to corrode her mind because guilt ate her from the inside. Doubts plagued her, and her past errors constantly replayed in her mind.

She climbed onto the wide handrail, staring at the cobblestones below.

She could jump off. It was high enough to kill anyone, but she wasn't *just* anyone. The Akumi king would keep her alive. He would heal her, the heated gush of magic flooding her entire body, and she would come out of it as if nothing had happened.

It only meant one thing.

She would never escape her fate.

The tiny flame inside her grew, and resentment slammed against the feeble containment she'd built. Why shouldn't she get angry? Sh'd lost everything—her freedom, her peace, even the right to choose her destiny. Anyone else would. Why not let it roar to life and be done with everything?

Her rage snorted and pawed. In her mind, a fierce bull flared its nostrils, releasing puffs of warm steam. Its wild, bloodshot eyes blazed with untamed fury. Its powerful hooves kicked the gates with loud thuds as it bellowed. Her barriers quivered under the relentless onslaught as the beast plowed into them over and over.

Kharis stopped trying, exhausted by her fate. Maybe it was better to surrender—to end it all—and let this beast gore her to death.

If death was how she got her freedom, so be it.

The gate shattered into a million sharp pieces, and Anger, the beast, stepped out, huffing the ground and glaring at her with hungry, bloodshot eyes.

Kharis opened her arms, closed her eyes, and braced for it.

"Breathe!"

Startled, she opened her eyes.

"*Breathe with me,*" the Voice requested. "*Please.*" A deep inhalation resounded in her mind.

She took a greedy breath, her heart drumming painfully. Anger bellowed its frustration as a more substantial and sturdier fence reappeared around it. Darkness consumed the beast, making it disappear.

"*Hold it for five... four... three... two... now out.*"

Kharis surrendered to the ebb and flow of her breaths. He'd opened the proverbial window, and a clean, crisp breeze had blown in. A soft smile lined her face.

"You came."

"*You needed me.*"

The Voice was possibly the madness, but his power illuminated her world. He banished the gray, dispelled the bleakness, and infused her life with vibrant colors. For six years, he'd been her one constant—a flicker of kindness in a world that offered none, a single drop of sweetness in a life steeped in ash.

"*Come down, please?*"

She did, a slow descent from the balustrade. Gentle fingertips made of mist touched her face with an appeasing caress. She almost melted at the soft pressure, hoping to lean into the nonexistent hand.

How could the unraveling be this enticing? If this was the madness, she didn't care.

She let go of everything.

Taika, the boy she'd loved, became a distant memory.

Sailing the seas no longer mattered.

The clamp on her chest vanished.

"*Why do you cry?*" His pleasant voice was a sweet melody floating on a hot summer night.

Phantom arms wrapped around her. "Because you came," she said. "Because you're here."

Perhaps she was going mad, but the loneliness that weighed her down disappeared when the Voice spoke. Maybe he was a construct of the madness afflicting every Djinnshirukh, but how could she ignore something so beautiful and beguiling when her life was gray and bleak, and he offered colors and cheer?

The silence between them stretched—a pause to let her catch her breath in the safety of arms she wasn't sure existed. Kharis smiled through her tears as warmth and security draped around her.

The Voice waited until her mind was quiet again. *"You should not be alone. Come with me."*

Maybe she was losing her mind, but when all else was horrid, this was a small piece of heaven—a promise, a crumb of hope.

"Yes," she whispered into the night. "Take me with you, please."

Kharis drew in one last, steady, deep breath, anchoring herself to the sensation of a phantom hand entwined with hers, and with her exhale, she let go of the world.

CHAPTER 3
SAYA, THE SORUKHIPA

Courage transforms defeat into resilience. - Poliormos

S aya's body snapped upright, pulled by unseen strings. She flicked her curls away from her face and rubbed the sleep from her eyes. Something felt wrong.

When the muslin curtains stirred in the breeze, and through the shifting veil, Saya glimpsed the terrace doors ajar —her sister standing just beyond them, still as stone. She untangled herself from the sheets, unease blooming in her chest, and got up.

"Khiri?" There was a beat of silence. "Is everything all right?"

Kharis didn't stir.

Her snake tattoos, typically invisible, pulsed faintly with an eerie glow beneath her shift.

Saya blinked.

The markings slithered like ink come to life with dark purpose.

Her heart knocked against her ribs. Was the night playing tricks on her eyes? She took a cautious step closer and squinted.

No. They were... moving!

A jolt snapped Saya back from her awe-induced dread.

14

Spear me.

The seals had glowed before, but they'd never moved. Not until tonight.

The Akumi king was attempting to break free, forcing Kharis's inked patterns to glow and shift, fighting the possession. Saya's Sorukhipial power stirred in response, ready to fulfill its purpose. Her magic rumbled in her chest. A deep vibration rose and coated her throat, saturating her vocal cords. Saya parted her lips, and her magic transformed into sound.

"*Khiri.*"

Like a silken thread, her voice glided through the air, wrapping around Kharis to pull her out of the spell. Saya's magic tugged, but Kharis didn't wake.

Saya's heart sank.

Her irresistible magic had faltered.

But she wasn't about to give up just yet.

Saya released another wave of magic—light, not sound. Molten gold erupted from her core and branched through her limbs. Fluttering gossamer ribbons unfurled from her body, twisting and twirling to weave a cocoon of glimmering gold dust that enveloped her sister—a necessary containment against potential failure.

"*Khiri, wake up.*" Saya's magic had become music again. She waited, hopeful.

It didn't work.

The failure confirmed a painful truth: Kharis had become immune to the once-formidable grip of the Sorukhipa's magic. Strength, speed, and self-healing were the Akumi king's gifts in exchange for a mortal body. Seeing Saya's magic as a disease, he eventually rendered Kharis impervious to the Sorukhipa's enchantment.

Now, Saya's only recourse lay with a blade forged by immortals.

She shook her head, unwilling to wield it—not now. Perhaps not ever.

Then hesitation crept in. Her sister's heat warped the air and blurred the world. Its fingers reached for her, mockingly—

daring her. As the Sorukhipa, she knew she could endure it; yet, for one breathless moment, fear brushed her thoughts.

But there was also no time to dance with doubt if she was to contain the demon.

Clenching her jaw, Saya stepped into the blistering radius of heat. The air shimmered with power as if a thousand fireflies had answered her summons—each flicker a vow, a warning, a prayer. Holding her breath, she wrapped her arms around Kharis from behind—skin burning, heart pounding.

Startled by the contact, Kharis emerged from her trance. The heat around her dispersed swiftly. The seals vanished, absorbed into her skin—invisible once more.

The delicate shroud of fine gold dust dissolved in the night.

Saya sighed in relief

"What happened?" Kharis asked after a moment.

"You were walking in your sleep again." A white lie.

Saya said little else, fearful of giving anything away tonight. She nestled her face against Kharis's, her cheek rubbing hers.

Kharis groaned softly, glancing at the night sky. "It's so hot tonight, don't you think?"

Saya didn't comment.

Her magic no longer affected Kharis. And if her sister ever lost control of the Akumi king's power, could Saya kill her before this demon burned the world to cinders again? The thought struck her like a swift arrow to the heart.

She tightened her grip on Kharis, forcing herself to think of nothing and banishing her spiraling doubts. Her heart thudded dully, but her fear coursed hot and wild through her veins.

Blessed Mother... I'd almost lost her.

CHAPTER 4
THE BOUQUET

Love neither has nor gives. Love simply is. - Poliormos

By the time Kharis woke the next morning, Saya was already gone. The Sorukhipa rarely lingered—her duties at the Royal Academy of the Healing Arts always came first.

If only Kharis could summon the same discipline.

With a loud groan, she threw off the covers and forced herself out of bed. Crossing the chamber, she parted the heavy curtains, and sunlight poured in.

Below, the villa's courtyard lay in tranquil order. Fragrant flowerbeds bordered the winding paths, and lemon and orange trees stood in neat rows along the walls, their branches heavy with blossom. Bougainvillea spilled in rich shades of merlot and magenta down the southern face.

A lone gardener worked in the distance—a young man focused on pruning the palm fronds, his wide-brimmed hat shielding his face from the relentless Zahari sun.

Kharis pressed her hand to the glass.

"Are you there?" Kharis whispered, hoping the Voice would answer.

None came. Not even the stir of a thought.

Maybe she truly was going mad.

Still adrift in that silence, she wandered down the sunlit corridor, the long stretch of windows gleaming beside her. She paused, resting her fingertips against the glass. It was already warm—the heatwave unrelenting, promising another blistering day.

A sigh slipped from her lips. Training would be brutal in this heat.

Servants had already parted the heavy curtains in the sitting room when she entered. She drifted toward a broad bay window, her gaze stretched across the Sendatorsum. The outline of the royal palace rose in the distance, partially veiled by tall oak trees. Her villa stood on the eastern edge of the Senda, connected to the palace by a private corridor few were permitted to use.

The windowpane shimmered faintly, catching her reflection and the wavering haze rising from the sun-scorched walls. Kharis's gaze lingered on the world she was forbidden to explore. A quiet longing crept into her chest.

But hunger tugged her back, and with a small exhale, she turned away from the window and toward the oak table, where her breakfast awaited.

The door creaked open.

A servant entered, and her sharp gasp cut through the stillness. Kharis froze mid-step, heart suddenly alert.

"Hello?" she offered a gentle smile, hoping to ease the woman's alarm.

The servant's mouth fell open in silent dread, her eyes widening in recognition. She blinked rapidly, processing *who* was in the room.

"Blessed be the earth and sun," Kharis said softly, keeping her tone even, her posture unthreatening, and trying, as always, to make herself small.

The servant whimpered, her words caught in her throat. Her fingers twitched, fear stealing her ability to move.

The woman's dread wrapped around Kharis like thorned tendrils, tugging at her skin. The stronger the emotion, the sharper and more agonizing the pull grew, as though her skin were truly being torn apart.

Kharis glanced away, seeking a reprieve from the pain. Like a rabbit freed from a trap, the panicked servant fled, her footsteps pounding against the floorboards.

Kharis's pain dissolved in an instant.

Emotions bled into her senses. She could taste sorrow, or hear rage like discordant music. Grief blurred her vision, stealing colors from the world. Fear could sting like nettles on her skin. Some scents coaxed, others clawed at her nose.

This was her life—until she broke the curse.

With a breath, Kharis turned back to her breakfast, resigned. She stuffed a boiled egg into her mouth, struggling to dispel the clouds hovering over her.

Six years of gray clouds.

No matter how hard she tried, people cowered in her presence, and most fled from her. Those who hated her watched her with a spark of revenge flashing in their eyes. After all, she was the Djinnshirukh—the Empire's monster.

How naïve she'd been, believing that she could pursue her dreams.

After breakfast, Kharis donned her uniform—always red, a color she hated—and attached her sword to her belt. She drew the blade with her thumb and then slid it back into its sheath, its click always satisfying... But why?

"Are you there?" she whispered.

There was no response, but she knew the Voice listened, quietly tucked in a dark corner of her mind.

A quick dash down the stairs brought her to the private passageway lined with lavender and rosemary. Their fragrance floated in the air, greeting her this morning.

A hummingbird darted through the hedges, its tiny wings a blur of motion. Its iridescent feathers shimmered as the little bird paused near her. Its rapid hum was audible in the stillness as it sized her up with its tiny black eyes. Then, it zipped back to the blooms, utterly at ease with her proximity.

Hummingbirds always hovered around her, glinting like little gems against the sunlight. Kharis couldn't help but smile at them—gorgeous little things, symbols of good fortune in Zahari lore.

Leaning over, Kharis inhaled the lavender, letting the scent settle over her, when a voice startled her from her quiet reverie.

"Your Highness?"

She straightened, her heart jumping in surprise. The young gardener stood before her, holding a small bouquet.

He took off his hat, offering a respectful bow. "Blessed be the earth and sun."

Suspicion swiftly flickered in her mind. "May they sustain us."

The gardener was no older than she. He was tall and lean, with dark locks framing a somewhat handsome face featuring brown eyes, a long, straight nose, full lips, and a dimpled chin. He wore the customary Sendatorsum livery: an ivory tunic with gold embroidery on the sleeves. Sturdy brown trousers and a lengthy apron, proudly bearing Zahar's coat of arms, a sun with seven radiant flares, completed his uniform.

Discreetly, she glanced around.

Given her exemplary behavior, the Crown had dispensed with her Velathari while she was within the Sendatorsum. She was now acutely aware she was alone with someone who could be seeking revenge. Her hand gripped her sword as she silently prayed she wouldn't have to use it.

"Is there something you need?" she asked, her voice tight.

The young man stepped back, his eyes lowered in respectful deference. He swallowed hard, his Adam's apple bobbing up and down, but he kept his hands out.

"I—I just wanted to offer these." He presented a bouquet of blue hyacinths.

Kharis arched an eyebrow. "Why?"

"They're blue," he stammered, "like your eyes."

Kharis blinked once, then again.

The Zahari considered her eye color ugly—unsettling, they would say, like the eyes of the dead.

Was he mocking her? Or worse, had someone set him up, a poor soul caught in the never-ending game of court intrigue? A game that too often made *her* the target.

"Did someone send you?" she demanded, mistrust sharpening her tone.

20

"No, Your Highness." He glanced at the ground, scuffing it with the tip of his boot. "I just thought... I wanted you to enjoy them." He lifted his eyes hesitantly, a smile spreading across his face.

A fluttery lightness bloomed in her chest. No stranger had ever smiled at her like that.

His bronze eyes shimmered in the sunlight, and the dimples carved into his cheeks gave his whole face a warm, easy glow. His pride reached her senses, its taste honeyed.

No fear. No pain.

Just... an enchanting bouquet of blue blossoms offered in kindness. Her senses could detect no other motive.

In a place where such heartfelt gestures were rare, Kharis found herself both charmed and uncertain about how to respond. All her senses were alive, not with pain but with a thrill she couldn't describe. She still kept her guard up. The Sendatorsum was not like the Iluna Forest, brimming with dangerous otherworldly creatures, but it was still a treacherous place.

"Thank you," she managed to say, accepting the flowers.

Delicate silver veins threaded the sapphire petals. She thanked the Blessed Mother for the kindness that relieved her otherwise stifling existence.

"Your name?"

The young man straightened, hands clasped before him. "Noam Willoway, Your Highness."

"Thank you, Noam." She raised the bouquet to her nose and inhaled deeply. "These are lovely."

Noam squared his shoulders and puffed out his chest as if hoping to make an even better impression. "If it were acceptable," he said, "I could cut more for you." He put his palms up. "But only if you wish, Your Highness. I wouldn't want to impose."

"I would enjoy that."

Noam's grin ignited a soaring sense of joy within her.

"How long have you been with us?" she asked.

"A little over a year now."

"I see." She pressed the bouquet to her nose one more time

while reflecting on the fact that, until today, she hadn't paid that much attention to her staff.

Hope flickered in his eyes, his smile quietly begging for attention. His emotions shimmered—colorful, tender, and infused with the garden's enticing scents. She'd forgotten how honesty manifested through her senses.

"I must head for my training." She clutched the flowers to her chest. "Thank you again for these."

"You're welcome, Your Highness." Noam bowed. "May the warmth of the sun's embrace bathe your day."

A slight tremor coursed through her body. No one had ever been this nice to her outside of Saya and Nana. "May it sustain us."

At first, the Djinnshirukh walked, filled with a tickle that made her heart sing. Before she knew it, she was running the rest of the way.

CHAPTER 5
DETOURS

Sometimes, the required road is the one viewed as an inconvenient detour. - Poliormos

Kharis crossed the Sendatorsum at a brisk pace, her boots thudding against the sun-warmed stone, the bouquet steady in her grip. She kept her chin high and her spine straight. *Walk tall and proud*, she reminded herself, echoing Saya's advice.

She skirted the edge of the central gardens, where lemon trees cast dappled shadows over marble paths. As the grand entrance neared, she slowed enough to breathe. Her grip tightened around the hyacinths. *Steady now.* A long, deliberate inhale filled her lungs, calming the storm of nerves rising inside her.

Then she stepped forward and crossed the threshold, the cool interior greeting her.

With an elegant, if somewhat brittle, smile, she greeted passersby with the customary, "Blessed be the earth. Blessed be the sun."

And just as she feared, the disgust hit her like a war hammer—sharp, painful, searing. She didn't flinch. Her smile held firm, even as frightened stares and hushed voices stirred in her wake. They came from the shadows of arched corridors, from behind silk-draped columns, and from lips barely moving as she passed—murmurs and curses dressed as prayers.

"*Blessed Mother, may she pass quickly...*"

"*Why is she in this section?*"

"*She will eat you whole.*"

"*Go away. Go away. Go away.*"

Never a smile or a kind word. Never a greeting for her.

Kharis quickened her pace, keeping her chin high and her smile wide—polished armor for a war she never stopped fighting. Once she turned a corner and was out of everyone's sight, she steadied herself against a wall, sucking in deep gulps of air to regain her composure. She waited, counting her breaths and allowing the pain to dissolve slowly. After a long moment, she resumed her pace, sticking to rarely used corridors to avoid people.

"One step at a time," she reminded herself.

Her destination was the secluded training chamber ahead of her. She pushed the ornate door open and froze.

Empty...?

An icy wave of dismay washed over her.

"Djinnshirukh?"

Kharis flinched, turning on a heel.

A young woman in green leather armor stood in the hallway—a zenka recruit. She stared at Kharis with a wary eye, keeping a considerable distance.

"Yes?"

"You're expected in the arena," the zenka soldier said, her voice steady despite how tightly her fear coiled around Kharis.

"Are you sure? I never train there."

The woman shrugged. "You're to report to General Aram Zhad. That's what I was told." After a hasty bow, the zenka soldier sped away.

Kharis's arms fell limp. Her joy collapsed like a paper flower dropped in water. "The arena...?"

The bouquet fell from her hands.

Of course. Everyone would be outside on such a scorching day. She cringed at the idea of facing more people and

suffering their hatred in silence. Her initial enthusiasm withered like a flower wilting under a blazing sun.

❧

His Serene Imperial Majesty, King Hröld, Son of the Sun, took a
quick detour. This morning, getting to the State Room to meet
with the Regia-Zenka would have to wait.

This wasn't how his day was supposed to start, but Saya's
request for an audience couldn't be ignored. Anxious, he
headed toward the large arena where Saya was waiting while
his retinue scrambled to keep up. What could it be this time?
Could it be—?

"Your Majesty?" one of the Regia-Zenka ministers, Lord
Miresma, asked.

Hröld halted mid-step, realizing he was deep in worrisome
thoughts. With his hands clasped behind his back, he turned
around, forcing a warm smile.

"I was wondering about the menu for tonight," Hröld said,
half lying. "Monk Anela is taking over the central kitchen
today."

Lord Miresma chuckled, his belly shaking as he did. "He
cares for your health, Your Majesty. He brings his knowledge of
the healing arts because your well-being is his utmost
priority."

The other ministers nodded their approval.

Hröld hummed, feigning his agreement, and resumed
walking with ministers and White Guard officers in tow.

The corridor spilled onto a large balcony overlooking the
vast training arena. On one side, imperial officers exercised in
their ubiquitous white uniforms. At the other end, mahazenka
guards in gray trained groups of recruits dressed in forest
green.

The commanders noticed him on the balcony right away.
Drums announced his presence, a wave of bodies spread
through the arena, and everyone bowed in unison upon a loud
command.

Hröld waved, his gaze sweeping over the sea of white and

25

gray until a single crimson figure caught his eye. Saya stood apart—her leather cuirass as red as an ember against ash. He motioned for her to join him on the balcony.

The ministers took their leave and strolled away. His White Guard escort, the Hesharat, remained.

The young woman ran up the stairs, and a slow smile blossomed on his face—his kind, loyal, and dependable Saya.

Not born to royalty, much less nobility, bhiksunim had brought the orphan to the Sendatorsum when she was a mere toddler. Breaking tradition, he adopted the Sorukhipa child, bestowed upon her the title of high princess, and decreed the same birthmark for Kharis and Saya.

"Asurûn." The formal Zahari word rolled off her tongue, a term reserved only for public ceremony and profound respect. "Blessed be the earth and sun."

"May they sustain us." He hugged her, the scent of jasmine in her hair soothing, then whispered, "What must you discuss with me?"

❧

A knot coiled tight in Saya's stomach, not looking forward to this conversation—what it implied—and pulled away from him.

"It happened again," she said softly, conscious of the Hesharat's presence standing within earshot. They were sworn to utter loyalty and discretion, but on this... She couldn't even trust them.

Hröld's shoulders tensed, rising as if to absorb a blow. For a breath, he looked older than his fifty-seven years. His fingers curled around the balcony rail, knuckles turning white.

"When?" His voice was low. Steady. But she saw the fear tightening behind his eyes.

"Last night." She concealed her concern behind a mask of duty and objectivity. "I woke her up, Tavah." The private word slipped free before she could stop it, its warmth and intimacy so at odds with the tense moment. "She came out quickly with my spell." Uttering the lie burned her, but if she didn't, she was sentencing her beloved sister to death.

Her father gulped, the tension visible in the column of his throat. "These are happening more frequently. Have you seen any sign that she can stop them?"

There was only one way to stop them.

Defeat weighed her shoulders down. "No."

A shadow passed over his face.

"Former Djinnshirukh went mad twelve to fifteen years after the resealment ritual." His voice quivered with dread. "Kharis is twenty, already pushing whatever is left of her luck. We must hide her condition. If the Regia-Zenka finds out—"

He couldn't finish the sentence. Glancing away, he focused on the arena—only for his eyes to widen as the color drained from his face.

Saya followed his gaze.

There was one more uniform in the arena—another crimson uniform.

CHAPTER 6
THE CRIMSON WARRIOR

In pursuing another's favor, one often loses sight of one's truth. -
Poliormos

K haris lingered near the arched entrance, contemplating what to do.

The Zahari sun peeked in through the open patches of fog, a molten eye peering down, alerting everyone that it would shine proud and fierce. On the horizon, dense thunderclouds gathered. A rainstorm loomed, thickening the air with rising humidity.

Kharis shielded her eyes, scanning the crowd for Saya.

Her fingers curled around the edge of a stone column, absently tracing the time-worn grooves. Anxiety churned in her stomach. *Walk in—or go home?*

Her breath came faster as indecision gripped her.

A sudden shiver crawled across her skin as though icy spiders skittered over her flesh. It came with a stale, musty scent and a bitter taste in her mouth. Sensing the intense gaze boring a hole in her back, she turned slowly.

Brown eyes with tiny black flecks stared at her. His wicked smile widened, sharp and menacing.

Some said he was disarmingly handsome—a man of forty-eight, with a velvety voice and an irresistible face. But to Kharis, he was vile and ruthless. His presence radiated an ugly aura that made the hair on her arms stand on end. Despite being a White Guard general, he wore impeccable black armor studded with silver rivets and buttons. The leather was intricately embossed with vines and swirls of twisty, thorny tendrils.

General Aghet Mendi.

"Imagine running into you here," he drawled, his tone mocking. "Do you plan to join us?" His eyes fixed on her hand, pressing against the column. "Perhaps you're better suited to be a decoration." He smirked, moving closer to her. "My quarters could use one as pretty as you. Care to come?"

Kharis pinched her lips, struggling not to utter something foul. That small flame inside her flickered—then flared.

Aghet's harassment was relentless, his barbs carefully crafted with a sinister intent—resealment. He thrived on her distress, seeking to unravel her composure and goad her into striking back. His words were bait, carefully laid to provoke a mistake—to give the Regia-Zenka the excuse Arjun Ghan needed to end her.

Some days, walking away took every ounce of restraint.

"You should accept my invitation." He leaned closer, breathing her in with revolting satisfaction. "I'll make it worthwhile," he purred.

Her body recoiled as his emotions smothered her senses like oil and ash—bitter, burning, invasive. A rancid taste flooded her mouth. The stench of rot violated her nostrils, forcing her to hold her breath. His voice droned on like a swarm of flies buzzing over carrion.

Aghet regarded the crowd with a curious hum. "This should be interesting. You. Them." He flicked his eyes toward the mass of soldiers ahead. "So much love to be had. And at the center of it, you, a pretty decoration." He chuckled softly. "I hope your sword is sharp. Six years ago, I saw it in action."

Kharis froze.

The whispers of vengeance still echoed through the palace corridors. They would never allow her to forget, live free of that day, nor escape the ever-present symbolic target rigidly attached to her back.

Aghet gave her an assessing look as he strolled past her. "You have something that belongs to my prince." He cocked his head, giving her a penetrating stare. "Soon enough, it will be his." His smile turned sinister. "Or perhaps mine?" He waggled his eyebrows. "The invitation to decorate my bedroom still stands." His cape billowed sideways as he disappeared among the crowd.

Kharis huffed at his threat. She was going to show him—show them all. Taking a deep breath, she squared her shoulders, conjured her courage, and stepped forward.

Spear me.

It wasn't a gathering of soldiers but an ocean of them. The first group stopped and saluted, but didn't return to their training, stunned to see her here.

What came next wasn't a wave. It was a storm threatening to sweep her off her precarious ledge. Their anger made everything brighter and jagged, distorting details to make them grotesque. Its metallic taste burned her tongue. But fear...

Fear brought on the thorny vines.

They crept slowly toward her, coiled around her ankles, then climbed up her legs and wrapped around her, tightening their grip, squeezing her breath out.

Her stride faltered.

Breathe, she told herself. With her eyes forward, she headed for the White Guard's section as instructed, one foot before the other, reminding herself that the pain was in her mind, not real.

The soldiers watched, frowning or raising eyebrows in her direction. Their whispers pricked her skin, so she picked up her pace to escape the onlookers.

Ahead, she spotted General Aram Zhad, an elite member of the White Guard.

Kharis summoned more courage, but her jar was already empty. She shrank as more eyes locked on her—more stares, more hatred, more pain. The vines constricted her with merciless force, the thorns digging deeper into her skin, prickling and burning. Her heart drummed faster. Her legs refused to move.

"*I can help you,*" the Voice said, gentle and comforting.

Kharis discreetly peered over her shoulder, only to see the soldiers exchanging angry comments, mouthing insults, and glaring at her.

"I must do this," she whispered, sweat rolling down her temples. "It must be me. I must show them."

"*Let me help you,*" he replied, his whisper alluring. "*You are not alone.*"

"I'm doomed if I can't do this."

All those eyes condemned her, demanding retribution. Hundreds and hundreds of them. A parade demanding her execution.

The pain became unbearable.

Fear pushed common sense aside. The memories of the massacre assaulted her. Her world began to spin.

"*Let me help you,*" the Voice insisted this time. "*Allow me to lend you a hand.*" A pause. "*Please.*"

She tried not to sink into despair, struggling to regain her breathing. But fear took hold of her, and the dark memories from her past danced before her eyes: Saya disappearing behind a wall of White Guard officers; her blade, dripping with blood; garnet rugs; crimson walls. Red splattered everywhere.

Doombearer.

A different vision assaulted her next. The rising heat from the sun-scorched ground blurred the edges of the arena. But the heat didn't make her skin crawl. Hundreds of dead bodies covered it, bathed in puddles of their blood. She'd killed them all.

Other visions flickered before her. Fire-stained fields. The charred remains of cities. A world turned into fire and ash, its glory now in ruins. If she couldn't control her panic, the Akumi king would awaken.

His power would be unleashed.

And he would be unstoppable.

Blessed Mother... She shouldn't be here. Couldn't be here.

The murmurs multiplied. "Doombearer. Doombearer." The title echoed like the relentless pounding of a funeral drum.

No, she reminded herself. *My name is Kharis. I'm not a monster.*

More tendrils twisted around her, their thorns jabbing her skin. The pain became excruciating, and the threat of paralyzing anxiety turned into a wave that shoved aside everything, allowing no other thoughts to enter the mind.

Her training always took place away from people. One of Yuna's trusted bhiksunim kept watch, always ready to assist her or call for breaks. Today, she was on her own, sinking fast into a panic attack.

The pain wasn't just in her mind. It burned her body. It scorched her soul.

She panted hard, eyes shuttering. "Please, help me."

"*Always.*"

Kharis felt a surge of cooling comfort.

A bright flash of dark red overwhelmed the fringes of her vision. Guided by the Voice, she leaped into the void.

CHAPTER 7

CRIMSON IS A CURSED COLOR

Fate's shadow looms long, but even in darkness, the will to defy burns brighter than despair. - Poliormos

G eneral Aram Zhad let out a sharp tsk. Princess Kharis was sauntering toward his section. A cold sweat invaded his body. *Why is she here and not with Salazar?*

He spotted the Sorukhipa on the balcony across the arena, standing beside the king. She wouldn't make it in time, would she?

Burning fires of Ifran.

Aram Zhad knew her story. It was best to avoid the Djinnshirukh altogether. His only hope was for Princess Saya to retrieve her sister. He glanced over his shoulder and caught her running down the stairs.

He pondered ideas to delay the inevitable.

Princess Kharis closed the distance, her cold, assessing gaze fixed on him. His heart immediately thumped against his ribs. This wasn't the match he wanted this morning. Venting a resigned breath, Aram Zhad walked toward her to create more space between her and his unit, signaling his men to stay back —that he would handle her.

Take it slow. Survive.

33

He approached with unhurried steps, hoping the delay would give Princess Saya the time to reach them.

"Good morning, Your Highness." He did his best to stay calm, breathing to still his galloping heart. His smile didn't waver. "Blessed be the earth and blessed be—"

"May they sustain us," the princess cut him off, uninterested, her eyes looking for someone in the crowd.

He was tempted to glance in the same direction. "I see you're ready to train this morning." His lips twitched, and he hoped it was because of a smile. "It's an honor to have you join us." A lie. A big one.

She peered over his shoulder, leveling on the balls of her feet. Her brow puckered, and her eyes darkened. Then, a broad grin lit her face.

Goose bumps crawled the length of his body.

"I'm glad to be here." Her voice had a dangerous edge. "Especially today."

Aram's smile never faltered. Although he wanted to check whatever caught her attention, he kept his eyes on her. Subjects of conversation swirled in his head, dashing past too quickly. He had to engage her a little longer and give the Sorukhipa the time to reach them. "I see you're in great health."

She quirked an eyebrow.

A sweat drop rolled down his temple, sliding down his neck and under his gorget. "It's such a hot day, don't you think?"

Kharis shrugged half-heartedly.

Blasted idiot, she breathes fire. The general swallowed hard. "Salazar and I have been discussing training strategies for you." It was worth a try to find out why she was here.

The Djinnshirukh frowned. He couldn't tell whether it was his comment because her attention was elsewhere, her gaze gleaming with something akin to loathing. Then, suddenly, a dark grin curled across her lips. Whatever she'd been looking for, she'd found it. Without a word, she drew her sword and strode ahead, eyes fixed ahead.

Aram blocked her way forward.

Her hiss snapped every one of his nerves to attention.

"Move," she snarled at him.

"Stand back."

She ignored him, moving to march past him.

He shoved her back. "I won't repeat it. Stand. Back."

Faces turned in their direction.

She angled her head, assessing the man before her. Her glare made him shudder. A beat of silence stretched between them. "Have it your way," she said.

She pounced.

Aram Zhad barely had the time to draw his sword.

He cursed.

Sparks flew as their blades collided. His muscles strained with the effort to force her back. The princess countered with swift parries, her sword whistling as she moved without hesitation to get past him and seek her target.

Her strength, speed, and agility were otherworldly. If she were serious, he would've been dead already.

He dodged her counters while preventing her advance. But the Djinnshirukh was ambidextrous, exceptional in combat, and the Akumi king powered her body.

Aram deflected her attacks and pushed her away, using the length of his blade to keep her at bay.

Her gaze betrayed a sense of urgency as if whoever she sought would slip away unless she could swiftly dispatch this obstinate obstacle standing in her path.

"Move it," she growled at him. "Get out of my way."

Where is she trying to go?

Aram cut the air with his blade, swinging it hard toward her. To his surprise, she dodged, sinking into the ground as his momentum swung him around, his back to her.

He realized his mistake and swore.

"I'm done with you." Already down, she threw a leg sweep, hitting his ankles hard and fast.

His left ankle cracked. His knee popped. A painful explosion shot up his leg, and a burst of formidable white light overtook his vision.

He braced for her hit. It didn't come.

❧

Saya blocked Kharis's advance with her Firegrazer sword, its supernatural hum filling the air.

"Khiri, he's down."

"Get out of my way." The rage in Kharis's voice could scorch the world. "Move it." Her eyes shimmered red, tiny flames dancing in them.

Saya clenched her jaw, holding her ground as their blades locked. Neither woman yielded their place. But Kharis was far stronger, and Saya's muscles screamed under the strain.

"Khiri, stop," she gasped, gritting her teeth as she drew on her Sorukhipial magic to bolster her strength. A controlled burst. Just enough.

But if she summoned too much—if she tapped too deep—she could trigger the resealment magic. Once awakened, Saya wouldn't be able to stop it.

"Khiri, please."

"I said, move it." Kharis's voice deepened into a threat. She shoved Saya, knocking her off balance. Saya quickly steadied herself, raising her blade, while Kharis began to pace like a caged predator. "Let me through," she snarled, her gaze sweeping the crowd with a fierce urgency. "Move."

White Guard officers had closed in to help General Zhad, lifting him from the ground. Healers were running to them with a stretcher.

Too many eyes. Too many witnesses. The Regia-Zenka would know of this by nightfall.

"Khiri, please," she whispered, desperation threading her voice. "You must snap out of this."

But Kharis was gone. A different set of eyes stared at her.

Saya's Firegrazer pulsed beneath her fingers, its power reverberating through the blade, surging up her arms in rhythmic waves. Her muscles trembled under the strain, aching from the effort of holding back.

Forged by the immortals to recognize the Akumi king's essence and imbued with the magic to defeat him, the sword sang, ready to fulfill its task: to strike down the vessel before the demon fully rose.

Saya's breath shuddered. Her grip faltered. She couldn't do it.

Steel flashed.

Kharis had lunged, taking advantage of Saya's hesitation. Her blade crashing against the Firegrazer with a resounding clang. The impact rippled through Saya's arms. The Firegrazer wailed. Kharis attacked again, moving with precise, relentless strikes against the Sorukhipa.

The two sisters clashed. Their weapons sliced the air with the power of those who wielded immortal magic. The Fire-grazer hummed fiercely, the metal singing each time it met Kharis's blade. But Kharis was intent on getting past Saya. Her strikes grew more lethal with every swing.

Saya's magic stirred, its call growing louder. *Blessed Mother.* Panic surged in her chest.

The soldiers watched—a rapt audience that High General Arjun Ghan would use as witnesses to call for Kharis's execution.

Saya's body moved on its own, years of training driving her steps, as her mind frantically sought a way to save her sister. Her beloved Kharis was lost to a firestorm, and someone else stared back through those ominous crimson eyes.

The Firegrazer hummed in anticipation—waiting.

Saya's blade clashed fiercely against Kharis's. A burst of shimmering gold dust erupted with the collision, and the blast pushed Kharis back, giving Saya the space she needed.

"If you protect her," she challenged the Akumi king, "you'd better shield her from this." Her magic morphed the Firegrazer into a short lance.

Kharis snarled, her eyes blazing as Saya hurled the spear. It cut through the air, turning into a bolt of gold dust once it struck Kharis's chest. Her body recoiled with the impact, her sword flying in the air before she crashed to the ground.

Saya sprinted forward, guilt gnawing at her, and gathered her sister's limp body into her arms. Her hand felt the faint rhythm of her sister's heartbeat, and Saya exhaled with relief.

Now, a raging fever consumed Kharis. The Akumi king had moved swiftly to heal Kharis's wound while refusing to relinquish the bodyhe'd possessed.

Saya squeezed her eyes shut, reminding herself she'd saved her sister from a crueler fate. Turning her gaze toward the group behind her, she said, "I'm so sorry, General Zhad. I should've gotten here sooner."

General Zhad, leaning against an officer, shook his head, a kind smile tugging at his lips as if he understood the terrible burden of her imposed destiny.

White Guard officers moved the soldiers away, commanding them to return to their sections. The crowd parted to let the bhiksunim through with stretchers. The Velathari approached, offering Saya their assistance and forming a protective wall around the princesses.

"What a match," one officer said, awe singing in his voice. "One more chance, and you would've had her, sir."

"Don't be ridiculous," General Zhad barked at the soldier. "Princess Kharis is the Djinnshirukh. Only the Sorukhipa can defeat her."

Saya's heart sank into a somber abyss. By nightfall, the Regia-Zenka would demand answers—and possibly, resealment.

CHAPTER 8
THE END OF ALL THINGS

Every ending carries the promise of a new beginning. - Poliormos

Kharis had jumped, but when her feet struck solid ground, she wasn't in the void. She recognized this dark place: a dark, damp tunnel she'd walked countless times in dreams and memory, but where was the void? A chill licked at her spine, seeping deep into her bones.

Tangled roots jutted from the earth like gnarled little fingers, clutching at her feet and making her stumble. She caught herself against the wall, her palms grazing over spider-webbed cracks. Slick, spongy mushrooms grew on the wider fissures, casting a faint, flickering glow that threw shifting shadows across the dam stone. Little things skittered across the moist ground.

It was quiet now, but Kharis knew what stalked this place, a relentless entity lurking beyond sight that would eventually detect her presence. Every shadow seemed to leap at her. Every whisper turned to thunder—

"Come," a child's voice called gently from that darkness.

Kharis flinched.

The echo dissipated as quickly as it had appeared, and silence once again reclaimed the tunnel.

Then came the hiss—low, vicious, distant. The tunnel's Shadow had sensed her. Awake, it was searching for the intruder.

The fine hair on her nape prickled.

"This way," the child urged again, more insistent this time. "Come."

With no better option, Kharis pressed forward, following this voice, winding through the narrow passage until it ended abruptly in a stone wall. A dead end. Her annoyance flared. Had she followed this voice for nothing?

Another hiss slithered through the air, louder, closer, followed by the rasping scrape of claws against the rock.

"Over here." The voice whispered, this time threading through a series of thin cracks in the rock ahead.

Kharis leaned closer. "Where are you?"

"Outside," the child replied.

Suspicion flickered in Kharis's chest, but she pressed an ear to the wall, her eyes narrowed to focus. "How do I—?"

A deep crack fractured the silence. The wall groaned. Kharis stumbled back as the rock split apart. The shaft filled with a choking plume of dust. Coughing, she fanned her arms to clear the air when a gust of fresh air sliced through the dust, revealing a gap wide enough to slip through.

She'd barely registered the opening when the hiss returned —a low, guttural sound reverberating along the walls. The Shadow loomed, monstrous and fluid, stretching in all directions. Cursing under her breath, Kharis shoved herself through the narrow crack, the jagged rock scraping against her body as she forced her way through. With a final heave, she stumbled into a small clearing in the woods.

She knew the tunnel's every twist—but leaving it was new.

Ahead, moonlight filtered through the dense canopy, its silvery glow cascading over the ancient trees and scattering across the forest floor. Behind her, the opening had vanished, revealing nothing but hard rock and twisted shrubbery as if it had never existed. An owl's hoot made her jerk, fists instinctively raised. The bird perched on a branch, its lambent eyes fixed on her with mild curiosity.

A child's soft giggle floated through the air. Her unseen companion was amused.

Kharis sighed heavily. "Where are you?"

"This way."

Kharis didn't move, waiting for the slightest hint of movement or a shift of shadow.

Ahead, a small figure flickered between the brush. The child then halted. "Will you help me?"

Kharis's guard was already up. Nothing here had ever offered help without a price.

"How?" Kharis asked warily. "Are you trapped here, like me?"

"Some days, I am." The voice, tinged with quiet sorrow, hinted at a girl. "Other days, I can leave."

Kharis tilted her head, uncertain. "Do you need help leaving?" The question felt hollow since she had no idea how to. "I'll help you." She bit her lip, waiting for a reply. When none came, "Do you have a name?"

A moment passed in loaded silence.

"This way." The girl's shadow darted from behind a bush and waved an urgent arm, urging Kharis to follow.

"Where are we going?"

"They told me to get you," the child replied, skipping lightly between trees and thickets as if she belonged in this place. "Come. They wait."

Kharis's blood chilled. *They?* That never boded well.

"Who?" Kharis pressed, but the child sprinted ahead.

Clicking her tongue, Kharis followed, weaving up a steep path. A pervasive metallic tang hung in the air, pestering Kharis's nose. Up ahead, a crimson glow outlined the child's silhouette. It couldn't be the sunrise, not with midnight stars still littering the heavens above.

Kharis slowed, a cold tingle spreading through her chest.

"Come," the girl called from the summit, her small arm swaying in a beckoning gesture.

Heaving a resigned sigh, Kharis scrambled up the last few paces, loose rocks shifting under her boots, but when she reached the flat summit, she sucked in a sharp, scorching breath that burned her throat. Ahead, dark, dense clouds veiled Sharan and smothered the stars. The sulfur stench clawed at her nose and throat, making her eyes tear. The air glowed scarlet, thick with ash.

And in the distance, a massive fire raged, swallowing the horizon and devouring the entire landscape.

"You must end it," the child gestured to it. "This is what they said."

"The fire?" Kharis stammered, hating how her body trembled with fear. "Did I do this?"

"I've been told that all the writings end with you, but if you don't finish them, you will end this world." She sighed with such sadness in her voice as she gestured ahead. "They want you to end this."

Dread crawled up Kharis's spine. The fire consumed everything in its path like a starving titan.

Ash flakes fluttering like midnight moths. Towering flames licked at the sky, their orange and crimson tongues twisting and writhing like vengeful spirits. Fire lightning struck in the turbulent air, starting new blazes. The intense heat spawned destructive fire whirls that moved with terrifying speed. In the horizon, mountains blew their tops, belching fire and smoke.

Searing dry gusts blew black hair strands off her face, and Kharis turned away, shielding her eyes with an arm.

"You must end it." The child's voice became a whispered echo as she melded into the night.

She'd known this place, but she wasn't sure how. Pristine meadows and ancient forests now burned. Once vibrant with life, the quaint villages had been reduced to smoldering rubble. The woods where she'd chased the wind and the trees had whispered their secrets were now nothing more than charred skeletons. The echoes of laughter shared with friends turned into a choking word.

Doombearer.

And in that desperate moment, her heart shattered, and her knees hit the stone.

Jarring sounds hit Kharis's ears: harrowing screams, the

thunder of hooves and paws hitting the ground, the clamor of birds escaping the blaze, the resonant boom of thunder. Explosions roared in the distance. Debris whistled past her ears in shrill, high-pitched skirls.

You must end this, the girl had said.

Her heart twisted as the heat stung her eyes. The command —so final, so cruel—left her heaving.

"What writings am I supposed to finish?" she screamed, utterly confused. "How do I end this?"

She screamed at the gods who had given her a task she didn't understand. She screamed and screamed until there was nothing else left inside her, until it shredded her throat, and she was but broken pieces scattered in a broken, unsavable world.

Panting, she staggered to her feet and wiped her tears, blackened by the ash they collected as they slid down her cheeks.

"If I must end it," her voice was low and menacing, "so be it. Let the gods watch. Let them tremble."

Usually dormant beneath her skin, her snake tattoos emerged, pulsing a fierce, molten red. The dam holding the Akumi king's power cracked, the fissures quickly spreading like fractured glass.

Kharis had been trained to suppress his magic. Now, she let it rise like a river swollen with sharp, jagged spikes.

Clouds gathered above, darkening the skies further. The hot wind picked up speed, swirling and merging into a turbulent vortex. Ash twirled in a frenzied dance. The ground rumbled beneath her feet like the slow, powerful beat of ancient drums. The vibrations thrummed through her bones as if the heartbeats of the world had answered her call.

Her voice surged, resonating as if ten thousand of her spoke in unison.

"I call upon the Fires of Creation."

The time had come for her to end this and start anew. Bolts of lightning clawed at the blackened sky, their brilliant flashes illuminating the swirling mass of smoke. The air hummed, alive with the crackling energy of a hundred storms. She raised her palms, ready to receive.

"I summon the key—"

Her words cut off abruptly when a pair of arms wrapped around Kharis from behind, and a heartbeat not her own pulsed against her back.

CHAPTER 9
THE VOICE

If you sit still long enough, you will hear love's gentle whisper,
exuberant and sultry as a warm summer's day. - Poliormos

The moment his touch met her skin, the storm in her mind dissipated like steam from a cup of tea going cold.

"I found you," a soft, silvery male voice whispered in her ear, the sound cascading into her mind like a cooling waterfall. "You must not wander unprotected."

The Voice.

"But the land—" she began.

"It matters not," he said. "Look."

Past the cliff, the valley lay in peaceful slumber, wrapped in the sweet scent of midnight flowers and the symphony of crickets. Wisps of fog drifted through the ancient woods. The tallest trees resembled islands floating in the mist. Above, Sharan glowed, serene and majestic, while Tung, the tiny red moon, trailed behind.

"Everything was burning," Kharis whispered. "The world was on fire."

"A dream within the dream," the Voice said.

Her shoulders slumped, and the urge to argue drained

away. Then, Kharis became aware of his steady, rhythmic breath. The realization struck her swiftly: The Voice was not in her mind.

He wasn't darkness gliding through her thoughts.

Or a deep, resonant whisper caressing her ears.

He was standing behind her as if he'd become flesh.

A shiver of curiosity, her ever-relentless vice, sparkled through her, igniting a thrill she wouldn't suppress. As his touch fell away, Kharis turned slowly.

The Voice was a mesmerizing dance of billowing black mist and shimmering stardust, shifting and rippling like the surface of a restless sea. Her mouth parted, but no words tumbled out. Her gaze followed the rise of the shimmering mist until it found his eyes—a blue so deep they bordered on black, flecked with silver like stars adrift in midnight. His was a glorious gaze, the one constant in a form that refused to hold shape.

A hesitant but genuine smile tugged at her lips. His eyes softened, the subtle shift in their glow tender as if he were smiling back.

His presence—otherworldly and vast—held her in thrall. "Is this your true form?"

He leaned in closer, his indigo eyes blazing with quiet intensity. "I shall make it whatever you wish it to be."

Frustration rumbled in her throat.

He leaned back. "Should I leave?"

"No." Her palms went up. "I didn't mean it that way." She shifted her weight, and her gaze slid to the valley. "It is you," her smile widened, "but how?"

"Why not?" His voice resonated with a deep, sensual timbre.

"Am I in Andaheimur?" she asked.

He chuckled softly, the sound low, rich, and tinged with amusement. "Perhaps."

Kharis groaned. "You certainly enjoy teasing me."

The Voice laughed, pleased. "I shall do more if you wish me to. Should I?"

Every nerve in her body snapped to attention. Was the

Voice... flirting with her? It stirred a strange, intoxicating warmth that settled in the pit of her stomach. And the most surprising part? She didn't want him to stop.

He inclined his head, meeting her gaze with quiet scrutiny. Waiting for her answer, she realized. When she didn't, he gently asked, "Are you well?"

"Yes," she whispered, finding it hard to tear away from his intriguing eyes and the universe collected in them. Warmth flushed her cheeks at his proximity. "Everything's fine."

His deep hum shook her heart. Even her soul luxuriated in that voice.

His gaze drifted across the landscape, and its mischievous glint faded. "I have wished for my freedom for as long as I have been imprisoned." His long sigh stirred the mist that shaped his face. "To wander this land once more."

His eyes found hers again, softer now. "But now, I am unsure I want it if it means leaving you." A few heartbeats passed in silence, the air thick with unspoken emotions. His voice dropped lower, raw. "You make me question everything."

Her mind, once foggy with thoughts of him whispering in her ear, sharpened into focus. "What do you mean? Wishing for freedom? Leaving me?" More questions jostled in her head, including a question that had nagged at her for a long time, pushing her to summon the courage to ask.

"Are you the Akumi king?"

His eyes burned with an unreadable emotion. "You have asked this before."

"And you've never answered," she scoffed, crossing her arms. "Maybe this time you do?"

The glow in his eyes guttered. "I am bound by punishment like him," he said quietly.

"For destroying the world?"

"No." His exhale was deep; centuries of pain carried in a single breath. "For saving it."

Kharis frowned, her confusion knotting tighter. The swirling haze shifted with a subtle shake of his head. "I was one of four who fought to stop him."

Her eyes widened. "Like in the song?" Her voice trembled with wonder as she recited a few verses. "A thousand years ago, four warriors came with their armies. They fought his darkness. They brought the sun. Four warriors came with their armies, and the battle was won."

She gazed at him, questions churning in her mind. "So, are you?"

"Yes."

Her voice faltered. "I don't understand. I thought you were him."

Another sorrowful sigh escaped him. "Not the Akumi king —I am the Pharos of Hegra."

"Hegra?" The name snagged in her thoughts like a thorn in cloth. She'd searched for this place in vain, but it didn't appear on any Zahari map.

Once, a ghostly woman had whispered, *"In Hegra, you'll find a way to end your curse."*

A traveling vendor had also echoed the name, his words cryptic as he held a dragon-shaped kite: *"A place so far away, it may not exist on your maps."*

Nearby, an owl hooted.

Kharis narrowed her eyes in thought. "I was told to go to Hegra. Would you take me there?"

A tendril of mist unfurled from his form, weaving delicately toward her. It lingered before her chest, curling as if to point at her heart. "I cannot, but you already have what you need to find it," he said.

Frustration crept into her voice. "Always with the puzzles." Her gaze lingered on his eyes, the only feature she could read, hoping for a flicker of emotion. Without a face to give her answers, she clung to the slightest shift in those indigo orbs. "Is that your name, Pharos?"

The Voice shook his head, the mist swirling faintly around him. "A title."

She tugged her bottom lip, studying his face. "So... you have a name."

The Voice tittered, his amusement rippling the air like a faint breeze. "You are obsessed with names."

THE DANDELION TREE, PART ONE

Kharis shrugged. "They're important, exemplifying our connection to others. In Zahari tradition, many change their names after a tragic event to signify a departure from their destiny. My tutors used to say it was a foolish custom, but there's value in hiding oneself from the god of fate."

He hummed thoughtfully. "I have had many; I know not which is mine anymore."

"If you allow it," she said, "I'll think of one for you."

His indigo eyes softened, the faint glow shifting to mimic a smile.

Her lips puckered slightly, her thoughts swirling. "If you're the Pharos of Hegra, the Akumi king—"

"—is imprisoned," the Voice interjected gently. "And while I can speak to you, you must reach out and speak to him. Our freedom depends on his."

A gentle breeze swept across the summit, stirring a small cloud of dust into a playful whirlsprite that danced briefly before fading under the moonlight.

"Without the Akumi king," she said, "I'm no longer the Djinnshirukh, but what happens to you?"

"Nothing." His deep breath rippled through the haze. "Because we made each other a binding promise."

Kharis's eyes widened in disbelief. "We?"

"I promised to search for you, and you, to wait for me." The mist billowed as if he were shifting his body. "You waited. I found you. Now we are together as it should have been."

She grimaced, still confused. "Why did we go our separate ways?"

"To end the One War, you bound yourself to the Akumi king."

"What...?" Kharis's voice quivered with incredulity.

His deep chuckle carried an infuriating fondness. Her annoyance flared. "That was a thousand years ago. Pieces of your story are missing."

"It is not my story, but yours."

Kharis squinted her eyes. The lack of a face made searching for the lie more challenging. "How so?"

"Yours was an act of compassion that defied the gods. You

sought to end the war, but instead, the world splintered. When you are free, all the writings will end."

"I've heard that before. What does it mean?"

"It is a task you must fulfill."

Her mouth fell open, finger pointing at herself. "Me?"

"Indeed." He nodded once. "All that was wrong will be righted when the immortal vessel dies."

Does he mean me?

"When the flames roam with might," he continued, "freedom will find its light. The spirits will join and transcend, and all the writings will end." Wisps of shadow rose and fell from his body, undulating like restless waves. He turned slightly, his misty form still shifting. "And now, we must leave this place."

"Wait," she protested. "I have questions, especially about these writings."

He didn't laugh this time. A heavy stillness had replaced the playful spark she'd expected from him, and an odd silence bounced between them. Finally, he spoke, his tone quieter. "Not all your answers are with me. Some belong to the Akumi king. Speak to him."

Before Kharis could argue, a gentle touch, soft as down feathers, brushed against her face. Instinctively, she reached out, her fingertips grazing what should have been his hand. The black mist rippled and curled around her fingers, elusive and intangible, confirming what she already suspected: that there was no physical body beneath the haze.

The sharp, insistent ache took her by surprise. She'd wished for a body to match the weight of his presence. Slowly, she pressed her palm against the swirling clouds forming his chest. To her astonishment, a warm, steady heartbeat thrummed against her skin, echoing against her palm like gentle waves lapping at a quiet shore.

"In this form," she asked softly, "can you touch others?"

"No." His voice betrayed how desperately he wanted to.

Six years of conversations played in her mind. In that time, the Voice had become a guide and a mentor, always there for her. Over time, the lines between mentor and friend blurred, and lately, she swore he flirted with her as if testing an invisible line.

"You've always protected me," she said. "Even advised and encouraged me."

"And I will continue to do so until my very last breath." His words carried the essence of an ancient, eternal promise. "Our time runs out," he said. "I must take you to the void." She could hear the longing in his voice—how he wanted more time with her.

A flicker of doubt clawed at her chest, sudden and sharp.

What if he wasn't what he claimed to be? What if this valley, this sky, even the steady thrum of his heartbeat, were nothing more than a delusion conjured by the curse rotting her mind? The unraveling always began with voices—sweet, seductive, and full of promise. What if the Voice wasn't her salvation... but the soft, velvet lure of madness?

His indigo gaze found hers again—steady, luminous, unreadable—as if he'd heard her thoughts. "Will you sing for me again?"

"Sing?" His request caught her off guard.

"Yes," the Voice said. "I find it enchanting." His pleased sigh rippled the mist. "Will you?"

Kharis smiled, her heart swelling. "Whenever you ask."

"Good."

A moment of silence lingered between them. "Will I see you again? In this form?" The timid note in her question carried a hope she couldn't suppress.

Another sustained exhale disrupted the mist around his face. "Taking a shape is a temptation I take upon myself, one that demands onerous effort—a price I willingly pay," he admitted.

Her brow creased with concern. "What sort of price?"

"Magic demands symmetry," he said. "I can occasionally summon enough to break away and be with you, but the magic that binds me always forces me back. Whatever time I spend with you here, I must spend away from you."

"But—"

"I am bound to you for all eternity," he said, drawing a

sorrowful breath. "I await the day we can be reunited. If not in this lifetime, then the next."

Her eyes narrowed sharply. "Huh?"

A warm current tugged at her ribs. Far away, her sister called her name—her voice, faint yet insistent.

CHAPTER 10
THE WAIT

The cruelest prison is built not of iron, but of the silence between what is and what could be. - Poliormos

While her soul remained trapped in Andaheimur, Kharis's body convulsed in the waking world.

"Khiri, please. Wake up," she whispered, brushing damp hair from her sister's burning forehead.

Saya exhaled in relief when servants rushed Yuna and her three most trusted healers into the bedroom. With their help, she stepped into the tub and submerged Kharis in an ice bath, praying the cold would draw her back.

"Let me help."

"No, Nana." Saya stopped her from stepping into the tub, teeth chattering. "This is my task."

"Darling, this is our task." She gestured to the bhiksunim, who were preparing tinctures in the adjoining room. "Ruha, Madi, Anya, and I are here to help you."

Saya was caught between the relief from Yuna's words and the creeping dread that often clouded her thoughts. Her tears finally spilled. "This must never make it to the Regia-Zenka—"

"And it won't," Yuna reassured her. "We will lower her fever, and Gutxi will soon be on her feet."

A soft smile graced Saya at Yuna's use of Kharis's nickname —Gutxi, her nana's little butterfly.

"No one will believe it ever transpired," Yuna added. "Allow Jordha to attend to the matter."

"But what if he can't?" Saya whispered. Fear was always present, leaving holes in her soul like silverfish through the pages of a worn book. "There were so many officers."

"There will be as many interpretations as there were witnesses," Yuna said. "But I trust General Zhad to remain discreet. He's a decent man, steadfast in his loyalty to the Crown." She paused, her brow furrowing as concern shadowed her features. "Saya, why was Gutxi in the arena?"

Saya stiffened, her thoughts a chaotic swirl. "I don't know." She squeezed her eyes shut as if that could keep her questions from rising. "She wasn't supposed to be there. Given the heat, we were scheduled to train together in the East Garden, but I was running behind."

"Why?"

Saya hesitated. "I had to speak to Tavah."

Yuna's expression shifted as she studied Saya with a sharp gaze. "Has it happened again?"

Saya barely nodded. "Last night." She glanced at the women in the other room and lowered her voice further. "My magic no longer awakens her."

Yuna's face paled. Her knuckles turned white as she tightly clutched the tub's rim. "Are you certain of this?"

"I confirmed it last night."

Yuna sank to the floor. "This... was not the first time?"

Saya shook her head—a single, grim gesture.

"I... I fail to understand." Yuna's brows knit together. "The Sorukhipa has always maintained control over the Djinnshirukh." She exhaled slowly, as though attempting to expel the fear within her. "You ought to have informed me sooner. This must remain a secret. No one can know."

"We won't be able to hide it eventually."

"I understand, my darling, but if anyone finds out, it will seal Gutxi's fate. We must conceal this at all costs to protect you both."

Resealment. Fear clamped its fangs on her. It was the same worry, day in and day out, except this time, nothing would save Kharis.

"Darling, you're shaking."

"I'm fine," Saya mumbled. She'd started trembling that day when she held onto her beloved sister on a blood-stained rug after the massacre. It never went away after that.

Yuna creased her forehead, a beat of silence passing between them before she asked, "Is Hröld aware that your magic no longer holds sway over Gutxi?"

"No."

"What about Hala?"

"He doesn't know, either."

Yuna's gaze sharpened. "Good. Ensure it remains so."

Saya wanted to scream. "Why was she at the arena? Khiri was supposed to go to the East Garden."

"It is all right. Our Gutxi is safe now." Yuna's hand moved gently through Saya's hair, her touch soothing. "In time, something else will arise to divert everyone's attention from this. So, please, do not let this trouble you."

Ruha came in. "Your Excellency, the tinctures are ready."

"Thank you," Yuna said, pushing herself up. "Let us administer an initial dose and move her to the bed."

※

Heat coiled around Kharis, the air crackling with a charge that prickled her skin. Tiny red sparks escaped her body, ominous little signs that the Akumi king was fighting for release. They zapped the servants fanning her, making them cringe every time. Saya also bore the uncomfortable little pinpricks, wincing and clenching her eyelids shut each time she checked Kharis's pulse.

"How is she doing?" Yuna inquired as she stepped into the room.

"Still unconscious. The fever remains high. She has a few green and yellow bruises on her body, but the purpling is already gone."

Yuna settled behind Saya. "For better or worse, the Akumi king shields her, always accelerating her healing. Cuts or scratches?"

"None. If she had any, they have healed already."

"Bless the Mother, then. Keep a close watch on the water clock. She's due for her next dose in another hour." Yuna exhaled deeply, her voice carrying a hint of weariness. "I've sent Madi to the palace. Hröld has requested an update."

"Is he coming?"

Yuna's quiet exhale spoke volumes. The king would not be coming. "Your tavah is occupied with this matter," she said evenly. "I've been informed that Master Hillal arrived some time ago."

"What do you think will happen?" A prickling sensation coursed through Saya's body. She paced the room, making a concerted effort to dispel the anxiety that fueled her fears.

"I don't believe anything will come of this," Yuna said. "Hala and Jordha will undoubtedly find a way to redirect attention away from Gutxi. The fact that Lord Mehta has not been summoned is already a favorable sign. It suggests this incident is being treated as a family matter rather than a threat to Zahar's security."

Saya frowned, slowing. "But... Master Hillal—"

"—Is an advisor your tavah trusts implicitly," Yuna said gently, cutting in.

Saya's steps stopped. "So he's listening."

Yuna nodded. "He is. And for now, that is all we can hope for."

CHAPTER II

A BOND SO SWEET

Love opens the hearts of the willing, illuminating their path and guiding them forward. For the reluctant, its formidable power overwhelms, blinding and pushing them despite themselves. - Poliormos

The evening gloom gradually enveloped the bedroom, and servants discreetly lit candles. The evening breeze brought the scent of jasmine into the bedroom.

"I must take my leave shortly," Yuna said. "I am expected at the Academy this evening, but Ruha will remain here should you require her assistance." Her gaze drifted toward the bedroom door, her features tight with concern. "Gutxi's fever worries me. It has never been this unyielding."

"She'll come out of it." Saya had to believe that with all her heart.

"The Akumi king's hold is strong this time." Yuna tenderly cradled Saya's face in her hands. "If you decide to enter Andaheimur, please have Ruha sit with you."

Saya rolled her eyes. "I promise, Nana."

Yuna's gaze hardened. "I mean it, Saya. Call on Ruha. Do not attempt it alone. I will not have you venturing into a place forbidden to mortals."

"Nana, I—"

"I won't hear it," Yuna said firmly. "Your entry into Välissa is already a transgression. Every time you go there, you defy all that is forbidden."

Saya growled in warning. "Nana—"

"Nana, nothing," Yuna snapped. "I have told you this time, and time again. I don't know the price you pay each time you enter Välissa and cross into Andaheimur to bring her back." Her voice broke, trembling with emotion as a sob escaped. "I cannot bear to lose my two darlings. I just... can't."

Saya wrapped her arms around the bhiksun. "I'll call on Ruha because otherwise, I'll never hear the end."

"Wise," Yuna said, a relieved smile softening her features. "I'll return in the morning to check on both of you. Should anything occur, send Ruha to fetch me immediately."

Yuna and Anya left, and Saya resumed her work with Ruha's help, repeatedly draping her sister in cold towels to lower her body temperature. Wisps of steam escaped them upon contact. The soft, sizzling sound startled the nearby servants, who shifted nervously, itching to flee the chambers.

"Ruha," Saya said. "We're in for a long night. Why don't you rest for a bit? I can wake you up in a few hours to swap places."

"As you wish, Your Highness."

"Thank you." Saya pulled Ruha into a tight hug. "Thank you for all your help."

Ruha smiled, her eyes soft and kind. After a quick bow, she retired to a nearby room. Saya slumped into a chair, every muscle spent.

General Zhad had been lucky.

The Djinnshirukh was a fierce warrior, a creature forged with ancient magic for one purpose only—to kill. They were relentless in their goal, fighting with harrowing viciousness. They slashed skin, broke bones, and cut limbs. Any warrior could.

But the Djinnshirukh also siphoned the souls of their slain enemies to strengthen themselves. As such, they could battle forever, not as otherworldly warriors but as demigods. And given their uncanny self-healing ability, the

Djinnshirukh could live forever, but such gifts always came at a price.

The Keeper of the South Wind also descended into a dangerous madness as the powerful and highly addictive Akumi magic slowly eroded their mind. The more they used it, the faster the unraveling.

Lying on the bed, Kharis looked as fragile as a twig that Saya could easily snap in two.

And yet, people feared her.

Her sister endured her unbearable loneliness in silence. Kharis pressed on, shoulders squared and chin high, reining in her power and muting any sign of threat. Her every gesture and word was a silent plea for understanding and acceptance. Yet, despite four years of unwavering, exemplary behavior, the whispers of fear and mumbled curses became shadows trailing after her.

Servants moved in and out of the chamber in a blur of constant activity, their disdainful murmurs swirling around Saya as if assuming she couldn't hear them. Fools. Saya couldn't understand how Kharis had borne it all. Day after day. Six years of it.

"Leave!" she shouted.

The servants flinched. Some stepped back while others halted mid-motion. The Sorukhipa had never lost her composure. They bowed in stunned silence, a few relieved to leave as they hurriedly exited the room and closed the doors behind them.

"She doesn't feed on souls. She doesn't eat people whole," Saya muttered. "Why can't they see that this blasted fate cursed someone with a gentle soul and a kind heart?" She shut her eyes to keep from crying. "Curse the gods for this. She suffers from nightmares and panic attacks. Anxiety constantly chokes her."

She fisted her hands, itching to hit something.

"I must protect her. I must defeat her."

The dichotomy of her role as the Sorukhipa tormented her.

"I want a life," she begged the gods. "A simple, boring life where nothing ever happens."

Could she perform her duty? Who would replace Kharis? How many more Djinnshirukh would she face as the Sorukhipa? These thoughts haunted her day after day.

If this was living, was death her freedom?

She snapped out of it, slapping her cheeks briskly. "Clear your mind, Saya. Let your fear flow away." She conjured her strength, caressing Kharis's face with endless affection. "There's no world where you aren't with me."

It was a promise the sisters had made to each other as children. She pressed her forehead against Kharis's, bearing the tiny sparks zapping her body. "I love you, Khiri, with all my heart."

With her mind made up, she stifled her tears, swallowing the rest with a deep inhale. "I'm coming for you, Khiri. I'll find you and bring you home."

CHAPTER 12
ANDAHEIMUR

The hands of those who dare to dream weave the threads of freedom.
- Poliormos

How many times had she entered Andaheimur? Saya had lost count.

Magic hummed all around her. Sounds dissipated until she became light as a feather and found herself floating in the dark oceans of Välissa.

Välissa, the in-between.

It would have been tempting to let its currents take her, to drift away and escape it all, but she couldn't leave her sister behind. Far ahead, a single point of light pulsed like a heartbeat—the door to Andaheimur. She swam toward it. The light rose to meet her—and swallowed her whole. The world unraveled... then rewove itself.

She emerged into a sea of gold, endless and swaying beneath a summer sun.

A playful zephyr created never-ending ripples on the amber fields of wheat. Perched atop the summit, Saya's curls danced with the soft breeze, tickling her forehead. The sky was clear, an endless expanse of blue. Granaries rose proudly like guardians of abundance while a web of canals and floodgates crisscrossed the fertile land.

A gentle tug brought her back, for such was the connection between the Djinnshirukh and the Sorukhipa, a bond forged by ancient magic. Saya focused on the sensation, turned toward it, and descended the dirt path toward the valley.

At first, the ground beneath her feet held firm, offering steady support. Then, without warning, it gave way. A jagged crack split beneath her feet, and the world dropped from under her. Saya plunged into the darkness, the air tearing past her as a strangled gasp wrenched from her throat. The fall was merciless—then came the impact.

When her lungs heaved for air, she lay on the hard floor of an underground water canal, where the sharp scent of wet stone saturated the air. A single flickering torch revealed a tunnel with a vaulted ceiling. One end stretched into the far unknown, shrouded in inky darkness. The other led to a locked metal gate, effectively sealing off the waterway exit.

The rhythmic echoes of droplets broke the silence, splashing onto her skin with a chilling touch. The water in the channel frothed and surged, crashing against the gate and spilling into the walkway.

"Khiri...?" Saya's voice echoed, reverberating off the slick walls before fading into silence. "Khiri, where are you?"

Except for the stubborn echo, there was no reply.

Her unease prickled at the edges of her mind. This wasn't the oppressive void that held Kharis prisoner. This... was an odd puzzle. The apparent solution was to open the gate and let the water flow, but doubt crept into her thoughts. It couldn't be this easy, could it? She took a few steps forward, scanning the walls for hidden mechanisms or traps. Her instincts screamed that something was off. Then, she heard it.

An icy whisper pierced the silence—a croaky, unpleasant sound.

Saya stopped, a chill coursing through her.

Slowly, she pivoted on a heel.

The black maw rippled and twisted, contorting into a tall shape with unnaturally long, gangly arms and legs. It had the gaunt silhouette of something that might once have been mortal. Charcoal and hardened ash appeared to have sculpted the body as if it had been forged in the relentless heat of an unforgiving blaze. Wisps of smoke curled and drifted from its body as though it still smoldered. Its features were barely discernible on the charred face, save for its eyes: two glowing embers that burned with an unnerving intensity.

"Khiri?" Saya hated how her voice betrayed her fear. "Is that you?"

The creature tilted its head slowly, assessing her with eerie intelligence. Clouds of swirling smoke ebbed and flowed around the monster, shrouding its form in a shifting black veil. Its eyes flared with a disquieting intensity as it silently observed her, their glow pulsing like a threat. Then, it lumbered toward her, each step a heavy thud. Its claws snapped into place with a sharp click, then scraped the rock wall as it advanced, the shriek of stone grinding against bone ripping through the tunnel with a grating, ear-splitting noise.

Saya clenched her teeth. "You won't make this an easy rescue, are you?"

The creature's eyes narrowed, its shoulders shuddering as if in a silent, mocking chuckle.

Saya increased the distance between them, summoning her Firegrazer. After a fierce shimmer, her sword appeared in her grasp. As she unsheathed the blade, it thrummed with power—a low, melodic hum rippled through the chamber like a warning made of music.

The creature shrieked in pain and fixed Saya with a venomous glare before unleashing a long, unnerving hiss. Then it lunged.

Claws slashed the air as Saya twisted, narrowly dodging the strike. She swung her blade, and the Firegrazer sang as it met whatever passed for flesh. The creature heaved a shattering, pained cry. Cracks rippled across its skin before it crumbled away in ashen flakes, revealing the smoldering core beneath.

Saya lunged, her blade cutting a swift arc, but the creature sidestepped, staying out of reach. It snickered before springing forward, claws gleaming. Saya twisted, but a sharp, searing pain tore through her shoulder as claws found their mark. She stifled her gasp.

The creature straightened, a smug expression narrowing its gaze.

With a pained grunt, Saya surged forward, swinging her blade. The monster slipped past the steel arc with uncanny grace and struck her from behind, hurling her onto the slick, wet floor.

Knocked from her grasp, her weapon clattered out of reach. The creature kicked it farther away and cocked its head, squinting as if smiling. Gritting her teeth, Saya pushed herself upright and lifted her hand to summon her sword, but before the weapon could reappear, the monster blurred forward with startling speed and seized her by the neck, slamming her against the wall.

The stench of sulfur assaulted her nostrils. The ember eyes, mere inches from her face, burned with a glare that seemed to pierce through her. The clawed hand tightened its grip, nicking delicate skin. The creature could have crushed her throat with ease, yet it assessed her, pondering something, sniffing her to confirm it.

Sensing an opportunity, Saya rammed her forehead into its face. The creature's grip loosened. It snarled and stumbled back, shaking its head. Saya followed with a harsh kick to its ribs, forcing it several steps away.

That was all the space she needed.

With a flick of her wrist, the Firegrazer reappeared in her hand. The creature dropped to all fours and vaulted toward her, claws flashing as it ripped through the air. Saya dodged, leather tearing behind her, and swung her blade.

The sword struck.

Charcoal flakes flew.

The monster swiped its claws, scoring Saya's face. Biting on the pain, Saya swung again, striking. The creature hissed and jumped back, fixing its glare on Saya, assessing their standstill. It narrowed its eyes, then took a few more steps back. Saya's heart raced with triumph at the signs that the creature was retreating. It edged backward and unleashed a high-pitched scream before vanishing in a blinding burst of fire and smoke before Saya could shield her eyes.

Spear me.

The creature's scream faded into eerie silence. The world had become a blur of dancing white spots. Her eyes burned, tears streaming down her face. She wiped at them, but the tears didn't stop. Where was that thing now?

A spark of magic hummed in her hand. She raised the Firegrazer, her grip firming around the hilt.

The unnerving moment stretched. The nicks on her cheek and neck burned, and blood seeped steadily from her shoulder, darkening the leather. With each breath, her chest throbbed— each inhalation more labored than the last.

A cold draft slithered through the tunnel, tingling the skin on the back of her neck. Her nose twitched at the musty scent clawing at her senses. Pivoting in its direction, Saya thrust her blade into that darkness.

The Firegrazer hummed, its vibration resonating through her bones.

The creature materialized, shocked to see the sword deeply embedded in its body. It eyed Saya with a labored wail. The hardened soot on its body cracked and crumbled, becoming a drizzle of ash landing on the floor. Large pieces followed, crashing to the ground and turning into billowing clouds of black dust. The smoke that engulfed the monster dissipated, and the exposed core, resembling molten metal, slowly reshaped.

Saya stared in horror at the resulting figure.

She'd run Kharis through with the Firegrazer.

Her face was pale. Scarlet stained her ivory teeth. The wound on her abdomen cascaded blood, trickling down her legs and pooling onto the floor. Her crimson eyes fixed on Saya with a shocked, painful glare.

"What have you done?" Kharis asked, her voice deep and hoarse.

The terror that had gripped Saya vanished: this was not her sister.

The creature growled, giving Saya a deliberate, angry shake of its head. "Why must it be this way?"

Saya ignored the comment. "Where's my sister?"

"Have you lost her?"

"You have trapped her," Saya shouted.

"Have I?" This version of Kharis arched a brow.

"Enough with the questions. Where is she?"

The creature ignored her, yanking at the blade with bloodied hands. The sword hummed, resisting the creature's effort.

Saya couldn't help but shake her head. "What are you?"

The fake Kharis cackled, amused. "Wrong question."

"Are you the Akumi king?"

The creature snickered.

Saya scowled. "I don't have time for games."

"Is this a game?" This Kharis fixed her with a questioning stare.

The sword's magic shimmered up her arms. Silver light bled through her hair and into her eyes, washing away their crimson hue. A silvery aura gathered around her, colder than winter.

"What's so amusing?" Saya threw at her.

Silver eyes now gazed at Saya with a jarring focus. "You are not her protector," the creature said. "I am."

Saya's aggravation flared. "I'm her Soru—"

"You almost killed her!" the creature shouted. It ripped the tunic open to show Saya the ghastly blackened wound on its chest, where Saya's magic had struck. "She lives because I took the hit," it snarled. "The one you delivered, so do not dare tell me you protect her." That silver gaze glowered at Saya, full of accusations. Then, for an instant, sadness enveloped it. "Why must you enslave her?"

Saya's anger swelled. "You're the one enslaving her," she shouted. "Tormenting her, possessing—"

"Why shan't you let her go?" this other Kharis shrieked, anguish casting a shadow on this version of her sister's face. "Why must you fetter her?"

Confusion rattled Saya's mind.

"If you love her so much," it said, "let her return with us."

"Return where?" Saya raised her chin, defiant.

This Kharis smirked, her lips curling with dark amusement. "The universe demands balance, Sorukhipa." Her silver eyes narrowed, boring into Saya with an unnerving intensity. "Yes, she is imprisoned, but you were the ones who did it, not me. You have trapped her in a world where she does not belong."

Saya kept her grip tight on the Firegrazer, but her mind reeled as the accusation sank in. "She's my sister."

"And she is mine," this Kharis hissed, thumping her chest.

Saya stilled, her mind suddenly quiet. No. That couldn't be true. Could it?

"You cannot stop what is to be," the creature warned. "And you cannot outrun fate, Sorukhipa. The spirits will join and transcend when the immortal vessel dies, and when she is finally free, all the writings will end."

"If we're the ones enslaving her," Saya blurted out, "help me set her free. Why fight me?"

This Kharis eyed Saya as if seeing her for the first time. The frost spell slowly branched into her chest, fracturing her skin as it hardened into ice. And yet, the creature seemed unpreoccupied. Her silver gaze narrowed, mulling something over. That otherworldly stare met Saya's.

"She loves you," the creature said, weighing this discovery. "And you love her." Her eyes widened as if something had become apparent. "Why is *she* with you?" this Kharis asked, contemplating this question.

"*Who* is with me?" Saya demanded.

The being paused, its movement so eerily reminiscent of her sister's.

"She is with her," the creature mused aloud, shaking its head. "No. She is her, but *you*...?" Her gaze sharpened, snapping back to Saya. "Why is *she* with you?" The words slithered from the creature's lips, brimming with menace. "You are bound to her by something stronger than fate, a thread I cannot cut." Her silver orbs turned into black voids. "A thread that upsets the balance of the Universe. A thread that has replaced me," she snarled. "A dangerous thread."

"Riddles won't help me—"

This Kharis lunged forward, impaling herself deeper onto the sword in a desperate attempt to reach Saya's neck. The blade's magic surged, freezing the monster mid-motion. The creature lingered there, immobile like a grotesque statue of her sister.

Slowly, the ice cracked and splintered, filling the tunnel with snapping, popping sounds until her body exploded, shards flying everywhere.

Saya crouched, shielding herself. The sharp projectiles melted upon striking the floor, releasing multiple plumes of hissing steam that gathered into a single black mass. It hovered mid-air as if appraising Saya.

"You cannot stop fate, Sorukhipa." Its voice boomed ominously. "In the end, she'll choose us. *Giltrandi elduru, adatari haguru.*" Its sardonic cackle filled the tunnel as the black cloud dashed down the endless shaft.

Saya kept her battle-ready stance, her gaze penetrating the shadows as she braced herself for another attack. Despite the sounds of sloshing water and the persistent drip, the vault was silent again.

The revelation had unnerved her. "Khiri's... the Akumi's sister?" Nothing made sense. Saya wiped the sweat from her brow and the blood trickling from the cut on her cheek. "All the writings will end when she is free?"

Flustered, she turned toward the darkest end of the tunnel. "What does that even mean?" she yelled.

Only the echo of her voice answered, soon fading.

Saya's gaze shifted to the imposing metal gate before her. "A riddle?" she muttered, a bitter laugh bubbling up. Rather than physically pull Kharis out of a dark void, she realized that allowing the water to flow again would free her sister from the Akumi king's hold. She spotted the lever, braced herself, and pushed down with all her weight, but the lever refused to budge, stuck fast in its rusted grip.

"Spear me now and gut me, too," she cursed loudly, finding satisfaction in the profanity.

She pounded on the gears to dislodge it, but only red dust came out, staining her hands maroon. "I am done with this riddle."

She unsheathed her sword. "Occam's razor, it is."

The Firegrazer hummed as Saya raised her blade and struck the gears. The collision resulted in a blast of magic that flooded the tunnel with resonant tones. Small radiant explosions disintegrated the rust. The gears groaned and rattled as the rusty prison released them. Saya put all her weight on the lever, clenched her jaw, and pushed it down until it finally shifted. The giant gate creaked as it slowly rose.

The water flowed once again, escaping its dark confinement.

Saya breathed a sigh of relief. Then she faced the tunnel's dark maw.

"You lost," she shouted. "I'm taking my sister home."

She lowered her sword as her breath shook in her chest. "Hold on, Khiri," she whispered. "Just a little longer."

CHAPTER 13
THE TASTE OF MEMORIES

Bittersweet are the steps as I walk into this darkness, but love's fierce light guides me, pulling on my hand. Your safety is my only reward.
- Poliormos

Kharis narrowed her eyes, suspicion prickling at her thoughts. "How long have we known each other?"

"Since the beginning of time," the Voice said.

His maddeningly casual response triggered a cough.

"I was twelve the first time I heard you." Her voice rose with the certainty of that memory. "You were a tiny flame hidden in the Royal Archives."

"Much earlier than that," the Voice said gently. "You have always remembered pieces."

Kharis's brows knitted. "What does that even mean?"

A wistful pause. "Each life leaves a trace. Yours may fade after each. Mine... remain."

She scrunched her face.

"I swore to find you in every timeline and universe—and I did," he said. "To end the One War, you defied the fate the gods had ordained. It was an act of utter defiance... and the truest expression of your stubborn heart."

A tendril of mist caressed her cheek, and Kharis felt his loving smile.

"You must let go of fear and leap into the unknown. When you do, we shall be reunited."

Sharan's ivory glow faded as a colossal shadow loomed on the horizon, inching closer until everything vanished behind a dark, impenetrable veil.

The Voice had moved them into the void.

Time ceased to march forward in this place. There was neither up nor down, and her senses melted into nothingness. Here, memories transformed into drops cascading into a vast, bottomless ocean.

And in the void, he became a voice haunting her mind again.

"*You should leave,*" he said. "*This is not a place where you should remain for long.*"

"Why would I go back?"

"*Why stay?*" he countered.

Wasn't it obvious? "To be with you."

"*Here, we would not.*" His disapproval rippled through her mind like a jarring echo. Then his voice softened, the tenderness seeping through his words. "*This place does not offer what you need.*"

"No, it doesn't," she said. The truth stung. "I need a place to start my life anew. A place where no one knows who I am or what I've done. Perhaps Hegra is this place." She exhaled, hoping with that breath to rid herself of everything. "I wish I could forget everything and live in blissful ignorance without memories to drag me down."

His soft hum caressed her thoughts. "*I understand why you would want this, but you would lose the sweetness in erasing the bitterness. Is that what you want?*" he asked. "*To forget the good moments, those tiny gifts of fate?*"

"Saya," she whispered into the darkness, her heart aching with the name. "She makes my life bearable, shining through my darkest days like the summer sun. If I were gone, she would finally have a chance at life. Anything would be better than what she endures because of me."

"*You should return.*"

"Why?" A sob lodged in her throat. "Everyone hates me. Why would I leave this place?"

"*Because your sister loves you*," he said gently. "*She is risking everything to rescue you as we speak.*"

Kharis let out a grief-stricken moan. "All I do is make her miserable."

"*Her hard work is in vain if you stay here.*" The sensation of tender fingers brushing her face followed, a touch so delicate that it soothed the sharp edges of her sorrow.

"It's quiet here," she murmured. "And peaceful."

"*Yes, but it is lonely, too. And your sister shall be lonely without you.*"

The ache in her chest deepened, and she moaned again, this time with all the weight of her heartache. "I can't face her. What will she think of me?"

A pause lingered between them. "*What would she think of you?*"

"That I'm weak. That I failed her—again."

"*Would she not think the same: that she failed you?*"

Kharis drew in a ragged breath. "Of course, she would, blaming herself for everything."

"*Then return and speak to her,*" the Voice insisted. "*Tell her how proud you are of her, that you love her, and that you would never be disappointed.*" He sighed ever so softly, the sound carrying a thousand unspoken words. "*She needs to hear those words from you as much as you need to hear them from her.*"

Kharis inhaled sharply, her heart wrestling with the decision. To return meant leaving behind this comforting shield that protected her from the hatred she faced in Zahar.

"If I remain here, no one will suffer. Saya will smile more, free of all the trouble I cause her."

"*Without you,*" he said, "*her smile shall be a mask hiding the hollow you leave behind. You are her light as much as she is yours.*" The Voice paced in her mind, a glimmering black cloud searching for the right words to sway her. "*Do you not love her?*"

"With all my heart," she shouted. "How dare you ask this?"

He didn't reply, but she could sense his mounting frustration, so she said, "Take my memories away—let this darkness swallow me and turn me into nothing."

The Voice faltered, his shock rippling through her.

"And remove my heart while you're at it so I can be truly numb—feel nothing, want nothing."

He seemed to recoil, unable to fathom what she'd asked. "*Even the gods feel.*" His words were quiet but edged with hurt.

"Really? Because they haven't answered any of my pleas." Her irritation bubbled over.

"*You received a lovely bouquet. Would that not be a reply from the gods?*"

An awkward hush fell over them, the end of it as far away as the other shore of an ocean.

"Let this place take the pain away," she begged. "Allow me to stay here."

Silence stretched between them. Then, at last, the Voice stirred, his tone wistful.

"*Once, it happened.*" The ghost of a smile weaved through his words. "*It was not a request but a challenge, an angry dare because I had lost my temper, but you? Oh, I shall not forget your lesson. It is a lovely memory, and I have no intention of parting with it. Is it painful to reminisce? Yes, but my recollections are also sweet, offering me hope.*"

Kharis stilled at the unexpected intimacy. He'd never spoken of his life before, but now, he'd shared something deeply rooted in his existence for the first time. He'd opened a door and lingered on the threshold, waiting to see if she would step through.

She feared the answer—but needed it all the same. "What do you remember?"

"*That you filled my void with stars and silver roses.*"

A chaotic scatter of pieces clattered in her mind. "Silver roses?"

"*Do you wish to forget that as well?*" A quiet challenge.

Kharis sniffed. "How could I forget something I don't remember?"

"*I was never allowed to forget,*" he confessed. "*I have tried. But the pain of an endless past is my punishment.*"

"And what about my pain?" she retorted.

"Yours is to forget. To begin again. Again and again."

She scoffed, not believing a word. "I live in the details of all the misery I brought. I wish to forget it all and have asked for your help." A pause. "The help you are denying me now."

The Voice didn't answer, his disappointment fluttering in the silence.

"I don't want my sister, Nana, or Tavah suffering because of me. I don't want to remember their tears or the pain in their faces. But it's not just them. I see it in every pair of eyes staring at me. Their loss, their sorrow, their grief. It clings to them as a reminder that I lived while everyone they loved died."

"Escaping is not the answer, and you know this. Staying here is a momentary reprieve, but to free your sister, you cannot be here."

"But—"

"Stop running away," he shouted.

She cringed, surprised he could feel such raw emotion. "Even you're unhappy with me."

His exhaled breath rushed through her thoughts like a strong wind blowing through a canyon. *"You cannot change what has been done,"* he said, softer now, more patient. *"But you have the power to decide what unfolds next."*

A ragged breath tore from her chest. "I'm afraid," she admitted. "Of facing what I've done."

"You are not defined by what has happened," the Voice said with familiar gentility. *"But by what you choose to do next."*

His quiet insistence was like a drop of water slowly cracking her defenses.

That weighty silence returned. His contemplative hum ended it.

"Your sister has opened the gate."

Kharis grimaced. No matter where she hid, Saya would find her, even if it meant traversing the unknown to break through insurmountable barriers. Her sister's duty as Sorukhipa was absolute. Saya wasn't free, either—not while this curse existed.

The Voice was right. Hiding served no purpose.

Kharis let out a heavy, sorrowful sob, resigned to her fate.

She'd once filled someone's void with stars and silver roses. Perhaps she could do it again.

"Fine," she grumbled. "Do it before I change my mind."

A sudden burst of light overwhelmed her eyes. The void vanished, and Kharis was hurled through space, falling and tumbling as if she were a fragile snowflake caught in the grip of a bitter wind. The descent felt endless until, with a jarring thud, she slammed back into her body.

Every sound hit her at once: the thrumming pulse against her ears, the murmur of a bustling city, her ragged breathing. A sharp pain jolted through her limbs as her senses roared back to life, too much, too fast. She gasped, struggling to steady herself as this reality crashed, wave after relentless wave.

"Khiri?"

The familiar voice glided into her consciousness and stirred Kharis's eyes open.

"You're back." A smile tugged at Saya's lips as she gently tucked strands of Kharis's hair behind an ear.

Drenched in sweat and drained of all energy, Kharis could barely whisper. "I made you cry again." Shame rode on those words. "Please, forgive me."

Saya sighed silently. "I should've come sooner."

Pools of glimmering silver blurred Kharis's vision until they spilled. "You always risk your life to rescue me."

"And I'll do it a thousand more times because you would do the same." Saya wrapped her arms around her. "Besides, there's no world where you aren't with me."

Kharis let out a feeble wail.

Saya tightened her grip. "I'm glad to have you back with the living, Khiri." She brushed her lips against her sister's hair. "I may hate my task as Sorukhipa. But you," she whispered, "you're the reason why it's worth bearing."

What would Saya have if she were gone? The question cut deep, and Kharis steeled herself, vowing to find a way to break the curse and put an end to this madness once and for all.

And she needed to act before the grim reality of resealment —her death—closed in on her like an inescapable shadow.

"I love you so much," Saya said, nuzzling her sister's cheek.

Kharis savored those words, more precious than gold. "And I love you more."

A quiet snort escaped Saya.

Kharis closed her eyes, and both women surrendered to their exhaustion.

CHAPTER 14
THE WAIT

Love is a chrysalis. In the wait lies a mesmerizing transformation. -
Poliormos

Hala's gaze swept across the State Room. The afternoon gloom had overtaken it, and servants quietly lit candles.

Prince Jordha paced the chamber, unable to sit for long. No older than Hala, he commanded the empire's internal security, orchestrating a vast network of spies and elite secret assassins. Tonight, he'd dispatched his finest Shadow Walkers to assess the damage.

Arjun Ghan sat at the table, fastidiously twirling his ring. The sight of him revolted Hala. Once, his uncle had overseen Zahar's armed forces, but three years ago, he stepped down in an enigmatic move buried in too much secrecy. His presence tonight only added to his simmering heartburn.

Master Hillal, who had come at his father's behest, sat on a bench with his back against a wall, enjoying the shadowy corner with his eyes closed. Prayer beads turned on his right hand.

Only one person was missing—Yuna.

Hala thanked the Blessed Mother for that.

Word of Kharis's presence at the arena spread fast, and

with hundreds of witnesses, the rumor mills had been churning since morning.

"What's the latest report?" Hala whispered when Jordha approached.

"Varying versions left the Sendatorsum and moved into the Zahar-Regia," Jordha said. "In one, Zhad missed a step and lost his balance. In another, Kharis hit him by mistake. But the most dangerous is that your sister attacked the general without cause."

Hala let out an unhappy breath. "If Khiri can't control the Akumi king, the Regia-Zenka will exercise its right to demand a replacement, and we all know what that means: her death and my ascension as Djinnshirukh."

A sharp shudder ran through him.

Jordha gave Hala a reassuring pat on the back. "I've got my people working on it." A hint of concern lingered in his voice. "But if she's going mad, we won't be able to keep it hidden for long."

Hala huffed. As long as Kharis lived, he was spared this task. He was the crown prince and would one day rule Zahar. Becoming the Djinnshirukh would impact that plan. "I wouldn't mind the power," he confessed, "but how do I stop the madness? It has afflicted every Djinnshirukh since their inception."

Jordha gave him a rueful smile.

A thousand years ago, King Owain ná Zahar had intended to save his only son by cheating the immortals with a commoner's child. They saw through the ruse and punished him by demanding True Blood as the sacrifice. Since then, the vessel could only be a child of royal blood, born of those who wore the Crown of Zahar. Otherwise, the resealment spell wouldn't work.

His mother, Queen Aghuti, had selected him as her successor, but he never understood why. A spare child, not the Heir Apparent, was always chosen. It should have been Götrid. His nostrils flared at the thought. Back then, Hala had dreaded the day—only for Kharis to be born carrying the demon. Convenient yet challenging.

He grumbled under his breath. "Have you found out why, in the fires, she went to the training arena?"

"No, and General Zhad confirmed he wasn't expecting her."

Hala felt his blood boil. "Then who did?"

Jordha didn't answer. His eyes merely flicked across the room to Arjun Ghan.

Hala's jaw clenched. "Proof?"

Jordha shook his head. "He never leaves a trail."

"Fires burn the man." Hala loathed that backstabber to death. Arjun Ghan adjusted the ring on his middle finger—the one carved with the Ghan family crest. He smiled faintly when Hala looked his way as if daring him to speak. He could delay the inevitable as long as Kharis lived, and keeping her alive was his goal.

Hala glowered at him, his biggest threat—a man intent on the opposite.

※

Hröld stopped pacing, closing his eyes for a moment, struggling to keep his anxiety from showing. "We could lose her today," he whispered to himself. "One misstep... and the Regia-Zenka will call for resealment."

He swallowed his tears, the taste of salt strong in his throat, and compulsively pinched the skin between his thumb and forefinger, silently crumbling while trying to figure out how to save his youngest child from potential execution.

Across the room, Arjun Ghan sat utterly still, his expression unreadable—save for the slow twist of the silver ring on his finger.

The hours had ticked by, time moving slowly as the evening gloom overtook the chamber. It was then that Prince Jordha entered.

"I have news." He was nearly breathless, shy of sprinting to the king. "The rumors are dying on their own."

Hröld frowned. "That Khiri attacked the general?" His voice betrayed how eager he was for confirmation.

"Yes, Your Majesty." Jordha smiled. "By tomorrow morning, the rumor will join the pantheon of unreliable gossip. The Regia-Zenka will certainly ignore it."

The weight that had tormented Hröld lifted.

Then, the chamber's side door opened, snapping Hröld out of his elation. Guards ushered one of Yuna's bhiksunim. Hala, noticing her arrival, gestured for her to approach. She leaned in, whispering in his ear. He nodded thoughtfully, absorbing every word. As soon as she finished, she exited as hastily as she'd come.

Hala turned to him, his expression bright. "Saya did it. Khiri's safe."

Relief washed over Hröld as he pressed a hand to his chest.

"Good news, indeed," he said.

CHAPTER 15
A SACRED DUTY

Hope is a sacred duty—guiding the willing with unyielding resolve.
- Poliormos

"Not that great, in my opinion." Arjun Ghan's gritty, unpleasant grumble ended the moment.

Hröld sighed quietly, doing his best to suppress the urge to punch that self-important expression off his face. He crossed the room and sat in his chair, addressing him. "Speak."

Ghan smiled smugly and cleared his throat. "We cannot ignore what happened. A highly decorated general was injured by her hand." His eyes widened as if he could taste victory. "It's clear she cannot control her emotions. Thus, she's an imperfect vessel. We must consider resealment."

Fully aware of the delicate palace maneuverings, Hröld maintained a neutral expression, careful not to betray his thoughts.

Arjun Ghan's nostrils flared with every breath he took, anxiously awaiting the king's response, one that Hröld would not provide yet. Flustered, Ghan turned around. "Hillal," he barked. "Make sense of this. Tell him that she's a cracked vessel. Weak. Useless. That resealment is the only option—"

"Asurûn!" Hala cut in.

Hröld lifted his hand to stop both men and drew a deep breath. "Hillal?"

Hillal met the king's gaze with a wary expression. Following Hröld's slight nod, Hillal stood up, vacating his shadow-soaked spot.

"Blessed be the earth and sun," he said.

"May they sustain us," Hröld replied, bracing himself for a fight.

Hillal rubbed his white beard, pondering. "Physical strength and agility are great attributes, but the Djinnshirukh must also possess the inner strength to keep the Akumi king in oblivion."

Hröld nodded, aware of this.

Hillal said, "If the vessel is weak—"

Hröld groaned under his breath, hating the moniker.

"—it forces the Sorukhipa to do all the work, disrupting a crucial balance between the Djinnshirukh and their guardian." Hillal clasped his hands behind his back. "A demon succeeds when it possesses its target, but exorcisms resolve these issues. We extract the demon and heal the mortal. However, in the Djinnshirukh's case, it's the opposite. We must keep the demon sealed, no matter what. When the seal fails, the only option—"

Hröld raised his hand to silence him.

Resealment. The tip of his stomach caught fire.

"What do you suggest?" he asked the monk, concealing the fear gripping him.

"Your Majesty, training her to be a weapon isn't enough." A discreet glance fell upon Ghan. "She requires specialized training, for she cannot yet enter Andaheimur, an ability every Djinnshirukh must master. Her training must avoid triggering anxiety, as this awakens the Akumi king, an excessively protective entity. Training should instead cultivate inner calm."

Hröld's lips went taut at the veiled reference. Ghan had abused Kharis's power to execute prisoners. Training, he'd called them. Three long years of secret sessions that ended the day Kharis, only seventeen at the time, stormed one of his proceedings with the Regia-Zenka, dragging a young prisoner behind her.

That memory burned him, and Hröld could barely hold back his impulse to lunge at Ghan and strangle him to death.

Hillal added, "With the right training, she'll return the Akumi king to his slumber." His smile softened, almost pleading with the king for his agreement. "That's my humble advice."

Hröld did his best to maintain his composure, surprised by Hillal's suggestion. He leaned back in his chair. Could it be that simple? He saw an opportunity to save his child's life. "How would this training be accomplished?"

Hillal answered quickly. Too quickly. "Let me take her to the Eliza."

Hröld blinked. For a moment, the chamber faded.

He was back in the aftermath of the massacre—the scent of smoke and charcoal thick in the air. Kharis had been barely fourteen, staring blankly as the healers washed the blood and ash from her. Saya had screamed herself hoarse, refusing to leave Kharis's side.

They'd been separated for only a few moments. And the world had almost crumbled.

Hröld gripped the armrests. His stomach burned, the fiery acid reaching his throat as he struggled to hide his ire.

If moving Saya to different chambers had awakened the demon, keeping his daughters geographically apart would destroy the world.

"I won't abide by their separation." The force of his voice reverberated through the chamber as the mask of His Serene Imperial Majesty, Son of the Sun, shattered.

"No, Your Majesty," Hillal said, his hands waving in a calming, appeasing gesture. "That's not my intention. I wish to take both of them with me."

Hröld blinked, the unexpected answer dampening his wrath.

"Over my dead body!" Ghan shot up from his chair.

Hala threw him a withering glance. "That can be arranged."

"I'm against it," Ghan yelled, red-faced, ignoring Hala's quip. "The Djinnshirukh must never leave the Senda. What will happen once she is out in the world? How do we stop her from—?"

"Enough!" Hröld's voice thundered as he slammed a fist against the armrest.

Ghan's expression darkened, anger sharpening his features. "Hröld," he warned.

Hröld fixed him with a cold glower. "I was magnanimous *once.*" His voice cut like ice, each word honed to a blade. "Do not test the last of my patience."

Ghan scowled, nostrils flaring, but aware of the threat, he sank back into his chair, fuming silently.

Across the room, Hala struggled to hide the smirk tugging at his mouth. Jordha, half-cloaked in shadows, leaned against the wall, his posture suggesting how he wished to walk away from the tense discussion altogether.

Hillal stood patiently, unshaken. His calm demeanor sparked a flicker of hope in Hröld's chest—hope at the possibility of a miracle.

"Master Hillal," the king said. "Explain your proposal."

PART TWO
A TASTE SO SWEET

CHAPTER 16
A TASTE SO SWEET

Hope is a guiding star for the willing and a persistent pebble in the shoe of the stubborn. - Poliormos

Kharis woke up with a groan, the thick veil of exhaustion clouding her mind. She sat up, slowly letting the world take shape with slow blinks as she rubbed her sleep-sodden eyes.

Scattered flashbacks flickered through her mind like shards of a broken mirror. As she pieced the images together and clarity sharpened her thoughts, she sank back into the bed with a gasp, her hair fanning across the pillow like a black cloud.

"Blessed Mother, what did I do?" She pulled the blanket over her head, the abrupt darkness a tiny void. "I'm never leaving this bed."

She wanted to scream, then cry. Hiding sounded better with every passing moment. "This is going to be the end of me."

"*Why?*" the silvery voice asked, calm yet probing.

"What do you mean, *why?*" she nearly shouted. "I attacked a general."

He sounded amused. "*You were sparring in a training arena. How is that 'attacking'?*"

"I'm the Djinnshirukh. Others won't see that."

"*Don't.*" His sudden flare of anger heated her body. "*I shall not let anyone hurt you.*"

"Many wish me dead," she scoffed.

"*And if any of them touch you, they shall pray for their death,*" the Voice growled, the sound dark and feral. Sharp claws clicked against a hard surface as he weaved through his words. "*You asked for my help, and I delivered. 'Thank you' is the only response I shall accept.*"

A blaze flushed through her. If the Voice had a face, he would glare at her with his arms crossed, daring her to argue with him, to utter one more word. He was right, though. She'd asked for his help—again.

"Thank you," she whispered, wetting her lips. "Did I hurt anyone?"

"*No.*"

The tension in her muscles eased. "Then why the anger?"

"*He was there.*"

Kharis stiffened, pulling the covers from her face. "Who?"

"*The dark one. The one who does not belong.*"

Kharis sifted through the blur—the oppressive heat, General Zhad, the soldiers—but something eluded her. A presence at the edge of her vision. No face, no form, just a shadow that pulled her gaze like a magnet.

"*He was the one we had wanted.*" His hiss was deep and rough, neither soft nor silvery.

A flicker of suspicion brushed her thoughts, and Kharis narrowed her eyes. "We?"

"*Your general blocked our way,*" he spat, each word sharp. "*We almost had him, but he stood in our way.*"

The fine hairs on her nape prickled. She hadn't seen anyone unusual—had she?

"Why do you want this... dark one?"

The Voice growled—a sound so vicious that it raised goose bumps on her arms. She could feel him pacing at the edges of her consciousness. His rage simmered until it lit a black blaze that threatened to consume her thoughts.

"Who's the dark one?" Kharis insisted, concerned.

An endless pause followed; the conversation was over. The Voice retreated to a dark corner of her mind to brood, his presence a smoldering black ember. Everything under his gaze would burst into flames if he had a face.

She scratched her head, primarily out of frustration. Sometimes, he answered her questions. Often, he left her with more.

Kharis got out of bed, dragging her hands down her face. "Where's Saya?"

Her bed was a mess of sheets and blankets, and even her clothes were piled on the floor. Saya always made her bed. Always. The Sorukhipa was a fastidiously neat woman... but not today. Kharis inhaled deeply to curb her anxiety.

She drew back the curtain, then groaned again. "Fires of Ifran. It must be midday. I'm in so much trouble."

The Voice offered no reply.

As expected, the king's summons arrived soon after. Uneasy and tense, Kharis pushed her untouched meal aside.

Her thoughts turned to General Zhad. Six years ago, he'd risked his life to shield the sisters from the dragon in the Iluna Forest. The thought that she might have harmed him made her stomach turn. She had to find a way to see him—and apologize.

After getting dressed, Kharis stepped outside her chambers, a thought needling her—Saya had left without a note. That, too, was a first today.

On her way out, Kharis's gaze lingered in the garden. The familiar rows of flowers swayed gently in the breeze, their fragrance wafting through the air, but she didn't spot the gardener. The garden felt strangely empty without him. Just a day ago, he'd gifted her a lovely bouquet. Disappointment pricked at her when she recalled she'd dropped it.

What was his name again? She tapped her clenched hand against her open palm when it came to her. Noam. Yes, that was it. A flicker of satisfaction tugged at her lips. She'd remembered it.

"Your Highness," a voice called out. "The Velathari are here."

Her smile faded.

89

The sentries snapped to attention as she neared the ornate iron gate. Beyond it, the Velathari stood waiting, their scowls etched with silent promises—any wrong move would be met with swift, unrelenting force. The hatred simmering beneath their cold stares never left.

Kharis clasped her hands and lowered her head, biting back the pain their emotions stirred within her. Without a word, she followed her overzealous escort. She kept her gaze low; the archers would be there. They always were. *I'm the Djinnshirukh, the Empire's monster.*

One persistent thought rumbled in her mind: Where was Saya?

※

Kharis strolled down a Sendatorsum's corridor, counting her footsteps in a futile attempt to steady her nerves. The Velathar's boots clacked off the perfectly polished marble floor, reflecting the surroundings. She imagined herself walking between two worlds, one real and the other an illusion shimmering beneath her feet. But which threatened to pull her under?

Opulence surrounded her. Fine tapestries and etched stonework adorned the lavish hallways. She walked past highly ornamented walls, exquisitely decorated columns and arches, sculpted stucco, and distinctive frescoes that poetically told the story of Zahar's turbulent beginnings.

She stopped before the large, ornate doors and sighed, aware of what awaited her.

Imperial sentries opened them, and Kharis entered the King's Chambers. She gulped when she saw her father sitting on the ornate chair, a replica of the one in the Throne Room. He was dressed in regalia, and the imperial crown rested on his head. Behind him, his Hasheret stood vigilant and fully armed.

Saya stood to his left in uniform, while Hala stood to his right in royal attire.

They didn't smile when she walked in, and a torrent of

goose bumps pimpled her skin. She bowed low, keeping her voice soft. "Blessed be the earth and sun."

"May they sustain us," was her father's response.

She stood in the center, her eyes fixed on the marble floor, feeling like a small creature awaiting its slaughter.

"I understand you went to the training arena yesterday," the king asked, his voice piercing the quiet.

"Yes, Your Majesty." Somehow, *asurûn* felt too informal right now.

"Why?"

That question baffled her. "Those were my instructions: to seek General Aram Zhad for training."

"Who told you?" His voice grew sharper, demanding.

Kharis grimaced, swallowing hard. She didn't even know the soldier's name. "It was a zenka trainee, Your Majesty."

"Which one?" His words were cold, biting.

Her heart jerked. "I—I don't know her name, Your Majesty." Her head was spinning; the walls were closing in. "I was pleased to learn I would be training under General Zhad. Saya and I owe him our lives."

"Did you even consider confirming this with General Salazar?" he asked, his tone edged with frustration.

Kharis gulped, her throat tightening. "I didn't think it would be necessary."

"General Zhad wasn't expecting you."

Her eyes widened as she lifted her gaze. "But—"

The king raised a hand, cutting her off. "These are the facts I have. General Aram Zhad wasn't expecting you. Your presence surprised everyone. General Salazar, who waited in the East Garden, worried when you didn't show up as scheduled. Someone told the messenger he sent to the villa that you were on your way, but the Velathari confirmed that you hadn't left yet. An unknown zenka trainee told you to head to the arena, but you didn't think it wise to confirm such a change in your schedule."

Her thoughtlessness would come with a new restriction.

Kharis returned her eyes to the floor. "Questioning orders often gets me into trouble, Your Majesty." A hint of defiance rode her comment. Question orders. Don't question orders. What was she supposed to do?

An uncomfortable hush fell over the chamber. Restlessness clawed at her chest as she braced herself for whatever punishment would be imposed this time. The metaphorical noose tightened around her neck. Tears stung her eyes, but after six years of crying, she was too tired to let them fall.

"You were framed," the king said, breaking the unbearable silence.

Her heart lurched.

"Someone intentionally placed you in the wrong place at the wrong time," he said. "Their only hitch to this plan was that your sister had asked to speak to me. As a result, we were on the balcony. If not for this, Saya would've been in the East Garden with General Salazar, and the outcome of yesterday's sparring would've been much more," he paused, choosing his words carefully, "problematic."

Kharis pressed her lips together, fighting to keep her composure. "Who would do this?"

"That we don't know." His hands gripped the armrests of his throne, knuckles whitening under the strain. The tension in his posture betrayed a suspicion he wasn't yet ready to voice aloud. "Prince Jordha is investigating. For now, stick to the approved schedule. Any changes will come directly from me or your brother. Is that understood?"

"Yes, Your Majesty." Kharis kept her head down, struggling to hold back the tears. Life in the Sendatorsum had always been a torment, but now, someone was plotting her downfall. It brought memories of zaldun Korshak, who had even followed her into the Iluna Forest to kill her.

"You're confined to the villa," her father said. "You may leave only for training with General Salazar—nothing else," he added, his voice colder now.

She'd expected this, but the weight of it still hit like a blow. Her throat tightened as she swallowed. "For how long?" She dreaded the answer.

"Until the inquiry is complete."

His words fell like a gavel. Her confinement was more than a punishment; it was a reminder of how precarious her position had become. All she could do was nod and keep her mouth shut.

An uneasy stillness hung in the air, drawn out painfully. Kharis kept her head bowed. The king had not permitted her to lift it, and while every fiber of her being loathed the Regia-Zenka and its suffocating rules, she wouldn't defy him. Her father had earned her respect, even when his decisions cut deep.

"Khiri," the king said, breaking the unbearable silence with her childhood nickname. "It isn't safe to have you here."

Kharis's gaze shot up, a cold dread settling over her.

"I was advised to send you to the Zahar-Eliza for a different type of training."

Her sharp inhale caught in her throat, panic seizing her.

"Master Hillal believes it'll be good for you. Hala and I intend to have the Regia-Zenka approve this journey."

Kharis staggered back as her world spun out of control. "Please." A stampede of images flashed before her eyes, swirling in a dizzying storm. She forgot to breathe as the floor tilted beneath her feet. "Please don't take me away from Saya." Fear's weight was crushing her. "Please."

She collapsed to the cold marble floor, her world crumbling, and pressed her forehead against it.

"I'll do anything you ask." Thousands of needles pricked her skin as panic draped over her. "I'll do whatever you demand of me. I promise to behave. I swear not to embarrass the Crown anymore. Please, I beg you. Allow me to stay with Saya." Her voice grew more ragged with each breath, her words barely holding together. Tears streamed down her face. "Please, please, don't exile me."

Before darkness overtook her, a pair of arms grasped her tightly, lifting her torso off the floor and enveloping her petite frame in a protective embrace. It exorcised the chill that had swallowed her.

"My darling child," her father whispered. "Saya is going with you. I won't have it any other way."

The world stilled, clicking back into place. Kharis's tear-filled gaze met her father's. "S—She's coming?"

He nodded, a gentle smile warming his expression. "It's the right thing to do."

Those words settled her galloping heart, and relief washed over her. She clung to her father and wept, but it wasn't anguish this time. She would be leaving the Ghak, and Saya would be with her. A thought this sweet had never occurred to her until now.

Suddenly, the doors flung open with a loud crash. A sharp gust flew through them, carrying the sound of angry boots. Guards or not, no force on this good earth could keep this woman from entering the king's chambers.

"Where is she?" Yuna's voice boomed across the room, filled with righteous fury and ready to engage in a yet-to-be-defined battle. Wide-eyed, the guards remained by the doors, but none had dared stop her. She halted abruptly at the sight of Kharis and Hröld kneeling in the middle of the floor.

"What's going on?"

"Nana." Saya's voice rang out from the dais, her golden eyes glowing brighter than the sun. "Khiri and I are going to the Zahar-Eliza."

"What?" Yuna's eyebrows arched sharply as she turned to Anong, who'd entered behind her. When Saya's words sank in a moment later, Yuna whipped her head back to the king, her expression shifting to unbridled fury.

"What?" she roared.

CHAPTER 17
MAYHEM AND MIRTH

Chaos wears a grin when joy takes the reins. - Poliormos

Kharis let out a sigh. Dinner would be a whirlwind of blissful chaos if they ever reached that point.

The arguing felt endless.

Yuna's voice filled the room as she pointed accusingly at her father and Hala. Anong stood close, barely keeping her from erupting as she clutched *her girls* protectively.

"This happened right under your noses," Yuna said, indignant. "I have begged you to allow me to take them away from Zahar-Ghak, and now you see why." Her arms tightened around Kharis and Saya. "You ignored me, yet when Master Hillal offered the same advice, you accepted it."

"Yuna—"

"Do *not* 'Yuna' me, Hröld. You should've known better. Where is the man who listens?"

"With you, all we can do is listen," Hala shot back, irritated.

"Hala Ghan," her voice boomed, "I have not granted you permission to speak."

Hala scowled, standing taller. "I'm the crown prince, and you shall address—"

95

"You're my nephew," she interrupted, waving her hand dismissively. "And I'm still displeased with you—"

"Yuna." Anong raised his voice, his eyes darting to Kharis and Saya. "Remember your place."

Yuna scrunched her face in frustration. She would never forgive Hala for refusing to defy the king's order to move Saya out of the villa, and how that inaction resulted in the massacre.

"We're here to celebrate a milestone for Kharis and Saya," Anong reminded them, his voice tinged with exasperation. "Could we please set our differences aside and cheer *for them* instead?"

The tension in the room shifted as Yuna, Hröld, and Hala faced him.

"They're going to the Zahar-Eliza," Anong said, casting the three a pointed look. "It's a significant moment for them—we should be celebrating, not squabbling."

Yuna's expression immediately brightened, a wide grin spreading across her face. "Ah! My voice of reason. I married well." She cupped his face with affection before turning to the sisters. "Now, my darlings, tell me, are you excited?"

Kharis bit her lip. "I am—"

Her stomach growled loudly. Laughter erupted around her.

"I haven't eaten today," she explained upon Yuna's questioning stare.

Yuna threw her arms around her. "What are we waiting for? Let us dine. Come, both of you." She pulled on the sisters, dragging them toward the dining room as if the men didn't exist.

Her father rolled his eyes in defeat.

Hala grumbled something unintelligible under his breath.

Anong simply smiled.

And like that, mayhem settled into mirth.

CHAPTER 18
DECEPTION AND DECEIT

A predator's patience is infinite when the prize is power. - Poliormos

Arjun Ghan stood by the window, his fingers tapping an uneven rhythm on the windowsill. Below, the plaza buzzed with evening activity: merchants hauling away their wares, evening servants arriving, and guards exchanging shifts.

But none of it anchored him. The whispers were inescapable, even here, far from the accursed Iluna Forest. They promised beauty and belonging. A lullaby of freedom, a home untouched by judgment. And some nights—like this one —he almost believed them.

Hröld, Yuna, and Hala toasted Kharis and Saya while he rotted away in his chambers, the uninvited ghost of the Senda-torsum. Ignored and forgotten, just like King Aram did with him. The forest never looked at him like that; its song never judged.

The bedroom door creaked open behind him, snapping the thread of thought. The confident stride was unmistakable. Aghet Mendi had entered.

"What happened?" Ghan demanded, a thread barely restraining his fury.

Aghet hummed, the sound smooth and resonant. "Luring

her to the training arena was easy. Pull the right strings, play on her fears, and she'll dance like a puppet. It was almost pitiful to watch." His tone darkened, a sneer creeping into his words. "But her cursed luck holds. The sister appeared uninvited and perfectly timed. Saya unraveled a meticulously planned endeavor."

Ghan clenched his hands, the nails digging into his palms. He welcomed the pain. It sharpened his focus.

"Saya," he hissed. "A well-executed plan foiled by a disciplined Sorukhipa. Why couldn't she be like Athon—arrogant, aloof, indulgent?"

He stared at his ring, at the emblem of the House of Ghan.

"And Kharis." The name dripped with venom. Bitter memories flared, including the ghosts of a night twenty years ago, when his hope turned to smoke. "Why did the demon choose her? She possesses the power I was meant to have, yet she wastes it as if it were nothing." He exhaled sharply, fogging the glass, and his eyes shifted to the White Guard officers marching past the palace gates.

"Aghet," he kept his voice low, fingering his gold ring. "We must act quickly; Jordha's onto us."

"Already done." Aghet chuckled with sinister satisfaction as he crossed the room, the silver buttons on his leather armor glinting in the flickering candlelight. "That zenka recruit won't be talking to anyone. What a terrible accident," he droned, expressing his disappointment. "It's unfortunate since she was quite useful."

He stopped just behind Ghan and leaned in, resting his chin on Ghan's shoulder to take in the view beyond the window. His breath brushed against Ghan's cheek—a warm, steady caress that chased away the chill that had settled deep in his bones.

Aghet asked, "What's the verdict?"

"Hillal's taking her to the Zahar-Eliza."

Aghet hummed, pensive. "An interesting challenge, I suppose."

"She can't leave," Ghan snarled. "If she goes, I'll lose her—

98

lose everything. As long as she's here, I have as many chances as there are days."

But once Kharis left...

"That blasted Kahurangi witch." His mind turned to the woman's prophecy before he unceremoniously snapped her neck.

The child of fire will slip past the gilded bars,
and wings of flame shall rend the stars.
Should she take flight,
no hand shall bind her, no chain shall hold.

The words clung to him like Indigofera ink, impossible to remove. He's been passed over—he, who had trained, sacrificed, and bled for the role and the Empire. Power was his inheritance. And if he couldn't inherit it freely, he would take it by force.

Aghet's voice dripped with confidence, his face a mask of cold calculation. "She won't leave the Senda, my prince. I won't allow it."

"Get me the Djinnshirukh. Alive." He gave Aghet a sidelong glance. "The resealment ritual needs her alive."

Aghet smirked, the gesture wide and cruel. "Broken?"

Ghan's lips shaped a faint, icy smile. "If necessary."

"She shall be yours." Aghet's lips grazed Ghan's. "But for now, let me make you forget all this hideous business." He clutched Ghan's hand, lovingly nudging him toward the bedroom.

For a fleeting moment, Ghan allowed himself to envision Kharis's defiance shattered and her power bent to his will. The intoxicating image was far more pleasurable than anything Aghet could offer. She would kneel in surrender, and he would take back what fate had denied him. Once he wielded the Akumi king's power, the world would be his.

A victorious grin spread across his face as he let Aghet guide him to bed.

CHAPTER 19
THE GRAVITY BETWEEN US

The stars whisper of hope, shimmering against the night, reminding us to dream beyond the darkness. - Poliormos

Kharis lifted her gaze, allowing the mesmerizing sight to wash over her. It was a clear night, and the glorious Silver River spread across the heavens. Lavender lingered in the evening air, its sweetness soft and soothing.

Dinner had stretched longer than she'd anticipated, but the memories brought a soft smile to her lips. Laughter and playful banter had punctuated the evening as the family engaged in endless discussions about the upcoming journey. Kharis and Saya had absorbed every word as their loved ones speculated on what this trip would mean for them. Yuna's grin had lasted all night, except when she shot irritated glances at Hala. Those two would never agree on anything.

The rhythmic crunch of gravel under Velathari boots brought Kharis back. They carried torches to light the passageway, the flames casting flickering shadows across the walls. She still pondered the archers' positions, wondering whether their aim would hold under such uneven light. A wilder part of her itched to test the theory by bolting down the path—but common sense struck her like a finger flicked to the forehead.

Saya marched in step with their escort, her face etched in quiet contemplation.

Would she ask about what had happened at the arena? The uneasy burden of secrecy settled on Kharis's shoulders. She couldn't speak of the aid the Voice had provided. Admitting his existence would terrify her sister. The last thing Saya needed was to learn that her sister was losing her sanity and the implications such knowledge held for Sorukhipa. Kharis couldn't subject her to such cruelty.

The Voice had mentioned a dark one before melding into her mind's shadows. He'd dropped a tiny kernel of information and disappeared. What did he mean by that? Even the Voice was silent now, brooding like some ancient shadow in the hollow of her ribs. She scratched her temple in frustration. She had to give him a name; it was annoying to call him "the Voice."

Kharis felt the weight of Saya's gaze—careful, steady, unreadable. The kind of stare that asked questions without words.

"How are you doing?" Saya asked.

Kharis's mental grumbling came to a halt.

"Sorry," Saya said. "I didn't mean to startle you."

Kharis waved a hand, unfazed. "It's fine." She glanced at the starry sky. A symphony of crickets serenaded the sultry night.

"Dinner was nice," Saya said.

Kharis nodded. "It was. Once we got to eating." A chuckle spilled from her lips. "I thought they would never stop arguing."

"So did I." Saya laughed softly. "So, how are you feeling?"

Kharis stifled a groan at the question, one she hated more than anything. It was always the first in Saya's probing inquiry. "Don't tell Nana, but I'm still dizzy."

"How come?" Curiosity glinted in her gaze.

Kharis tipped her head. "I don't know how to describe it. 'Dizzy' is the best I can come up with."

Saya hummed thoughtfully. "You were trapped in Andaheimur. Your soul is still adjusting to your body."

"I wasn't trapped."

"I had to go in and free you." Saya's annoyance finally spilled over, and her true feelings surfaced. "That's the definition of being trapped."

"Fine," Kharis snapped.

Saya halted in her tracks, hands balling into fists at her sides. "Don't do that."

Kharis frowned, uncertain. "Do what?"

"Dismiss me like that," Saya shot back, her voice rising. "Acting like it's you against everyone."

Kharis stepped back, her sister's words striking hard.

"You must temper that reckless tendency of yours," Saya pressed. "And stop telling me it's fine, fine, fine. It's not *fine*."

Kharis stood still, her arms hanging limp by her sides. "Saya—"

"You must let me in." Saya's gaze locked onto hers. Anger and pleading made her golden eyes glisten.

Kharis blinked, confusion creasing her brow. "What do you mean? Who else do I have but you?"

"We used to talk all the time."

Huh? "Saya, we still do."

"Not as we used to." Saya's stare bore into her. "We talk, yes, but I don't know what goes on in that head of yours anymore." She huffed, crossing her arms. "Now we talk about the weather."

Kharis cast a glance at the Velathari, their faces blank and unyielding. She shoved her hands into her pockets, trying to hold back her frustration. The leather was cool to the touch, carrying the bite of the night air.

"What do you want me to say?" she asked, her voice strained, like a bowstring ready to snap. "I make you cry. I make you angry. You worry so much that it consumes your entire life, so why would I burden you with even more of my problems?"

"Because you're not alone." Saya grabbed Kharis's arms, pulling her close. "Because I'm your sister." She choked back a sob. "Because I love you dearly."

Kharis sucked in a breath. "I love you, too, but I can't saddle you with all my troubles. You deserve a life."

"I'm your Sorukhipa." Saya's grip tightened, almost shaking Kharis. "You are my life. Don't you get that?"

"Of course I get it." Kharis's voice wavered, then sharpened. "I get it every time I step outside. You're spared the hatred when they all look at me. I've heard the whispers, Saya. *'The Sorukhipa faltered. If she'd done her duty, the Djinnshirukh would be dead. Fewer lives would've been lost.'* That's what they say. That I should've died—that you should've killed me."

Kharis's words landed like daggers. Stunned, Saya stood frozen, at a loss for how to respond. The silence between them stretched painfully until a soft whimper escaped her lips.

"Never say that." Saya threw her arms around Kharis, her body trembling as sobs racked her frame. "We're in this together, do you hear? Together."

Kharis remained still, her chest tight, every shaky breath from her sister carving deeper into her guilt. Tonight was no different—her sister was finally venting the fear from a training session gone awry.

And once again, Kharis had made her cry.

Not a day passed without the wish to undo it all—to take back the choices that had led to the massacre. Those memories stalked her like a never-ending nightmare. Most days, she could bury them in training, pushing her body past its limits until there was no space left to feel or think. But during quiet moments like this, with tears and trembling arms wrapped around her, the past surged back—merciless and unrelenting.

Saya didn't deserve the consequences, yet she bore them, suffering the fallout of the horror Kharis had unleashed.

The Djinnshirukh tilted her head, seeking solace in the stars.

Kharis and Saya were like the moons, pulled and pushed away by the gravity of the cosmos—always orbiting each other, never free.

Sharan shone brightly, its ivory glow casting a soft light over the night. Tung had crossed over, giving Sharan its red eye. On this night, when they met, it felt as though they paused to watch the world below.

What would they see?

Kharis tightened her embrace, inhaling the scent of jasmine and orange blossoms that always clung to her sister. It reminded her why she would fiercely do anything to free her sister.

Above them, the Silver River stretched across the sky, a shimmering garland twinkling in the darkness. The North Star winked at Kharis, reminding her that every journey began at a crossroads. She fixed her gaze on the heavens, her heart aching as a sudden shower of shooting stars streaked across the sky.

She wished on each one, not for her freedom, but for Saya's. That someday, her sister would laugh without fear and love without duty. If there was a way to set her free, Kharis would find it—even if it meant breaking every chain herself.

CHAPTER 20
THE GARDENER AND THE DJINNSHIRUKH

Love is a timid flower, slowly unfolding its petals to reveal the beauty within, leaving a heady trail of wonder and magic. - Poliormos

After the incident with General Zhad and the threat it exposed, the king had confined Kharis to the villa until further notice. It felt strange to be restricted, but oddly, she welcomed the quiet. At least here, she didn't have to endure the stares of people who despised her.

Kharis wandered through the garden, her cloak brushing against fragrant blooms. Three days after the announcement, the news still clung to Kharis's thoughts like tiny jewels encrusted in fine brocade. The Zahar-Eliza—a place steeped in mysticism and draped in the ancient lore of the immortals. And she was going there.

She settled in a quiet, secluded corner, tightly pulling her garment around her. The morning sun had crept above the horizon, its lavender and coral rays painting the sky in soft hues, gently waking the world.

A hummingbird with stunning cobalt and emerald feathers darted playfully among the orange blossoms. It moved swiftly through the air. Then, as if spotting her, it hovered above Kharis, its tiny wings a joyful blur. Each graceful dip and twirl coaxed a smile from Kharis, and her heart swelled with a sweet lightness she hadn't felt in days. She closed her eyes and let the sun's warmth gently kiss her face.

"Your Highness?"

She shifted on the bench, startled. Standing before her was Noam, clutching a flower arrangement with both hands, his grip a little too tight.

He stammered, his cheeks flushed. "I didn't mean to interrupt."

"You didn't." She hoped her smile would confirm it.

Noam exhaled, relieved. "I made this for you."

The flower crown drew Kharis's gaze. Noam had carefully woven Hellebore blooms, interlacing sprigs of fragrant rosemary and laurel with colorful ribbons. Impressed by the intricate craftsmanship, she accepted it from his outstretched hands.

"Thank you," she said, lowering her gaze. "It's beautiful."

"It's for the Lorea Festival," he said.

Kharis's smile faltered. While the realm prepared to celebrate the winter solstice, she was confined and unaware of it. Resentment tugged at her, and she realized how distant she'd become from the world her father ruled. She studied the arrangement on her lap—the colorful blooms, bright green leaves, and silky ribbons masterfully woven into a circlet crown. How long had it taken him to make this?

Outside of Saya, no one had ever made her something so thoughtful. The gifts she typically received were often obligatory, mere tokens designed not to please her but to curry favor with the imperial king. Noam had taken the time to craft this lovely arrangement to celebrate a festival she knew nothing about.

Did he want something? The thought still crept in— unwelcome, familiar. No one ever gave the Djinnshirukh anything but scowls. Yet, instead of greed or rot, a harmonious hum filled her ears. Joy sparkled behind her eyelids, golden and bright, crisp as winter.

Standing against the morning sunlight to shield her eyes, Noam gazed at her with wonder and hope.

To show her appreciation, she placed the crown on her head.

"How do I look?" A smile danced on her lips.

Noam's eyes widened, his shyness momentarily forgotten. "Like a goddess." The words slipped out, and realizing this, he stepped back and bowed, his face flushing. "Please accept my apologies."

Genuine appreciation tugged at her heart. "I appreciate the compliment. You have a talent for creating beautiful things." She gestured to the flower crown.

Noam stilled, his eyes shimmering. "I'm glad you enjoy it, Your Highness." His voice wavered but was filled with sincerity. He lowered his gaze, and the flush on his cheeks intensified. "I—I've admired you from afar and wanted to make something for you."

Her heart skipped a beat, the sensation crashing over her like a giant wave sweeping her off a rocky breakwater. She instinctively braced, shoulders pulling tight as if preparing to deflect a blow. Not because she feared him, but because compliments and kindness always landed like ambushes.

She was torn between wanting to hold on tightly and allowing the currents to take her away. Blessed Mother. This emotion was overwhelming, overtaking her body in a dizzying fashion. And gods above and below, she didn't want it to end.

Kharis caught the flicker of hesitation beneath his sincerity. "Your Highness," he said, daring to meet her gaze. "You're the most radiant bloom in this garden."

A bold risk. A step beyond the careful lines he was meant to follow.

The bolt that jolted through her pushed all thoughts aside. Her heart vaulted, wanting to race past her throat to jump out and land on Noam's hands. Kharis gazed at him, having forgotten how to speak. Her brain had gone blissfully blank; no muscle in her body moved, yet every nerve was alive, firing a glorious tempest.

He stiffened when she didn't utter a word, his bronze eyes widening as his brow creased. "If I overstepped—"

"No." Her mouth spoke of its own accord. Even her brain

had betrayed her, leaving her at a loss. Blessed Mother above. "Your words meant the world to me."

That much was true.

His warm smile revealed adorable dimples on his cheeks.

Her heart melted at his down-to-earth handsomeness. Kharis admired his bravery; who else in the Senda would dare approach the terrifying Djinnshirukh?

And then she remembered her role.

A shadow crossed her thoughts, and her smile faded. Did he know who she was? If he didn't, his flower gifts would stop once he learned the truth.

"Your Highness...?"

Kharis felt the sting of tears. This had to be a cruel prank. Plenty of zaldunak were eager to see her humiliated—and what better way to fuel their mockery than by being caught with a gardener? Her mind flashed to courtly laughter and whispers in silk-lined halls. *"What an idiot,"* they would say. *"Thinking anyone would ever love her."*

She lifted her gaze, struggling to stifle the tears that threatened to spill over.

Noam flinched, his expression shifting as he noticed.

"I did offend you." He dropped to one knee, lowering his head. "Please, forgive me."

"No, you didn't. I..." What could she even say? "I'm burdened with other concerns."

His eyebrows drew together, and his features softened. "Even if this is preposterous for me to say," he said gently, propriety warring with compassion, "if it were helpful to you, I would listen."

Kharis stilled.

His mint-scented honesty wrapped around her, melting the edges of her doubt and hinting at possibilities.

"I don't wish to offend," he said, "and I know my place, but perhaps"—he pressed his lips, uncertainty flickering in his eyes—"I could be a friend. One who listens."

The silence in her head felt absolute.

A friend? The idea that this could be a cruel joke persisted.

Yet honesty had always been a soft, soothing melody for her, rising in pitch like the first notes of dawn.

"Most ignore my presence, Your Highness," Noam said. "After all, who pays attention to a gardener?"

The sadness in his smile gave Kharis pause. She'd only learned his name days ago, yet he'd been working at the villa for a year. How many moments had she overlooked, lost in her thoughts, while he quietly tended to the beauty around her?

"I volunteered to work here." His confession surprised her.

Silence settled between them.

Servants balked at working in the villa, and some were likely coerced into it; the allure of a higher salary was never enough to tempt them. The Djinnshirukh terrified everyone except this gentle gardener. Curiosity crept up behind her, urging her to dig deeper.

"Why?" she asked, her brow drawing into a frown.

Determination shone brightly in his eyes. "I wanted to see for myself."

"And?" she scoffed, crossing her arms.

He gazed at her with such kindness that it pushed her thorns back. "They were wrong, Your Highness," he simply said. "All of them."

It was a land-shattering earthquake, his words shaking the foundations of her perception.

"I know it's absurd for someone like me to make such an offer," he said, "but if you were ever in need of a friend—"

"Yes."

Her response escaped her lips before her mind could catch it. Her lonely heart had pushed her to cling to this unexpected lifeline and hold on tightly.

Noam's eyebrows arched.

"Yes," she repeated, a little more firmly this time. "I would love to learn what happens outside these walls. Having someone to talk to and ask questions."

His eyes searched hers, and his smile grew. Kharis felt a flicker of hope ignite within her. Maybe, just maybe, people like her were given a reprieve from their fate.

"It's not preposterous at all," she said. "I would appreciate having a friend."

"Then, a friend you'll have." His excitement sent a thrill through her. He rose to his feet, his hands clasped before him, and bowed slightly, preparing to return to his task.

"Noam?"

He halted.

Kharis summoned her courage as Noam had. "Would you tell me about the Lorea Festival? I have a little time before I'm expected for training." She fidgeted with her cloak. "Would you spare a little of yours?"

Noam turned around slowly, looking like she'd offered him Zahar on a silver platter. "Your Highness," he said. "I have all the time in the world for you."

The joy in his gaze sent a pleasurable shiver running down her back.

Blessed Mother of all.

He sat on the ground, cross-legged, his eyes wide and eager. "The Lorea Festival honors the flowers that bloom in winter," he said. "It's a tribute to women, life, and renewal. For hope endures through the darkest night. During the festival, young men offer flower crowns to young women—like the one you wear now—because, on that night, they become our queens."

He lowered his eyes, a timid gesture Kharis found endearing.

The longing in his voice lit a small fire inside Kharis. "Tell me more."

For the first time in a long while, Kharis wasn't thinking about fire, fate, or fear: just a boy, a story, and the warm, fragile promise of something beautiful. And so, the Djinnshirukh and the gardener chatted under the approving gaze of the sun, her quiet smile brightening their conversation.

CHAPTER 21
PETALS AND PROMISES

Flowers are kisses from the stars on this blessed earth, infusing the air we breathe with their heady aromas to uplift our souls. - Poliormos

The melodious humming confirmed it.

When Saya entered the solar, Kharis had already finished her breakfast, a bright smile lighting her face. It was a familiar gesture, yet touched with something new—lighter, freer. Saya had noticed the shift in her sister's demeanor since the Zahar-Eliza announcement two weeks prior, subtle at first yet growing with each passing day.

Kharis was undeniably happy, enjoying her confinement. She rushed to training, hurried back, and retreated to the garden to read. Going to the Zahar-Eliza suited her. Then again, leaving the Senda suited Saya just as well.

"You're up early—again." The sun had not risen yet.

"Good morning to you, too," Kharis replied, cheerfully gulping down her tea.

It had been two weeks, and Saya still couldn't believe the transformation. Kharis's joy was a bright new season—spring in the middle of winter—a refreshing change from the shadows that had lingered over her for so long.

"May the earth and sun bless you."

"May they sustain us," Kharis replied, serving herself more tea while watching how the sweet cream collected at the top.

Saya couldn't help but stare. Kharis's happiness made the silver in her eyes gleam. For the past two weeks, Kharis had been humming or singing, rising before dawn to sit in the garden, soak in the morning light, or relax before the evening call for dinner. Saya cherished the blissful aura her sister exuded.

"You're in a good mood."

"It's a lovely day." Kharis winked.

Saya made a grumbling noise, aware there was more to her sister's "lovely day" comment. "You're up to something."

Kharis's smile widened as she added a spoonful of honey to her tea. "I am not."

A whimsical sense of mischief coiled around her answer.

For a moment, Saya faced the other sister: the Khiri from the past, who laughed with prankish energy; the defiant queen of rascals who had gotten them into so much trouble; the Khiri who had vanished the day of the massacre.

Saya's body quivered with happiness; she'd missed that sister so much.

"You got up before me, which is quite rare. In fact"—Saya pointed her fork at her—"for the last two weeks, you've beaten the sun. I've never seen you be," she pursed her lips, searching for the right word, "committed to an early start."

Kharis chuckled. "Why not?" She stretched her arms up and exhaled, satisfied. "We've had great weather. Not too cold yet. And in the early morning, the scent of hellebores and cyclamen is intoxicating."

"Enjoy it," Saya said. "We leave for the Zahar-Eliza in three months."

A sudden cloud shaded Kharis's gaze. It was there, then it was gone. "I better get started." She got up with a full cup of tea.

Saya cocked her head. "Where are you going?"

Kharis inhaled the tea's sweet cardamom aroma. "I'll finish my tea in the garden, then train with General Salazar. You?"

"Tending the sick with Nana—our usual morning walk

through the academy. My training with Salazar is later in the afternoon."

"May he be gentle with both of us."

"Doubtful," Saya said.

"I'll take his training any day." Kharis's gaze got lost in a place only she could see. "He's demanding and rather strict, but his praise is genuine."

Saya understood. Under Arjun Ghan, Kharis was always useless. Salazar did his best to conceal his smile when he demanded they repeat their drills. There was a visible sense of pride when he assessed them. Kharis was correct. His praise was freely bestowed, urging Saya to do more and better.

"I'm off," Kharis said. "May the earth and sun bless you."

"May they sustain us," Saya said to Kharis's back as she dashed out of the room, her cup spilling tea on the floor. Saya sighed, amused, but seeing her sister this happy and light-hearted was the only blessing she could've asked for.

With a grin that reached her eyes, Saya dove for her breakfast: a large, crisp rice flour crepe stuffed with spicy potatoes, onions, garlic, and green peas rolled to perfection. The crunch it made when her fork broke a piece was music to her ears.

§•

Kharis nearly broke into a sprint, her grin refusing to fade. She shot a cautious glance over her shoulder and, satisfied, straightened her posture and walked purposefully through the garden until she found her target.

Noam had crouched by the jasmine hedges, collecting flower clusters in a small hemp bag.

A warm familiarity settled over her. Over the past two weeks, these encounters, filled with conversations about a hundred different topics, had become their routine. Kharis had come to cherish these moments when she could lose herself in the company of someone who answered her endless questions with patience and humor.

"Good morning." She hoped not to sound too eager.

Noam smiled and got up, wiping his hands on his apron as he bowed.

"I brought you tea." She presented the steaming cup with a timid smile. "I figured you could use some." This was her daily morning excuse to see him.

"Bless the earth and sun," he said, curling his hands around hers as he took the cup.

His touch stirred her entire body to life. Her heart, bouncing wildly inside her chest, burst into song. Kharis somehow strung her words together. "M—May they sustain you."

Curiosity gleamed in his eyes.

"Us," she corrected herself, a flush of warmth dancing across her cheeks. "May they sustain *us*."

"Us," he repeated, his voice sending a shiver of pure contentment coursing through her entire being.

Would there ever be an "us"?

He blew on the cup, the steam wafting off, and took a sip. "It's quite flavorful. Thank you."

Her mind raced as she scanned the garden for a hint of what to say next. A surge of nerves flooded her, trapping her in a whirlwind of indecision. All the dialogues she'd rehearsed, each meant to impress the young man, vanished instantly. Her eyes darted between him, the cup, and the jasmine clippings.

He caught her gesture. "I'm collecting these so I can dry them."

"Oh?" Kharis angled her head, her curiosity rousing.

"I clip these and deliver them to the kitchens. The blend can infuse teas, perfumes, or aromatic oils." He fished a small organza bag from his pocket and handed it to her. "I made this one for you using flower clippings from your garden."

Her heart fluttered as she pressed it against her nose. "It smells divine."

His smile spoke of pride. "I used winter jasmine, alyssum, and chamomile for this one. It's an old recipe from where I come. You can place it under your pillow to keep bad dreams away."

"You remembered." He'd noticed her exhaustion one

morning, and she'd attributed it to nightmares. That had been the extent of it. "I appreciate the gift, and yes, I'll use it." She rolled on the balls of her feet, hands clasped behind her back. "Finish your tea before it gets cold."

His smile always put her at ease. She watched him savor the hot drink, wondering whether she should tell him about the Zahar-Eliza. And why wouldn't she?

"Noam?"

He lifted his gaze, lazily licking the cream off his upper lip. Every coherent thought in her mind evaporated, her focus drawn to his mouth.

"Your Highness?" He gazed at her with concern.

"W—Would you like more tea?" The words tumbled out, a poor excuse to cover the moment of adoration she'd let slip.

He assessed the sun, peeking from behind the hills, its deep red and orange fingers parting the indigos. "It means you would leave." His gaze shifted back to her. "And I'd rather enjoy your presence a little longer."

Blessed. Mother.

Kharis longed to leave the Ghak and escape the suffocating confines of the Senda, but the thought of missing their conversations and losing the light Noam brought into her life filled her with a bittersweet ache. In a world where Saya was her only friend, Kharis appreciated Noam's presence and unique worldview, especially when his perspective was delightfully addictive.

"Noam," a subtle frown puckered her brow, "my sister and I'll be leaving the Senda soon."

His forehead creased. "When?"

"At the beginning of spring. We're being sent to the Zahar-Eliza for training."

He tilted his head, letting sunlight kiss his face. "It'll be good training," he said. "The Zahar-Eliza's an in-between—a mystical place between the mortal and spiritual realms. The Hatorisaita guides those who enter. Training under him is a profound honor."

"The Hatorisaita?"

Noam's nod was solemn, his voice infused with reverence.

"The temple's Grand Master. The gods selected him, and their power resonates within him like a sacred drum."

Kharis nudged a boot against the path. "I thought it was a place for more focused training."

"It is," Noam said. "Many say emerging after a year in isolation is a rebirth. Like being given a blank canvas on which to rewrite their fate."

That idea thrilled her, imagining what she might write on hers.

"Your Highness?" Noam hesitated, eyes lingering on the cup. "My best friend just married my sister. They're heading back to Urrun soon, and there's a small farewell gathering. I was wondering if... maybe you'd like to come with me?"

He said it so quietly she almost wasn't sure she'd heard him right. A rush of emotions flooded in. In all her years in the Senda, no one had ever invited her anywhere.

"Where is it?"

"On the outer Zahar-Regia ring." He bit his lip. "So... would you?"

Her answer should be *no*.

She was confined to the villa and forbidden from even leaving the inner ring. Every rule, every shadow, every eye would say *no*.

And yet...

With Noam, the world felt different. Brighter. Possible. Flirting with fate—*with him*—was reckless. Dangerous. Yet, for someone who'd been denied freedom since birth, this invitation felt like a door swinging open.

"It was never my intention to fluster you." He raised his hands in apology. "Please, forget I—"

"Yes."

The word slipped out swiftly, ahead of common sense.

Noam's eyes widened, his eyebrows lifting in surprise.

"Yes...?" he whispered, as if afraid to believe what he'd heard.

Kharis tilted her head to gauge the time, hiding the emotions warring within her. "Let's discuss it tonight." Blessed Mother, she was doing this. "If I go, there will be conditions."

"Anything." He stared at her, his gaze infused with optimism. "I'll do whatever you ask of me."

Anticipation tickled her in ways she didn't quite understand. The allure of adventure stirred deep within her with a need to quench her curiosity and participate in something so clearly forbidden.

It was ridiculous.

It was undeniably wrong.

And she couldn't wait.

Suddenly alive, a grin played on her lips as an ineffable sensation wrapped around her as if made of luxurious silk. Was it hope? Joy? Defiance?

The distant blaring of trumpets signaling the change of guards shattered her thoughts. "I must leave soon," she said, "but tonight, when everyone's asleep, come here and we'll discuss it. The patrol cycles consistently on the hour, so wait for your chance to enter, and no one will spot you."

Noam stared, speechless. Kharis doubted he'd heard anything after her "yes."

When she took the empty cup from him, their hands brushed again, sending a thrill through her that was hard to contain. She dashed back to the villa as Noam's singing lingered in the air.

CHAPTER 22
ALES AND TALES

*Joy is intoxicating, a warm rush of euphoria, a vibrant embrace. -
Poliormos*

Kharis navigated the tunnel, praying she wouldn't be caught. Her footsteps echoed against the wet stone, the air thick with the scent of moisture. Puddles dotted the uneven ground, and her boots splashed through them as she pushed forward. She'd draped her cape around her shoulders to keep it from getting wet, and the fabric rustled against her ears as she scurried.

The Djinnshirukh reached the end, and her eyes narrowed at the sight of the heavily rusted metal door. She wedged her torch into an iron bracket, the flame casting long, restless shadows across the walls. Then, slowly, she opened her hand, palm facing the flame. The fire leaned toward it as if it were its home. With a soft hiss, it vanished into her skin. Darkness immediately swallowed her whole.

Kharis listened to the steady thrum of her breath as she waited for her sight to adjust. She shouldn't use her magic, for it would hasten the unraveling, but the need to sense beyond what her sight could offer tugged at her. Against her better judgment, she gave in, letting her magic drift outward like a whisper in the void.

Nothing larger than a mouse stirred, and no warning flares ignited in her mind. She probed further, her magic questing silently for the pulse of life, the faint echoes of mortal heartbeats, or the tang of emotions that could paint unseen presences in the tunnel.

There was only a deep, all-encompassing stillness. No one lurked nearby. No one had followed her. Relief tasted sweet.

The door was a different issue. Time and neglect had sealed it shut, its iron skin blistered wth rust.

With a determined grunt, she grasped the handle and pulled. The hinges groaned in protest, refusing to move. With a quiet breath, she summoned her magic. Stardust flared across her palms, pale and glittering like moonlight. She pressed both hands against the iron, and the door shivered. Whispers of her power seeped into the corroded seams, coaxing them apart. When the metal softened, she steadied herself and pulled again—this time with her otherworldly strength. The door shrieked open, metal scraping against metal.

The overgrown shrubbery that clung to the other side reached for her like clawing hands. Twisted vines tugged at her hair and clothes, snagging her as she fought through until she finally emerged into the open air.

Noam was pacing when he caught sight of her.

"There you are." A sigh of relief escaped him as his shoulders slumped. His eyes searched hers. "Are you all right?"

"Yes," she said, brushing stray hair from her face and pulling on a leaf. "Why wouldn't I?"

Noam tilted his head toward the tunnel's entry, his brow furrowed. "I didn't believe that you would use that."

She smoothed her hair and lifted a shoulder, unfazed. "There are several underground drainage and water reclamation canals," she explained. "As well as the sewers."

His face contorted with a hint of guilt. "I didn't realize how much effort and trouble this would take."

Kharis brushed off his concern. She didn't have the heart to tell him this was an escape route for when the Senda came under siege, its existence long forgotten. She preferred to keep it that way.

With another grunt, she closed the gate, gathering the vines and foliage to conceal it. "There." She dusted her hands. "It took me longer than expected. I had to avoid a few guards on my way here. Skulking around comes with some minor challenges."

Noam's brow creased.

"One of the mastiffs found me," she chuckled, "but after a good scratch behind the ear and a nice meaty treat, he left me to my own devices without a bark."

Noam stared at his feet. "I'm sorry."

"About what?" Kharis refastened her cloak, letting it fall past her shoulders. She then adjusted the knit cap to hide her jet-black hair and drew on her hood.

"Mine was a selfish request," Noam said. "I should've known better."

"I did say yes." She smiled at Noam, hardly containing how glad she was to spend time with him.

"And when you did," he whispered, "I forgot how to breathe."

She chuckled softly, cheeks heating up. "From here on out, I alone am responsible for what happens to me. I hardly ever leave the royal compound, so an opportunity to see how the rest of the world lives was hard to pass."

He stared at her, but she couldn't tell if disappointment clouded his eyes. Sharan's moonlight was playing tricks on her.

"So, where do we go?" she asked, hoping to change the mood.

"Follow me." He gingerly took her hand. "I don't want you to get lost," he explained.

She didn't snatch it away, and in that moment, she swore his disappointment melted away.

His calloused hand, so large and warm, swallowed hers. As other thoughts popped into her head, she thanked the clouds concealing Sharan so Noam couldn't see she was blushing. Both quietly left the riverbank and headed toward the outer Zahar-Regia ring, where Senda servants, workers, and soldiers lived.

Lanterns hanging from eaves added to the twinkling stars

over this section of the imperial city. Their soft light enveloped the open food stalls, their vendors infusing the air with tantalizing aromas, from roasted chicken skewers and savory meats rubbed with toasted cumin to the scents of spicy curry, sugar, and mint. Laughter permeated the atmosphere with a surprising sense of community.

Kharis had never expected the vibrant energy blanketing the neighborhoods. She'd imagined them to be as dull as the evenings at the palace.

Music and singing spilled from open doors and windows, and a kaleidoscope of colors flooded the lively streets. People bustled, from groups enjoying late dinners at sidewalk stalls to artists setting up impromptu performances under the stars. Zenka guards patrolled the streets, never minding the young couple rushing past them.

Out here, the night was mysterious and magical. Kharis drank it all, thirsty for more. Yet, beneath her awe, a thread of guilt whispered Saya's name, warning her this joy might cost too much.

Noam navigated this labyrinth of humanity, his hand clutching hers tightly. Kharis walked alongside him, her hood drawn low, shielding her face from prying eyes.

As they turned on a bustling street, four zenka guards emerged from the crowd, their blue-trimmed leather armor making them stand out.

"Your Highness," Noam warned, his voice steady but low. "Don't look, but—"

"I see them," she replied, her hand tightening around his. "Let's keep walking."

Her heart pounded. A single misstep, a glance of recognition from a guard with a keen memory, and she'd be dragged to the dungeons. Then would come the spiral: political intrigue, ruthless schemes, and something far worse: a storm that would swallow everyone she loved—including this kind gardener.

And yet, Noam's hand in hers felt like defiance. Like freedom.

One of the guards called out, "Hey!"

Kharis flinched. Noam cursed.

The guards veered toward them with purpose, cutting through the crowd like hounds scenting prey. A tall man with a scar bisecting his right cheek stepped in front of them, tapping the blunt end of his spear lightly on the cobblestones.

"Are you Noam Willoway?" he asked, his voice rough as gravel. "You match the description."

Kharis's breath snagged, her mind racing for a lie, an escape, anything.

"Y—Yes," Noam answered, trying to stay calm. "Is there a problem, sir?"

The guard's gaze lingered on Kharis. Her hood cast deep shadows over her face, but she felt his scrutiny—sharp, probing, *too long*. Her pulse roared in her ears.

His expression was unreadable. Then, with a sudden shift, he smiled.

"You're late."

Noam blinked. "Sir?"

The guard's eyes twinkled with dry amusement. "Wish Commander Loria our best on his wedding," he said, then nodded toward Kharis. "Perhaps yours will follow his?"

Noam let out a shaky laugh, squeezing Kharis's hand. "We'll pass on your wishes."

"From Captain Joriv and his unit," he said, gesturing to the guards behind him, who murmured their well-wishes. "Better get going," Joriv added, already turning away. The others chuckled as the crowd swallowed them.

Kharis and Noam exhaled in unison. "That was close," he said. "They must know my friend."

Her gaze followed the patrol. "As long as no one realizes who I am, all will be well. Shall we continue?"

Noam nodded, his grin and color returning. "Let's."

CHAPTER 23
TWIRLS AND WHIRLS

Joy is rebellion in rhythm, a refusal to stay still when the heart has found its song. - Poliormos

Together, Kharis and Noam weaved through the bustling streets. Narrow three-story townhouses cluttered every space imaginable until merry music floated in their direction.

"We're almost there," Noam said.

Ahead, a building with a stone foundation and external wooden beams in a grid pattern displayed a wooden sign that read The Porcupine.

A few individuals, identifiable by their attire as Senda workers, stood near the sturdy entrance, eagerly chatting. Some recognized Noam and waved at him. Kharis gulped, pulling her hood closer.

"It's good to see you this evening," one said, curiously glancing at Noam's companion for a moment too long.

"Eru, Nasir. Good to see you, too," Noam said after a quick two-finger salute, pushing the door open and tugging Kharis along.

Amid flickering torchlight and the cozy embrace of rough-hewn timber walls, the tavern burst with life. The air brimmed with the aroma of roasting meats and spiced ale. Patrons huddled around worn wooden tables, tankards clinking in raucous toasts. A fire crackled in the hearth, shadows dancing across warm, laughing faces.

The tavern keeper—a broad-shouldered man with a thunderous laugh—moved with surprising grace behind the counter, sloshing frothy ale into jugs and ladling steaming stew into wooden bowls. The scent of garlic, saffron, and slow-cooked lamb filled the air.

Serving women wove through the crush of bodies, skirts swaying as they balanced trays of drink and fare, ducking stray elbows and sidestepping drunken feet with practiced ease.

The energy was contagious. The scents spoke of simplicity yet felt decadent, like forbidden fruit.

Minstrels strummed guitars and flutes while tambourines and bodhran struck a steady pulse, weaving tales of far-off lands and mythical creatures mingled with stories of courage and love. Before the small dais, people twirled to the tempo, skirts flying, boots stomping, and laughter bubbling like spring water.

Blessed Mother. Dancing.

Kharis thought she'd died, and Andaheimur's door had opened to this tiny piece of heaven.

"Nom!" a voice boomed in her ears. "There's my best man."

A pair of strong arms wrapped around Noam, patting his back. A broad-shouldered, thick-necked young man, tall and wrapped in too much muscle, pulled away and held onto Noam's shoulders with a smile that revealed how happy he was to see him. Then, his curious eyes locked on Kharis.

"Sebastian," Noam began, "this is—" His eyes suddenly widened, a flicker of panic flashing across his face.

Blasted. They hadn't discussed names.

"Hya," Kharis said swiftly, cutting in before the silence could stretch. She forced a small, confident smile, the name rolling off her tongue. "Hya, as in Hyacinth," she added, recalling the first bouquet Noam had ever given her. "But don't you dare call me Hyacinth," she warned Sebastian.

Sebastian blinked.

"Hya!" he shouted. "Good to meet you!" And those burly

arms wrapped around her so tightly that, for a moment, she feared he would snap her in two. He lifted her, shaking her as if she were a doll. Kharis squealed, startled.

"Sebastian!" A female voice behind them sounded irked.

"Look, Marissa. Our boy Nom brought a girl." He lowered Kharis. "Finally!"

Marissa smacked his arm. "Don't break her then."

Sebastian laughed.

"I'm so sorry," Marissa said. "Please forgive him," she told Kharis before facing her brother. "Is she the one who received your Lorea flower crown?" she asked with a playful smirk, then faced Kharis. "He spent an entire afternoon assembling it. I've never seen my brother so obsessed with a task—"

"Issa..." Noam glared at her.

Marissa stifled a laugh and rested her hands on her voluptuous hips. "It's lovely to meet you. I'm Noam's sister." Then she shot Noam the "you're keeping secrets from me" stare. Saya would do much worse if she ever found out Kharis was at The Porcupine.

Sebastian leaned toward Noam as if sharing a secret. "Your girl's pretty."

Noam's face turned bright red, and the dim light did nothing to conceal it.

Marissa arched an eyebrow. "You know we can hear you, right?"

"Don't let her go, Nom. Snatch her right away"—he squeezed Noam's shoulder—"as I did with my lovely Marissa." He lunged for her, hands clutching Marissa's waist to lift her off the floor. He lowered her, giving her the most seductive kiss Kharis had ever seen.

Sebastian pulled away from Marissa long enough to turn to Kharis and wink. "He bites." He tilted his head toward Noam. "Be on your toes."

"No, I don't," Noam griped, turning to Kharis. "I don't bite, I swear. He's making everything up as he goes."

And Sebastian, apparently with a few ales already in his head, laughed and laughed, entertained to see his friend utterly embarrassed in front of his sweetheart.

"Come." Sebastian grinned, throwing an arm around Noam's neck and dragging him along. "There's a tankard with your name on it, my friend." He turned to Kharis, his voice teasing as he gestured for her to follow. "There's one for you, too."

Holding steins, Noam led Kharis through the crowd toward a booth. Once she sat down, he slid beside her. Sebastian joined them, and being bigger and broader, he took up all the remaining space on the bench, pressing Noam against Kharis. His smile at Marissa confirmed he'd done it on purpose.

"Sorry," Noam mouthed.

Kharis gave him a curious look. "Nom?"

He rolled his eyes. "My childhood nickname."

Kharis giggled at that.

"You don't have to drink it." Noam tipped his chin toward her mug. "Don't feel obligated. The flavor," he hesitated, "may not be to your liking."

"I've never had ale." With that, she took a confident gulp... and almost spit it out. But by the third swig, she'd discovered the earthy warmth beneath the bite, and finished the mug before she realized.

The usual filters containing her world began to fade. A second tankard appeared, courtesy of a winking Marissa. With each sip, her worries began to fade. Zenka patrols or being recognized? Gone. Laughter floated in the air, and Kharis let go.

Noam had to be the most handsome man alive. Bronze danced in his gaze, gold in his hair. His smile, given without conditions, lit a fire inside her. Suddenly, the desire to have a seductive kiss with Noam sounded practical and common-sensical.

"How did you meet Sebastian?" She hoped the conversation would free her mind from the metaphorical gutter.

"Childhood friends. We came from Urrun."

His dimpled smile returned her mind to the gutter, and she luxuriated in the pleasurable tingle that heated her core.

"He requested a transfer, and when it was accepted, I came with him to try my luck in the capital."

"Transfer?"

"Yes, from the Urrun Garrison. He now commands one of the Zahar-Homa gates. And I found work at the Sendatorsum as a gardener."

"I see. So, he married Marissa, and they're returning to Urrun."

He nodded. "The garrison's commander retired and spoke highly of Sebastian with his superiors, recommending him for the post. Seb and Marissa then asked me to return with them, and I almost said yes."

Kharis wasn't sure what to make of that. "Why didn't you?"

Noam's teeth snagged his bottom lip. "I enjoy my work." He took a long drink from his mug, then gazed at her with an intensity that made her gulp. "And I enjoy tending to your garden."

The moment stretched as their eyes met, and everything around them disappeared. Only Noam existed, sitting beside her, half his body pressed tightly against hers. The heat he radiated overwhelmed her senses. She wanted to run her fingers through his hair and curl her arm around his neck to draw him closer...

Yes. Kharis was ready for that kiss now.

The music started again, jolting her out of her daydreaming. Her body bristled, but Kharis brushed the feeling off.

"Would you dance?" Noam asked, his lips brushing her ear.

Kharis stiffened, aware of her prohibition against dancing, but before she could manage an excuse that didn't come out as rejection, Sebastian yanked on them, dragging them by their wrists to the dance floor.

"Marissa!" he yelled over the noise.

She was by Sebastian's side swiftly, her hips already swaying.

"I don't know any steps," Kharis told Noam, hoping for a way out of dancing.

"Just follow what I do." He offered an encouraging smile. "The steps are simple." He took her hand before she could say anything else, and they joined those already on the dance floor.

Everyone linked hands in a circle, moving rhythmically to the left in time with the music. As the tempo quickened, so did the pace of their movements, the circle spinning faster and faster. Kharis's laughter rose above the din, light and unrestrained, swept up in the joyous rhythm. Suddenly, the music softened to a brief lull, and Noam released her hand, stepping back to face her.

When the lively melody resumed, Noam circled her with nimble, intricate footwork. His hands remained clasped behind his back, his movements precise yet playful, and his gaze never left hers.

"Now, your turn," he whispered.

Mimicking what the women did, Kharis clapped her hands as she moved around Noam. Since Marissa had done it with such a seductive flair, Kharis decided to do the same, swaying her hips as Marissa had and never breaking eye contact with Noam. He watched her with a sense of hunger, and she was sure he would pounce on her next.

Thank you, Marissa.

The moment the tempo shifted, Noam's arm slipped around Kharis's waist, pulling her closer. A thrill rippled through her as they twirled, their bodies moving effortlessly in sync. They spun right and left, the musical beats guiding every step. The tavern faded into a blur, the world shrinking to the two of them as they moved as one.

It was intoxicating.

She'd never been allowed to dance before, and now she was completely swept off her feet, literally and figuratively. Spinning in Noam's arms made her feel weightless, invincible. The music wrapped around her, lifting her with each turn and spin, melting away doubts, duties, and concerns. If death was supposed to come for her, it seemed to have gotten lost in the labyrinthine outer ring.

Kharis let go, no longer worried about leashing her magic. Noam's grin mirrored hers, a shared understanding that this moment was theirs alone.

And in that moment, something else began to stir in the air.

With each step and beat of her heart, an unseen current unfurled from within her. Kharis felt as though she was weaving her rhythm into the fabric of the night. The vibrant music became a tangible power seeping into the foundations of the humble tavern, compelling everyone to dance, clap, and sing.

Magic had slipped free.

Flames danced taller in the hearth. The air, already rich with the scent of savory spices, took on a magical sweetness as if they'd stepped into a wild meadow brimming with fragrant wildflowers. Each musical note created a rich melody that made everything warmer and brighter.

The Porcupine swelled with it. Caught up in this current of joy and music, more customers came in, the crowd thickening. Strangers clasped hands and spun, dancing with abandon. Laughter rang out as the magic of the night bloomed like wildfire and carried Kharis away.

Soon, the time came to celebrate Sebastian and Marissa.

The tavern had thinned, and the music was quieter now. Everyone raised their tankards, clinking. "To the happiest bride and groom in the Ghak," everyone shouted.

A guest with a twinkle in his eye raised his mug. "Here's to enduring love and unforgettable adventures!" he proclaimed, earning smiles and nods from those around him.

A woman leaned in with a mischievous grin, her arm around Marissa's waist. "To your many evenings brimming with endless bliss." Naughty hooting and clinking punctuated her words.

Noam, beaming with joy, raised his tankard. "You've finally convinced my sister, the fool that she is." A burst of laughter rippled through the crowd. "May your journey be filled with love and understanding. Seb, love her for the rest of your days." His words resonated with sincerity. "Or I will hunt you down."

The crowd erupted with a chorus of chuckles and funny cackles.

"With the support of cherished friends and family," Sebastian's eyes crinkled with happiness, "and the love of the most

gorgeous woman in Zahar"—he drew Marissa to his side—
"anything is possible."

More good wishes and heartfelt words floated in the air.

Noam found Kharis's hand and clutched it, his thumb
gently brushing her knuckles. A moment that defined how life
should be. They gazed at each other, his soft smile on her,
hoping in their silent conversation that this moment would
never end.

"Hya!" Sebastian had found them. "Dance with me."

Before she could refuse, and granted, who could refuse this
giant, Marissa appeared out of nowhere to drag Noam, and the
four returned to the dance floor. As her feet found the rhythm,
she knew she'd carry this night with her—no matter what
came next.

CHAPTER 24
HEARTS AND HOPES

Love is the silent force that turns ordinary moments into extraordinary memories. - Poliormos

"I t's late." Sebastian was in lecturing mode. "You take her straight home, do you hear?"

Noam dipped his chin in assent as if he knew there was no point in arguing with his now brother-in-law.

"She's pretty." Sebastian didn't care that Kharis was standing beside Noam. "Maybe kiss her." He scratched his chin as he pondered further instructions. "But then you take her home. No funny business." He squeezed Noam's shoulder, expecting a response.

"No funny business," Noam parroted.

"Good!" Sebastian said. "We respect our women."

"It was nice meeting you," Marissa said. "Please make Noam happy," she whispered. "I know he'll make you happy."

Kharis's lips twitched. She hoped it was because she was smiling.

Sebastian's warning hung in the air. "Straight home," he shouted as Kharis and Noam walked away.

They strolled through the streets, watching vendors close their stalls and patrons lingering in animated conversation before heading home. A lonely musician sat perched on a weathered crate. His fingers danced across his guitar strings, rousing sweet melodies. He watched the pedestrians with a hopeful glint, hoping for a few more coins before calling it a night.

"What about a song for your lovely wife?" he called out to Noam, a playful grin tugging at the corners of his lips as his fingers coaxed a romantic tune from his instrument.

With a nod from Kharis, Noam tossed the man a coin. Soon, a beautiful song filled the air, the minstrel's pleasant tenor drawing the attention of several passersby.

Kharis and Noam listened quietly until the minstrel finished his song. The final note hung delicately before the crowd broke into applause, and the jingle of a few more coins punctuated the minstrel's grateful bow. "That's it for tonight, folks," he announced.

As the crowd dispersed, Noam reached for Kharis's hand, and together, they resumed their walk through the quiet, lamplit streets.

"Did you enjoy yourself?" he asked.

"I didn't want it to end." And this was the truth. "I've never enjoyed myself as much as I did tonight." She couldn't contain her smile. "It was a lovely, magical night." She meant it, her wonder genuine. The night had been something out of a dream. "Thank you for inviting me."

Noam smiled, his eyes warm. "Thank you for agreeing to come." He slowed, his thumb brushing her hand with quiet reverence. "May I?" His gaze searched hers for permission.

Kharis nodded, though uncertain of his request.

Noam lifted her hand to his lips, pressing a gentle, lingering kiss on her knuckles. She stilled, her breath catching as her gaze locked with his. His lips on her skin shocked her, wildfire spreading through her body.

Her throat tightened, suddenly dry. Ale sounded like something she needed.

"I've wanted to do this all night long," Noam murmured, "wondering what it would feel like." His smile softened with gratitude. Kharis didn't pull her hand away, unsure what to do or expect. Noam simply held it, clutching it with both hands to his heart.

She tipped her chin up, drawn to the soft look in his eyes. Noam leaned in slightly, his gaze tracing the lines of her face with an intensity that sent her thoughts into a whirl. A flush of heat crawled up her neck, and for a fleeting moment, her mind filled with thoughts of seductive kisses and wild, unspoken desires that she'd never given much weight to before.

Noam didn't press her for more. His eyes searched hers as if memorizing every detail of her features: her eyes, the curve of her lips, the way her breath caught ever so slightly under his gaze as if that were enough for him.

Then, "I could stare at your eyes all night long."

Her wild mare of a heart galloped, running inside her ribcage. The moment felt suspended in time, charged with a thrilling tension.

And yet, beneath that nervous excitement, there was a quiet warmth, a connection that didn't demand anything from her. Noam held her hand as though nothing else mattered to him. He leaned in closer, his nose barely brushing her ear. His voice dropped to an intimate, velvety murmur. "Your scent," he said. "It reminds me of the stormy seas of Urrun—deep, restless, and full of power."

His warm breath against the delicate arch of her ear stunned her, and a wave of sensations she hadn't anticipated crested over her. How could something so mundane be so intoxicating? But when his cheek brushed against hers, she knew she was gone. She'd jumped into the swift currents of this wild ocean and let it carry her away.

Kharis could see the hunger in Noam's eyes—his longing and unspoken passion—tempered by unyielding restraint. He was waiting, she realized, for her permission. Noam, made of leaves and petals and as fragrant as a rain-soaked garden, would never force himself on her. He held himself back, offering her the choice. The power to decide what came next was hers and hers alone.

Choice. The thought sank like a stone, creating ripples that spread through her mind.

This moment was bewildering in a world where strangers dictated the course of her life, planned her every move, and offered her no options. It was scary, yet also exhilarating, like standing at the edge of an imaginary cliff, toes curling over the precipice, heart racing at the thrill of the unknown.

Giddy and weightless, she was back on the dance floor, twirling with Noam, as something intensely magnetic charged their every breath. This was an invitation to choose and leap—or not.

And in that swirling chaos, she realized how addictive that feeling was.

To cross that line.

It was such an enticing thought. If she did, there was no turning back. That was the nature of forbidden fruit. One bite, one single taste, and there was no turning back.

Their eyes met, both hoping and wishing for the same: to cross that line.

"Noam?" she whispered.

His gaze softened. "Yes?"

"Would you kiss me?"

His smile widened. "Yes."

He leaned in slowly, cautiously, brushing her lips with a featherlight touch. It was a barely-there touch, a careful first step to allow her the time to change her mind. To Kharis, it was an explosion of every sensation possible. The heat that surged from her core became an overwhelming flood that overtook her.

If a simple touch did this, what would an actual kiss do?

She was dizzy and drunk again; joy tasted like spicy cloves and sweet nutmeg.

"Should I continue?" he asked, eager yet waiting for her command.

This temptation was pleasant torture. Every muscle tensed in anticipation. Her eyelashes fluttered, expectant. Blessed Mother, the fires of Ifran should take her now. Her grin, brighter than Sharan's, was her answer, her permission—her sign of consent.

"You should," she said.

A gleam lit Noam's eyes. "You're the loveliest woman I've ever met," he whispered, nibbling on her earlobe. "The most beautiful." He began a slow, deliberate journey from her ear to her mouth, tracing soft kisses along the way. "The most enticing."

Kharis was melting in Noam's body heat.

"My, my." A grating voice cut through the air.

It shattered the spell.

Kharis flinched, her senses snapping back. Noam straightened immediately, his body tensing as he turned toward the voice.

"What do we have here?" A group of men emerged from the shadows, their faces twisted in amusement.

Noam stepped before Kharis, shielding her and raising his palms in a gesture of appeasement. "We don't want any trouble," he said. "We're on our way home."

The apparent group leader cackled a gritty, unpleasant sound that grated against Kharis's nerves.

"Home?" The man chuckled darkly. "It looked like you were about to eat her right here."

Noam gave Kharis a gentle nudge, urging her to start walking.

"Why in such a rush?" the same man said, his tone menacing.

The group was closing in.

Kharis glanced over her shoulder. Her training—etched in her muscles, burned in her brain, and inked on her soul—kicked in. She counted four heavy-set men, burdened by so much weight that they would be slow like molasses. Drunks who, emboldened by too many ales, now flaunted courage.

Easy targets.

One kept his hand in a pocket, probably fingering a dagger. They cackled and hooted discordantly, making crass comments about the body she hid under her woolen cloak.

"Take it off," one slurred. "Let us see the goods."

"We'll double whatever he's paying you," another said, swaying slightly.

"Let's get going," Noam whispered to Kharis, the anger in his voice sharp.

"How did such a loser land a pretty girl?" one of the men said. "What a waste."

"I'm escorting her home," Noam insisted, urging Kharis to keep moving. "Please," he said calmly but firmly. "We don't want any trouble."

"Then you won't mind sharing, won't you?" the leader said.

He swaggered forward, a greasy grin spreading across his face while holding onto the bulge between his legs. "You're better off with me, sweetheart. I know how to use this."

The other three snickered, their eyes leering at Kharis as the taunts continued. A different fire ignited within her. How many times had they done this if they were already tasting victory? As the thorny vines emerged from nothingness and coiled around her, she decided enough was enough. She squared her shoulders. Her heart pounded with the steady thrum of readiness, her mind clear and sharp.

"Noam," she said. "Close your eyes."

He jerked his head back to her. "Why?"

"Because I don't want you to see what I'm about to do."

His eyebrows knitted. "Don't do anything you'll regret," he begged her, his whisper tinged with more than concern—genuine fear for her.

She realized Noam knew about the massacre. Of course, he would. Who in the Senda wouldn't know about it? And yet, despite knowing about it, he'd invited her to celebrate with his sister and best friend. With a smile directed at him, Kharis unfastened her cloak and gave it to him. "Please hold on to it. I don't want it getting dirty."

Noam's eyes widened, speechless.

"Don't forget," she said confidently. "Close your eyes."

CHAPTER 25
BREWS AND BRAWN

Love is the silent force that turns ordinary moments into extraordinary memories. - Poliormos

Kharis pulled on her knit cap, limbered her neck, and cracked her knuckles. Then she faced the four men, wiggling her fingers.

"I'll show you how I use these."

The leader let out a sinister laugh, pleased with the idea. "Then get closer."

Moving as fast as lightning, she lunged, the four men barely registering the blur. Her fist found a face, and the brutal punch hit below the jaw. The owner of that face stumbled and collapsed to the ground, knocked out cold.

Dodging a clumsy fist, she sent the second man crashing to the ground with a leg sweep. She slammed her elbow on his torso, and air whooshed out of his chest in a hideous gasp before he fainted.

The third surged forward. His wail got stuck in his throat with her kick to his groin. He bent over, hands holding onto his manhood, and her boot not only broke his nose but sent him kissing the ground.

The leader, stunned, glanced at his three friends, piles of

flesh sprawled on the ground, and turned to her with wary eyes.

Kharis grinned. "I thought you wanted to show me how you use that." She gestured to his manly lump.

The man stepped back.

"What?" She lowered her voice, faking her disappointment. "Have you changed your mind?"

"You filthy txakurra," he growled.

Kharis dusted her sleeves. "Even your cursing is dull."

"This isn't," he snarled, pulling a dagger from his pocket, the blade glinting faintly in the dim light.

Kharis angled her head, assessing a blade no longer than the man's hand. A sharp laugh nearly escaped her, her eyes narrowing in amused disbelief.

"You intend to stop me with that?"

He lunged for her, swinging the weapon. Kharis sidestepped his attack and kicked the back of his knee. The man wavered, his balance lost, but undeterred, he got up and swung again. She leaned back, dodging the blade's arc. Her boot heel connected with his back when the momentum of another swipe turned him around. A sharp exhale escaped him as his body slammed against a wall. The thud of fatty flesh meeting stone came with a pained, "Oof!"

He slid to the floor, shaking his head in a daze, then realizedhe'd stabbed himself in the thigh with his blade. His face blanched as the pain overwhelmed him. A dark stain with an offensive scent soon bloomed between his legs.

"That doesn't look good," Kharis said, genuinely concerned about the wound. "Someone should check it. Do not pull on the blade, or you'll bleed to death."

Pulling a silver whistle from under her leather jerkin, she blew on it, a series of short, high-pitched sounds slicing through the quiet. The reply came immediately. A similar whistle echoed a few streets away. Kharis whistled again, this time longer, more urgently. Then she dashed toward Noam.

"Run." She yanked on his wrist.

"Wait!" He picked up her knit cap from the ground, and

both melted into the gloom as more whistles broke the stillness of the night.

With fire coursing through her veins, they ran, darting around corners and traversing the sleepy neighborhoods through dark alleyways, their breaths coming in ragged gasps. They weaved between carts and wagons and jumped over a lone sleeping drunk, constantly glancing behind them to ensure zenka guards weren't pursuing them. Together, they leaped over crates and barrels and raced toward the riverbank.

The cool breeze from the river soon greeted them, and relief poured out of her.

Noam leaned on his knees, catching his breath. "What was that?" He gestured to the item hanging around her neck.

"It's a zenka whistle." She pulled on the chain to show it to him. "They're used to alert other patrols of emergencies. Blow on one; before you know it, you're surrounded by zenka guards. At night, the patrols are always in fours, and this whistle is standard with their uniforms." She pressed her lips, wondering whether to reveal another flaw. "I stole one." Glancing away, she scratched her cheek. "It's handy to have."

Noam snorted, a grin tugging at the corners of his mouth. "I'm glad you had it."

"Here." She pulled it over her head and handed it to him. "In case you need it on your way home."

He stuffed it into his vest pocket, then handed her the knit cap. "It fell during the fight." His expression changed from lightheartedness to concern. "Are you hurt?"

Kharis shook her head, but Noam took her hands, gently turning them over. His gaze shifted back to her face, and for a moment, she couldn't quite read the expression in his eyes. Fear? Defeat?

"I'll help you with the gate," he finally said, tipping his chin toward the tunnel entrance.

"Right." Disappointment patted her head. She glanced up at Sharan, the moon now high in the sky. It was past midnight. What should have been a perfect evening with a lovely kissing opportunity had been ruined. *Curse those idiots.*

Noam shoved against the weathered gate, muscles taut

with effort, muttering curses under his breath. He threw his weight into it—more forcefully than necessary—jaw clenched, breath sharp. He wasn't just wrestling rusted metal but grappling with the storm still roiling inside him. Since the fight, he hadn't said a word. Beneath his silence stirred the quiet ache of not being the shield he believed she deserved.

Aware that he was working out his frustration the only way he knew, Kharis held back and watched.

After a few grunts and shoves, the door finally gave way. He stared at it, hands on his hips, his breathing ragged from the effort. When he gestured for her to go first, she stepped forward but stopped short when he followed her into the tunnel.

"What are you doing?" she asked, raising an eyebrow.

"I'm taking you back," he said, no hesitation in his tone.

"There's no need—"

"Yes, there is." He met her gaze, calm and steady, leaving no room for argument. "I never want to see you in danger ever again."

With a sigh, Kharis stepped aside and let him close the gate. The metal creaked in protest, hinges grinding with the reluctant shriek of age. Rust flaked to the ground like autumn leaves.

"How did you open it on your own?" Noam grunted, pushing harder, unwilling to let the gate win. The strain in his body mirrored the turmoil he hadn't yet put into words.

Kharis stifled a smile. He didn't know the Djinnshirukh possessed otherworldly strength. Still, watching him try so hard stirred something soft and unexpected in her.

"Let me help," she offered. "Together, we can close it."

His lips thinned, but he nodded anyway.

They pushed against the gate, and it shuddered in protest before reluctantly yielding. The rusted metal scraped against itself with a harsh, metallic shriek, releasing a cloud of maroon dust.

CHAPTER 26
KISS AND BLISS

*Like a sudden breeze on a quiet day, love whispers its presence with
unexpected tingling, leaving us breathless. - Poliormos*

"There." Kharis brushed off her hands. "Closed."

A chill hung in the air, lingering briefly before it
dissipated, while the darkness inside the tunnel bore
down heavily.

"I can't see anything past my nose," Noam said.

"Give me a moment," she said. "There's a torch somewhere
around here. I can light it, but—" The inky maw didn't conceal
the hesitation in her voice. "Don't be scared, please?"

"I won't."

Kharis bit her cheek. "That's what you say now." She
paused. "So, promise me you won't be scared or run."

Noam's boots shifted, gravel crunching softly beneath
them. "I saw you fight four men who were larger than me. You
moved like the wind, and it appeared you were playing with
them, that you could've easily—"

A sudden, heavy silence settled between them.

Suspicion crept in. Was "killed them" the part he'd left out?

"Noam?"

"Never mind me," he said. "I'll never fear you. Ever. I won't
run."

No invisible thorny tendrils coiled around her throat or tore at her skin. The absence of the familiar pain relieved her; Noam wasn't lying.

"Good," she said, letting her magic flow freely.

The soft glow of silver stardust shimmered around her fingers. Embarrassed that Noam could spot the dragon scales that always came with it, she waved her hand in the air, hoping the movement would mask them. Instead, the motion left an ethereal silver contrail that glowed like something out of a dream.

"It's like a silver ribbon," Noam said, awe in his voice. "It's beautiful."

Kharis froze, but the word lingered in her mind.

"Could I touch it?" he asked softly.

Hesitation flickered in her chest before she slowly extended her hand toward him. Noam took it, his fingers cradling it with care, his gaze mesmerized by the shimmering light that danced across her skin. He caressed her scaled skin with the same fervor with which he tended the garden.

And for the first time, she didn't fear the magic she held. Under his gaze, she became aware of every little detail that made her who she was: her scales, glowing like jewel-like petals, acting as her armor; the magic racing beneath her skin, pulsing at her fingertips; her magical seals lovingly embracing her form; her heart drumming to a song only she could hear.

He thought it was beautiful.

And that word became her chant, her spell, her command. Kharis gently pulled her hand away, and the stardust ignited, engulfing her fingers in a sudden burst of crimson and amber flames. The fire flickered and danced, casting shadows across Noam's face as he stared at her, his lips parted in astonishment.

He looked at her not like a man staring at danger, but as someone witnessing a miracle.

Kharis didn't move, her heart racing as she swallowed hard, bracing herself for his reaction. But the pain she'd always associated with dread never came. Instead, something else sparked in her chest—an unfamiliar emotion, not painful but warm. Pleasant, even, and her senses danced to it.

"Does it hurt?" Noam asked, his gaze still fixed on the dancing flames.

"No." Kharis shook her head slowly, a small smile crawling onto her lips. "It feels nice, like sitting near a fireplace on a chilly night." The warmth seeping into her cheeks also felt nice.

Flames curled around her fist. As she opened her hand, they leaped—obedient and sure—catching the torch in a single breath of light. Shadows scattered, driven back by her will alone.

"It's mesmerizing," Noam murmured, stepping closer. "All of you." His eyes never left hers. "Hya," he whispered, the word delicate on his lips. "May I call you that?"

"Yes." A playful lilt danced in her voice. "But only you can call me Hyacinth."

Noam didn't laugh; his intense gaze filled with something more profound. "May I?"

Kharis bobbed her head, intrigued. Noam took the hand that had been wreathed in flames, his fingers gliding lightly over her skin, now free of scales, as if to confirm she wasn't burned.

"You aren't scared?" she asked.

"I swore I'd never be afraid of you." The world suddenly slowed. He brought her hand closer, tenderly kissing her fingers, one by one, as though he were savoring the taste of magic on her skin.

All her words jumbled into a tangled mess.

Noam's eyes lifted to hers, and his voice, soft but clear, pierced the haze. "Do you still wish me to kiss you?"

He leaned in close until his moist breath tingled her lips. He stood in that line, eagerly awaiting her "yes." His eyes locked on hers, and the world remained utterly still. Noam smiled, his eyes radiant. His thumb caressed the back of her hand, and the gentle touch drew goose bumps over her skin.

Heat curled deep in her stomach.

"Noam?" Her throat tightened. Her voice cracked.

A soft smile parted his lips as if he knew what came next. "Kiss me."

"As my princess commands."

His kiss was warm and tender, velvety lips pressed against hers. He nibbled on them, coaxing them, enticing them to open for him.

Her mind spun, every thought swept into a whirlwind of sensations. Skin against skin. It was a revelation. Crimson and gold heat surged through her, a fire so fierce she could lose herself in it—melt in it. When Noam wrapped his arms around her, drawing her close, the rising winds became a wild tempest.

Passion urged her to close her eyes and let go.

His tongue swept against the seam of her mouth, and she parted her lips, wanting more of him. Her breathing quickened, and a soft moan escaped her, his name a whisper at the end of it. He quivered at the sound of his name, and a deep, seductive groan dragged through his breath.

Her hands, no longer limp by her sides, clutched possessively, pressing him closer to her as her body moved with him, both swept by the same current of passion and desire.

His kissing grew hungry and frantic, tasting her, his tongue dancing with hers.

"Hya." His voice filled her mouth amid strangled breaths. "Hya."

Kharis curled her hands around Noam's neck, getting lost in the exquisite pressure building inside her. He groaned and pressed her against the wall, gazing not at the princess or the Djinnshirukh, but the woman he held in his arms.

"I love you," he breathed out. "I'm madly in love with you."

A tight shudder rolled through Kharis at his confession. The sudden intensity took her by surprise. A pang of guilt rose to threaten the moment—to remind her that she didn't deserve any of it—but Noam's expression, tender and brimming with devotion, exorcised it.

"I've watched you from afar." His voice trembled with emotion. "Never once imagining that you'd ever look my way. Sometimes, you came into the garden, and I hid to listen to you sing. Other times, you sat on the bench by the jasmine, and the sadness in your expression wrung my heart. I worked tirelessly, hoping to catch you smiling at the flowers and somehow ease your pain."

He inhaled sharply, his gaze searching hers. "I don't know when it happened, but soon, I was praying for a chance to cross your path. To see you. To wish you a good day."

Her eyes widened in astonishment, her heart pounding like a wild drumbeat.

"I knew it was foolish of me to have such dreams," he said, his voice softer now, almost fragile. "Me, a lowly gardener, a commoner, but when the opportunity came, I gathered every bit of courage, and you...? You didn't turn me away. You took the bouquet and smiled; it was the most beautiful sight I'd ever seen."

The glow in his eyes revealed how significant that moment had been for him.

"That alone would've been enough for me," Noam said. "But when you wore my flower crown and asked for a friend, I thought I had died and gone to Andaheimur. Every morning, you greeted me with a cup of tea."

He chuckled softly, the memory bringing a fond smile to his face.

"A cup of tea in exchange for answers to your questions about everything outside the villa's walls." His smile brightened, a glowing sunrise of a grin. "I couldn't wait to see you, speak to you, and bask in your presence."

He paused, taking a deep breath to steady his emotions. Wonder threaded through his words. "When you agreed to come with me, I couldn't sleep for days."

Leaning in, his cheek brushed tenderly against hers, the closeness sending a shiver through Kharis. "And now I get to hold you in my arms," he whispered. "A divine vision made flesh."

Kharis's heart raced, her emotions swirling in a terrifying and exhilarating way. She'd never expected his confession or the feelings it stirred. Tears welled up in her eyes, blurring his face. She allowed herself to be swept away by his honesty and passion.

Noam awoke the hunger she'd been forced to leash as the Djinnshirukh. The world around her faded as her heart beat in unison with his. Overwhelmed, she clung to him, her fingers digging into him as if anchoring herself to this moment.

A smile broke through her tears, and she whispered, "Kiss me, Noam. Kiss me hard."

He did.

His mouth devoured her as if the fences around him had shattered, and horses, wild and fast as the wind, ran freely into the meadows of her mind.

A wild shiver rippled through her, and her heart pounded against her ribs, flooding her with unbearable warmth. The caress of his lips, the stroke of his tongue—each touch unraveled her thoughts. He kissed her like a man dying of thirst who had finally found a spring: each taste a prayer, each breath forgotten in the hunger to know her.

His kissing set every inch of her body aflame.

This pleasurable heat was everywhere. Blessed Mother above. She wanted to erupt and burn—for this all-consuming blaze to take them both.

He pressed against her, his hips grinding against her, the hard ridge between his legs arousing her desires. She surrendered to a primal urge, wrapping her arms around his neck, hoping for better leverage to press harder against him. He groaned, swiveled his hips, and plundered her mouth, sucking on her bottom lip, then dragging his mouth down the line of her throat, leaving a moist path on her skin as if he were a painter, and she, his canvas.

Kharis kissed Noam as if her lake of longing had no bottom. She moaned, immersed in every sensation he'd awakened. Gulping every moment he gave her.

For six years, a darkness she couldn't exorcise had enveloped her. Her world was cold and barren, and love was a word whispered in fear. All she knew was pain and sorrow and guilt. Nightmares framed her nights, and fear drove her days.

But this kind young man loved her, and by the fires of Ifran, she was going to push past everything to touch the sun and feel its warmth.

If this were all she got out of life, she would take it and never look back.

"Noam?" Her hand slid into his hair. "Take me."

Noam froze, his body going still against hers.

"Spear me," he murmured, a hint of shock dancing in his voice.

Concern curled in her stomach. "Noam?"

His breath caught. "J—Just give me a moment." A pause. "Please?"

He rested his forehead against hers, pressing her into the wall behind her. His breathing was hard and heavy, each exhale brushing her skin and tickling her nose. Kharis could feel the restraint vibrating in his body. It confused her.

Why had he stopped? Had she said something wrong?

Her heart drummed faster as she searched his face for an answer.

"Oh, Hya," he breathed softly, his voice full of something she couldn't quite place. He finally opened his eyes, and their gazes locked. The hunger was still bright and undeniable, but he'd reined it in. His expression softened, his hand rising to caress her face.

"Everything's fine." His thumb brushed tenderly over her cheek, his touch gentle and full of unspoken emotion. "I don't want to rush this—us." His lips curved into a smile filled with unbridled joy. His voice lowered to a warm whisper. "I want to take my time with you, Hya."

This other name, the one that was only theirs, became a tantalizing melody. It tasted of roasted meat and spiced ale and was fragrant, like a garden in spring.

Kharis, the Djinnshirukh, belonged to the Regia-Zenka.

Hya belonged to Noam.

"Say it again," she said. "My other name."

His eyes showered her with all the love he could summon. "You're Hya, my lovely, lovely Hya." With each word, he pressed a kiss to her forehead, her cheeks, the tip of her nose, and finally, his lips met hers, soft and lingering. Every kiss became a promise and a declaration of how much she meant to him.

Tears sprang from her eyes, unexpected little soldiers suddenly free, and she kissed him back, tenderly and affectionately. Her stormy seas gave way to calm waters.

Noam slid a few hair strands off her face and gently tucked them behind her ear while his eyes explored every detail of her face.

"Did I hurt you?" He wiped her tears with a gentle thumb.

She shook her head.

"Why did you stop?" she asked. Would others have stopped?

Noam gently cradled her face in his hands and kissed her once more, lingering long enough for his promise to sink in. "Because I'll do it properly when I make you mine." His fingers traced her features. "We won't hide in a dark, dirty tunnel. It'll be in the open, under a radiant Zahari sun, after celebrating our joy with friends. It shall be done on a warm bed brimming with fragrant rose petals."

Joy was sweet and salty. Hope was fresh and crisp.

"When I make you mine," he said, his voice low and seductive. "I will be slow and deliberate, acquainting myself with every inch of your glorious skin. I'll make you see the stars and the moons."

His kiss was sweet, gently nipping on her bottom lip. "When the time comes, I'll do whatever you wish as often as you want because I want to make you as happy as you deserve." He sealed his promise with a tight embrace, pulling her close. With her face half-pressed against his chest, she could feel the steady drumming of his heart.

"It's late," he said, his voice a soft rumble that vibrated in his chest, "and your absence will soon be noticed."

Kharis heaved an unhappy sigh. Her gaze lingered on him, filled with reluctance. She wished the night could stretch forever.

She started down the tunnel. "Are you truly coming with me?"

"As if you needed to ask," Noam huffed, offended. "Show me the way."

He removed the torch from the bracket and intertwined his fingers with hers, their hands fitting together as if they were made for each other. His eyes sparkled affectionately, and his smile made her heart flutter. With a gentle tug, Noam urged her to lead, and with their joined hands, they strode into the darkness, the torchlight dancing on wet stone.

CHAPTER 27
MOONLIGHT ESCAPADE

The stars were witnesses, the shadows our allies. We wove through like whispers of the wind. With laughter still on our lips and danger at our heels, we let the moonlight guide our reckless hearts. -
Poliormos

Kharis and Noam moved swiftly through the tunnel. On occasion, Kharis glanced at Noam, his face illuminated by the torch. Concern wrinkled his forehead. That she'd used this secret pathway clearly caused it.

"This way." Kharis tugged on him, turning left when the path forked ahead. At the tunnel's end, she pressed her palm against a sigil etched into the wall, ancient magic pulsing beneath her fingertips. With a low groan, the rock shuddered and split, revealing a narrow gap wide enough to slip through. A gust of cold, damp air rushed in to meet them, clinging to her skin as they stepped out into the open.

Noam shivered beside her, his breath misting in the air. "It's quiet." His gaze darted across the shadowy expanse around them.

Kharis allowed a small smile. "Few come this way. The catacombs of the ancient kings and queens lay beyond here." She gestured ahead, her voice lowering. "Many fear trespassing on sacred ground and earning their wrath and the curse that comes with it."

Noam swallowed hard, and she stifled a laugh behind her hand, unable to keep a straight face. "Don't worry. I'm already cursed, so you're safe."

His wide-eyed expression shifted, his eyes narrowing at her. "Seems you're not afraid of earning my wrath either," he shot back, a glare crossing his features.

The laughter that would've bubbled up from her faltered. If Noam hated her... "I would never survive your wrath," she said, a truth slipping out before she could stop it.

Noam's expression softened instantly as he took her hands. "Never talk like that. You matter to me. But more than that, you should matter to yourself." He pulled her closer. "To me, you're not a curse but a blessing. Remember that."

His sincerity made her heart soar. She was ready for another kiss.

The sharp rustle of bushes shattered the moment. Noam flinched. Kharis blinked. A raccoon burst from the under-growth, spared them a bored glance, and skittered across the path, vanishing into the shadows.

"We must get going." She pressed her hand on a weathered stone block, and the entrance closed behind them. The gap blended seamlessly into the wall as if it had never existed.

Noam stared at the now-solid wall. "How did you know about this?"

Kharis exhaled quietly, her thoughts drifting back to the long, sleepless nights she'd spent poring over old scrolls and forgotten maps in the Royal Archives. "I've learned to read between the lines, listen to the whispers no one else hears, and ask the right questions." She paused, glancing at the wall. "It won't work for anyone since magic is required to open it." With a tight smile, she gestured to herself. "Come, we're not done yet."

Noam's brow furrowed, bewildered. "There's more?"

Her tone turned apologetic. "These are the old servants' quarters. They are no longer used, except for storage. Our destination lies on the other side."

Noam blinked. "You did all this to come with me?"

She shrugged, a faint smirk playing at her lips. "What can I say? I love a challenge."

They moved swiftly, hugging the shadows. The faint flicker of sparse torchlight cast long, wavering silhouettes that they used as cover. Kharis kept her senses tuned to the slightest noise, her pulse quickening as she scanned for any sign of a patrol.

They crept down a loggia, slipping between its columns, and paused at a corner. Kharis leaned out, her eyes narrowing as she checked the path ahead. Her heart stilled when the distant murmur of guards' voices drifted toward them, growing louder.

Blasted. They're early.

Pressing a finger to her lips in warning, her gaze darted around until she spotted the dense myrtle hedges lining the walls. Silently, she dragged Noam behind her and dove into the bushes, pressing him against the wall, then flattening herself against him. She pulled his cloak over them, hoping the darkness and tangled greenery would hide them.

Soon, the sound of clacking boots was upon them.

"Nothing ever happens around here," a male guard said, his sigh punctuating the casual stroll past Kharis and Noam.

The female guard tsked. "I'll take this route any night. Ruk and Argi patrol the Royal Archives, and you know how that goes."

The male guard voiced a shudder. "Have they encountered the ghost?"

The woman chuckled. "Argi swears by it. Ruk, though, denies everything."

"This place," the man muttered, spitting on the ground. "Strange things happen on most nights."

Kharis grinned, feeling no guilt about causing a few of those disturbances.

"Like what?" the woman asked. "I've heard the rumors, but honestly? Nothing ever happens on my patrols."

"I prefer it like that. Boring. Quiet. Easy. I make it home in one piece, thank you very much."

The woman laughed, amused. "Ah, Boas, I bet your wife wears the trousers at home."

"And yours doesn't?"

A sharp thud struck the stone—the butt of a spear hitting the ground close to Kharis's face.

"You better believe it," the female guard said. "My wife loves it."

Another thud. Alarmingly closer to Kharis's face this time. She flattened herself further against Noam, pressing into him as if he might absorb her entirely. Noam said nothing, but his pulse quickened against her spine, his breath catching. She felt him—unmistakably aroused—his desire pressed tight against her. Heat flushed through her, like fire licking across bare skin.

"Leah?" Boas suddenly paused, sniffing the air loudly. "Do you smell that?"

"Smell what?" Leah drawled, bored.

Boas took another exaggerated whiff. "Grilled meat and ale?"

Kharis stiffened, pressing the fabric of Noam's cloak tighter against her nose. *Spear me.*

"Seriously?" Leah groaned, exasperation creeping into her tone. "Are you hungry already?"

"Oh, come on." Boas heaved an annoyed sigh. "I'm telling you, something's cooking out here. Can't you smell that?"

"Boas, if this is another one of your—?

"Where's the dog?" Boas's tone shifted, the playful lilt gone.

Kharis's pulse spiked, cold fear settling in her stomach.

"Havok," Boas shouted.

A sharp whistle followed. A bark echoed from the distance. *Blasted. Blasted. Blasted.*

Kharis grabbed a large enough rock from the ground, careful not to rustle the leaves, and peeked through the hedge. The guards had moved a few steps away, their backs to the bushes, searching for the dog in the dark. Channeling magic into her hand, Kharis hurled the stone toward the opposite end of the courtyard and dunked back. She heard it crash against a small copse of trees, sending a startled swarm of birds flapping into the sky.

"Who's there?" Boas shouted.

Boots clattered over the cobblestone as the guards ran toward the noise.

Kharis's pulse throbbed in her throat. The rush hadn't subsided, but she couldn't afford to freeze now that the guards were distracted.

"Follow me and stay low." Her voice was barely a breath.

Together, Kharis and Noam crawled, using the hedge for cover. Kharis scanned ahead for an escape route. She had to find another way—

A heavy body crashed into her back, forcing her face into the dirt.

A warm tongue dragged across her cheek, leaving a sticky trail. Kharis blinked in shock. Havok's massive tail wagged furiously, a whip scattering tiny white petals and filling the air with their fragrant scent.

She spat leaves and dirt while pushing Havok away. His tail stiffened when he noticed Noam behind her. A low growl rumbled from the hound's throat, his hackles rising.

Fumbling with her pockets, Kharis found the piece of meat she'd saved from her meal at The Porcupine. "Is this what you want?"

Havok's ears perked up, forgetting all about Noam. His nose eagerly pushed on Kharis's hands. "You must catch it, though." Moving swiftly, she threw it far.

Havok shot off, fast as an arrow, a blur of black fur dashing across the courtyard. The commotion caught the guards' attention.

"Havok!" Boas yelled, chasing after the dog.

"Enough with the running, Boas!" Leah's frustrated voice rang out after him. "What happened to a quiet patrol?"

Kharis didn't waste a moment. Grabbing Noam's arm, she yanked him in the opposite direction.

A concealed gate hid behind a dense curtain of ivy. Her fingers shook as he fumbled with the keys. The first one jammed. The second rattled uselessly in the lock. The third—

nothing. Her pulse pounded in her ears. "Oh, come on, come on." She forced in the last key, heart skipping a beat. The mechanism caught. Then, at last—click.

She shoved the gate open just enough for them to squeeze through.

She pressed it shut behind them and locked it, leaning against the wall. Her chest heaved with quiet relief, and she allowed herself a moment to catch her breath. Her body still tingled where it had touched Noam's. Pressed against him in the dark, her pulse had betrayed her. And his... had matched it.

Noam's voice broke the stillness. "Did you go through all this just to meet me?"

She gave a breathless laugh, flicking her eyes back and forth to ensure the path ahead was clear. The thrill of escape pulsed through her, but a quiet thought whispered: *How long could you keep outpacing the consequences?*

"This is nothing." She motioned for him to follow. "Come. We're almost there."

Noam exhaled a quiet, exasperated groan—probably directed at her.

CHAPTER 28
THE WARNING

The prelude to an impending storm lies within the somber veil of dark, heavy clouds. Heed their warning, for dismissing the winds that may sweep you away is unwise. - Poliormos

Kharis and Noam slipped through a narrow alley, skirting along as Kharis guided them through forgotten corridors, hugging the walls. Every creak of wood and flicker of shadow kept her senses highly alert, her pulse a steady drumbeat in her ears.

Finally, after skulking and winding through ancient oaks, they reached the villa. Kharis scanned the area, waiting for the gap between patrols. When it was clear, she pushed through the back gate, and they slipped inside. The tension drained from her body. Navigating the Senda alone was a breeze, but bringing Noam along had raised the stakes. Yet the thrill of it invigorated her in ways she hadn't expected.

"We made it." A hint of satisfaction curled at the edges of her comment.

Noam didn't utter a word. He wrapped an arm around her and kissed her, igniting a new fire within her. Their bodies melded together under a cascade of jasmine, its heady fragrance mingling with the rush of desire.

Kharis pulled away before she lost her senses.

"You must go now. If the patrol stops you, tell them you delivered herbs to the kitchens. The bakers start bread production around this time, so they'll believe that."

He angled his head, regret thinning his lips. "You do this often?"

"I'm the Djinnshirukh, Noam." What else could she say? "I make it my business to know what happens around the Senda."

His features softened, and his fingers brushed against her face. She leaned into the touch before pulling back.

"Leave," she insisted.

He sighed, reluctant. "Leaving you is the worst part of my day." He turned to the side gate and pulled his hood over his head. "But seeing you at sunrise more than makes up for it." His gaze lingered on her face, his smile growing. "No flower blossoms as you do. None is as sweet nor matches your grace or courage."

Kharis opened her mouth to respond, but Noam gently touched her lips, silencing any protest before it could form.

"None," he affirmed before tenderly kissing her again. With a wink, he quietly slipped into the shadows.

Kharis's heart fluttered. The taste of his kiss lingered on her lips—warm, indulgent. She closed her eyes, letting the sensation wash over her.

"Why am I denied this joy?" she asked the night.

Above her, the Silver River gleamed in the sky. The stars shone brighter as if answering her plea, reminding her there were as many possibilities as stars in the heavens.

She moved through the villa like a silent shadow, grateful that the servants slept and that Saya was still at the academy. Scaling the sturdy trellis, she slipped into her chambers through the terrace, unseen and unheard. Once in, Kharis unfastened her cloak, letting it fall in a heap on the floor. Her boots, trousers, leather vest, and vambraces followed, marking a trail behind her as she shuffled toward the washroom.

Unaided by candlelight, Kharis pumped the lever a few times, filling the washbasin with cool water. She splashed it over her face and neck, the remnants of Noam's kiss still tingling on her lips. The rest of the water chased away the heat in her body, washing her skin clean of passion and tension. Once done, she slipped into her sleeping shift and padded toward the bedroom, her mind beginning to drift.

"Khiri?"

Kharis nearly jumped out of her skin, stumbling back and almost losing her footing.

An oil lamp flickered to life, illuminating Saya's frowning face. "Where were you?"

It swiftly became clear that Saya had been in bed when Kharis had entered their bedroom. She opened her mouth, struggling to form words, so she gestured toward the wash-room, hoping that would explain everything.

Saya's glare lingered on Kharis, waiting for an honest answer. When none came, her attention dropped to the discarded clothes on the floor. She picked up Kharis's cloak and took a deliberate whiff. Her expression shifted. When Saya looked at her, her golden eyes glowed with a power that felt anything but human.

Her disappointment struck Kharis like an arrow.

"I left the academy early," Saya said, her voice too steady. "Imagine my surprise when I didn't find you here, especially since you're confined to the villa." Her tone sharpened, a pointed edge cutting through her words. "Tavah hasn't lifted your punishment, so naturally, I set out to find you."

Kharis's heart sank, dreading what was coming next. "You didn't."

"I couldn't alert the guards of your disappearance, could I? So I used my third sight."

Kharis swallowed hard. It was formidable Sorukhipial magic. No Djinnshirukh could ever hide from it. A chill coursed through her as her secret lay bare before the one person she didn't want to disappoint.

"I'm sorry." Even as Kharis uttered her apology, she knew it wouldn't be enough.

Saya dropped Kharis's cloak and sat on a chair, crossing her legs. "Why would my sister violate her confinement and roam the outer ring when we aren't even allowed past the inner ring?"

The urge to flee tugged at Kharis.

"Tell me." A quiet menace pierced Saya's voice, the calm before a brewing storm. "What was so important that it warranted a few dangerous lies?"

Kharis's pulse stuttered, her gaze falling to the floor to escape Saya's intense scrutiny. Noam was her secret, but Saya was her sister, her Sorukhipa. What if she said she'd gone out for a breath of air? What if she stretched things just a little?

But this was Saya, the one person she never wanted to deceive.

So instead, softly, hesitantly, she said, "I went to the west end. I heard servants talk about some fun celebration." She hugged herself, hoping for the touch to ground her. "So I followed them."

Saya arched an eyebrow, smelling the lie. Her narrowed eyes bore a hole in her head. The silence that followed was suffocating.

"I was curious." Kharis's voice edged toward desperation. "Don't you want to know what goes on out there?" The question was a plea to tap into Saya's sympathy and end this interrogation before it dug too deep.

Saya's expression didn't waver. She flicked her eyes back and forth between the disheveled pile of clothes and Kharis, her lips pressed into a thin, angry line. Kharis could see the sharp intellect behind Saya's gaze, piecing everything together, including the parts Kharis hadn't shared.

"You used the tunnels," she said.

Kharis's stomach twisted. The faint trace of stagnant air clung to her garments. "Yes," she whispered.

Saya closed her eyes for a beat, rubbing the skin between her eyes, weary and frustrated. When she looked back at Kharis, her gaze was colder, sharper. "Your actions impact the Crown," she said, tone icy and cutting. "What you do is our business, Kharis. My business, too."

Kharis gulped, shame prickling at the edges of her resolve. Her heart hammered painfully in her chest, and she counted heartbeats, hoping to steady herself. Saya's expression was worse than any punishment she could ever receive.

Saya's gaze hardened further. "Zenka guards brought a man in tonight. Stab wound. He claimed it was from a fight with a prostitute. Black hair, fierce. The other three men with him were pretty beaten up. One was missing teeth; another had a broken nose. The third, a broken rib." Her eyes bore into Kharis, unrelenting. "They all told the same story—how a woman half their size beat them to a pulp."

Kharis didn't move. She didn't even dare to breathe, as if any motion might shatter what little remained of the fragile trust between them.

"I've looked the other way before," Saya said, the hurt bleeding through despite her best efforts to stay composed. "When you slip out at night, I don't say anything because I know how this place, this role, suffocates you."

Her shoulders squared, her golden eyes shimmering. "But you aren't invisible," she said. "Tonight, you crossed a line."

Saya's voice hardened. "You broke your confinement—the one Asurûn, His Imperial Majesty, imposed for your protection, because an unknown faction wants you resealed. Instead, you went to the outer ring for gods know what reason, got into a fight with four drunks, and stabbed one of them."

"It was self-inflicted," Kharis protested as if that could lessen Saya's anger.

"Who do you think the Regia-Zenka will believe?" Saya's glare pinned Kharis in place. "If things had gone wrong, you would have sealed your fate, mine, and that of Hala's children."

Saya's words struck her, each a harsh blow. Alnaar's bright laugh, Laila's songs, even little Gad's clumsy toddling—gone, swept away in this flood. Kharis's lips flattened into a thin, trembling line. She searched for any defense or justification but found only empty silence. Not even the Voice would help her now.

"Say something," Saya demanded, her voice low and rough. The flicker of anguish in her eyes was a red-hot poker burning Kharis.

But what could she say? No words would undo what she'd

done, and no excuse could soften the truth crackling ominously between them. Saya's words hung over her like sharp little daggers. Kharis remained rooted where she stood, her silence as damning as any confession could be. She'd crossed a line, and they both knew it.

"I don't need to remind you of the stakes," Saya said, her voice sharp. "If any Regia-Zenka minister got wind of what you did tonight, you wouldn't escape resealment." Her anger blazed through every word. "Such a mistake would've been costly for all of us."

Saya's hands fisted at her sides, trembling as though she barely held herself together and could hardly resist the urge to strike out and break something. Kharis had seen Saya angry before, but this other Saya, stripped of restraint, was terrifying.

"The consequences would shatter my heart, Khiri," Saya shouted. "They would destroy Nana and Tavah."

The mention of Nana—kind, steady Nana—hit Kharis like a slap. The image of her weeping, hand pressed against cold marble, gutted her.

Saya's tone grew cold and bitter, her nostrils flaring with barely contained fury. "Is that what you want?" she said through gritted teeth. "A lake of tears by your tomb?"

Saya's rage was justified. Kharis swallowed hard, deserving every scorching ounce of her sister's wrath—wishing she could die.

"Those four men were drunk enough that their story didn't amount to much," Saya said. Her temple vein pulsed visibly. The forceful rush of air from her nose betrayed the storm raging just beneath the surface. "I have asked you—warned you—to curb your recklessness, yet you keep ignoring me."

Her glare's severity intensified.

"You got lucky this time." Her voice turned low and menacing, her words landing a final blow. "Next time, you won't."

The silence that followed was thick, fraught with unspoken tension. Saya exhaled sharply as if expelling her lingering anger and rose to her feet, making the tension in the room snap taut again. "It's late, and I'm exhausted."

Seething, she stomped toward her bed with an audible huff of frustration.

"Good night," she muttered, her tone clipped and final, the words a door slammed shut. The muffled grumble of unintelligible words escaped her as she pulled the covers tightly around her, cocooning herself to keep out the world and Kharis with it.

The conversation was over. No opinions were welcome.

Kharis didn't move.

A cold silence had swallowed the room. She stared at the floor, her thoughts chaotic, knowing that no apology could undo what she'd done.

Her reckless tendency. She couldn't deny it. Luck had been on her side this time, but that luck wouldn't hold forever.

Riddled with guilt, Kharis snuffed the lamp and slipped into her bed, curling up under the covers. She didn't fall asleep as quickly as Saya had.

Deep down, she feared dreaming of all the things that could've gone wrong this evening or of the consequences that would sweep everyone in its wake. One misstep and the storm would blow everyone she loved off this precarious ledge.

And yet, something else kept Kharis awake: the sensation of Noam's lips against hers as he whispered his confession. It stirred a warmth inside her that refused to fade, no matter how hard she tried to push it away.

Temptation hovered at the edge of her thoughts, waving at her from a distance, beckoning her to follow her heart and return to that dangerous, thrilling dance. Even knowing the risk, she felt the pull, a spark that glinted in the night, urging her to come closer.

A flash of lightning lit the chamber for a heartbeat. A slow rumble of thunder followed, curling through the villa. Outside, the wind picked up, lifting the muslin curtains. The scent of rain thickened the air.

How long could she resist?

How long could she hold back the tide of emotions that came so naturally to others but were a forbidden luxury to her?

How long?

CHAPTER 29
THE GARDEN

To love another is a conscious act of will, steadfast and deliberate, transcending the fleeting allure of whims and temporary enchantments. It stands resilient, even amidst the calm seas of contentment. - Poliormos

Saya was gone when Kharis awoke the next day. Noam wasn't in the garden, either. Was this his day off, or had he gotten into trouble? That fear kept Kharis company.

"Are you there?" she murmured.

The Voice didn't answer.

On her way to training, Kharis strained to catch snippets of the guards' sparse remarks or the servants' gossip, hoping for any mention of a gardener. Nothing. And so, her thoughts twisted like a mess of weeds and vines, her concern growing.

The day passed in a disjointed blur, hours slipping faster than she could track. Guilt shadowed her like a specter, grinning from the edges of her mind.

By early evening, Kharis sat on her usual bench in the garden, hoping the familiar fragrances would ease the tightness in her chest.

Saya wasn't back from the academy, but Kharis feared that when she did, the silent treatment would continue. She picked at the sleeve, thinking through the growing rift. Why couldn't she tell Saya about Noam? Above all, Saya was her beloved sister. They'd been through thick and thin. So why not tell her?

No! She shook her head to throw the thought away.

The memory of Saya's fury from last night stopped her cold. Confessing would only make matters worse. Saya would never understand. Not this time.

And Kharis wasn't sure she could bear to see the betrayal in her sister's eyes again.

Besides, the idea of holding onto something precious that was only hers glimmered in a corner of her mind. Always prudent and bound to duty, Saya would see fault in her relationship with Noam. After last night, she'd go straight to Nana —and Nana, without pause, would send Noam away.

In a world where nothing was hers and every choice was dictated by others, holding onto Noam wasn't just an act of rebellion. It was an act of survival.

She closed her eyes, letting the last of the afternoon sun spill over her face.

The silvery voice rippled through her mind. *"Did you enjoy yourself?"*

Her eyes snapped open. Her pulse quickened.

"Are you mad at me?"

"Why would I?" His voice was as smooth as a lake under the moonlight.

Her heart thudded faster now. It was one thing to keep secrets from Saya, but hiding something from him? Embarrassment tightened the knot in her chest. "Because I kissed him?"

Silence followed, and her mind whirled with dark thoughts. Was he jealous? Angry? Disappointed? And why did she even care if the Voice was a sign of the Djinnshirukh's madness?

"Did you enjoy yourself?" he asked again.

Shame heated her cheeks. "Yes."

"Then I'm glad," he replied, smooth and composed.

Her stomach twisted. Didn't he care about her? She remembered the last time they spoke. His words had skirted too close to something tender and intimate. He'd flirted with her—poked at an invisible line just to see where it led. Now, he sounded almost indifferent, which bothered her far more than it should.

Her nostrils flared. "You said we'd made a promise to each other. I would wait, and you would search for me."

"*We did.*"

Her hands curled into fists. Why wasn't he mad when he'd hinted at more, promising to do more than tease if she allowed it? Was he asking for permission, then? She wasn't sure of anything anymore. The Voice could be vague and riddle-prone on most days.

She bit her lip again. "It doesn't bother you that *that* was my first kiss?"

"*My kiss need not be your first,*" he replied, his voice as steady as ever, the ghost of a gentle caress trailing her face. "*I want it to be the only one you shall ever want.*"

His words ignited a spark that coursed through her veins. Her heart leaped into a wild cadence, beats caught between disbelief and a fluttering thrill.

She swallowed against the dryness in her throat. "You wish to kiss me?"

"*I do.*"

Her words tangled in the knot in her throat. How could she kiss a shadow that lived in her mind? How could something so intangible ever feel satisfying? But if he did... would the kiss be gentle? Or fierce?

"You said we were bound for all eternity," she murmured, the memory threading through her thoughts. "That you awaited the day we could be reunited."

"*You remembered.*"

"How could I forget?" Aggravation rose in her chest. He wasn't angry. He wasn't disappointed. She wanted him to be jealous and show the world she was his—

The thought struck her like a wayward ball. *Blessed Mother, what am I thinking?*

Regaining her composure, she said, "You were quite eloquent." She mimicked his voice. "'If not in this lifetime, then the next.'"

"*Indeed,*" he replied, unshaken. Pleased, even. "*If we are destined to be together, why would I be concerned with the man you kissed last night?"*

Her frustration bubbled over. "Wouldn't you be jealous? I would."

The admission slipped out, startling even her. The mere thought of the Voice sharing tender words, intimate moments, or kissing someone else made her blood boil. Then she caught herself—again. Why in the fires was she even thinking this? He was the madness.

But the Pharos of Hegra laughed, pleased with her confession. The rich, low sound rippled through her mind like a whisper of wind, brushing against her thoughts and rousing emotions: longing, yearning, confusion.

"You need not be concerned." His voice wound through her mind, softly rustling errant thoughts. *"I do not need anyone else. My promise to you stands. I am yours until my very last breath."*

His luminous words lingered in her mind, carrying a devotion even the stars couldn't match. *"I vowed to search for you in every timeline and universe. I swore that I would find you, and I did. You pledged to wait for me,"* his voice thickened with emotion, *"and you did."*

A part of her, the foolish one, had expected—wanted—the fervent kiss that should have followed his confession. Warm lips against hers, arms pulling her close, a melding of curves, an entanglement of limbs, a sharing of breaths. Her reckless heart demanded a kiss that matched the depth of his devotion.

Noam's kiss still burned on her lips. He was a tangible connection to a world of flesh and blood.

But the Voice... the Voice was infinite. He was a constellation, a night, and devotion spun from timeless threads. The Voice was everything. Affection. Support. Courage. An eternal presence etched into the core of her being. A kiss from him would change her world forever.

But he was also nothing. She couldn't kiss or hold him.

"You're annoying," she said, slightly irritated by the wonderfully pleasing heat behind his words.

He chuckled, the sound indulgent—playful even, like

sunlight brushing against shadows. *"And you continue to be delightfully impatient and stubborn."*

His teasing stirred everything within her. His hummed melody resonated softly in her mind as if to say goodbye without words. Slowly, his voice faded like a breeze blowing away the mist.

He'd remained a mystery, lacking even a name, yet teasing her like a shadow out of reach. The Voice could be firm and kind, but he also got her wild heart beating fast. Everything about him would be perfect if—

"Your Highness?"

Noam, pushing a cart piled with soil, had stopped before her.

He was real, someone she could touch and kiss.

The Voice, as seductive as he was, couldn't give her that. He was boundless yet untouchable. Infinite yet fleeting.

Before the madness claimed her, she would seize her time with Noam. And she would not let him slip through her fingers, unlike Taika.

"Your Highness?" His brow furrowed in concern. "Are you all right?"

Noam's voice cut through the noise, returning her to a wonderful reality.

"My apologies," she said. "I'm tired." She grinned at the recollections—dancing, kissing, hiding from guards.

Conflict flickered across his face. "I—I'm not allowed to work when you're here."

"Says who?"

"The villa's steward. My work happens when the garden isn't being used—"

"Nonsense," Kharis interrupted, rising to her feet with mock authority. "I'm here to supervise your work personally," she declared, straightening her cloak. "And to ensure it's done to my satisfaction." She winked, adding to the playfulness in her tone.

A small smile tugged at his lips, and his gaze melted into something gentler.

The urge to throw herself at him and kiss him shook her. She reined herself in, taking a measured step back.

"Show me what you're doing," she said. "Please?"

Before Noam could answer, a voice echoed across the garden. "Your Highness."

The moment shattered. Kharis turned sharply to find a servant on the balcony, waving her arm.

"Your escort is here," the woman added.

"Of course they are," Kharis muttered under her breath. Waving in acknowledgment, she turned to Noam. Their moment had faded like the colors of a sunset.

Sighing, she said, "I'm scheduled to have dinner with my brother. It's a dull event, but I get to spend time with my niece, Laila. She's five and exceedingly adorable."

He tilted his head slightly, curious. "You like children?"

"I love them."

His smile turned warmer and softer. Kharis fidgeted with her belt, her fingers nervously tracing the embossed leather. For days, the question had lingered on her tongue, and now it pushed forward, impossible to ignore. Her voice was quiet but resolute when she said, "Come with me to the Zahar-Eliza."

His eyes widened. "Me?"

She nodded, barely containing her enthusiasm. "Many will join the royal caravan: merchants, pilgrims, travelers. You could easily blend in."

Noam ran a hand through his hair, uncertainty flickering across his face. "Wouldn't you have an escort?"

"That I can't avoid," she admitted, "but we also agreed not to have soldiers or servants once we reached the temple." She dropped her voice to a whisper. "We leave for Zhegama at the start of spring. Come with me."

Noam hesitated, rubbing his face. His brow furrowed, doubt gathering behind his eyes. "Wouldn't I... distract you from your purpose?"

Kharis stepped closer. "You won't. I'll make sure of it." Her voice was steady, sure. "Just think about it. When we leave the Zahar-Eliza, we'll have a clean canvas on which to paint our fates together."

She paused, her breath catching.

"Will you?" Hope burned brightly in her heart. "Come?"

Noam looked at her, searching her face as if trying to gauge the weight of what she'd offered. Then, slowly—deliberately—a smile tugged at his lips.

"As if you needed to ask."

Joy and relief flooded her instantly, the current too strong to resist. "Then leave the details to me."

A flicker of warmth returned to his eyes. "Will I see you tonight?"

Kharis grinned, the answer free and radiant. "As if you needed to ask."

CHAPTER 30
THE BLUE HIBISCUS

Flowers speak of love silently, in a language known only to the heart. - Poliormos

The morning sun cast soft rays through the high windows, heralding a new day.

Kharis halted and took a deep breath before pulling on her new crimson armor. The elaborate, boiled-leather cuirass featured segmented pauldrons and metal rivets that secured decorative pieces to the main plate. Squaring her shoulders, she retightened the buckles on her vambraces, cinched her belt for the fourth time this morning, patted her sword, wetted her lips, and pushed the doors open.

Those inside the training room turned.

A few eyebrows raised in surprise.

General Salazar threw her a fatherly smile.

Aware of the attention, Kharis lowered her gaze, waiting for this odd wave of emotions and their effect on her senses to fade. Seeking a distraction, her fingertips caressed the exquisite blue hibiscus flower adorning her left ear. Intricate silver veins wove through the velvety sapphire petals. Noam's gift was mesmerizing, its color matching her eyes.

General Salazar crossed the distance. "You look lovely this morning, Your Highness."

"You think so?" she timidly asked, hoping today to be seen as a woman, not a monster.

"It's a striking blossom," he said. "Hard to miss. And yes, it's as beautiful as the one who wears it."

It surprised her to hear this. Salazar didn't dispense compliments freely. "Good work" was about the most he'd ever verbalized.

He clapped his hands. "Time to get started." With hands on his hips, he surveyed the White Guard officers already warming up for today's training. "Officer Hark," he called out.

"Yes, sir." The officer turned.

"You're with Her Highness today."

With a quick bow, the officer approached and got into position.

A few years older than her, Officer Jonah Hark had an impressive build—tall and strong, head topped with dirty blond hair. He noticed the flower in her hair, studied her head to toe as if seeing her for the first time, and turned to Salazar with a concerned stare.

"Sir?"

Salazar exhaled sharply as if he already knew Jonah's issue. "That's a lovely flower," he pointed to it, "and she," he gestured to Kharis, "is your task. Train the Djinnshirukh princess as you've done previously. As usual, attack with all you've got. Don't let the flower confuse you." He narrowed his eyes, a thought suddenly crossing his mind. "And do *not* get any ideas."

Kharis almost rolled her eyes. Jonah blushed and got into position. Salazar turned to Kharis, leaning in close and speaking through gritted teeth so that the message was only for her. "Focus on control."

She understood the warning. Resealment.

Upon Salazar's signal, Jonah lunged. Their swords clanged. Kharis countered and parried, but she could tell the damage was done. Jonah attacked with hesitation, abruptly aware that he was sparring with a woman, not a soldier, and that he should be rolling on a bed with her instead of doing this.

Wrath lit a fire inside her. How was it that a flower granted her the humanity they'd all ignored until now? The thought seared her, stoking a different fire.

Her sword clashed with Jonah's, blocking his attack. A swift, precise kick to his thigh caused him to falter, his face contorting in pain. Seizing the opportunity, Kharis channeled her otherworldly strength down to a trickle and struck Jonah's chest with the flat of her hand, sending him crashing to the ground. The ensuing thud reverberated throughout the flooring as the blow forcefully expelled air from his chest.

Without haste, her blade was pressed against his neck.

"Do you yield?" she asked.

Sprawled on the floor, Officer Hark didn't move. His chest rose and fell, his widened eyes shining with an intensity that made her pause. His gaze burned with something unfamiliar— admiration, surprise... Lust?

"Hark!" Salazar bellowed from the other end of the room, his deep voice shattering the tension.

Jonah Hark blinked, quickly smoothing his expression, but not before his gaze flicked to her face one last time. Salazar's boots thudded heavily across the room as he marched toward them, his gaze dark and stormy.

"What did I tell you?" he barked, glaring down at Hark as though the man had insulted his ancestors.

Jonah scrambled to his feet, his face flushed with embarrassment. "General—"

"Save it." Salazar cut him off with a dismissive wave of his hand. "Get up and dunk your head in ice water." He jabbed a finger toward the exit, his tone brooking no argument. "Maybe that will get the right one thinking."

"Yes, sir." Jonah shuffled to the door with a ruby-red face, one hand rubbing the back of his head as though hoping to massage away his humiliation.

General Salazar huffed, his annoyance radiating off him like heat.

"Tsk-Tsk," a silky smooth voice uttered. "What is this I see?"

Salazar turned, his displeasure immediate. His bushy gray eyebrows furrowed so deeply they nearly met.

"General Mendi," he drawled, his revulsion sharp, as if he'd bitten into something rotten. "To what do we owe the honor of your presence in my training room?"

Aghet Mendi, unbothered as always, approached with his usual air of pompous confidence. "Isn't Officer Jonah Hark one of your best?" His eyes glinted as they flitted to Jonah's retreating form. He paused theatrically, lifting his hand to count on his fingers. "I mean, he was beaten in," a beat of silence, "three steps? That's a new record."

A self-serving smile flashed across his face, a weapon crafted with pure arrogance. Salazar's hands curled at his sides, but the general didn't rise to the bait.

Aghet's gaze slid toward Kharis, and a wicked gleam flickered in his black-flecked eyes, the man never one to refrain from mockery. Yet, when his eyes landed on Noam's gift, that sharp smile vanished as quickly as it had appeared.

"What is that?" He moved toward her with unnerving speed, a blur of motion that settled mere inches from her face. He tilted her chin to the side to study the flower. "A shame if something so delicate were crushed beneath a boot."

Kharis slapped his hand with a force that echoed through the room. "Don't ever touch me," she hissed, her voice brimming with venom.

Aghet didn't flinch. Instead, he hummed softly, the sound curling around her like a noxious fume. His wicked smile slithered back into place, and he leaned closer, his breath brushing against her ear as he whispered, "I bet you would love it."

Kharis pushed him back with a snarl. "Don't you have something better to do with your prince?"

His eyebrows lifted, but his smug confidence never wavered. "Oh, I do all sorts of things with him," he replied, his voice silken and vile. "I could do them with you. Interested?"

The urge to spit in his face grew, but Kharis chose restraint, barely, and stepped away.

Aghet only laughed, his sinister grin widening as though her anger fed him. He watched her with a satisfaction that made her blood boil. She gritted her teeth, her hands clenching at her sides. He knew how to unsettle her, and she hated herself for giving him that power.

"General Mendi." Salazar's boots stomped purposefully against the wood floor, his approach deliberate, his imposing frame protectively stepping between Kharis and Aghet with a forceful bump to her shoulder, a subtle but clear signal to move away. Kharis stayed where she was, her chin lifted stubbornly. She didn't need his shield, and not from the likes of Aghet Mendi.

"Is there any reason you're here?" Salazar asked, his tone brimming with restrained fury. "Perhaps there's a message you must deliver before you're on your merry way?"

Aghet's smile sharpened as his greedy gaze roamed the room. "I wanted to spar with someone."

All the officers instinctively stepped back, their hesitation rippling through the room. Even Salazar's stance stiffened. They knew of Aghet's reputation—a ruthless general who treated sparring matches as opportunities to inflict pain. Yields meant nothing to him; he often ignored them, leaving soldiers bruised, bloodied, or worse.

"The Djinnshirukh is without a training partner," Aghet crooned. With his hands neatly clasped behind him, he leaned into Salazar like a giddy child begging to play with a shiny toy. "And that won't do."

Salazar's exhale flared his nostrils, his body a wall between Aghet and his intended prize. "The Djinnshirukh doesn't train with just anyone," Salazar spat.

Aghet chuckled softly, the sound oily and smug. "Oh, I'm not 'just' anyone, General." He tilted his head, his dark gaze lingering on Kharis for too long. "The Djinnshirukh should decide for herself... if she's not afraid."

If she backed down, she was permitting him to humiliate her again. This was his game. And she would never win it—unless she flipped the board.

"I'll wipe the floor with your ass in three steps," Kharis blurted, the words escaping before she could stop them.

Salazar's head whipped toward her, his eyes opening so wide they could've popped out of his skull.

"Feisty." Aghet's gaze gleamed as he peeked over Salazar's shoulder. "I like that."

Kharis's lips curled in disgust, her skin crawling under the weight of his leering approval. Worse, she'd jumped into his trap willingly.

Fires burn me now.

Aghet eyed the flower again, something in his gaze giving her pause. Whatever it was, it wasn't good.

"General Salazar," Aghet said, his voice deceptively light, though his eyes never left Kharis's face. "Will you referee?"

A muscle twitched along Salazar's jaw. "I would rather see you leave," he bit out, the words bristling with venom.

"Now, now," Aghet chuckled darkly. "We can't disappoint the Djinnshirukh, can we?" He even bumped shoulders with Salazar as if they were old friends.

Salazar turned, his face mottled with exasperation. He swore under his breath, his expletive quite colorful and loud enough that a nearby officer stifled a cough.

"Doesn't she look pretty with her flower?" The smirk on Aghet's face widened, its curve deliberate. The way he uttered "pretty" turned the word rancid.

An invisible grip coiled around her neck. The gorgeous bloom, once a symbol of something sweet and tender, had become a beacon for Mendi's predatory gaze. If he found out who gave it to her... Her heart lurched with that thought, and the intangible vise squeezed harder with each breath.

Aghet drew his sword, his grin flashing a perfect row of white teeth. The sharp, metallic "shing" of the blade leaving its sheath reverberated in her ears. The implied threat pulled her out of her anxious spell.

"Are we going for two out of three?" Aghet asked casually. "I'm feeling magnanimous today. What if we go for three out of five?" He turned halfway, casting an amused glance at the gathered officers. "Place your bets. The odds are great today."

Like a match striking dry tinder, his haughty smile ignited a slow burn of anger within her.

"I am the Djinnshirukh," she told him, her voice lowering

an octave and turning lethal. "I am the weapon forged by immortals to destroy the Akumi army."

"Officer Ghan!" Salazar barked sharply, his heated voice reverberating with authority. "Step away—"

"Aaw, Salazar," Aghet cut in with a mock pout, a cruel glint dancing in his eyes. "Let her have her fun."

"Enough with the games," Kharis snapped. Her hand curled tightly around the hilt of her blade, her knuckles white. "Prepare yourself, Mendi, because I intend to show you how good those odds are."

Aghet stilled, his eyes sparkling like he'd received a delicious offer.

"Finally," he breathed, the word practically dripping with pleasure. He lowered his blade slightly, just enough to prepare himself, eager and dangerous. "No more games, then."

CHAPTER 31
THE BLOOM AND THE BLADE

Do not be tempted to unleash a storm simply because someone you hate dances in the rain. - Poliormos

Kharis got into position, her focus narrowing to the man before her, General Aghet Mendi.

"Ghan!" Salazar barked, his voice sharp as steel. "Control—"

"Absolutely not," Aghet cut him off, his shout a crack of thunder. His eyes danced with a dark thrill when his gaze fixed on Kharis. "Don't hold back on my account, princess."

She sized Aghet up, every muscle in her body taut like a drawn bowstring. All else faded. Salazar's reprimand, the officer's murmurs, and even the sound of her breathing. The world shrank until there was nothing but Aghet, his twisted grin pulling her into his game.

Then it came.

A resonant voice rumbled through her bones as if from some far-off realm. The sound shattered through the barriers of her mind like a war horn, slipping past every magical and mental containment to find her.

The scent hit her next. Acrid, choking sulfuric smoke curled into her nostrils, forewarning of who lurked in the dark.

"*Are you ready?*" His voice was deep and menacing. A voice

she shouldn't listen to. The Akumi king slithered into her mind like a smoldering ember searching for dry tinder to ignite.

She froze—just for a breath. She'd been taught to suppress his magic at all costs because it quickened the unraveling and stole years from her life. Because his magic was terrifyingly dangerous. And so was he.

Kharis didn't care anymore.

Her target was ahead—despicable Aghet Mendi—and she intended to make good on her promise.

"Yes," she growled back. "I am."

The roar inside her head almost split it open.

Raw power surged through her, devouring thought and breath. Her body buckled beneath it, but if she resisted now, it would shatter her.

Kharis's pulse spiked, her mind fraying at the edges. Her panic flared, but it was too late.

When she surrendered, his magic surged deeper—piercing her to the marrow. Her lungs heaved, desperate for air, as fire licked through her veins. Her muscles strained, stretched too tight beneath her skin. Her heart thundered—an explosion with every beat—until the rhythm of it eclipsed everything else.

As her hearing sharpened, Aghet's breathing resounded in her ears with a relentless whoosh. Her nostrils flared, catching his stale, metallic scent. It burned its way into her awareness, transforming into an unmistakable trail. She would find him even if the world were plunged into utter darkness.

"*You are mine,*" that resonant, sulfur-infused voice snarled.

Did he mean her or Aghet? She couldn't tell, but his searing hatred, burning through her, wasn't a threat but a promise.

Salazar's voice tore through the chaos, barking orders. "Ghan! Mendi! Stand down! Both of you!"

But the sound was faint and distant, as though he were calling from the end of a long, narrow tunnel. No, she realized. His voice had dragged through space from another world.

Ahead, Aghet sported his haughty smirk. Her anger flared. The officers, her doubts... Everything faded like mist dissipating in the wind.

Aghet's sword gleamed as he lunged forward. She met his attack, a resounding clash of metal against metal. The blow sent tremors down the blade to his arms, and he winced.

"Too hard?" She teased him with a mocking pout.

"Is that how you prefer it?" He sneered. "Hard?"

Kharis shoved him, building her distance. Her blade sliced through the air, aiming for an opening in Aghet's defense. He parried skillfully, even when her relentless assaults forced him back each time. Their swords sparked as they danced across the training chamber.

She drove Aghet toward the wall, her focus sharpened. Victory was within her grasp.

Then the glint in Aghet's eyes shifted—dark, satisfied, victorious.

Kharis's heart stuttered. Too late, she'd realized she'd done precisely what he wanted.

For a fleeting moment, the word resealment flashed before her eyes like a terrifying shadow crossing the sun.

Before she could recalibrate, Aghet twisted his wrist with a flourish, and the sharp flick sent her sword spiraling through the air. The blade hit the ground, the clatter echoing off the walls.

The crowd gasped.

Kharis barely hid her shock.

Aghet tilted his head, a slow, predatory grin spreading across his face as he savored her shock. He thrust his blade, aiming to run it through her. Kharis sidestepped, but his blade collided with the thin metal plates underneath her armor and sliced through the leather. Using his momentum against him, she grabbed his arm and, in a fluid motion, turned, pulling him off balance.

With a powerful surge of energy, she heaved him over her body.

Momentarily weightless, Aghet arced through the air before gravity reclaimed him. With a bone-jarring thud, he crashed onto the floor. Gasping for breath, he lay sprawled on the ground, stunned by the unexpected move.

A sword was on his neck before he caught his breath.

Kharis's hand shook as she fought the urge to sink it into his throat. The blade kissed his skin, a thin red line blooming across his throat.

Aghet grinned as if he'd won.

"Yield," she snarled, but the command wasn't directed at Aghet.

The Akumi king was fighting her, demanding Aghet's death and driving her to plunge the sword into him.

"Yield," she shouted, her knuckles white from how tightly she gripped the hilt to stop herself.

Aghet, still on the floor, stared at her with curious eyes as if aware of what was happening. He didn't move or speak; he simply smiled at her.

"I said, yield." Her voice cracked like thunder.

A cacophony of voices rose behind her—shouts, commands, gasps. Salazar's voice boomed through the chaos, but his muffled words barely reached her. The ground trembled beneath her boots, sending ripples through her stance. The air around her crackled with an unbearable heat that licked at her skin.

Inside her, the demon's power clawed, rising like a tide that couldn't be stopped. It pushed against her ribs, pressing at the seams of her body as if she were a brittle shell.

The invisible seals that bound his power stirred beneath her skin, writhing like serpents roused too soon. They pulsed with frantic urgency, as if sensing a threat they could no longer contain—tugging, coiling, tightening their grip around her flesh to hold him back... and to delay the thing she was becoming.

Before her panic took over, the Spirit Kin queen's soul awakened, and her magic met the Akumi king's head-on, universes colliding. The explosion resounded in her head, overwhelming all her senses. Pain gushed through her, an unleashed torrent cascading through her body as if a colossal faucet had been wrenched open. It blinded her to the world, snatching away sounds and colors in its merciless wake.

Kharis staggered back, dropping Aghet's sword.

Aghet didn't wait.

He slammed his full weight into her, his shoulder driving into her ribs and swooshing all the air from her lungs. They hit the ground hard, rolling in a chaotic tangle of limbs—elbows jabbing, knees digging, bodies fighting for dominance.

Her primal instinct flared to life. She shoved him off her and sprang to her feet. But before she could step away, his hand clamped around her ankle and yanked. Kharis fell face-first, the impact sending shockwaves through her skull.

The world spun, caught in a savage whirl.

Her body moved before her thoughts caught up. She kicked, her heel connecting with Aghet's head. He grunted, the hold on her ankle loosening, and she used the chance to scramble to her feet, chest heaving, teeth clenched.

The air vibrated as the shouting around them intensified.

Aghet lunged again like a predator that had tasted blood. His fingers tangled in her hair, yanking her head back with a brutal jerk. Pain screamed through her scalp, and she cried out. Moving through it, she twisted her body sharply and drove her elbow into his face.

The crunch of bones announced she'd met her mark. Aghet's perfect grin shattered as his head snapped back, blood spraying in a fine mist.

Aghet attacked again. She barely blocked the blow.

And at that precise moment, the Akumi king seized her body—and shoved Kharis out.

CHAPTER 32
THE BLOOM AND THE MONSTER

Beware the wish hastily made—for the gods may grant it, and with it, the ruin you failed to foresee. - Poliormos

Suddenly, Kharis stood outside her body, a silent shadow watching her physical form battle Aghet. Was this what it felt like to be possessed? To be made into a weapon instead of choosing to be one?

This other Kharis twirled and flipped, easily dodging Aghet's strikes in a mesmerizing display of elegance and confidence. She glided like a phantom on the wind, as if merely playing with an increasingly frustrated Aghet, who couldn't land a punch or a kick.

It was beautiful, an electrifying impression of ferocious grace.

But it wasn't her.

He was fighting Aghet using her body.

A shadowy figure lingered at the edge of her vision, watching the chaos unfold. "We should end this," he said, his voice silvery. "Before it worsens." His disapproval clamped around her.

Kharis pursed her lips, her frustration rising. "He asked for it."

"Yes, he did." The Voice's disappointment was sharp enough to cut. "And you gave it willingly to him."

The truth stung, its bite worse than any bruise she'd received today.

"Think of your gardener," the Voice said, quietly but pointedly. "Do you not wish to kiss him again?"

A chill crawled down her spine, freezing her to the core. That old, gnawing fear returned. The Regia-Zenka had sent Prince Rawiri away for good. Noam could be next.

And then it hit her. She'd fallen for Aghet's trap as he'd intended—a trap to force her resealment.

"Help me, please," she said, now desperate. "I don't know how to return."

The Voice didn't answer, letting the silence stretch. His words thundered in this liminal space when he spoke. "You must never enter a battle without a plan for retreat."

Kharis swallowed hard, shame pooling in her stomach. "I didn't see this until—"

"You did what he wanted," he warned, his tone sharp with mortification. "And until you temper your anger, you shall always fall for his traps."

Her heart was at a full canter. "You're right," she said. "Aghet won this round." Her throat burned as if she'd swallowed ash. "I'm begging you. Please, help me." She bowed deeply.

His soft exhale ended the silence. "Do not unleash a storm because someone you dislike is dancing in the rain."

Her voice barely held together. "Help me set this right."

The pause felt endless, his silent judgment hanging in the air.

"As you wish," he said. "He shall not let go without a fight, so brace yourself. This will hurt."

Before she could reply, a sudden, brutal force yanked her back with violent speed. Her soul slammed into her body, and pain exploded in her muscles, each nerve shrieking in agony. A searing burst of silver light engulfed her vision, leaving her gasping and trembling.

Amid the chaos, Aghet's fist found her face, and she staggered back from the impact. The world reeled. When her senses finally snapped back into place, an unyielding ring of officers had closed in, pressing her against the wall. Across the room, five more struggled to restrain Aghet, who fought their grip even as blood streamed from his nose.

Her legs trembled—the shock still humming through her —but she forced herself upright. She couldn't collapse yet. And not in front of Aghet.

Salazar was screaming in her face, but with her soul settling back into her body, she heard nothing. Her eyes, however, honed in on Aghet, whose wicked grin never wavered as his gaze locked onto hers.

"Do you yield?" A muffled set of sounds slowly drifted into her mind. "Officer Ghan, do you yield?"

Then Salazar's voice exploded in her ears. The tip of his nose grazed hers as he unleashed a torrent of furious curses and spittle that surged in her direction. Beneath the fury, stark fear shimmered in his eyes.

"Yes," she managed to answer. "I yield."

The press of bodies loosened around her, and Kharis wiped at the blood on her lip.

The burn of power had retreated, leaving behind the ache of strained muscles and the chill of dread. Somewhere, a sword clattered to the floor. Her heartbeat still thundered in her chest, but the fire inside her had been replaced by something cold and hollow. Every officer staring at her saw not a princess, but a threat.

Aghet snatched his arms from the restraining officers and straightened his black leather cuirass. With a malevolent flourish, he raised a hand to reveal the prize cradled within his possession—the hibiscus flower.

"That's mine," Kharis said. "Give it back."

"This?" Aghet scrunched his nose at her, wincing through his pain. "This is now mine."

"Give it back," she growled.

"Stop playing with boys," Aghet scoffed, "and I might consider it."

Boys? An icy sensation cascaded down her back.

"Mendi," Salazar roared. "Return the flower."

Aghet's sleeve wiped up the blood trickling from his nose. "Why?" He studied the blue hibiscus with amusement. "Wouldn't this be the only way to deflower her?"

"Mendi!"

Everyone in the room stood at attention at the sound of that voice and the rage blazing through it.

The *Wall of Zahar-Ghak* had arrived. High General Arjun Ghan entered with deliberate, thunderous steps, hands clasped behind his back, his piercing brown gaze sweeping the room.

Aggravated, his sharp eyes narrowed on Kharis. "This better be worth the interruption to my work."

He walked toward Aghet first, hands still behind his back.

Aghet lifted his adoring gaze. "My prince—"

Ghan's fist collided with Aghet's face with a sickening thud, sending him crashing to the floor. Aghet lay there, hands clutching his face, eyes squeezed shut as he braced against the sharp wave of pain. After a moment, he propped himself up on his elbows, sliding back until his body met a wall. Stunned, he stared at the high general, massaging his face like a wounded animal.

"We've spoken of this." Ghan's voice rumbled, deep and dangerous. "She is a princess of the realm, and you will show her the respect owed." His words surged through the chamber, his voice a scorching sound. "Second. You're not to approach her. Ever."

Aghet lowered his head, consenting to the high general like a docile lamb.

"Salazar. Mendi. You stay." Then, with a voice like a whipcrack, Ghan bellowed, "Everyone else, out."

His words lashed the air. The officers saluted and filed out in haste, their boots striking the floor in a sharp, retreating rhythm.

Ghan pivoted slowly. He scrutinized General Salazar for a long, tension-filled moment. He shifted his focus, and his intense gaze found Kharis. He advanced toward her, each step resounding in the silence.

She hated the bastard. She also feared him.

He towered over her, his eyes filled with endless loathing. The jagged scar running from his forehead to his jaw—an angry river of ruined flesh—twitched. "What is the meaning of this?"

Salazar said, "Sir—"

"I did not ask you, did I?"

Salazar pinched his lips and lowered his head. "No, sir."

Ghan glared at Kharis. "I am waiting."

After all these years, she'd returned to being that scared fourteen-year-old girl in a muggy training room. The sting in her eyes announced tears. She swallowed them along with the lump of fear lodged in her throat.

"General Mendi challenged me to a sparring duel."

Salazar confirmed it with a nod. Ghan pursed his lips. "Who won?"

Her breathing hitched. She knew no answer would ever satisfy him. Silence wouldn't be her salvation, either.

"No one," she said, keeping her tone even when fear dried her mouth.

His weighty silence permeated the air, stretching for an uncomfortably long moment. Her pulse hammered in her ears, each shallow breath feeding the fear coiling inside her.

"And the flower?" Ghan glanced over his shoulder at Aghet, still on the floor. "It isn't standard uniform."

She gulped. "It was a gift."

Ghan arched an eyebrow. "From?"

Dread ignited in her chest, and she clenched her hands to keep them from shaking. She knew she was breathing, but pulsing white spots danced before her eyes as if the air weren't reaching her lungs. All blood drained from her head, and she was suddenly dizzy, the world spinning to the tune of *useless, useless, useless.*

One word from her, and Noam would be imprisoned.

Fate swooped in like a starving vulture.

Kharis stood upon a crumbling precipice, acutely aware of the grim choice before her: to save herself or Noam, to leap into the abyss, or push Noam off. Cruel and relentless, fate would never allow her happiness until she atoned for her wrongs.

She closed her eyes in defeat. Why did she ever think she could be happy?

Noam. Saya. If she had to choose, it would always be them, so she took a deep breath and readied to jump off the cliff.

"From me," Salazar said.

Kharis opened her eyes.

"It was my fault." Salazar squared his shoulders, eyes forward, chin high.

Ghan tilted his head to the side, assessing Salazar with a narrowed gaze, unconvinced. His eyes darted back to Kharis, then to Aghet. His face was unreadable as he pondered the pieces of information he had with a stare that missed nothing.

Arjun Ghan observed them as if he could smell the lie.

He hated her, and that emotion wreaked havoc on her senses. It tasted bitter in her mouth, and a pungent odor stung her nostrils, leaving her throat raw. Every nerve ending screeched. Ghan didn't conjure thorny vines. His hatred manifested as a swarm of fire ants, each bite searing her skin.

He leaned in, his breath hot against her ear, carrying the venom of his words. "This changes nothing. You are a useless monster, Raven Spawn. Nothing more."

The slurs tore at the threads of her soul. Raven Spawn—a cruel nod to the rumor that she was Athon's daughter, not Hröld's—cut the deepest. She gritted her teeth, desperate to stay in control and keep the monster at bay despite the rising tide of anger.

He pulled back, his scorching glower never wavering as if the force of his loathing could incinerate her on the spot.

"Useless," he repeated, the word falling from his lips like a curse.

His face contorted into a grimace, every line etched with disgust. He glared at General Salazar, his lips curling into a sneer heavy with disappointment. When his gaze returned to Kharis, it lingered with an unspoken judgment that made her stomach churn.

Then he smirked with his usual cruelty.

"Aghet," Ghan said. "Let's go."

Aghet rose, dark eyes glaring at her, and followed his prince, but before he exited, he tucked the crumpled flower behind his ear and offered her a mocking pout.

Outside, angry footsteps struck the marble with wrathful precision, breaking the silence. Then a door closed.

As soon as they were gone, Kharis staggered back, her legs barely holding her weight. She steadied against the wall, her entire body shaking. Why had she been so careless, allowing vanity to drive today's decision? Why would she ever think happiness was possible? The tears she swore she would never shed cascaded down her cheeks.

Her old mentor, Master Rawiri, was a Kahurangi prince protected by the Commonwealth of Nations. Noam was the son of a blacksmith from Urrun. Who would protect him if Ghan got his hands on him? Blessed Mother, what had she done?

No. Monsters never enjoyed happy endings.

She wanted to scream, to let her body erupt in flames and burn everything in her path. To end it all.

And before she did, General Salazar threw his arms around her.

"Don't let Mendi get to you," he whispered, his voice choked with emotion. "Just don't." He inhaled, collecting himself. "It's only the two of us."

Knowing what he meant, Kharis let go, weeping in his arms. The cold, disciplined general holding her not like a soldier, but like a grandfather trying to shield what little remained. Her sobs came in waves—gasping, broken, raw.

She'd lost more than a lovely flower.

She'd lost the hope that came with it—the quiet possibility of love, of softness, of a future shaped by her own hands.

Her dream of a life with a kind gardener melted away.

And soon, so was the last of her freedom. After this, the Velathari would tighten their hold. Her privileges would be stripped away. More officers. More eyes. More walls.

She was behind the line now.

And everything she'd almost touched had already begun to vanish, never to be grasped again.

CHAPTER 33
GHAN AND AGHET

Love, when driven by fault or folly, is not love. - Poliormos

The angry click-clack of Ghan's boots reverberated off the marble floors. His sentries caught sight of him and, upon their salute, opened the double doors to his study. Ghan crossed the threshold, shaking with barely suppressed fury.

The heavy doors closed behind Aghet, shutting out the world.

Ghan sank into the high-backed chair, steepling his fingers as seething fury coiled in his gut.

Aghet leaned casually against the doors, arms folded across his chest, one ankle crossed over the other, radiating an air of effortless insouciance. When Ghan didn't utter a word, he pushed himself off the doors, massaging his face.

"Did you have to strike me so hard?" Aghet asked.

What could Ghan say? Thathe'd enjoyed doing it? "How else do we keep this stupid ruse?"

Aghet ignored him, running his tongue through his teeth to assess the damage.

That gesture suddenly aroused Ghan.

"Take that thing off," he grumbled, his eyes fixed on the crumpled flower. "You look ridiculous."

"I beg to differ." Aghet batted his eyelashes, teasing him, always eager to push boundaries.

Ghan loved that about Aghet. He also hated it. "Aghet." He clenched his jaw.

"Fine." Aghet placed the flower on the desk with an exaggerated sigh. "It enhanced the color of my eyes," he said mockingly. "At least agree to that."

Ghan huffed, his gaze narrowing on the wilted bloom. "What's your issue with it?"

Aghet snarled. "Can you not see it?" His voice bristled with anger. "Someone gave it to her."

"Salazar—"

"Not Salazar," Aghet groaned, dropping into his chair. "When have you ever seen him bother with flowers?" His eyes gleamed, hungry for a chase. "Someone else gave it to her."

"Then find who did it." Ghan kept his voice steady, trying his best not to sound too eager—not in front of Aghet.

Aghet rested his elbows on the desk as he cradled his head. "Can I?" His eyelashes fluttered with mock innocence. "Find the one who gave her this soft, stupid, hopeful thing?" He laughed darkly. "What action should I take once I locate the flower thief?"

Ghan didn't answer right away. It would reveal too much if he said what he truly wanted—to grind their skull beneath his boot. He frowned, though, for he had ideas.

"Why would I care?"

Aghet puckered his lips. "Don't you want to know who's stealing her attention with flowers?" he crooned.

The room chilled a fraction. Light filtered through the windows, striping Aghet's face in harsh lines. His gaze glittered, but something razor-sharp now hid beneath the glint.

Ghan raised an eyebrow, his expression carefully schooled. "I want the Akumi king. Nothing else matters."

"The Akumi king..." Aghet hummed, his gaze drifting, his face softening as if savoring a memory.

A flicker of jealousy slashed through Ghan. What thought held him so entranced?

Aghet inhaled slowly and deeply, as if, with that gesture,

he could relive the moment. "His power still buzzes inside my chest." He exhaled, eyes half-lidded. "I almost gave her to you. One more tug, my prince, one more poke, and she would've been yours."

Ghan's jaw tensed. "Why did you?"

Aghet's ominous eyes glimmered. "The opportunity presented itself. Besides, she's such a predictable woman. Push the right buttons, and she becomes as pliable as the petals in this flower. Such an easy target."

Under the desk, Ghan's fingers curled into a fist. "We hadn't planned this, Aghet."

The playfulness in Aghet's face vanished. "Once, you swiftly dealt death upon your foes with attacks as precise as savage. I watched you battle fearlessly, driven by a thirst for blood that spoke to me. Where has that man gone?" He explored Ghan's face as if searching for a ghost. "When it comes to her, you falter and flail," he said. "I'm curious to understand why."

"This again?" Ghan clicked his tongue, annoyed.

"Yes. This again." Aghet leaned forward, his fingers drumming a slow, deliberate rhythm against the table. "What is it you hide?"

Ghan stiffened, his thoughts abruptly returning to a sentence in a letter from six years ago: "Olhan is the man who sired you." True Blood didn't run through his veins. It never did. His father was a nobody—a name in a letter. A secret the former imperial king took to his grave, not to save his mother from the embarrassment of a secret affair, but to avoid the obvious soubriquets: a cuckold king and a bastard prince.

"Gone somewhere, my prince?" Aghet drawled, coaxing his attention back with a slow blink.

Ghan's nostrils flared. He stopped his ring twirling. "You can do this, right?"

"The resealment ritual?" he scoffed. "Of course I can replicate it." He pinched his lips, tapping a finger on the desk. "You've said repeatedly how you want this power, and I almost gave it to you today. Why bother with the shell containing it?"

Ghan's chest rose, an unconscious gesture to regain his calm. Aghet caught it.

"What power does she have over you?" His eyes narrowed into slits. "You get so close, then back away. Why? I thought you wanted it."

"And I do." Ghan struck the desk, and the items on it rattled slightly. "With the Akumi king, I would be invincible. But rushing it jeopardizes our plan."

Suspicion narrowed Aghet's gaze. "What about thirty-five years is rushing it?" His expression hardened, waiting for Ghan's answer.

Ghan held his stare, his lips twitching in exasperation. How could he tell Aghet that it was useless to pursue this now? And if he did, would Aghet leave him? Once, Ghan had lusted after all that power. Now, he focused on ending her so she wouldn't burn the world to ash. Aghet, who craved the thrill of battle and thrived on chaos, would never understand this. Would he turn against him? Would he follow her instead? That thought burned him like acid.

"It was splendid when she truly let go and fought me with everything," Aghet said with a dark lilt.

Ghan refocused.

"The taste of it was so enticing, I couldn't stop," Aghet said, admiration sparking in his eyes. "That power is real, and the immortals contained it in such a worthless vessel—"

"Aghet," Ghan warned.

Aghet's eyes flashed, his expression darkening. "You threw all those prisoners at her." His gaze brimmed with envy. "Why didn't you let me play with her back then?"

Ghan's posture shifted—more rigid, less teasing. His fingers stopped drumming, curling instead into the edge of the desk.

Anger twisted Aghet's handsome face, menace coiling behind his eyes like a beast stirring awake. His entire mien shifted, and an undercurrent of violence crackled between them.

"Why have you kept her from me?" he hissed.

Ghan's face hardened. "Why would I allow it? So she could kill you?"

"Kill me?" A harsh chuckle followed. "You underestimate me. Do not assume that a creature like her could beat me," he said. "Strength and agility are not enough if the will is lacking. She matters not; only the prize residing in her does."

Ghan's clenched hand trembled. "Her body must be alive for the resealment ritual to work."

"Then maim her," Aghet snarled, his eyes flaring with a dark, unnatural glow. "What are you waiting for? What holds you back?" His gaze sharpened. "Once you possess that power, we'll be on a different plane. The world will kneel at our feet."

His eyes widened with awe, as if he could already see it. "Nothing will keep us apart ever again."

Ghan frowned. "Again?"

Aghet barked a laugh. "The excitement bested me."

His gaze fixed on Ghan—but his expression shifted, as if caught by a distant thought. "The Akumi king's magic hums through her," he said quietly, almost reverently. "That resonance is sublime, a harmony unlike anything I've ever encountered." Aghet's eyes turned inward, the memory overtaking him. "She reminds me of..." His words dissolved, leaving only the shadow that passed across his face.

Ghan scowled. "Reminds you of who?"

"Never mind." His shoulders shuddered as if trying to erase it.

A muscle in Ghan's jaw ticked. What name had nearly spilled free?

"I can still feel his magic prickling my skin." Aghet moaned as if the taste of it were glorious. "I can't get enough of—"

"Do not approach her." Ghan raised slowly from his chair. "Do not give the Crown the opportunity they seek to execute you. Besides, she's mine." He walked around his desk to tower over him. "Mine, do you hear?"

Aghet pursed his lips into a displeased pout.

"Do you understand?" Ghan asked, his voice dangerously low.

Aghet glanced away, resting his head on a hand, elbow

leaning on the desk, and heaved a frustrated sigh. "I also faltered," he said, cutting through Ghan's hazy fear. "I killed the others without hesitation, and yet, when it came to you, I couldn't."

Images from a ghastly war with Kahurang replayed in Ghan's mind.

"That day," Aghet said, "I almost killed you, and yet, I chose to stitch the gash on your face. Something about you conjured my need to protect you, so I sat beside you until you woke up."

Ghan remembered the eager eighteen-year-old Aghet Mendi, son of a tailor. He'd smiled at him as if he belonged on that dreadful battlefield more than Ghan did.

"Since then," Aghet continued, "you've inundated every facet of my conscious existence, inhabiting my waking thoughts, weaving through my dreams, and haunting even my darkest nightmares, and I must know why."

His gaze narrowed.

"We're so alike." He rose, meeting Ghan eye to eye. "You're different, unlike them." He took in Ghan's scent, brushing his nose against Ghan's ear and breathing quietly, immersed in the experience.

Ghan didn't move, but his throat tightened. Aghet's whisper was like silk on steel. Somewhere in the distance, a wind gusted, rattling the latticed window with the same quiet fury pressing beneath his skin.

"Your fragrance is unique, as if you're not of this world." He traced his fingers down the column of Ghan's throat. "It arouses me so." He bit on Ghan's bottom lip, gently pulling on it. "It drives me wild." He kissed his scar affectionately, from forehead to chin.

"Aghet." Ghan glared at him. "Do not get close to her. Ever."

Aghet's smile vanished, the shift like a cloud swallowing the sun. He pulled away to face Ghan fully. "Why?"

Ghan anchored his hand on Aghet's belt and yanked, their chests touching. "Because your eyes should be on me, not her."

Aghet stilled, his dark gaze intense and unflinching. "And

yet," he said softly, his voice edged with challenge, "your eyes are on her... not me."

Ghan's jaw flexed.

"Then don't give me a reason to look away," he growled. "You're mine—and only mine. I won't repeat myself."

Aghet angled his head slightly, a thoughtful hum vibrating in his throat, his lips curling faintly. "Yours." He closed his eyes as if tasting the word to decide whether it suited him. "Such a strange concept."

When his eyes opened, they gleamed with sly amusement. "Jealousy does not become my prince."

"Aghet," Ghan growled, a warning rumbling low in his throat.

A wicked grin parted Aghet's lips, a devilish promise lingering on them. "I'll behave," he purred. "I'll even apologize."

CHAPTER 34
THE WHIP OF FATE

Love is like the sea: sometimes calm, sometimes turbulent, but always powerful and captivating. - Poliormos

"N om!"

Noam, who was heading to the tavern for lunch, turned. Sebastian waved an arm and ran toward him, parting the bustling crowd, concern etched on his face.

"I've been waiting for you," Sebastian said.

Noam arched his eyebrows, curious, noting that Sebastian had left his post and his guards were covering for him.

"Hey," Sebastian said, rubbing the back of his neck—a sign he was gearing up to ask something awkward. His eyes flickered with hesitation as if he knew the question wouldn't land well. "Are you working at the villa today?"

"Yes." Noam grimaced, confused. Sebastian's unease made the question more puzzling. "Why are you asking?"

"What about Hyacinth? I mean, Hya, and please don't tell her I used her full name," Sebastian stammered. "Does she work there, too?" His voice carried fear.

Noam blinked, his mind racing to catch up with the sudden shift. "Seb, what's going on?"

"Stay away from the princesses' compound."

Noam's eyebrows shot up. He opened his mouth to complain—

"The soldiers were talking about it." Sebastian glanced over his shoulder and lowered his voice. "Something bad happened this morning, so stay away, please?" His hands gripped Noam's arms, fingers tightening with urgency. "Please?"

Noam's breath caught, his voice trembling. "What happened?"

Sebastian shook his head, eyes wide with worry. "I don't know the particulars, but it's connected to the Djinnshirukh princess."

A cold knot twisted in Noam's stomach.

"During the sparring training, she lost control. It took five White Guard officers to pull her away from one of the generals training with her. The word floating around is that she almost killed him. The High General had to step in. That's already bad enough, Nom." Fear and awe danced in Sebastian's eyes. "The Wall of Zahar-Ghak. The hero who delivered our victory against Kahurang."

Noam went still, his heart hammering his ribs. Fear, like a tiny seed, sprouted tendrils that coiled around him.

"That princess is dangerous." Sebastian's voice deepened. "Stay away until this blows over."

Noam felt the blood drain from his head, the world suddenly tilting under his feet.

"Nom?" Sebastian's voice broke through the haze, pulling Noam's gaze back to his.

"Does Marissa know?" Noam's voice came out higher than intended. He hated how fear clawed at him, tightening its grip.

"Everybody knows." Sebastian raked a hand through his hair. "Everyone's spooked, Nom. Talking about it. About her."

He hesitated, then added, "Six years ago, she—"

"I'll be careful," Noam snapped, desperate to end this conversation. Every instinct screamed at him to run to the villa to see for himself that she was well—to hold her in his arms. She would never attack without cause—not his Hya, who loved his flowers and the sound of his voice.

Noam's brows drew together. "She wouldn't..." The sentence withered in his throat. She wouldn't hurt someone—not unless provoked. Not her.

"Nom, please." Sebastian's brow creased with worry. "Come back with us to Urrun. Bring Hya, too. Your mavah will love her."

"We've spoken about this." His words came out harshly.

Sebastian flinched, taking a step back. Regret immediately gnawed at Noam's chest. Ashamed, he looked away. His fists clenched at his sides, nails digging into his palms as he struggled to contain the fear and frustration threatening to spill over.

"I get it," Sebastian said. "You enjoy your work, and it pays well, but I hate the thought of leaving you behind after this incident." He shook his head. "If something were to happen to you—"

"Nothing will," Noam cut him off, his jaw tightening as he forced the words out. "Nothing."

"Nom." Sebastian locked eyes with him, his hands squeezing his shoulders. "Promise me you'll be careful—"

"I already said I would," Noam replied, brushing Sebastian's hands with a sharp motion.

Sebastian recoiled, shocked. Noam turned and stormed away, anger simmering beneath the surface—angry at a world that didn't understand his Hya. And right now, she needed him.

❧

Noam stood at the iron-wrought gate, counting twice the guards who usually guarded the villa. They stood like titans, clad in gleaming breastplates that caught the sunlight, a stark departure from the usual leather armor.

"Where do you think you're going?" one of them said.

"I work in the garden—"

"Not today," the same soldier said. "By order from His Highness, the crown prince, laborers without his summons aren't allowed in. You"—he pointed at Noam—"were not summoned."

"But the garden—"

"Would you like a taste of my boot?"

Noam regarded the soldier and sighed, frustration and longing laced in that rush of air. "When will I be allowed to enter?"

The soldier, his demeanor as rigid as his armor, replied curtly, "When the crown prince decides."

Noam's gaze remained fixed on the magnificent villa with a sense of loss. His Hya needed him, but the security was excessive, with a substantial fence of soldiers and archers in position. Sneaking in at night would be impossible now.

His sense of uselessness gnawed at him, deepening the hollow in his chest.

He thought of Marissa. Perhaps she could enter the villa and check on her? He quickly dismissed the idea. Sebastian would scream at him for even suggesting it. Worse, it would expose Kharis and Noam's secret love affair.

Another soldier approached. He leaned into Noam, his tone sympathetic. "Listen, the Sendatorsum boasts countless gardens, each needing tending. Surely, you can find one to earn your wages. But this one," he gestured toward the villa, "it's off-limits for your safety."

Noam nodded, not at the guard but at defeat.

He turned away, pushing the cart down the path. She wouldn't know that he'd tried. That he'd stood there, reaching for her from the other side of a wall he couldn't scale. The wheels creaked on the stone, each turn a betrayal. That was the sound that followed him—not her laughter.

CHAPTER 35
THE THORNS OF LOVELY FLOWERS

The thorns in lovely roses are reminders that each flower bears the scars of its journey. - Poliormos

Since the incident with Aghet Mendi, the days had blurred into a week, then two. On the upside, Saya was talking to her again. On the downside, her confinement had been extended indefinitely. A wistful sigh escaped her lips.

Kharis couldn't stop thinking of Noam. Was he safe? Did he know? Did he hate her now? She could still feel his breath against her cheek—how tenderlyhe'd whispered that she was his joy. That familiar fear crept back into her thoughts. Would he stay away for good?

The knocks on the door brought Kharis out of her gloomy haze.

"What is it?" She lowered her book, not even bothering to open the door. Why would she? Besides, servants preferred it that way: an extra layer of defense against a violent Djinnshirukh.

"There's a messenger at the gate for you," the woman's quivering voice drifted through the door.

Hope suddenly shone brightly. "From?"

"The Regia-Zenka, Your Highness. A letter to be hand-delivered."

That brought the black clouds back. Why would she ever think it could be Noam? A gardener would never be allowed past the gate, much less summon a princess of the realm.

"I'll be down shortly." She set the book down, dreading the moment.

Kharis exited the house and crossed the path, heading for the wrought-iron gates where an entourage of White Guard officers awaited.

A sudden chill gripped her, bringing back that unsettling, prickling sensation. With a determined breath, Kharis gained her composure, ignoring the crawling feeling all over her skin. She squared her shoulders, lifted her chin, and kept walking.

The villa's sentries thumped their spears in salute upon spotting her. Clad in black, the officer standing outside the gates turned slowly.

"General Mendi." Her voice, a deliberate cascade of frost, hinted at nonchalant boredom while she wore a cloak of indifference.

Aghet sneered, perhaps playing the same game, and approached the gate with a scroll. "I'm here to offer my earnest apologies." He bowed, the movement perfunctory.

She didn't trust his gesture.

No one else would notice the shift—but she felt it. The colors around him dimmed, as if the world itself recoiled. The faint scent of rancid wine bloomed in the air, sour and cloying, curling in her nostrils. Her curse whispered that he was lying.

Her gaze dropped to the scroll he held.

He smiled, all too pleased. "I'm delivering your new orders in person, given you are"—his gaze roamed the space behind her—"confined to your residence."

She didn't bother with a "thanks," her eyes flicking to an officer to take the scroll on her behalf.

Aghet snatched it away before the woman could grab it. "My orders were not to give it to you," he snapped at the officer, "but to the Djinnshirukh princess." He smiled like a hunter catching the scent of his cornered prey.

"And you shall give it to Officer Mayam," Kharis remarked

with disinterest, turning around. "I don't have time for games this morning."

"Yours is a lovely garden," Aghet said, darkly wicked. "The blossoms are exquisite."

Kharis halted at the sinister sweetness in his words, her back still to the gate as fear flooded her veins.

"You must have exceptional gardeners," Aghet added with a dark fascination. "I should inquire about their services."

Every muscle in Kharis's body froze.

"Yes." Aghet Mendi's voice dripped with disturbing amusement. "I should find out who handles your villa."

Kharis clenched her jaw, aware of the game at hand.

"Suit yourself." She forced a deliberate calm in her voice to mask any hint of her dread. "General Mendi, I remind you that you're not allowed to be here, not even to deliver apologies."

"Ah, the frost still lingers." Aghet faked his disappointment. "It appears you're unwilling to offer forgiveness." His tone conveyed the ghost of a malicious grin. "And here I thought that my gesture would warm your heart."

If Kharis could, she would burn him to a crisp.

"Officer Mayam," Kharis commanded with finality. "Fetch the scroll. I've wasted enough of my time here."

She strolled away, resisting the urge to rush back into the house. The awful sensation of hundreds of tiny spiders crawling beneath her skin threatened to shatter her composure. Relief trickled in as she got farther from Aghet.

She couldn't pinpoint what about him triggered this visceral reaction. It wasn't the usual response she received from others: not the bitter or sour tastes, the invisible thorned tendrils that threatened to rip her skin, or the jarring colors that warped the world. This was different, darker, leaving her unnerved in a way she couldn't ignore.

Once inside, Kharis took the stairs two at a time, nearly stumbling in her haste. She reached the nearest window and threw a glance outside. The general and his escort march were already disappearing down the path.

Noam's safety hung in the balance. She had to move—now

—before Aghet Mendi uncovered who had given her the blue hibiscus..

If he did, Noam wouldn't survive the questioning.

And Ghan wouldn't just interrogate him—he'd kill him. Of that, Kharis was certain.

"Haleen!" Kharis called out from the landing, her voice sharp.

A timid servant peered from the hall below. "Y—Yes, Your Highness?"

"Send for Her Excellency Yuna. I must speak to her, and only her."

The woman ran.

CHAPTER 36
RECKONING

True reckoning begins not with judgment from others but with accepting one's truth. - Poliormos

K haris tried focusing on the book, but her hands wouldn't stop shaking.

The sitting room doors swung open with a quiet creak, and Yuna stepped inside, her gaze sharp and searching. "I received your message. What happened?"

Kharis put her book down and ran to her, wrapping her arms around the bhiksun. "Aghet was here."

"What?" Anger shook Yuna's body. "He is not allowed near you or the villa."

Kharis exhaled her frustration. "He came to offer his apologies."

"That bastard. Always looking for a way to lure you in." Yuna pulled away slightly and exhaled slowly. "I must calm down. Nothing good comes from anger." The tension ebbed off her face. "One of these days, Mendi will grow overtly confident, cross a line, and the Regia-Zenka will finally have the excuse to send him away for good or, better yet, execute him.

"Aghet Mendi is a dark presence that surrounds all of us," she went on. "I'd rather see him dead. Many in the Sendatorsum will celebrate his death." She exhaled sharply, a rare glimmer of rage breaking through her usually composed demeanor. "Never mind how my brother protects him. The control Mendi exercises over Arjun is a growing concern. He has Arjun tightly wrapped around his insidious little finger."

"Nana?" Kharis feared even uttering the question. "Is the Zahar-Eliza off the table now?"

"Oh no." Yuna shook her head firmly. "I suspect Aghet's little stunt was meant to derail it, but he failed spectacularly. General Salazar stated that he taunted you, that he asked Aghet to leave, and that Aghet attacked you when you stepped away after disarming him. Salazar ordered him to stand down, and Aghet ignored the command. That's when he called on his officers—fifteen witnesses, mind you—to intervene and pull you apart. Jordha worked with Salazar on the report that was presented to the Regia-Zenka. Your father"—she bit the inside of her cheek—"shared it with me. That's how I know."

Yuna breathed out her frustration. Kharis's heart sprinted like a panicked horse careening toward a precipice.

"Gutxi?" Yuna's brow knit, her gaze sharpening. "You're worrying me. The messenger said your summons was urgent. What happened?"

"I kissed a boy," she blurted out before she could second-guess herself, lowering her head. "Many times."

Yuna's voice remained steady. "And who is he?"

She hesitated, eyes shuttering. "The gardener."

A long silence stretched between them. Kharis felt its weight, her heart sinking with each heartbeat. This rule had to be the worst she'd ever broken. She wanted to vanish, bracing for the anger—and crushing disappointment—of the woman who had always loved her like a mother.

"I see," Yuna said softly, her voice devoid of judgment.

Kharis lifted her gaze, perplexed. "You're not angry with me?"

Yuna tilted her head with a long sigh, and the faintest smile tugged at her lips. "I, too, kissed a boy I wasn't supposed to. Many times." The warmth in her smile reached her eyes. "So why would I be?" She reached out, cupping Kharis's cheek and brushing away a stray tear with her thumb. "It's a testament to your humanity."

A shuddering breath escaped Kharis as relief washed over her. For a fleeting moment, she felt like she wasn't drowning anymore.

Yuna sat, gently guiding Kharis to settle beside her on the cushioned bench. "Is this what you wanted to tell me?"

Kharis's stomach clenched. "Aghet must never find out."

Yuna hummed thoughtfully, a flicker of discontent darkening her composed features. "The messenger claimed he was here to deliver your new orders. How gallant of him," she remarked with regal sarcasm. "He was sniffing about, wasn't he?"

Kharis confirmed it with a nod.

"What does Saya think of this?"

The question hit harder than anticipated. "Saya doesn't know," she said. "Nor must she ever."

"Why?" A wrinkle formed between her brows. "Why would you hide this from her?"

Kharis curled her fingers so tightly that her knuckles ached. "And tell her what? That she's not the center of my world when I'm the center of hers? She didn't ask to become the Sorukhipa, but now, she's enslaved to me. Where's the justice in that? I'm supposed to find a way to free her from this fate, not add to it."

She swallowed a sob, the ache in her chest sharp. "I can't burden her with this."

A quiet sorrow crept into Yuna's expression as she gently patted her lap in invitation. Kharis curled beside her, laying her head on it. "You didn't ask to be the Djinnshirukh, either," Yuna said, stroking her black hair.

"Stupid curse." Salty tears trickled down her cheeks. An impending storm was drawing near, the thunder of fate rumbling ominously.

"Do you love him?"

The words caught in Kharis's throat, strangled by grief. "Yes."

"Then we must do everything we can to protect him. No

one must discover your transgression. I fear how the Regia-Zenka may view this."

Resealment.

Everything always boiled down to that one word.

"I'll do anything to protect him." Her guilt returned in full force. Sitting up from Yuna's lap, she faced her. "Noam's innocent. He... It was my fault for encouraging it."

"It's nobody's fault, my darling. Why would I blame a bird for singing or a flower for blooming?" Yuna's gaze grew distant, her mind caught in a memory before she refocused. "Do you understand what this means?"

Kharis's resolve wavered like a flame in the wind. Did she?

Yuna's tone remained gentle but firm. "With Mendi on the prowl, it is a matter of time before he figures out who this lad is and what he means to you. I fear how Arjun will play such knowledge against you and your gardener." She paused, her voice softening with sorrow. "And my brother... is a cruel man."

Kharis's breath snagged in her throat, downright terrified for Noam. He'd been a rainbow after a storm, warm sunlight after a cold winter. He was a glimpse at what life could have been—should have been—if not for the curse that had turned her into the monster that instilled terror in everyone—the creature with the power to destroy the world.

She'd hoped for a lovely flower to soften her image and make her seem less of the abomination everyone feared—a foolish indulgence because fate had played a cruel trick, twisting her hopes into a nightmare. She was confined to the villa until further notice, and all workers had been dismissed, leaving only a skeleton staff of uneasy servants who didn't want to be there. But what hurt most was the thought of Noam hearing of it—and choosing not to return. How could she blame him?

Shame was a relentless weight on her soul.

Shame and guilt and regret.

"Are you willing to go through with it?" Yuna asked.

Noam deserved a life untainted by the shadows looming over hers. How could she drag him down as she sank into the abyss? Love was joy, but it also implied sacrifice and came with painful thorns. She would carry this pain with her, but so long as Noam lived, it would be worth it.

She drew a shuddering breath. "Even when it breaks my heart."

Yuna's expression faltered, sadness flashing in her eyes. She nodded solemnly, her hand lifting to caress Kharis's cheek with the tenderness only a mother could offer. "I'll arrange it, then."

The last remnants of Kharis's world collapsed. She curled up in Yuna's arms, mourning the loss of a sweet dream and lamenting the tangled web of lies and secrets that now surrounded her.

CHAPTER 37
LOVE'S JAGGED EDGES

True love is not about perfection; it is hidden in flaws and sacrifices.
- Poliormos

Disguised as a servant, Kharis followed Yuna, heart thudding beneath the fabric of her borrowed kirtle. They left the Sendatorsum before daybreak, cloaked in secrecy and aided by servants loyal to Yuna and Anong.

"I'll do my best to cover for you," Anong had told them. "Do not linger." He'd kissed Kharis's forehead with fatherly affection and Yuna's lips sweetly.

Now, Yuna hurried through the tunnel, torch in hand, moving with the sure-footed ease of someone who had traversed this underground path countless times. The women rushed, navigating its twists and turns. A set of worn wooden stairs leading to a small trapdoor halted their advance. Yuna raised her hand and knocked on it—two sharp knocks followed by a tense pause and a third quieter knock. Footfalls and creaking noises resonated from above. The wooden hatch swung open, and a flash of light pierced the blackness.

"This way, Your Excellency," said a male voice.

A large hand came into view, assisting Yuna and Kharis up the weathered steps and bringing them into a narrow three-story townhouse in the outer Zahar-Regia ring. Two warrior monks sporting long purple tunics over their mahogany-rich skin loomed protectively over the family: a husband, a wife, and three children. With a nod from the husband, the wife swiftly nudged their children into another room.

One of the monks, a tall man, stepped forward and bowed to Yuna. His voice carried a faint accent as he spoke. "We leave upon your command."

"Thank you, Salam," Yuna said. "Let's proceed."

With the door slightly ajar, he peeked out into the street. "It's clear. The zenka patrol will take about an hour to circle this neighborhood again. We must be swift. If they spot any irregularities," he cast a discreet glance toward Kharis, "they'll stop us."

"Understood." Yuna's sharp eyes swept over everyone in the room. "This plan hinges on not being found out." She then faced Kharis, her expression softening. "Are you ready?"

Was she ready for what she had to do? Could she face the consequences? What if the plan failed? This family would be in danger. What about Yuna, the servants, and bhiksunim who had risked so much to help them? And Saya, unaware, would be caught in the aftermath.

Leaving the house also meant crossing an invisible line and closing a door forever.

There was no return from this.

But Noam deserved to live a life without danger. A life away from this madness.

With a sharp inhale, she nodded, secured her braid under her knit cap, and pulled the hood over her head.

The group slipped out through the townhouse's back exit, blending into the predawn shadows that stretched between the narrow alleys of the Ghak.

Yuna tugged her along.

Kharis was thankful for her nana's hand, a lifeline of unwavering support that anchored her to this world. Guilt left her with so many holes that she feared she would drift away.

The chilly, moist air pricked her cheeks. Clouds dense with rain hung low, somber sentinels watching the world.

The group crept through the narrow alleyway. Amina, the

female warrior, took the lead, pausing at corners to ensure it was safe to proceed, while Salam guarded the rear. Their cautious footfalls barely made a sound on the damp cobblestone path, each step splashing the hems of their cloaks.

As the sound of squawking seagulls grew louder, Kharis's heart pulsed in her throat, about to leap out.

"Halt!" Amina commanded, raising her hand before rounding the corner.

"What is it?" Salam asked.

Amina jerked her chin, her accent thicker than Salam's. "Zenka patrol." She clicked her tongue. "Something happen. They not move."

Yuna looked back at Salam. "We must reach the docks in time."

"I do," Amina said, gliding past them. "I draw them away." Like a ghost, she melted into the shadows. Salam shifted into her place, watching, waiting.

"Nana?" Fear made Kharis's voice high-pitched. "I don't know if I can do this."

"Gutxi," Yuna said, gripping Kharis's hand reassuringly. "Love always comes with sacrifice, but it isn't perfect. Love has flaws and rough, jagged edges, too."

A commotion broke out—sharp voices, hurried footsteps. The zenka guards turned, rushing toward the disturbance.

"Now!" Salam motioned them forward while the path lay unguarded.

They darted across the open street, weaving through clusters of people, their heads low and their footsteps quick. In moments, they slipped into the next alley and vanished into its waiting shadows. Soon, it widened into a quay, where the bustle of activity surrounded a ship ahead. The ship's bow bore the carved figure of a phoenix, wings spread wide, rising, like her, from the ashes.

Crew members moved swiftly, securing the rigging, adjusting the sails, and readying the masts for departure. Shouts and commands rang through the damp morning air, blending with the rhythmic creak of wood and rope. The ship's silhouette shifted with the rolling waves while mist curled and drifted, veiling the harbor in ghostly shrouds.

Three figures waited near the gangplank as the ground crew hauled the last cargo aboard in a soon-to-end parade of crates, bags, and barrels.

Kharis stopped in her tracks as logic and passion battled each other.

He lowered his hood—and smiled. Everything dissolved when she saw his face. The world narrowed to the sound of her breathing, the thump of her heart, and the open arms waiting for her.

Kharis let go of Yuna's hand—and ran.

CHAPTER 38
THE ZENKA WHISTLE

*Love places another's happiness above your own,
even when it breaks you. - Poliormos*

Noam knew her shape, the way she stood, how she moved. Her scent invaded his senses—wild and salty like the stormy seas of Urrun. He knew, even without seeing her face, that it was her. She ran to him as if pushed by the wind, and he wrapped his arms around her small frame.

His lips crashed onto hers, a frantic kiss devouring her. He took everything about her into him: the way she tasted, how her body fit perfectly in his arms, and the feel of her lips, warm and soft as they met his.

When he pulled away to gaze at her, the cold, unforgiving morning air clung to his skin.

"Hya," he whispered, tightening his grip. "Come with me."

Her muscles tensed at his request.

"Please," he begged her as he pressed her against his chest.

"Noam." Her voice quivered. "I can't go," she said, as if swallowing her desire to say yes and run with him.

"They'll come after us but also target those you love," she said. "We can't hide or live in peace. The Crown will place a bounty on our heads, and when they find us, for they will, they'll execute you on the spot." She gazed at him. "Worse.

They'll execute anyone extending their kindness to help us. There's no happily ever after for us, but life awaits you once you get on that ship. You must leave now before the 'us' gets you killed."

Her tears flowed, liquid diamonds tracing a glittery path down her cheeks. Noam didn't know what to say or do to stop them—to stop everything. The right words escaped him. The appropriate gesture to ease her pain, or even coax the faintest glimmer of a smile from her, failed him.

His heart ached as he held her, his fingers trembling against her back. "How can I leave you behind?" he murmured.

"You must," she said. "Your life is all that matters to me."

Noam inhaled, resigned to this moment with her. He understood the risks. If others found out he existed, there was no telling what they would do to him to get to her.

"You must leave Zahar-Ghak." Kharis caressed his face with tenderness. "If anything were to happen to you, I'd never forgive myself."

He squeezed his eyes shut, the pain too much for his heart to bear. His sobs punctuated their kiss, a silent exchange of love, pain, and longing. He tasted the salt of her tears, savoring the last few moments he would ever have with her, resting his forehead against hers as their breaths mingled.

"I promised to return this to you." Noam pulled the silver zenka whistle from his pocket. Taking her hand, he placed it on her palm.

Kharis shook her head. "No." Her sapphire gaze met his bronze orbs. "Keep it. Let it protect you for as long as you live. Keep it so you won't forget me."

"Forget you?" Pain edged his voice. "How could I ever? Can't you see—you're entrenched in my soul, woven into my every breath? This farewell... It's like dying."

Her lips quivered as if searching for words to make this better. Regret laced her gaze, and it burned him intensely. Because of her past, there would be no future for them. The injustice of it shook his body and soul.

She closed her hands around his, her voice so low, so weak, so filled with pain. "Keep the whistle close to your heart.

Whenever you blow it, think of me." A quiet smile parted her lips.

He glanced away, hiding how his heart had fractured, but nodded, his tears falling freely. She wrapped her arms around his waist, and her scent enveloped him one last time. Noam clutched the whistle tightly, his sobs wracking his body. "I'll never forget you. I'll carry you in my heart, always."

"Nom?" Sebastian approached the couple. "We must leave." He gestured toward someone atop the gangplank, waving their arms and yelling for them to get on the vessel.

Marissa settled by him, her face heavy with worry.

Kharis cradled Noam's face one last time. "I never told you."

"Tell me what?" His forehead wrinkled.

"That I love you. I—I thought we would have more time."

Noam moaned, pressing her against him, hoping to seal her inside his body and take her with him. "Oh, Hya." He hugged her tightly one more time. One last time. "As if you needed to tell me."

"Noam?" Marissa's eyes flicked between Noam and Kharis. Then her gaze lingered on Kharis, and her expression shifted from confusion to realization. With trembling legs, she curtsied. "Y—Your Highness."

"Please, don't," Kharis warned.

Sebastian frowned, his gaze darting between the woman in Noam's arms and Marissa. "Hya?" His face paled as understanding crashed over him. "You're the Djinnshirukh of Zahar."

Kharis's voice broke with quiet desperation. "You must take him away," she pleaded. "No one must ever know."

Sebastian inclined his head, and his grip tightened around Noam's arm. "We must go, Noam," he said, his voice now firm, speaking not as his best friend but a Zahari commander. "You must board the ship."

The bhiksun stepped forward, meeting Sebastian's gaze. "If you value your life and that of your loved ones, no one must ever know." Her tone hovered on the dawn of a dangerous threat. "No one."

Sebastian offered the woman a crisp head bow. "On my

honor and life, it'll be as you wish, Your Excellency." He then turned to Kharis, meeting her eyes with a solemn promise. "I will protect him, Hya. I swear it."

Noam faced Kharis, his eyes taking in everything about her. "No matter what happens, I'll always be there for you. Nothing will ever change that." He clutched her arms. "I will never forget you. I'll plant hyacinths in my garden and always remember you whenever I look at them. And I'll blow the whistle, hoping its sound finds you, so you know I'm thinking of you."

Kharis smiled as fresh tears filled her lovely eyes. "Since I can't, you must live for both of us." She kissed him again. "Live and love," she whispered, "so this sacrifice isn't in vain."

"Nom," Sebastian insisted, tugging on him. "They'll leave without us, and you must be on that ship."

"He won't be alone," Marissa told Kharis. "I swear it to you." She turned to her brother. "Noam, we must go."

After one final kiss, Sebastian and Marissa tore Noam away from Kharis.

"I love you," were his last words to her as their fingers unclasped. "I will love you always."

Marissa pulled on him, and Sebastian nudged him from behind to climb onto the gangplank. When the three boarded the ship, Noam's gaze fixed on her as the crew hoisted the ship's sails and the anchor groaned out of the water.

His heart shattered into a thousand pieces, just like dandelion seeds exploding from their blooms. A lifetime wouldn't be enough to collect them, floating directionless at the whim of fickle winds.

His beloved Hya stood on that weathered dock, grief twisting her face as tears streaked down her cheeks. He loved her, the most exquisite flower in his garden. His chest heaved, a sudden rise and fall, as this farewell finally sank in.

Once this ship sailed, it would be the end of everything.

He would never kiss or hold her as they danced the night away amid spirited jigs, foamy ales, and laughter.

This was goodbye—the end of a lovely story. The pain that erupted from deep inside crushed him.

Noam's grip tightened on the ship's rail, his knuckles aching.

"Hya!" he shouted.

It was a plea. It was a wish. It was a curse directed at cruel gods.

"Hya! I'll always love you!"

❧

The wind carried Noam's voice, and it reached her ears. He called out to her; his name for her was a fragile lifeline that would endure even the fiercest storms.

The sails gobbled up the winds, swelling with a loud swoosh. The dock creaked as the ship sailed away from it, slowly gliding down the Ibaia. The vessel met the strong river currents, gained momentum, and swiftly took Noam away from Kharis.

When she heard the whistle, its sound became a prayer lost in the vast expanse of the world, and her heart broke into a thousand shards. And while her heart shrieked at her, desperately trying to make her run to Noam, a gentle hum caressed her from deep within her mind.

"Why?" Kharis shouted at the gods above and below. "Why must it be this way?"

The Voice lingered in her mind, a quiet presence hoping to comfort her.

Ancient magic swirled inside her as if the waves of an endless ocean sought to reach the shores. But this pain inside her chest, like nothing she'd ever experienced, stole her words. It brushed harsh strokes in her mind, all in gray and black.

"Why?" She directed her accusation at the god of fate.

Kharis didn't hold back her howls as the distance between her and Noam became an insurmountable chasm. She found it hard to breathe, her grief overwhelming.

The river barge carrying her beloved gardener soon became a speck in the distance.

Like that, Noam was gone.

A distant memory rose from the darkness, where it had

been imprisoned. This had happened before—a long, long time ago. In it lived a tormented farewell and one last kiss, slow and deep, before saying goodbye with a promise sealed by magic.

An anguished voice buried under the mists of time echoed with celestial certainty: "*This is not the end,*" he'd yelled at her between sobs. "*This is a new beginning. We are bound to each other, you and I.*"

In that memory, eyes the color of midnight—so deep a blue they bordered on black—gleamed with the power of stars and moons. They shimmered with unshed tears and held hers, unblinking.

His voice was raw with anger and desperation. "*I bind myself to you and shall search for you in every timeline and universe,*" he'd vowed, the words ringing with unyielding determination. "*I will find you.*"

The grief in those eyes resembled the grief reflected in Noam's stare.

There would be no more flowers and quiet chats in a lovely garden, no more arms to hug her, no more kissing him. Eyes the color of roasted chestnuts would never gaze upon her again with sweet affection.

Kharis felt as if her heart had been ripped from her chest. This pain, new and yet so ancient, engulfed her. When she acknowledged that Noam was gone, a sustained, grief-stricken wail escaped her lungs. But it wasn't his name that escaped her lips.

"*Farrádh!*"

Her knees buckled, and she crumpled to the ground. Her pain urged the heavens to weep with her. The magic inside her erupted, surging as if from a different world altogether. It pulsed outward with each sob, carrying her sorrow to the clouds so that the gods themselves would feel her grief.

The clouds above flashed with a crack of lightning, answering her anguish. Salty drops cascaded from the darkened sky, fallen gems that tasted like her tears. They struck the ground and shattered into a million glimmering shards of light. The world rippled around her as invisible waves of magic unfurled from her body, urging the gods to cry with her.

The heavens rumbled with the deep, mournful echoes of thunder. Another lightning bolt speared the dense clouds, dancing in bursts. Its brilliant arcs pierced the darkness, revealing the raw, torn edges of the distant storm-tossed clouds, so like the jagged edges of a shattered love.

Rain shrouded the quay in a gray cloak. The wind howled louder, drowning her cries.

Far across the city, another heart suffered Kharis's grief, too.

CHAPTER 39
LIGHTNING AND LOSS

There comes a grief so vast, it splits the spirit like a tree beneath lightning—leaving it standing, but never the same. - Poliormos

During her training at the palace, Saya stopped in her tracks.

A powerful traveled through the bond with her sister. Saya lowered her sword, immersing herself in the flood of emotions. They came like clumps of ice on a wild river, collecting and crashing against the rocks.

"Your Highness?" General Salazar asked.

These waves crested, wild and fierce, spilling out of their causeway. The tears that jumped out of Saya's eyes surprised her. The tug she felt was a cry in the dark—a desperate wail from a soul that sought to become whole again.

Khiri?

Grief dragged Saya along as if she'd been caught in its disorienting wake, pulled by its currents. The scent of salt and wet stone ghosted through her nose.

"Your Highness?" Salazar's voice was sharper, lower. "Are you all right?"

Saya wiped her face, pondering why such profound yet unexpected sorrow had engulfed her. It had overwhelmed her so quickly and intensely that she could barely breathe. When she faced Salazar, who stared at her with a wrinkled forehead, words failed her. But she knew that the tears gushing from her eyes weren't hers. Kharis was making the entire world cry with her.

Salazar's brow creased, unspoken questions swimming in his eyes. He was about to ask when a furious gust of wind slammed into the windows, flinging them all wide open. Fat raindrops pelted the room, drenching everyone inside with a sudden spray.

"Spear me," Salazar cursed, hastily closing the nearest window. "Another blasted winter storm," he grumbled, moving to the next one, wrestling against the wind, and shouting, "Get the servants to dry the floor."

The potent roll of thunder rattled Saya's bones.

Footfalls sent tremors through the flooring as officers moved to close the rest of the windows.

The rain, relentless in its attack, beat on the glass as if those drops were fists trying to break through to reach Saya.

The flash of harsh and violent lightning brought Yuna back. An unexpected torrential shower had swept in, catching everyone off guard. Thunder rumbled its anger, rattling windows and wooden stalls. Raindrops pelted the ground with their relentless staccato.

The storm burst upon them, and rain poured torrents, blurring the world. The wind howled through the alleyways and whistled past the eaves as if it were mourning with her niece.

People dashed in a frantic rush, their hurried footsteps splashing on the wet pavement. Some clutched bags tightly to their chests, running toward the safety of nearby buildings, while others hastily pushed carts, their contents swiftly covered with tarps to shield them from the watery onslaught.

Sharp, cold gusts blew through the streets, tugging at clothing and hair, making the chill in the air even more biting.

Yuna clutched Kharis's arm. Her niece obeyed the firm tug

to get up, but Gutxi's heart was another matter. One half was on that ship, and the other half lay on the cobblestones, broken.

"You loved him," Yuna whispered. It wasn't a question. It was a bitter realization.

Kharis didn't reply, wet black hair plastered to her forehead. Her silver and sapphire eyes glimmered, the colors mirroring the storm that now blew upon them.

When it mattered, Kharis thought of the young man, not her feelings or desires. It tore her niece to pieces to do the right thing, but the young gardener's life had mattered more than her happiness.

Many years ago, when it mattered, Yuna thought only of herself and Anong, not her subjects or the Empire. She walked away, abandoning Aghuti and Arjun. That old, persistent sense of guilt returned to poke at her.

"Your Excellency," Salam said, touching Yuna's arm. "We must go."

Yuna nodded and gently pulled Kharis's cloak closer around her. Despite the urge to hug and comfort her niece, she took her hand and tugged, their figures swiftly melting into the rain-streaked shadows.

PART THREE
SHADOWS AND WHISPERS

CHAPTER 40
WHEN THE WRITINGS END

Love does not falter in the presence of turmoil; instead, it grows stronger, proving its boundless and enduring nature. - Poliormos

Kharis stood on the balcony terrace, a gentle breeze stirring her raven-black hair. The sun had risen to kiss the morning sky, coloring everything in shades of pink and gold. She watched an older man lead a woman through her duties in the garden, both wearing the same gardening uniforms. She was likely Noam's replacement.

A lump formed in her throat.

Turning away, Kharis clutched a letter, its parchment rough against her fingers, and carefully concealed it within the folds of her cloak. With her Velathari, she left the villa and headed to the academy to see her nana, who would ensure it reached a young gardener in Urrun.

Life pressed on relentlessly, indifferent to her ache

Even as her heart lay shattered—its pieces scattered like dandelion seeds in the wind—Kharis knew she could no longer remain still. The spring equinox was two months away. The moment of balance. Of breaking and becoming. And when it came, she would leave the Ghak.

She'd tasted life and love—and there was no going back from that. Moving forward was the only choice now, but as long as she was bound to the demon, her life would be on pause. If she didn't break the curse, death would be the only mercy left to her.

❧

The doors creaked open, and the archivists' eyes bulged in shock.

"Y—Your Highness?" a young woman stammered, her hands trembling on the heavy tome she held.

"Blessed be the earth and sun," Kharis said, her voice ringing against the towering bookstacks.

The archivists replied with a disjointed, "May they sustain us." Then, silence.

Kharis was acutely aware that they were scared to see her. The metallic taste hit her first. Then came the sharp thorns.

Her gaze roamed the space, taking in the tall bookshelves brimming with scrolls detailing the history of Zahar.

The accounts of former kings, queens, Djinnshirukh, and Sorukhipas lay here. The wisdom of the Forest Kin immortals awaited her. Rolls of prophecies and weighty tomes beckoned her to approach.

In this place, she could forget the world while absorbed in her one task: ending the Djinnshirukh curse. Here, the pain in her heart would become a muted ache. Although she'd often slipped in at night to avoid prying eyes, she wouldn't hide anymore. This place was hers by birthright, and no one would chase her away. Not anymore.

Her fingertips itched to dive in—once the pain abated.

Eventually, the burning sensation faded. The thorny vines withered. Kharis breathed in relief.

"To what do we owe the pleasure, Your Highness?" another woman, the most senior of the group, asked as if it were a rarity for a royal to visit the very place that held her lineage and history.

"These are the Royal Archives, are they not?" Kharis asked, her tone icy.

"Yes, Your Highness." The woman peeked behind her, hoping for support. None came.

The archivists stepped further back. A few scampered off, probably to hide.

"Your name?" Kharis asked.

The woman smoothed her coiffed gray hair and cleared her throat. "I am Keeper Brenna, Your Highness."

"Keeper Brenna," Kharis said, her smile soft, her eyes sharp. "I want every prophecy connected to the Djinnshirukh and the Sorukhipa brought to me."

More silent glances were exchanged. "All of them?" Brenna asked.

Kharis quirked an eyebrow, her patience wearing thin. "Yes. Every single one. Even the ones you hide."

"We don't hide..." Brenna's words faltered under Kharis's sharp glare.

Crossing her arms, Kharis's narrowed gaze studied the men and women who dared not meet her eyes. "If you fetch my brother to come and get me, I'll burn this place myself."

Everyone froze.

"I am not to be disturbed," Kharis said, her voice cutting through the tense silence. "Is this clear?"

"Of course," Brenna bowed. "We're at your disposal." She turned on her heel without missing a beat, clapping her hands sharply to stir the room into action. "You heard Her Highness. Let's get to it."

The archivists sprang into motion, suddenly eager to follow Kharis's command without delay.

Satisfied, Kharis smiled. "Thank you," she said, her tone softening a little. "Your help is appreciated. I'll be in the private reading room."

Kharis sauntered quietly past the aisles, aware that Brenna was still bowing behind her.

❧

A few hours later, Kharis's desk was buried under baskets overflowing with scrolls and neatly stacked piles of books.

229

The flickering sunlight streamed through the upper window panes as she skimmed through texts with the same diligence that had marked her night explorations. She devoured each scroll and book as her eyes scanned for a clue or a whisper of the immortals' spell that had created the Djinnshirukh and the Sorukhipa.

The blasted spell remained elusive.

Letting her annoyance ebb, she unrolled another scroll and read it. The last line caught her attention right away.

> *All that was wrong will be righted,*
> *When the immortal vessel dies.*
> *Tear asunder the seals that contain it,*
> *Let the flames roam with might.*
> *Let it all be destroyed so freedom finds its light.*
> *Let the world revel in fire.*
> *Let it be consumed again,*
> *So the spirits, once joined, transcend,*
> *And all the writings end.*

"And all the writings end," Kharis recited aloud.

A melodic hum curled at the edge of her thoughts, glimmering with stardust and midnight.

"It's your favorite quote," she whispered, amused. Before Kharis could reach for her quill to take notes, a young archivist entered the room, bringing her another basket.

"This is the last of the scrolls on the information you requested, Your Highness," he said, keeping his distance. A mop of brown curls framed an enthusiastic smile and curious eyes.

"Name?" she asked.

"I'm Apprentice Serem. Keeper Brenna assigned me to attend to you personally." He sounded so proud of it. "Is there anything else you need?"

"What do you know about this prophecy?" she asked, handing the scroll to him.

He read it and nodded. "Ah, yes. This is the oldest prophecy we have in storage. It is a copy of the original, mind you. Given its age, a thousand years old, we keep the original in the vault."

"Is this a faithful copy?"

"That it is, Your Highness. We don't change a word, even when there are obvious errors in spelling or syntax." He shuffled around the table, searching for books among the piles.

Kharis watched. His fear had faded, replaced with scholarly enthusiasm. The taste of it, apples and cinnamon, teased her tongue. She could deal with this emotion. Picking two books, Serem handed them to her. "These two volumes go into the details, providing various interpretations. You may find them quite useful."

Kharis smiled, her hand caressing the book on top.

"Is there anything else?" Serem asked, flashing a much-too-eager grin.

Kharis suspected he was doing his utmost to keep her from setting the archives ablaze. She couldn't help but wonder if the others lingered outside, holding their breath as they listened, desperate to ensure the Djinnshirukh remained calm and content while poor Serem bore the burden for them all.

"This one doesn't follow the same format as the other prophecies," she said. "It doesn't start with 'The fates have revealed' or 'The gods have shown me,'" she mimicked a dangerous-sounding voice about to utter doom and destruction.

Serem laughed.

"What do you make of it?" Kharis asked, resting her head on the palm of her hand. "Is it a prophecy or something else?"

Serem fidgeted. "The books I selected might—"

"No, Serem," she sighed, her smile soft. "I want your opinion first."

He scratched his cheek, taken by the request. "I agree that it isn't written as a prophecy." He chuckled nervously. "It appears to be structured more like a promise." His initial apprehension melted away as his academic fervor took over. "'All that was wrong will be righted' is the promise. The condition for its fulfillment comes in the next line: 'When the immortal vessel dies.' Now, if we assume the 'immortal vessel' to be—"

He clamped his lips, eyes darting away.

"Serem?" Kharis pushed.

Serem wavered, probably pondering his mortality. "If the Djinnshirukh is the immortal vessel referenced here, this could be a promise to end the contract that set the spell in motion. However..." His teeth snagged his bottom lip.

Kharis sighed, drumming her fingers on the table with annoyance. "However, what?"

"We've had sixty-seven Djinnshirukh, to be exact. You're number sixty-eight." He stared at her as if she would understand the implication of his comment.

Kharis exhaled loudly because she didn't. "And what exactly do you mean by that?"

Serem handed the scroll back to Kharis. "All the other Djinnshirukh are dead." He scratched his temple nervously.

That knowledge made her sad. "Men and women who chose their roles upon their eighteenth birthmark, none of them making it past thirty-five."

"You broke the mold, Your Highness, being born a Djinnshirukh."

"So was my sister," Kharis added, voice flat. "Born a Sorukhipa."

Serem nodded solemnly. "And Lord Athon, too."

Kharis had forgotten about him—another baby with golden eyes. Now he was gone. Dead in the prime of his life. She shook her head to dislodge the thought because that couldn't be Saya's fate, too.

"So," she said. "You were telling me about the dead Djinnshirukh."

Serem flinched. "Ah, yes, of course. They're all dead, which begs the question... If the condition is met when the immortal vessel, that is, the Djinnshirukh, dies, wouldn't everything be righted about now?"

Kharis squinted, following his logic. "Go on."

"The Djinnshirukh cannot be 'the immortal vessel' referenced here. Otherwise, all the wrongs would've been righted when the first Djinnshirukh died. Maybe this isn't a prophecy about undoing the spell. Maybe," his finger tapped his mouth, "this is something entirely different."

"What are these wrongs, Serem?"

"That remains a mystery, Your Highness."

A flicker across her mind told her the Voice was listening—watching. Not intervening, not guiding, but present. Always present.

Kharis pursed her lips, rereading the lines on the scroll. "So, assuming I die, immortal vessel here, I'll somehow let my flames roam, burn the world," she chuckled cynically, "and the spell ends. Of course, with the world destroyed, we won't need the Djinnshirukh, won't we?" She sat back, tilting her head on the backrest. "What a riddle this is."

Serem's lips twisted apologetically into something that resembled a smile. "The text reads like a promise, Your Highness, but the identity of the immortal vessel remains an enigma."

"Why is this prophecy even connected to the Djinnshirukh?" Kharis asked. "I don't see the term mentioned at all."

"This scroll was the last page of the immortals' treatise with King Owain ná Zahar. A son for a weapon."

"Or a daughter," Kharis said, quieter this time.

Serem's expression shifted, flickering with something more profound than scholarly interest. He inclined his head slightly, a gesture of quiet acknowledgment—a silent concession.

"What if this piece wasn't part of the treatise?" Kharis asked. "What if this page were mistakenly placed with the treatise? A page that wasn't supposed to be here."

His gaze softened. The weight of history seemed to lift, replaced by something gentler. "We are keepers, Your Highness," he said quietly. "Interpretation belongs to the scholars."

She shot him a flat look. "Convenient."

Her eyes slid to the two books he'd handed her. "And these shed light on the prophecy?"

"Indeed. You may find the authors' insights into the prophecy of interest."

Kharis tapped her fingers on the table. "I would like copies of these to take with me."

Serem nodded. "We shall get the scribes on it right away."

Then, abandoning royal protocol, Kharis stretched, her arms reaching high above her head with a loud yawn. "I'm starving," she said, "and my training awaits. You can put everything away, but keep these two books in reserve for me. I'll be back tomorrow."

He chuckled, then blushed at the blunder.

Kharis narrowed her eyes, a suspicion dancing in her mind. "Your vowels are a little more rounded than how we would pronounce them. Where are you from?"

"Almarim, Your Highness."

Of course. He was too nice to be from the Ghak.

"Before coming here, I apprenticed at the Almarim palace and served Her Highness Princess Götrid."

That name blistered her stomach. "And now you're here. Did she get rid of you?"

"Not at all." He waved his hands nervously. "Her Highness recommended me for this post."

Kharis hummed thoughtfully. Serem tilted his head, a curious expression crossing his face. He had that look, pondering something he wasn't sure he should ask.

"What is it?" she asked.

"Are you searching for a spell that ends the Djinnshirukh curse?"

"I am." Her answer was swift and unequivocal. Since she was twelve, she'd slipped into these halls in the stealth of night to find how to undo the blasted curse. And if she couldn't find her answers in this lifetime, at least she could leave clues behind for the next Djinnshirukh.

"Everything that has a beginning also has an end," she said. "A thousand years ago, an immortal from the Spirit Kin clan chanted a spell that started this cycle. Wise as they were, they would've never created such a spell without a counter to end it."

Deep within her, the Voice shifted in silent approval.

234

Serem agreed with a crisp nod. "Princess Götrid felt the same way."

That got a rise from Kharis.

"I'll see what else I can find and have it ready for you tomorrow."

"Perfect." Kharis rose from the chair, locking eyes with him. "Will you continue to assist me?"

Serem's nod was shaky, hovering between academic curiosity and fearful apprehension.

"Good." She gave him a small, approving smile. "I look forward to seeing you."

"Your Highness?"

"Yes?" Kharis placed scrolls back in their respective baskets.

"You didn't mean what you said about burning this place, did you?"

Kharis burst into laughter. "Of course not, Serem. A thousand years of Zahari history are preserved within these walls. I would be a fool to destroy it." Her gaze softened as she added, "Even if I'm the Djinnshirukh, I'm not the Akumi king. I have no intention of burning this place, or the world, for that matter. So rest assured, the Royal Archives will endure for another thousand years."

CHAPTER 41
THE GENERAL FROM CECCHIO

Love is an endless act of honest and quiet grace. - Poliormos

"Only one month to departure," Hala mused.

The arrow of time had flown swiftly. Soon, his sisters would begin their long journey into the Zahar-Katea—a vast mountain region whose jagged peaks shaped the spine of the world. The caravan would take nearly three months to reach Zhegama, the region's capital nestled high in the cliffs.

The general trailing behind him said nothing. On any other day, the silence might have suited Hala, but not today. He'd been hoping for a remark, something to keep the conversation going—a distraction.

They reached the Academy of the Healing Arts, and Hala slipped inside quietly, doing his best to avoid notice. The last thing he needed was to cross paths with Her Excellency. His head already throbbed with too many concerns, and Yuna would only add to them.

Yuna could've become his mother. That thought made him shudder. As crown princess of Zahar, she was to be married off to Hröld had she not eloped with Anong some forty years ago. That alternate reality haunted him, a reminder of the twisted paths fate could still take.

Hala drew a deep breath, steadying his nerves. Everything was falling into place, and the journey would carry Kharis far from Arjun Ghan's deadly grasp.

That man was like a cat with more than nine lives. No matter how often Hala threw him off the proverbial roof, Ghan always landed on his feet.

Hala shook his head to dispel the frustration. Ghan's relentless scheming grated on his nerves, and the constant pressure to outmaneuver his uncle festered like an open wound. As long as Kharis lived, Hala lived.

And for twenty years, that plan had worked.

Yet... How long before the Akumi king had to be resealed again?

He could almost feel the crushing weight of fate looming over him, but he buried the rising panic. There was no room for weakness when the stakes were so high.

Thankfully, the Regia-Zenka had disregarded Ghan's argument that Kharis's resealment was necessary after the incidents with Aram Zhad and blasted Aghet Mendi.

Sending Kharis to the Zahar-Eliza was the best move. Isolated from the rest of the world, Kharis would be safe. One more year to keep her alive. It also bought him time to untangle the curse hanging over them. He wouldn't need to worry about Arjun Ghan if he could find a way to break it and free himself for good.

Hala kept his pace, his steps measured and commanding, radiating the expected confidence of the Zahari crown prince. He cast a quick backward gaze, subtly tracking the general following close behind.

He caught sight of Saya, who was engaged in conversation with a few bhiksunim.

Saya... So much more malleable than Kharis.

The irony wasn't lost on him. Saya's keen intellect was prodigious, but her kindness, loyalty, and unwavering dependability made her a wonderfully predictable person. Better still, their goals were aligned. Saya wanted Kharis to live as much as he did. In that respect, she was an ally. An unwitting one, but an ally, nonetheless.

On the other hand, Kharis's reckless curiosity was a wild card in his carefully laid plans. She was unpredictable, driven by questions and impulses that could shatter everything if left unchecked. That made her dangerous.

But steady, trusting Saya was the key to keeping Kharis in control. If Saya believed in him, she would unknowingly be the tether keeping Kharis under him, and Hala would ensure it stayed that way.

Yuna wasn't around, and he breathed in relief. Cunning and defiant, she was another dangerous player on the board. Her influence over his sisters could unravel everything. Her presence was a constant threat, a reminder of her power over the family.

He glanced over his shoulder, gesturing for his general to follow him.

"Ah! Just the person I needed." He approached Saya with quick steps. "There's someone I want you to meet."

Saya turned around, smiling warmly. Her group bowed and scampered off in various directions. "My apologies, brother," she said. "I was settling the healers' schedules."

"I fully understand." Hala pressed his hand to his heart with a proud grin. "Not long ago, you were a child running amok in the palace. Now, you command everyone's respect at the Academy."

Saya blushed, aware of the man standing behind her brother.

Hala noticed immediately. "Sister, this is General Reza Zhegur of Cecchio."

The general stiffened, pressing his helmet too tightly against his body. He squared his shoulders and bowed in an overly formal manner.

Hala eyed him curiously. Why was he so nervous? Saya kept her polite smile, but was she trying to stifle a laugh? He almost chuckled.

"General Zhegur, this is my sister, Princess Saya Ghan."

Saya tilted her head in acknowledgment.

"General Zhegur will handle security logistics and lead the royal cavalry to Zhegama." Hala knew Saya would appreciate the involvement in planning their journey. It was another game piece he could add to his board.

"It's nice to meet you." Saya quickly bowed. "Blessed be the earth and sun."

Reza Zhegur's gaze lingered on her face, speechless. His hazel eyes widened as if he couldn't believe he was facing the princess.

"General Zhegur?" Saya asked.

The man flinched as if waking from a dream, visibly embarrassed by his lapse. "May they sustain us." He cleared his throat, offering her another formal bow to hide his noticeable blush. "It will be an honor to escort you."

Amused, Hala's gaze darted between the two before returning to Saya. "Khator spoke highly of him, leading to his selection."

Saya was visibly surprised, her brows arching. "Our brother isn't one to shower people with praise. His compliments are rare, better than jewels. Therefore, we'll be in capable hands."

"Good. I'll arrange a meeting so you can discuss logistics and security with General Zhegur." Hala clapped his hands once. "You leave soon."

Her eager smile was all Hala needed to know his overture had paid off.

"With introductions in place," Hala said, "we take our leave, sister. You appear busy."

"It's always busy at the Academy, but I would make time for you."

Hala grinned and threw his arms around her. "This is why I love you so much."

"I love you, too," Saya said, "and because of that, I have these for you." She took a handful of aljaicin from a pocket sewn into her delantal and gave it to him. "I keep some for the children. One never knows when these might be needed." She winked at him.

His chuckle slipped free. "You know me so well."

She turned to General Zhegur. "Would you like some?"

The general shook his head, his smile slightly awkward,

making Hala wonder if the refusal was simply out of politeness. Saya noticed it, too, because she gently took his hand and gave him some. "If not for you, then for your children."

"I—I'm unmarried, Your Highness, and no children."

Saya's cheeks flushed crimson. "Please accept my apologies. I shouldn't have assumed."

"No, please," General Zhegur replied quickly, his voice soft. "I can share them with my officers. A few enjoy aljaicin."

She smiled quietly. "Glad to hear, then."

The general bowed again as if the daze of a fine liqueur had draped over him. Without a doubt, Saya's beauty had mesmerized him. Hala rolled his eyes. Men seemed to fall apart around the Sorukhipa, and Reza Zhegur was no exception.

"Blessed be the earth and sun, sister," Hala said, turning around while waving at her.

ॐ

"Blessed be the earth and sun, Your Highness," the general said, his voice a tad softer than expected.

"May they sustain us," Saya replied.

Thick eyebrows framed his hazel eyes, the left one bisected by a faint scar that added a hint of ruggedness to his otherwise composed demeanor. He was tall and broad-shouldered like all Zahari generals, with a firm jaw and chiseled features. Unlike most Zahari men, he didn't wear a beard. Without one, he appeared younger than expected for a general, perhaps in his late twenties.

His cape swung back and forth as he marched away, looking overly stiff and dignified. It made her giggle.

He struck her as warm and honest. An excellent choice, she supposed. The fact that Khator had highly recommended him didn't escape her notice. She wouldn't be sharing this with Kharis, though. Her sister would never forgive her siblings for their silent absence.

"Saya, darling. There you are." Yuna strode forward with a group of apprentices trailing behind her.

"You missed Hala."

"Pfft. Good." Yuna flicked the loose end of her kashaya over her shoulder. "Then my headache was averted."

Saya wasn't sure whether to laugh or frown.

"Are you ready to see the patients?" Yuna asked, eyes darting to the group behind her.

Saya responded with a sharp nod.

"Perfect," Yuna said, a satisfied smile tugging at her lips. "Let's go."

CHAPTER 42
THE CONSTELLATIONS BELOW

*Undeterred by setbacks, courage is the force that propels us onward.
It refuses to yield to the shadows of defeat. - Poliormos*

The bright afternoon light greeted Hala as he descended from his carriage. The visit to the Academy had gone well. This would top it. Before him, in all its glory, stood the impressive Zahar-Homa. Built by the immortal races, the ancient wall now stood as a proud witness to Zahar's history.

Hala spotted the inspection unit and joined them.

Eventually, he lost track of time.

When he refocused, the sun was soon to kiss the distant horizon. The inspection team had identified a few needs. Tomorrow, the work would continue at the palace to discuss funding and repair priorities. Satisfied, the group was packing up when a voice addressed them.

"I found you."

Startled, Hala turned only to see Kharis wearing a triumphant grin. He shook his head with a snort, walked over, and hugged her.

"This is the outer ring, sister," he whispered in her ear, unhappy. "You're not supposed to be here." He pulled away, a quick smile on his face to ease the inspectors' anxiety, an annoying game in this situation. "What brings you here?"

Kharis grinned mischievously. "I heard you were inspecting the Homa and couldn't resist the chance to join you up here." She dusted herself off.

Hala sighed. "You're in uniform." A white one, not red. "Did you finish your training?"

"Yes."

He noticed the Velathari's absence, and his frown took a life of its own.

"I climbed over there to search for you." She patted her daggers with pride and pointed to a section behind her. "Nobody saw me."

"Khiri, you could've—"

"None of it, brother." She held her palm up to stop the lecture.

He grunted. The lecture would come later. Grabbing her hand, he scrutinized it. The skin was scraped and rough, with minor cuts and bruises not healed yet, and she was still chewing her nails down to the nub.

After the incident with General Mendi, her confinement to the villa had been extended. When allowed to leave, she'd thrown herself into training and reading at the Archives as if trying to occupy every waking moment. Now, she was on the outer ring, wearing a white uniform, probably stolen, and without her blasted Velathari.

"Why would you climb the wall?"

She snatched her hand away. "Blame Salazar. Always lecturing me." She emulated the general's voice when scolding her. "You're too loud. You're too quiet. You breathe too hard. You don't breathe enough." She inhaled deeply. "So, I came to see you." She flashed a grin. "No one spotted me, not even the guards. I'm calling it training."

Hala almost screamed at her. "Training, you say?"

"Yes." For a moment, a wall higher than the Zahar-Homa came up between them, but it vanished as quickly. "General Salazar says I'm not stealthy enough, so I'm practicing." She covered the lower half of her face with one arm as she tiptoed around, not making a sound. "See? Stealthy. I'm ready to be a Shadow Walker. Let's visit Jordha."

Slightly amused by her antics, he motioned the inspectors to go on ahead of him.

"Come on, stealthy creature of the shadows. Walk with me. Let's take one last look, shall we?" He gestured for her to follow him toward the west-facing side to watch the sunset's last moments.

"Next time," he patted her head, "use the stairs. And I fervently hope you didn't sink your daggers into the wall's mortar."

Kharis groaned at the lecture.

Hala threw his hands up. "Khiri, we're here to repair it, not damage it."

"Yes. Yes. We love the Zahar-Homa."

She chuckled at the icy stare he shot her.

Where had the child gone? Twenty years old already. Or was it twenty-one?

"Laila has been asking about you," he said. "I'm sure all the packing keeps you busy, but visit her before leaving." For whatever reason the Blessed Mother had, Laila, his five-year-old, had attached herself to Kharis. And despite the intense arguments with his wife over this, he loved Laila too much to keep her away from Kharis.

Conveniently, Kharis's schedule was always packed.

"She'd love to spend time with her beloved aunt." Hala batted his eyelashes as Laila did whenever Kharis was mentioned, making her laugh. "She thinks the world of you," he said. "No one can deny that."

"And I love her back. Does that mean you're inviting me to come over?" She poked him in the side.

Ticklish, he flinched.

"Your wife dislikes me."

He shrugged. What else could he say? "You're my sister, and Laila's your niece. She adores you, so yes, come and visit. And don't mind Aya. She's pregnant and close to her due date.

Nothing is comfortable for her now. Even my voice annoys her lately."

"So that's why you're here today."

Another chuckle bubbled up his chest. He waited for another witty remark, but she fidgeted with her baldric.

He recognized that gesture. "Khiri?" His voice softened. "What is it?"

Kharis bit her lip, wrestling with her thoughts. Anxiety flickered across her face.

"Khiri...?"

"Do you think it will ever happen to me?" she blurted out.

Hala raised an eyebrow, not understanding. "What?"

"You know." She bit harder on her bottom lip as if the words were more difficult to say than she thought. "Children?"

Ooh. A shiver ran down his spine. Female Djinnshirukh weren't encouraged to bear children. She'd been told this. He didn't know what to say. He'd never imagined her having these thoughts. What had changed?

The earlier levity vanished, and the air between them grew tense.

"What do you mean?" His voice lowered.

"Never mind. I didn't mean to put you in a tough spot."

"What spot?" His voice lost its sharp edges. "If you're—"

"Forget it," she cut him off. "When can I visit?"

The uncomfortable silence became a widening chasm. Hala pressed his lips together, feeling guilty for not knowing how to respond. Kharis remained quiet, her elbows resting on the battlement as she stared at the horizon. Her gaze was distant, lost in thoughts he couldn't reach. He swore her eyes glistened.

"Khiri?"

She smiled at him, but it didn't reach her eyes. The chance for an honest conversation, for her to truly open up to him, had slipped away. Hala silently berated himself. This wasn't how he won her trust.

They faded into a silence Hala didn't know how to bridge.

The sky burned with its final bursts of deep red, slowly giving way to shades of mauve and purple.

"I see why you love it atop the Homa," she said.

In the distance, people were lighting lamps, and the darkness gave way to a constellation of golden stars across the capital. "I had forgotten how beautiful it is up here," she said. "We're gods reveling in our creation."

They stood in silence, the cool night air brushing past them as the vast city stretched below, lights glittering like fireflies.

"I'll miss this," she murmured.

Hala remained quiet.

Kharis brought her fingers to her mouth, about to chew on her nails again. Before he could slap her hand away, she brought it down. "Hala?" She paused, struggling with a thought. "Please, don't hate me."

Those words broke him. "Why would I?"

"I keep embarrassing the Crown." Kharis paused, and Hala did his best to listen. "Life was as it should've been, and then, I was born." Her voice quivered. "If you hated me..."

"For starters, I don't hate you and never will. You're my baby sister." He slung an arm around her, pulling her close. "I regret I can't do more because I would instantly take this burden away from you." And this he meant. "I hate how you suffer in silence while working hard to ensure everyone else thinks you're fine. You may fool others, Khiri, but you can't fool me."

Hala waited, hoping she would open up to him, but no words came. Instead, to his utter surprise, she buried her face in his chest, her sobs breaking the silence. He held her close, his eyes drifting to the quiet distance.

The White Guard officers pivoted to face the other way.

After a while, Kharis broke the embrace and wiped her tears, smudging her face. Hala sighed. "Your hands are dirty." He pulled a silk handkerchief from his pocket and gently wiped away the smudges. "Honestly," he teased, flashing a wide smile.

"I couldn't use my sleeves." She flaunted her not-red leather vambraces.

He shook his head. "What are we doing with you?"

She burst out laughing, her eyes still shining with tears.

"Come, let us return. The carriage awaits."

She wiped her face again, new smudges streaking her face. "Hala?"

He turned.

"Could I visit General Zhad?"

He arched an eyebrow. "Whatever for?"

"I can heal him," she whispered.

Hala froze, letting those four words sink in.

Self-healing was intended only for the vessel. But if she could heal others...? He maintained a calm expression, though curiosity stirred within him.

"Whatever do you mean?"

"It would help." Her eyes pleaded for this chance. "I've heard he isn't back from his leave."

Hala didn't answer right away, his brain whirling with possibilities.

"I could be useful," she said. "Show that I'm not a monster."

He clutched her arms, brown eyes meeting blue-gray ones. "Are you positive about this?"

Kharis gave him a faint nod. "But no one must know."

One of his eyebrows lifted. "Not even Nana?"

Kharis nodded again with a nervous, sideways glance. Hala savored this piece of information. *Not even Yuna.* He offered her a soft smile, curbing his sudden need to grin broadly. "I'll arrange it, then."

She offered a shy smile and tilted her head in a quick bow. "Thank you."

"Come. Let's get going." He put his arm around her, a big brother propping up his little sister as they walked toward the stairwell. "I haven't seen the Zahar-Eliza in years," he mused. "Have you finished packing?"

"Almost."

"Hmm. I wonder which route would be best this time of year." Hala filled the silence with his ramblings about the convoy, the various plans, and the adventures to be had, too excited to stop. The thrill running through his veins at her confession was a wildfire igniting dry brush, consuming him with an unstoppable, fervent blaze. She could heal others. His heart raced as he salivated at the idea of commanding that power.

The White Guard, silent bodyguards, followed them.

Below the wall, darkness had given way to a constellation of twinkling lights.

CHAPTER 43
TIDINGS AND TETHERS

Destiny rarely asks for permission; it arrives dressed as duty and leaves with your heart. - Poliormos

Saya awoke before dawn, too excited to sleep. In less than a month, the sisters would leave the Ghak and go to a mystical place in the mountains. Kharis, sound asleep, deserved her rest this morning. *Nothing's scheduled for her.*

Saya donned her uniform and ran to the palace. Her White Guard escort, some still half asleep, barely kept up with her.

After overseeing the packing of carts and wagons and finalizing details with General Zhegur and palace clerks, Saya rushed down the hallways, eager to tell Kharis everything. She rounded the corner and nearly collided with her father and Lady Khostuna.

"Ah, perfect timing," the king said, his face breaking into a bright, eager smile. "This saves us the trouble of summoning you." He opened his arms wide, and Saya stepped into his warm embrace.

"Asurûn," she sighed, content.

He stepped back, his sharp eyes scanning her face with paternal pride.

"I was telling His Majesty," Lady Khostuna said, "that I

cannot stress enough how thrilled the hazenkas are about this caravan. A venture of this magnitude is unprecedented."

Saya's sharp gaze caught the gleam in Khostuna's dark eyes. She had a striking personality. Her tall, lean frame gave her an air of authority that was impossible to ignore.

"The hazenkas have unanimously agreed to join the royal convoy," the minister said. "This is a lifetime opportunity to establish trade partnerships with the mountain region. The Ghak is abuzz with anticipation."

"The benefits are undeniable." The king's tone brimmed with satisfaction. "Trade will flourish, but this expedition's true achievement lies in strengthening diplomatic ties with the Zherikh-Umea nation."

Khostuna's voice dropped into a conspiratorial tone. "This is Empire-building at its finest." She paused, then continued with a sly smile. "The Regia-Zenka also resolved another matter. Did we not?"

"Indeed." Hröld straightened, his expression one of pure delight. "The lack of a Mahazenka Court in the Zahar-Katea region." He turned to Saya, eyes gleaming. "This will be resolved when my daughters settle in Zhegama."

"What?" The word escaped Saya in a rush, her pulse drumming in her ears. Her mind reeled as her father's words crashed over her. "Settle... in Zhegama?" Had she heard right?

Her father chuckled, clasping her shoulder with an affectionate grip. Lady Khostuna gave a brilliant exposition on why you're perfect for the roles, and the Regia-Zenka has offered its final blessing. I believe you're ready for this responsibility. Once you return from the Zahar-Eliza, you and your sister will represent the Crown and the Empire with grace."

"I... Um... You planned this?" Saya's gaze darted between them. When? How? Why? Was Khiri ready for this? Her shock gave way to a flicker of excitement.

"The caravan will accomplish many things"—her father smiled proudly—"but none greater than this."

Saya's emotions swirled—shock, joy, disbelief, and anxiety tangled with curiosity and awe. She could only nod, her life having shifted unexpectedly and irrevocably. And that... That was beyond anything she'd ever dreamed.

"We shall discuss at dinner," he said. "I expect you and your sister to join me—"

Saya threw her arms around him, the force of her embrace catching him off guard. "Yes, dinner," she said breathlessly, pulling away, her body alight with a newfound energy. "Khiri!" Her eyes widened with anticipation. "I must tell her!"

She bowed respectfully, and with that, she dashed off, her laughter trailing behind her as she waved a quick goodbye.

CHAPTER 44

THE TASTE OF LIES

To see what lies beneath is a gift—until it demands a price too steep for mercy. - Poliormos

Since his encounter with Princess Kharis, General Aram Zhad had spent time in his chambers with his left leg elevated, unable to put any weight on it. The princess's blow had caused a severe ankle fracture and knee dislocation.

As the days blurred, he was less hopeful about a potential recovery.

At times, his officers would visit, keeping him informed of the latest news. They played xakea, a game where the players aimed to take over the other side of a checkered board using colored disks. Playing it demanded his complete focus and attention, requiring him to anticipate his opponent's moves while using clever strategies to capture their pieces and advance his own. With time on his side, this game kept him sane.

Always in motion, he was now bound to inertia, watching birds fly in and out of the garden, envious of their freedom.

By mid-morning, he was a restless mess.

"The crown prince is here to see you, General Zhad."

Aram snapped out of his angst. The servant moved aside as his wife, Zadya, led the crown prince in.

"Please don't," Prince Hala said when Aram attempted to salute him. "There's no need for formalities, General Zhad," he said. "We hope everyone in your household is in good health."

"Yes, Your Highness." Aram bowed his head with deference —the best he could do. "We're all well."

The Royal House always announced its visits, never imposing its presence without proper notice. But Prince Hala had come unannounced. Aram's head whirled, pondering the reasons behind the secrecy.

Am I being relieved of my duties?

With little fanfare, Prince Hala moved a chair closer to Aram and sat beside him.

"How are you doing?"

Aram, still off guard, stumbled on his response. "I—I'm doing well, Your Highness."

"We apologize for the intrusion," the prince said. "It wasn't our intention to surprise your household. The welfare of one of our esteemed generals is of great concern to the Royal House. Therefore, we're here to see what else we can do to make your recovery more comfortable."

"Your Highness, a royal healer was already assigned to look after me. I couldn't ask for more."

Prince Hala smiled and swung in his chair to face Zadya. "We've brought provisions for your household. Would you direct your servants to help bring them in? It's the least we could do to repay the imposition the Royal House has caused yours today."

Aram gave Zadya a reassuring nod, and she motioned the servants to retrieve the goods, closing the doors behind her.

"We'll ensure the King's healer stops by to see you more frequently," the prince said. "Your recovery is certainly one of our current priorities."

Aram appreciated the concern, but hesitated before speaking again. "Your Highness, how's the princess doing?" He remembered how determined she was that day—the anger in her eyes as she searched the crowd. "I couldn't stop her." He, who'd faced a dragon to rescue the princesses.

Prince Hala put his hand on Aram's shoulder. "There isn't

anything anyone could've done. We are, at best, mere bystanders. However, there's an important reason for our visit today, one that couldn't wait."

He walked toward the door.

"As we mentioned," the crown prince said, "the Royal House is interested in your health and recovery." He pulled a hand from the other side and closed the door. "On the matter of the princess, you may ask her if you wish."

The crown prince brought a veiled woman in opulent finery into the chamber. When she lifted the veil, Zhad's eyes widened. His lips moved to utter her name, but no sound came from them.

Gone was the dirtied uniform and messy long braid. Not a trace of grime and sweat covered her face.

Red. She was always clothed in red.

Today, she wore a lavish purple gown adorned with gold-threaded designs, tiny glittering crystals, and billowing sleeves accented with blue. Gold and silver bangles coiled around her wrists. Sapphire earrings dangled from her ears. An elaborate choker necklace hung around her neck. An ornate tiara with pearls and small gemstones adorned her head.

Princess Kharis glided into the room like a goddess, haunting and magnificent.

"General Zhad," she said, a soft smile framing her face. "I hope you and your family are well."

She... She's lovely.

Aram was speechless. He never thought a human lived inside the crimson uniform. Now, he stared at a beautiful woman, not the dreaded Djinnshirukh, and the transformation took his breath away.

"I—I'm doing well," he stammered, unable to tear his gaze away.

"May I inquire about your injury?"

Timidly, he shifted in his seat. "Yes, of course. What would you like to know?"

Her eyebrows drew together. "What have the healers said about your recovery?"

He searched her expression and posture for any hidden

meaning beneath her words. "I suffered a dislocated knee and a fractured ankle that will take time to heal." If it ever did. "The herbs and tinctures keep the pain at bay and reduce the swelling."

The princess walked closer and sat beside him in the same chair Prince Hala had been sitting in.

"May I see them?" she asked.

Aram paused, but without saying much, he uncovered his leg. Dark blue and purple bruising radiated from his swollen ankle and knee.

"These injuries are my doing," she said. "I can't forgive myself for harming a loyal subject like yourself and the anguish this has caused your household." Her hands, clasped on her lap, glowed—tiny embers flickered beneath her skin as if a fire burned under her fingertips. "Today, I'm here to right my wrong."

She gently placed one hand on the bruised ankle and another on his knee. Aram flinched, watching with apprehension. She grew still, eyes closed. Her hands emanated a surge of warmth, soothing the needle-like stings that troubled him. The painful throbbing dissolved, and the tight pressure gave way to comfort. The blue and purple bruises turned green and yellow.

The crown prince didn't just smile. He watched, rapt.

Her hands stopped glowing, and their soothing warmth dissipated.

A tingling silence filled the room, broken only by his shallow breath. "It's gone," Aram whispered, half to himself. "All of it." He touched his leg as if it belonged to someone else.

The princess rose from the chair, taking a few steps back. "Please accept my heartfelt apology for the pain I've caused you. I cannot change what happened, but I fervently hope you'll lend the Royal House your service and loyalty and continue to light our path."

She knelt before him, and her forehead touched the rug.

Aram reached out to stop her. "Your Highness, please, don't—"

"Ours was a simple visit, General Zhad," the crown prince

said, cutting him off with a kind smile. "The princess was never here, and you'll never speak of this."

Aram's gaze darted between the crown prince and the Djinnshirukh princess. "On my honor and life, Your Highness."

He stretched his foot cautiously. The movement no longer came with the brutal jolt of torn muscles, ripped tendons, and bone damage. The ache and pressure that had accosted him were gone. A swell of hopefulness overtook him. He would walk again, ride his horse, train soldiers—serve the Crown.

Soon, the visit was over.

Using a cane and cautious steps, Aram bid the royal carriage goodbye. He would need to regain his strength, but he could walk again.

As the carriage left, Zadya scolded him. "The healer told you not to move, walk, or put weight on the leg."

"The swelling's gone, wife, and so is the pain." He drew her closer to him.

She hummed, not entirely convinced. "And who was the woman?"

"Of no importance to us."

CHAPTER 45
THE BLACK SHADOW

Some truths, once glimpsed, unravel all comfort. - Poliormos

Saya burst into the villa, her heart a rapid thrum of excitement. The steward, a stout woman with a stern face, a tight crown braid, and wrinkles to match her age, greeted her with her usual formality. "Your Highness."

"Where's Princess Kharis?" Saya asked.

The woman froze as if Saya's question had turned her to stone, and Saya's frustration flared. Why did they always react in this manner? Fear was the only emotion her sister ever evoked among the staff. If given a chance, they'd work somewhere else.

Saya softened her tone, forcing patience into her voice. "Did the princess leave a message?"

The steward's fingers twisted the fabric of her dress. "None, Your Highness."

A sigh escaped Saya as her excitement faded and unease crept in.

Where are you, Khiri?

Saya furrowed her brow. Kharis had done this before, an escapade a few weeks ago cloaked in bothersome secrecy. But the recollection of her attempted escape six years ago bubbled to the surface. Back then, she'd almost jumped into a ship approaching the Stoneberry drawbridge. The fear of a repeat had become a relentless shadow.

Her first lesson as Sorukhipa echoed in her mind, a truth as immutable as her role: "A Sorukhipa always knows the whereabouts of their Djinnshirukh."

Ignoring all her other responsibilities, she bolted for the mirador, climbing the spiral stairs in twos.

Her training had centered on one fundamental truth: the force that had created all life had shattered itself to birth the universe, weaving everything into a web of interconnectedness. As the Sorukhipa, Saya possessed an elevated perception, a magical third sight that revealed these hidden connections. With it, she could locate the Djinnshirukh.

Saya reached the top of the watchtower, open on all sides, and her fingers tightened around the wooden rails. She pondered the risk. Using her third sight was dangerous—she could lose her vision, but the urgency tormented her.

With her mind made up, she focused on her breathing and released a wave of her magic. The world around her dissolved. Layers of reality unraveled like gauze, peeling away until she stood alone in a vast, otherworldly field. The air shimmered with delicate, luminous strands connecting all things, seen and unseen.

All around her, delicate clouds of silver mist floated in the endless expanse, each pulsing softly with life—human souls.

A discomforting pressure settled behind her eyes.

Gossamer tendrils unfurled from her body, twisting and spiraling in every direction. They moved with a will of their own, brushing past the silver clouds until they found what they sought—a wisp of red, distinct from the others. They coiled around Kharis, giving Saya a sense of her sister's location.

The Sorukhipa frowned.

"Why is she in the middle ring?"

This section of the imperial enclave housed the lower nobility, Regia-Zenka ministers, and Zahari generals. It was the second time Kharis had left the inner ring, and that secrecy worried Saya.

Worse, Kharis had broken a rule—again.

Saya was about to end the spell when the red wisp coiled around one of the silver wisps in a protective embrace. Saya's breath caught, fear and fascination tightening her chest. Kharis's wisp pulsed, flashes shifting from crimson to silver and back to crimson in a dance of exquisite magic. Then, it released the silver wisp and slowly retreated as if her task were complete.

Saya stared in disbelief, her mind struggling to process what she'd witnessed. The realization struck her, cleaving her heart like a blade.

Kharis had healed someone.

Who? Why? That couldn't be right. Kharis wouldn't risk it —not without her.

Confusion clouded her thoughts while the sharp sting of betrayal burned deeply.

Suddenly, something felt off—a faint disturbance rippled through the fragile balance of unreality. Her eyes darted, searching, until they settled on a shadow lurking at the edges of her vision—a small cloud of black mist pulsed, rising and falling in a rhythm that eerily mimicked the beat of a heart.

Having never seen anything like it, Saya strained her eyes to focus on it. The pressure behind her eyes became painful. Her grip on the rails tightened, her nails clawing the wood.

"Hold it, Saya," she grunted. "Find out what that is."

The black wisp wrapped itself around a silver one and swallowed it whole.

Saya gasped in horror.

This black wisp swayed, savoring its meal, then slowly turned toward Kharis's location as if sensing her.

Saya's magic thrummed in alert. The tremor it generated rolled along her body, leaving her in waves that rippled the air and enveloped her in a shield of shimmering golden dust. The onyx wisp detected Saya's magic immediately. It wavered, caught in a contemplative dance, torn between another enticing meal or facing the one who'd discovered it. Saya could feel it studying her, appraising its enemy.

The heartbeats ticked by as the pain behind Saya's eyes became excruciating. Tears brimmed at the edges, her vision blurring. The magic fueling her third sight was expanding within her skull, pressing against her eyes, threatening to force them from their sockets—

The entity shot forward toward her with stupefying speed.

Saya's shield expanded in response, and the shadow collided with it before it could retreat. The black mass screeched, its high-pitched sound jarring, as it disintegrated, shredded into vapor by her protective magic.

Saya gasped, the pain behind her eyes now unbearable.

But the black wisp was gone.

She'd destroyed it.

A bolt shot through her skull, sending painful shockwaves through her body. She wheezed, the sound thin and brittle, and collapsed to the ground, the impact jarring her bones. Her magic flickered, fading into a soft drizzle of fine dust.

Then darkness swallowed her vision. "I've gone blind."

Panic stabbed her chest, tightening its grip like a vise. Her heart thudded, fear crashing over her. But Saya fought against it, forcing slow, steady breaths.

"Fear leads to deception," she recited, clinging to her mantra. "And deception leads to darkness." Over and over.

Gradually, the panic ebbed, and a growing flow of calm replaced the receding tide.

Her breathing steadied.

Her heartbeats slowed.

And ever so slowly, the darkness lifted.

Faint outlines and shapes began to emerge from the void as if unseen hands were removing thick layers of dust. The world sluggishly regained its clarity. Sunlight pierced her sensitive eyes, triggering another rush of tears.

Steadily, her body reverted to a lower level of perception and reality.

Sprawled on the mirador's floor, her eyes darted left and right as she pondered whether moving was safe.

"That didn't belong in this world."

She cupped her mouth in shock. Still dizzy and in pain, she gripped the rails and hauled herself up, turning toward the place where she'd seen it. An icy shiver ran through her.

The outer ring.

And that meant only one thing.

Whatever that was... it had been hunting.

CHAPTER 46
THE SHAPE OF SILENCE

When the world steals your voice, let silence become your sword. Let it be your power. - Poliormos

Kharis kept her veil in place, watching the world through the thick lace as the Zahar-Regia blurred past.

"You did well," Hala said. "I didn't know you could heal others. It was... phenomenal."

Kharis stiffened. He sounded curious—but beneath that curiosity, a colder emotion slithered, grazing her skin like a caress edged with ice. Dangerous. Calculating.

"How long have you known?"

Kharis wetted her lips, her eyes never leaving the view outside the carriage. "It isn't my power," she said quietly. "It only happens when the Akumi king allows it."

Hala hummed, a sound stretched taut with thought. "Then why today?"

She shrugged, hoping to end the conversation with that single gesture, and threaded her fingers together in her lap to hide their trembling. *Blessed Mother, why did I suggest this to him?*

Regret curled like a specter at her side, grinning at her misstep. She'd vowed never to use magic without Saya to anchor her to this world. But today, she'd broken that promise.

And now Hala knew of her healing ability.

She didn't know what stung more—her betrayal or the fact that he'd witnessed it.

"Well, I believe your ability is fantastic." Hala's lips quirked, her brother lost in the myriad thoughts buzzing in his head. "Imagine its potential, Khiri. What we could achieve."

She shivered at his "we." Sickly-sweet ambition tinged his excitement, clinging to her skin like sweat and oil. Revulsion twisted in her stomach. All she wanted was to get home and scrub it away until not a trace of it remained.

His voice filled the carriage, but she heard none of it. She focused instead on the horses' rhythmic clop and the slight rattle of the wheels over the cobblestone. Outside, market stalls rolled past, bursting with color, shouts, and the scents of cardamom and fenugreek.

And beneath it all, the bitter aroma of betrayal lingered.

"Don't you think?" Hala asked.

Another shrug. Empty. Detached. She hadn't heard a word.

Hala's voice dipped lower. "You're awfully quiet." His gaze flicked to her hands, still clasped tightly in her lap. "What are you thinking?"

She adjusted the veil as if to smooth her composure. "Nothing."

A lie. One more added to the pile.

"*Must you lie to your brother?*"

The silvery voice glinted at the edges of her consciousness. Disappointment dulled its usual warmth. Curiosity tinged it red, but a quiet sadness washed everything else gray.

A second voice followed—bass-like and dangerous, seeping through the cracks of a formidable magical containment to growl at her. This voice wasn't soft or silvery but resonant and powerful, scraping against the inside of her mind like rusted chains. The silvery voice was familiar, and quiet wonder cloaked his concern, but this other voice, as ancient as the world itself, rumbled like the end of days, hungry for revenge and destruction.

"*Trust no one*," the Akumi king said, angry and resentful. His rage poured in like molten metal, tainted with smoke and sulfur, churning her stomach.

Bile caught in her throat. Sweat pricked her brow. Her vision swam.

"*No one*," the voice repeated, now louder, demanding a reply.

Kharis kept her gaze fixed on the window, her eyes unblinking. She straightened, burying her thoughts beneath the lace, and said nothing.

Not to Hala.

Not to the Voice who loved her.

And certainly not to the god who wanted to burn the world.

Her silence was the only power left to survive.

CHAPTER 47

LITTLE LIES

Small lies may seem harmless, tiny seeds planted in fertile soil, but they grow into tangled weeds, choking the truth and the one who planted them. - Poliormos

Hazenka Captain Marya Levandran rubbed her chin, displeased with the discovery. A body had been found in the outer ring alleyway, and Hazenka patrols were now combing the area for clues.

The midday sun baked the cobblestones, where blood had dried in jagged streaks, dark as rust. The alley reeked of refuse and rot. Flies swarmed the body they'd claimed.

"This isn't the first one we've found," Marya said, annoyed enough to wring someone's neck, and studied the area with narrowed eyes. "It's noon. The main street's quite busy. Are you telling me no one heard anything?"

"Correct, ma'am," Sergeant Orlen Dëtka said.

Marya huffed, arms crossed, foot tapping. "Perhaps they knew each other? The victim never suspecting he'd be killed." She assessed the alleyway. "A lovers' quarrel? A business gone wrong?" She groaned loudly, prompting a few hazenka guards to shift uneasily. They knew their captain's sharp mind had hit a wall. "I hate not having a single clue," she muttered.

She crouched by the body and pulled the cloth off the

body's face. "A slashed throat." She bit her cheek, thinking. "The face sports a nasty gash on the left side. One eye is missing, too."

She tsked, frustrated.

"A fight?" she pondered. "But why take the eye?"

"Could be symbolic," Dëtka offered. "Or a warning. Either way, this wasn't an impulse killing."

Marya shot him a look. The lack of clues and the frustration connected to this investigation burned a hole in her stomach. She covered the body, turning to the hazenka guards. "Question everyone in this neighborhood. I want clues."

The guards saluted swiftly and scampered. With the muscle to rival the burliest of her men and a no-nonsense demeanor to match, her mounting frustration only meant one thing: she wouldn't be buying them ales at the tavern tonight.

"It's the same as with the other bodies," Sergeant Dëtka observed.

Marya hummed in agreement, tilting her head as if the heavens might offer answers. "What does it mean? A signature?" She stood with a creak of bone, lips pursed. Only forty birthmarks behind her, and she was already getting too old for the ugly parts of this job. "Has anyone identified him?"

Dëtka shook his head.

Her headache intensified. "Dëtka," she elongated the vowels in his name with menace. "We need clues."

"I'll get on it, Captain." He noticed her contemplative stance. "What are you thinking?"

She exhaled loudly. "Something's off. Something we aren't seeing." She rubbed her chin again, a tell-tale sign of her mounting annoyance. "This location isn't far from the main street, but no one saw or heard anything. How?"

"Maybe the killer was hiding, waiting for him?" he said.

"It's more than that, Dëtka." She grunted her aggravation. "It's another body. I don't want to draft this report. The commander wants answers—a conviction." She massaged her temples, trying to forestall the headache. "All I have is one more body." She let out an exasperated moan, mainly to keep from cursing. "Have the body taken to the morgue," she ordered a soldier nearby, then turned to Dëtka. "Hopefully, someone misses him soon enough."

"Doubtful," he said. "The princesses leave the city in three days... and the capital's already caught in the fever of it."

Marya tsked and gave him a sidelong glance. "You're a ray of sunshine."

The royal caravan had the city in its grip—buzzing with excitement, heavy with ceremony. Crowds had flooded in from the region to catch a glimpse of the procession. Vendors lined the streets. Zenka guards were on high alert, barking orders and shuffling patrols. There were more people, more movement, more noise than usual—and somewhere in that chaos, a killer had vanished. Finding him would be like chasing smoke in the middle of a blaze.

"Captain?" A hazenka guard stood beside her, handing out a set of papers. She skimmed the first, stamped it with her seal, and then leafed through the others.

"Is this it?" she asked.

"We haven't finished sweeping the area," the guard said. "But the others are questioning the neighbors and merchants. All the deceased's items have been collected and listed here." He gestured to a particular page. "He had valuables with him, but none were taken."

Marya huffed in sarcasm. "Great. He can rule out theft." She turned to the guard. "Ensure the rest of the reports are on my desk by tomorrow morning."

The guard saluted and walked away. Dëtka, who had crouched by the body, watched him leave. "Captain?"

Marya knew what that tone of voice implied and stuffed the parchment in her pocket. "What is it?"

Dëtka jerked his chin, urging her to come. Checking they were alone, he lifted the body's arm to show her something wedged in the vambrace.

Marya salivated at the potential find. "Now, what's that?" Using her pocket knife, she managed to pull it out after a few tries. "This man fought his assailant. It's how this got lodged in the leather." Her jaw clenched at the implication. "Yet no one claims to have heard a peep."

Dëtka's eyes popped open. "It's a—"

"Shush." Marya studied it for a long moment, holding the item between her forefinger and thumb to confirm her suspicion, then glanced behind her. "Keep this quiet."

"But Captain—"

"Spear me deeply and gut me, too."

Dëtka arched his eyebrows at the profanity. "Ma'am?"

"This isn't good. We must be discreet." She leaned in closer, whispering in his ear. "This is a button in an imperial officer's uniform."

Dëtka's eyes bulged, whispering back. "The killer's an imperial guard?"

"Not any imperial guard." Her gaze fixed on the engravings on the silver button. "A White Guard officer."

"Spear me, too," Dëtka muttered. "We're going to need more tea."

She quirked an eyebrow. "Tea? Really?" Alcohol would've been her choice. "As I said, not good at all." Marya Levandran shook her head. "Not a word of this gets out, understood?"

Dëtka nodded, his eyes tracking every turn of the button in her hand. Her thumb brushed over the engraving once more, then again.

Silver. Pristine. Official.

Small yet revealing a gleaming hint of corruption. "Let the murderer think they've gotten away with this," she said, slipping the button into a small pouch. "Let them feel safe."

Her gaze drifted toward the end of the alley, where pedestrians passed by, oblivious to the truth unfolding in the shadows. Marya understood all too well—small lies could grow into uncontrollable fires that had burned cities before, and the Unification Wars proved as much.

"We'll find out who did this," she muttered, more to herself than Dëtka. "Justice will prevail, and the imperial city won't burn this time."

PART FOUR
THE JOURNEYS

CHAPTER 48
LONG LIVE ZAHAR!

*The power of love is revealed not in grand gestures but in the small,
consistent acts of kindness that shape our world: the subtle warmth
of a smile or the quiet support in times of need. - Poliormos*

D eparture day had arrived.
With the spring equinox came two celebrations.
One was the princesses' twenty-first birthmark,
adding to the caravan celebrations across the city. Fiddles
thrummed spirited jigs in city streets and squares, inviting
listeners to sway to their lively rhythms. In the taverns, foamy
ales flowed. In the zenka guilds, last-minute preparations were
ongoing for their groups to join the procession at the
appointed times.

Kharis's heart was about to leap out of her throat. After
months of careful planning, this day was finally unfolding.

The palace's grand foyer echoed with the soft murmur of
conversations, laughter blending with the chatter. The clicking
of heels, the occasional jingle of jewelry, the rustling of fabrics,
and the shuffling of shoes on the polished floors danced along
the marble floor. The subtle scent of perfumes and colognes
blended with the aroma of freshly cut flowers.

Kharis swept her gaze across the space, taking in all the

activity with bittersweet amusement. "I must be dreaming," she said. Twenty-one years had flown, and a year had been added to the memories she prayed to forget.

Saya wore a knowing smile. "I promised you that one day we would leave this place together, on our terms. That there would be no need to run away. Rather than arguments, there would be a celebration." She tilted her head toward the assembled crowd to emphasize her point. "Thank you for your patience."

Bitter memories churned through Kharis's mind. Prince Rawiri's banishment. Her failed attempt to flee. The massacre. The Iluna Forest.

"Seven years ago, my world fell apart," Kharis whispered.

Saya's steadfast love had kept her afloat when she was sinking. The sweet memory of a gentle gardener became a drop of water for a parched garden. Tears blurred her vision, but she quickly wiped them away, refusing to let them fall. Noam lived, and that was enough.

"Saya?" she fidgeted. "I'm sorry about everything."

Saya's eyebrows arched in surprise. "What is this about?"

Kharis glanced away. "I had to protect someone from General Mendi."

Saya stared, her brow furrowed, clearly confused about the unexpected turn in the conversation.

"It was about the incident with Mendi," Kharis confessed.

Saya's eyes widened in understanding. "All I know is what General Salazar shared with me."

"He told you?"

"That you showed up to training wearing a flower? Yes, he did. All the officers did. Some still poke fun at Jonah Hark."

Kharis grimaced, embarrassed.

"General Salazar said you wanted your flower back, but Mendi kept it to spite you. It hurt to be left out, but I'm sure you had a good reason." Saya's eyes flicked to the crowd. "If this person must remain a secret, I won't press you, but you did the right thing if you were trying to save them from that prick."

Kharis lowered her head. "I'm still sorry."

"I know you are," Saya said. "Your heart is as big as this

world." She pulled Kharis into an embrace as tight as their bond. "If I did something to make you lose your trust in me," she whispered, "I apologize. I'll do whatever it takes to regain it. Say the word, and it'll be done."

Kharis didn't reply.

"I wanted you to know that," Saya said. "Maybe next time, you'll ask for my help. I'm here for you. Without judgment or conditions. Together forever." A small smile tugged at her lips, the memory of their childhood promise as vivid now as it was then.

Kharis held back her sobs. Noam's goodbye had shattered her heart, but Saya's endless affection was slowly helping to piece it back together.

She pulled back enough to meet Saya's eyes. "There's no world where you aren't with me," she said.

Saya grinned, her golden eyes sparkling. "I love you, Khiri."

Kharis closed her eyes, letting her sister's warmth infuse her soul. "And I love you more."

⁂

Hala wove through the crowd, exchanging pleasantries as the morning sun spilled over the plaza, draping it in golden warmth. The murmur of voices had shifted from initial greetings to more engaged conversations.

The Regia-Zenka ministers were present. Even Master Hillal, surrounded by bhiksunim, got caught in the festive atmosphere. Everyone was here except one. Arjun Ghan's absence should've made Hala happy, but the blasted man never did anything without a motive. After a quick scan, he spotted Jordha. Discreetly, he used hizkuntza, a signed language.

"*Where's Ghan?*" he asked.

"*In his quarters,*" Jordha signed back. "*All is safe.*"

"*Good. I hope he's dead.*"

Jordha guffawed so loudly that he startled a Regia-Zenka minister near him.

"*And Aghet?*"

Jordha gave Hala a dangerous smile. "*Ghan sent him to Almarim three days ago.*"

"*Odd.*" That piece of news gave Hala some pause. His spies had spotted Mendi leaving the markets on the outer ring three days ago. "*Why Almarim?*"

"*No clues yet.*" Jordha shrugged his apology. "*But my Shadow Walkers tell me he took the long route.*"

Hala laughed, pleased. Aghet wouldn't cross the Ghetu Plains by land but sail on a barge down the Ibaia River. If no storm hit their ship once they entered the Zaharkayo Straits, they would reach Almarim a month later.

"*I hope someone throws him overboard, and he drowns,*" he signed to Jordha.

A royal attendant approached him, snapping him out of his pleasant visions of squalls and ocean storms. "Your Highness, everything is ready. We only need your signal to begin."

And so, it begins. He turned to Jordha, who shrugged with a tight smile.

Hala threaded through the crowd, offering brief nods to the guests, but didn't pause until he reached the king. "Asurûn, it's time to get started," he said.

"Already?" The king's brows knitted. "This is such a bitter-sweet moment." He shared a complicit glance with Yuna and swiftly embraced his daughters, holding onto them longer than expected.

"Asurûn?" Kharis said, her voice muffled by the tight embrace. "You can let go."

He pulled away to gaze at her. "Are you in a rush to leave me?"

"Never." She smiled back. "But the hazenka leaders may organize an uprising if we delay."

"That they would." The king broke the embrace with a loud chuckle and cupped the sisters' cheeks with affection, eyes glistening despite the broad grin. "As members of the Royal House, make us proud. Your successes become our successes."

"Saya, Gutxi," Yuna said. "The Academy will be quiet without you. It'll also take longer to go through the jar of aljaicin." Her eyes pooled with tears. "They won't be as sweet without your company. My darlings, I love you dearly, and if your mavah were here today—" Her voice faltered for just a beat. "She would be brimming with pride, as I am right now." She hugged them tightly, and a sob escaped her.

The king gazed at the women as if etching this moment into his memory. "Are you ready?" he asked.

"Yes!" Kharis and Saya answered in unison, bumping shoulders with each other.

He quickly nodded to Hala, saying, "Let's begin."

With the signal given, trumpets echoed throughout the plaza.

Outside, endless rows of courtiers, attendants, soldiers, and servants readied to bid the princesses farewell. Their White Guard escort and two mounts awaited at the other end of the plaza.

Hala and his father descended the grand staircase. Kharis and Saya followed, sporting their royal uniforms: armor, pauldrons, and vambraces made of the finest, crimson-stained boiled leather. The long plume in their helmets matched the color.

Upon reaching the bottom, Hröld cleared his throat, his voice quivering at times. "Today, I grant you my leave so you may embark on your journey forward. Not a day will go by without me thinking of you. May the Blessed Mother guide your steps and light your path forward. My beloved daughters, grow strong in grace and kindness." He paused for a breath too long. "And return to me," he finished softly, sorrow wrinkling his forehead. "Go forth to the Zahar-Eliza."

Hala stepped in next.

"Saya," he said, marveling at how she resembled him more than Kharis. "May the sun always warm your face. Promise me you'll take diligent care of yourself and your sister."

Then he hugged Kharis. "May the sun warm your face, too, and until we meet again, may the gods keep and protect you both." He stepped back, and mischief sparkled in his words next. "I have a surprise for you once you reach the East Wind Gate."

❧

Hiding in his chambers on the third floor, Ghan stood by a large window, cradling a steaming cup of tea. He watched with a scowl as the royal procession made its way down the grand staircase, the sight of the crimson uniforms stirring a deep-seated disdain that tightened his lips. Everything he'd stitched together was fraying, one seam at a time. He sipped his tea. Bitter—like all things lately.

"It's done, Your Highness." A male servant drew his attention.

Ghan pursed his lips, unsure whether to be glad or not. "Is the uniform repaired?" he asked.

"Yes, Your Highness, and done as you requested, with the utmost discretion."

"Good." His fingers rasped against the windowsill. Rage simmered under his ribs, begging to consume something—someone. "I don't know why Aghet loses buttons from his uniform."

"General Mendi trains hard to serve the Crown. It's expected."

"I suppose." He sipped from his teacup again.

"Is there anything else His Highness needs?"

Ghan exhaled slowly, his mind racing with unresolved anger. "No, Danel. Nothing else." After a moment's pause, he added curtly, "Thank you."

The servant bowed and closed the door behind him.

Ghan's lips thinned into a grimace as he fought the urge to hurl the cup across the room. "Where are you, Aghet?" he muttered, frustrated. He hated his absence. He hated not knowing—the lack of control.

Returning his gaze to the fanfare on the plaza, Ghan's brow furrowed deeper. Seeing the two crimson uniforms only inten-sified his displeasure. He struck the glass, his gold ring leaving a star-shaped crack, small and spreading.

❧

Kharis's gaze swept across the plaza to where their horses stood. Inhaling deeply, she steadied the rush of anticipation thrumming in her veins. "We'll reach the Zahar-Eliza in three months." With a confident smile playing on her lips, she turned to Saya. "Today, we begin our first chapter."

Saya's grin was alive with the same fire Kharis felt in her bones. "Then let's write it, sister."

The sisters donned their helmets, the long red plume wavering in the gentle breeze. Once they mounted their horses, they raised their right fists. The crowd went silent. Together, the sisters shouted with all their might.

"Long Live Zahar! Long Live King Hröld!"

The crowd roared the same response, and the trumpets resounded once more.

Saya turned to General Zhegur and gave him a nod. "We're ready."

"So are we, Your Highness." Settling his horse to Saya's right, he signaled the cavalry officers to ride forward.

Trumpets and clamor greeted the convoy as it paraded through the imperial city. Zahar-Regia guards lined the streets, and people stood behind them, waving small Zahari flags or throwing flowers in their path.

When Kharis and Saya approached the West Wind Gate, adorned with imperial banners, they spotted Hala's surprise.

Alphorns lined the top of the ancient wall, and the soldiers blew on them as soon as they saw the princesses. The deep, whirring resounded like a haunting wail—joy and sorrow intertwined. Their notes hit Kharis, and an explosion of memories inundated her. She was finally free of her shackles and the suffocating cage in which she lived, but she was also leaving her father and her nana.

She became keenly aware of her royal status and rode tall, a proud Zahari princess, trying not to display her emotions.

When the royal convoy crossed under the impressive West Wind Gate into the capital, memories of Noam danced in her mind, and a jolt of grief struck her heart. Once, she'd walked past this gate with Noam on their way to a tavern, and on that magical night, they'd danced, toasted to love, and kissed.

She could leave Ghan and Mendi behind and never look back, but leaving those she loved tore her heart apart.

"Long live Zahar," she recited as she sobbed. "Long live King Hröld."

CHAPTER 49
NOMADS

Not all stories of freedom are sung with joy. Some are ridden out in dust and ache. - Poliormos

The first two days went by uneventfully.

The caravan slowly wound its way north, following the western shores of the Ibaia River—an extensive line of covered wagons, packed animals, soldiers, mercenaries, merchants, bhiksunim, travelers, and pilgrims headed for the Zahar-Katea region.

This journey was a thrilling new world for Kharis. Each morning, the bustle of life on the road greeted her, the air rich with the murmurs of excited chatter. At night, their camp came alive with music, laughter, and myriad stories amid flickering fireflies.

It was a whirlwind of wonder, filled with intoxicating sights, sounds, and scents. The vibrant colors of the merchants' wagons, the intriguing stories of fellow travelers, and the sheer scale of the caravan were all feasts for her senses.

With the passing of days, the landscape shifted from the vast grasslands of the Ibaia Plains, endless stretches beneath the open sky, to the rolling forested hills that hinted at the gradual elevation gain.

But enchantment, like dust, settled fast.

Soon, the novelty wore off.

The once-enchanting music became a constant backdrop; the once-thrilling hustle of the camp became predictable, and the caravan's pace became less an adventure and more a monotonous rhythm.

Kharis learned that riding was more than sitting in a saddle and letting the horse do all the work. Despite her blisters, she had to hold the reins firmly, direct the animal with her legs to keep it from wandering, and maintain her place within the caravan. Her inner thighs chafed, her joints stiffened, and her sitting bones hurt even with a thick cushion. The princess did her best to carry her weight on her legs, but after three days, they'd screamed in agony.

"I can't move my legs anymore."

"Hang in there," Saya said. "There will be a break soon."

Kharis slumped her shoulders in defeat. "When I get off Pendragham, I'll be a pile of flesh on the ground."

Saya's eyes lacked their usual spark as she absently stroked Ephron's neck, her fingers brushing through the horse's coarse mane. "Hala didn't add horseback riding to our training because we were supposed to use the carriage—"

"No," Kharis interrupted, her voice firm. "I want to see the world from atop my horse, not hidden inside a carriage." She slapped her thighs to ease the tingling and rubbed her buttocks, already numb.

The Sorukhipa rolled her neck until a satisfying crack provided relief. "Nana gave me a salve for sore muscles that should help."

"I'll massage some on your legs tonight," Kharis said. She shifted on the saddle, hoping for comfort that remained elusive, and refocused on the distant horizon to get her mind off it. By the time she reached her bed, her soreness would be gone, thanks to the Akumi king. For Saya, Nana's salve provided a small measure of relief from her misery.

Kharis huffed, irritated. The acrid smell of horse sweat, leather tack, and the constant buzz of flies was wearing on her patience. "How many more days ahead?"

Saya grumbled something under her breath. "It's months, sister."

"Hmph." Kharis gave Saya a nasty glare, cursing under her breath.

"What are you mumbling about now?"

Kharis scrunched her face. "You're so… gormish."

"What?"

"Gormish!"

Saya arched a tired eyebrow. "Why are you making up words now?"

"I'm not." Kharis's tone sharpened.

Saya threw her a scowl, her patience visibly thinning. "That word does not exist."

Kharis sniffed, eyes straight ahead. "It's not a word. It's a curse."

"That curse does not exist."

"Stop being so gormish."

Saya dragged a hand down her face. "Don't talk to me." Wincing in pain, she urged her horse to ride next to General Zhegur, leaving Kharis to wonder what life would be without her grumpy sister.

Over the years, she'd overheard the officers talk about the military camps on the outskirts of the Empire. They would share stories of their journeys, the bonds of new friendships, and their adventures. They were happy, laughing about those funny memories.

This wasn't one of those. Kharis was dirty and worn out. Laughing wasn't even in her vocabulary. The road… was endless.

No one had mentioned that freedom would smell like horse sweat, collect dust in her lungs, and feel like bruised bones.

CHAPTER 50
THE SHADOW DRIFTS

Shadows sometimes drift like smoke, unseen until the fire is upon you. - Poliormos

By the fifteenth day, the reality settled in—two and a half months still stretched out before them. The sisters realized that life in a caravan wasn't as romantic as books made it out to be. Kharis wanted to arrive *and stay* in Zhegama.

General Zhegur taught them to pack and unpack more efficiently (he'd deemed their tutors' lessons useless) and to start campfires using flintstone and steel. During the day, he discussed potential stops with Saya and Kharis, pointing out the pros and cons of each location. Saya listened, nodding and humming. Kharis yawned.

Under the general's direction, the sisters helped set camp every evening, learning to be more self-sufficient in preparation for their arrival at the Zahar-Eliza, when neither servants nor soldiers would help them with chores. When it was time for bed, Saya reached for the wagon to pull out their bedrolls, and Kharis assisted, carrying the thick blankets.

This evening, however, she couldn't help the chill that crept along her spine. The familiar heat at her fingertips surged, sharpening her senses. Every rustle in the underbrush had her turning, and every susurrus of the breeze amplified her concern. Her gaze roamed the shifting shadows, searching for signs of a lurking presence.

"Maybe it's nothing," Kharis muttered, on the verge of abandoning her search, when a sudden jolt of magic coursed through her in alarm. She was being watched.

"Saya?"

The Sorukhipa, unrolling their sleeping mats, asked, "What is it?"

"We're not alone." Kharis discreetly raised one hand, her fingertips glowing like tiny embers.

Saya frowned. "I'll never understand how you feel these things before I do."

"It's a survival mechanism." Kharis pushed her magic back until the glow faded. "The Akumi king always protects his vessel."

Saya unleashed a wave of her magic, allowing its tendrils to roam. The patrol moved about, chatting with guards stationed at strategic points as they marched past them.

"I don't sense anything unusual."

"What if they're masking their presence?" Kharis dropped their blankets on the bedrolls.

Saya shook her head thoughtfully. "Magic doesn't exist outside of us two... and the Iluna Forest, and that place is across the other shore of the Ibaia Sea." She crossed her arms, her brow furrowing. "Our security detail is in place, but we have a lot of people with us, making it hard to discern friend from foe." Shifting her weight, Saya peered over Kharis's shoulder. "I'll speak to General Zhegur. Maybe it's nothing, but sweeping our area won't hurt anyone."

"Thank you," Kharis said before glancing at the woods.

The soft crunch of leaves beneath Saya's boots followed in her wake. Kharis reached her back holster to test the readiness of the daggers secured in it. Her fingers found the hilt of one, and with a smooth, practiced motion, the blade slid out without a sound.

A sudden rustle from her left made Kharis spin, eyes narrowed toward the tall bushes.

"Who's there?"

Silence answered. A whisper of leaves stirred in the evening breeze. Kharis tightened her grip.

She gripped her dagger tightly. "I said, who's there?" Her voice cut sharper this time.

To her right, a sudden commotion made her flinch. Birds burst from the treetops, wings slicing the air, their cries splitting the night with shrill calls and fleeting shadows.

Then—another sound. A distinct crunch of twigs to her left.

She didn't hesitate.

Her blade sailed through the air and embedded itself into a nearby tree trunk with a resounding thunk. Undeterred, she drew her second dagger.

"That was a warning," Kharis shouted. "I'll hit my mark with the next one." She raised her blade, readying for another throw. "Reveal yourself or face the consequences."

A bhiksun sprang from behind the thicket, struggling to climb a muddy gully beyond her campsite. "Don't hurt me." He held his arms up, clutching large lotus flower pods in trembling hands. The flickering campfire revealed the color of his muddied garments—maroon.

"My apologies, Your Highness." Fear etched the lines on his weathered face as words stumbled past his lips. His rough breaths came out in gasps as he fought to regain footing and clear the slippery climb.

Kharis recognized him as Botan from Master Hillal's sangha and narrowed her eyes in irritation. "What are you doing here? This is not your section."

Bhiksun Botan shifted nervously, lotus pods swaying in his grasp. "I was collecting these." His voice shook as he offered her a glimpse. "The seeds are tasty but also useful in treating various ailments." He scratched his face, a sheepish gesture betraying his embarrassment. "I'm unsure how, but I—I lost my way back from the riverbank. "

"Be more careful." Kharis raised her dagger. "I almost threw this at you, and I never miss."

The color drained from the poor man's face, realizing what

he'd narrowly escaped. He dashed back to his camp section, uttering a litany of apologies.

Kharis grumbled under her breath, swiftly retrieving her dagger from the tree. Her magic stubbornly refused to fade, and her fingertips remained warm and tingly.

Then, an odd tug rippled through her.

The fleeting sensation left her momentarily disoriented as the ground beneath her shifted almost imperceptibly. Unease prickled her awareness. She gripped the dagger's handle and readied to throw it again.

The scent of stench assaulted her nostrils first. That all-too-familiar sensation of tiny legs skittering across her skin returned, and a shudder raced down her back.

Only one person had ever triggered such a response from her, and Ghan had sent him to Almarim.

A fleeting shadow to her right caught her eye, a dart of movement barely registering in the dim light of dusk. She pivoted sharply, her instincts taking over as both daggers flew from her hands. The thud of their impact followed, striking wood, not flesh.

A sound reverberated in her ears like a hum.

Kharis felt another tug—an invisible thread pulled taut within her soul—and she turned. The air rippled outward. Then, just as suddenly, the hum was gone. The thread had snapped.

Taking stock of herself, Kharis scanned the surroundings.

The shadow had drifted like smoke. But was it gone?

Whoever they were, they'd vanished into the darkness, leaving only an unsettling silence in their wake. That crawling sensation on her skin faded swiftly, and all shadows melted into the night. Her frustration lingered because their nearby guards had remained oblivious to what had transpired as if they'd been in a different world altogether.

She sniffed at the thought, aggravated.

Yanking the daggers free, she sat by the campfire, her grip tight on their hilts, waiting for Saya.

CHAPTER 51
THE LOOM OF FATE

Kharis hadn't slept well. Last night's unease clung to her like the dust from this journey: relentless.

Last night, she'd been heard, her concerns not brushed aside. And that was rare. General Zhegur's voice had cut through the evening lull as he sternly lectured his unit. Even the Voice was impressed. Standing beside her, Saya had watched, but her expression was ambiguous. Was it pride? Respect? Curiosity?

After one more apology from the general and his assurance that it wouldn't happen again, Kharis and Saya went to bed, except Kharis didn't sleep much.

Even the crisp air couldn't loosen the tension in her shoulders. Someone had been watching her. She blinked against the light and pushed herself upright. The distant clatter of camp activity echoed like drumbeats through her skull.

She was glad for her cup of spicy tea, curling her hands around the warm cup. Sitting with her back against a log, she let the early morning sun exorcise the chill in her bones.

"Blessed be the earth and sun," Master Hillal greeted her.

"May they sustain us."

"How are you doing this morning, Your Highness?"

"Tired and stiff but doing well," she replied with a wry smile. "My apologies for the paradox."

Hillal chuckled. "No need for them. At my age, riding in a carriage is the best option. Ah, but to be young and ride a horse again." He sighed. "Tell me, are you dizzy or short of breath?"

Kharis shook her head. The altitude was beginning to affect a few in the caravan.

"What about your sleep?" he asked. "Any disruptions?"

Kharis squinted, suspicious. "Will you be asking me to sleep in the covered wagon?"

Hillal burst out laughing, his shoulders rising as he did. "Nothing of the sort. I also enjoy falling asleep under the stars."

"Thank you." She smiled, gratitude softening her attitude. "For everything."

A flicker of curiosity flashed in his eyes. "Everything?"

"I understand you suggested this journey." She blew on the steam rising from her cup. "Without you, Saya and I would be at the Senda, staring at walls."

Master Hillal settled on the log beside her. "Your Highness, I often ponder why a tiny baby was burdened with such a challenging task. The Blessed Mother is wise and chooses her children well, yet I couldn't help but wonder. It is, perhaps, what we do best: question, contemplate, and reflect. I see you haven't lost the ability."

"I'm not allowed to question my circumstances, Master Hillal."

Hillal leaned forward, his gaze steady and kind. "I beg to differ. If anyone has earned the right, it is you."

She smiled and took a long sip. He sipped, looking askance at her. "You're quiet this morning, Your Highness. I had expected at least three questions from you by now."

Kharis chuckled. Five would've been her number. "Do you ever feel you don't belong?"

He pondered her question. "Now and then. You?"

"It's a constant for me."

Hillal regarded her with a thoughtful expression. "If I may offer advice. You bear the soul of the Akumi king, a creature from Andaheimur, yet your form is rooted in the mortal realm. It's a paradox to reside in a body bound to this realm while

287

housing a soul yearning to return to the spirit world. This likely accounts for what you've been grappling with."

"Master Hillal?" She hesitated, aware that giving voice to her fear could make it real. "Am I truly a Doombearer?"

He tilted his head, observing her. "I see a young woman brimming with all sorts of interesting questions, always curious about the world. Such a woman doesn't strike me as one bent on its destruction."

Kharis brought her knees to her chest and rested her cup on them. "But I've made mistakes before. Terrible ones."

"And who hasn't?"

That got a rise from her. Hillal glanced at her over the rim of his cup, a quiet smile tugging at his lips. "A Doombearer wouldn't hand aljaicin to the children in this caravan. Nor would she clap to the rhythm of evening music, joining in the laughter of those around her. You care too deeply to be the destroyer of worlds."

His words pierced her armor, but didn't banish the gnawing doubt.

"What if... what if it happens later?" She hated how small she sounded. "What if, one day, I become... it?"

Hillal rested the cup on his lap, his contemplative gaze lingering on the morning activity. "After a thousand years of imprisonment, perhaps the Akumi king has let go of his anger, and rather than brood over vengeance, he has accepted his fate. If I were him, I would ponder how to break free and return home."

Kharis let out a deep breath, a pang of empathy stirring within her for the Akumi king, trapped in an endless cycle of resealment. "Will he ever return to Andaheimur? Or is this his perpetual fate?"

Hillal sighed. "I've often wondered what lessons he must glean from his punishment and what role we must play in his imprisonment. It's hard to tell what will be, but nothing will stand in fate's way if he's to return."

Kharis watched the camp's bustle, her mind skipping ahead. "Is there a way to end this curse?" she asked. "To allow him to return?"

Master Hillal paused mid-sip, his eyes softening with contemplation. "That," he said after a thoughtful silence, "is a question I have asked myself."

Kharis leaned in slightly. "And?"

His gaze drifted toward the distant peaks. "At the Zahar-Eliza, there is a library. I've heard it houses ancient tomes, some of which have remained untouched for centuries. Some probably written by immortals. If answers exist, they may be found there. The Forest Kin were infinitely wise, sharing their knowledge with us, and the Royal Library houses many of their writings."

Yet she didn't find spells to undo curses there.

"Before retreating to Andaheimur," Hillal said, "they bestowed important gifts on us."

Kharis nodded, aware. "The Zahar-Sendatorsum, the Zahar-Homa, and—"

"The Zahar-Eliza," Hillal and Kharis said in unison with the utmost reverence.

Kharis had read about the Forest Kin. Their touch radiated warmth, bringing life back to the earth with a mere caress. Their bond with nature ran as deep as their beauty, intricately tied to the forests they nurtured.

"I would've loved to live when they walked among us," she said, half-lost in her imagination. "To experience how it was when the land brimmed with magic, and for a chance to ask them all sorts of questions."

"We can only imagine how long your list of questions would be, Your Highness."

Kharis smiled. She couldn't help her insatiable need to understand the world.

And in line with such curiosity, she asked, "Why did the Akumi attack? What led the Akumi king to war? I can't fathom it being a mere whim, a *let's-destroy-the-world-today* sort of fancy. I wonder if, after a thousand years, the Akumi king regrets his actions."

Twenty-seven had died by her hand on the day of the massacre, and that guilt burned her daily. How much worse would it be after having destroyed the world?

Master Hillal sifted through his memories. "The Ancient Writings don't tell us, Your Highness. The answer, however, could beat the Zahar-Eliza library. Perhaps this journey is not just about training you to enter Andaheimur." His eyes gleamed with wisdom. "It is about finding answers to your questions."

Answers. The word settled like a stone dropped into deep water. She had plenty of questions, but no answers.

"How did the immortals vanquish him?" she asked. "Why would they seal him, and how did they do it? And why would they think he could become a weapon to fight his own? Wouldn't there be a better punishment for him? And what reason would he have to start the One War? He advanced, burning the world in his wake. That tells me he had a purpose, but what was it? And who was the Akumi king? I mean, did he even have a name?"

Hillal laughed, a subtle arching of his eyebrows betraying his amusement. "I was wondering when your questions would appear."

Kharis flashed an apologetic grimace. "I've been told I ask too many."

"As you should. I'll worry the day you stop. In that respect, you're very much the king's child."

Her eyebrows arched at that.

A soft laugh rumbled in his throat. "His Majesty also has a habit of asking many questions. To study the universe is to delve into the reason for one's own existence. The same is true for the Akumi king. Maybe he's here to find answers to his questions."

Hillal rested the mug on his lap. "Life's a tapestry," he said. "Each thread serves a purpose. I've often wondered about the conditions for leaving the Loom and whether I would be content as a solitary thread adrift in nothingness or as a part of something intricate."

He took a sip, lost in momentary reflection.

"Perhaps our purpose is to remain in the Tapestry," he said. "To strengthen it, infuse it with color and vitality, and enrich it in ways we cannot fully grasp. The Akumi king is not exempt from this task. If our role, including his, is to contribute to the Weave, wouldn't it be best to do so as a resilient and vibrant thread?"

Kharis let that question settle between them, pondering how she contributed. Was it possible to undo what had been done and start again? If a mistake was made along the way, how did the Weaver fix it? She was about to ask Master Hillal when a bugle announced the first call. The caravan would be moving soon.

"And so begins another day." Hillal stretched his back, bones creaking, and rewrapped the loose end of his maroon kashaya over his shoulder. Brown eyes full of wisdom and fatherly affection gazed at her. "And remember, not every answer leads to the path we expect."

Kharis nodded with a tired smile.

Glancing at the sky, he said, "If you feel dizzy or faint, please let me know. Do drink the Zherik-Umea tea. It will help with altitude." After a nod, he walked away, heading for his carriage.

A resilient thread. That thought made Kharis wonder. Was her thread strong and vibrant? Made of cotton? Wool? Linen—?

"Khiri!" Her sister snapped her out of her contemplation. "Get ready," Saya called. "We'll ride soon."

The Djinnshirukh grumbled, not eager to face another long day riding on a horse. Suddenly, being a single thread floating in nothingness sounded good.

CHAPTER 52
WATER AND ITS MONSTERS

The river only answers with its currents. - Poliormos

After a month and a half on the road, the caravan halted at the twin rivers—the Little Ibaia's churning rapids and the Isa's glacial-blue expanse. Barges and ferries groaned under the weight of wagons and beasts each time, swaying as handlers barked orders. Porters rushed to secure goods, wary of the treacherous Little Ibaia's currents that had claimed many before. Every rope was tightened, and every plank was checked twice, making the crossing a slow and painstaking ordeal.

Kharis lingered far from the riverbank for the crossing. The annoying prohibition was absolute: no open water could come into contact with her. Not even the spray. Saya knew this better than anyone.

When Kharis stepped onto the barge, covered from head to toe in too much fabric, Saya hustled her into the cabin, eyes flashing with quiet urgency. Grumbling in frustration, Kharis would remain inside, forbidden even from standing by a window to catch a glimpse. She doubted Saya breathed freely until the crossing was complete.

Two weeks later, they would have to repeat it all to cross the much calmer but deeper Isa River.

*

After the river crossings, the mood changed—somewhat.

The White Guard officers still shared dreadful tales about the monsters inhabiting the Ibaia Sea's swamps and marshes. They spoke of the v'leta, blood-drinking creatures luring people to their deaths by taking the shape of whatever they desired most. The dangu dragged people into a watery grave with long, vine-like fingers. The leagh, a horse-shaped creature that appeared during foggy weather, enticed people to ride it, but they couldn't jump off it, drowning as the animal plunged into the river's waters.

If water created life, why did it house such horrid monsters? It made no sense.

"Why are the officers' stories so frightening?" she grumbled. "Don't they know any love stories?"

"They have their orders," Saya said, taking one of the bedroll blankets and giving it a brisk shake. "They'll keep you as far as possible from the rivers. So, of course, they'll share horror stories." She patted Kharis's cheek with a teasing glint in her eye.

Not far, the inland sea's waves lapped at the shore, their melodious whispers reaching Kharis.

"The Ibaia calls to me." Kharis gestured in its direction, her voice tight with frustration.

Saya arched an eyebrow as a flicker of amusement played on her face. "Calls to you?"

"Parrot," Kharis mumbled under her breath.

"Watch it, Teppe." Saya tsked, leaning forward to poke her sister's cheek, a smirk tugging at her lips.

Teppe. Prince Rawiri's nickname for Kharis—his little badger.

The Djinnshirukh lifted a corner of her sleeve, took a sniff, and grimaced in disgust. "Gah! Why can't I enter it? What's the worst that could happen if I bathed in it?"

Saya paused before taking the other blanket from Kharis. "I don't know, and I have no intention of finding out." She crossed her arms, her chin high. "I look the other way when you dance or go on midnight strolls, but the water prohibition stands."

Kharis grumbled, though it was less about the restriction and more about feeling trapped. Saya, ever gentle, placed a reassuring hand on her shoulder. "I fear losing you if you did."

Kharis's nostrils flared. "Of course you would. I'll drown if no one teaches me to swim."

Saya sighed. "If you want to bathe, I'll have soldiers bring water, and you can use the covered wagon. But going to the river is out of the question."

Kharis sniffed, mildly aggravated.

"Besides," Saya added, "ghosts and monsters aren't real. They're just cautionary tales to scare people into common sense."

Kharis wanted to believe her. She truly did. "Wouldn't the Akumi king be the same?"

"The Akumi king is a fallen immortal. Ghosts and monsters have no business in the mortal realm. To interact with them, including your Akumi king, we must enter Andaheimur."

Kharis scratched her temple, recalling the ghost she'd met in the Royal Archives as a child. "I can't enter Andaheimur."

"And hopefully, we'll remedy that once we're at the Zahar-Eliza." She finished setting up their sleeping mats, and her tone turned serious. "I'm more concerned with mortals, who are far more dangerous than these so-called spirits inhabiting a place you can't enter."

Saya was right. The Djinnshirukh was one of those dangerous mortals. *Doombearer.* The thought lingered, unwelcome, gnawing at the edges of Kharis's mind.

Saya clapped, startling Kharis. "Come. Let's sleep."

Kharis lay on her sleeping mat, her blanket up to her nose, shielding herself from the unsettling thoughts in her head. The faint rustle of branches and the soft chirping of night insects should've been comforting, but instead, they set her on edge, each sound sharpening her awareness of the shadows stretching around her. Images churned relentlessly in her mind: pale, ethereal immortals watching from the trees; restless ghosts flitting just out of sight; and bloodthirsty v'letas and dangus lurking, waiting for the unwary. For her.

A soft breeze brushed against her face, carrying the moist scent of the Ibaia Sea. Goose bumps rose, every nerve alert. Her heart thudded steadily, ready to gallop at a moment's notice. She scooted closer to her sister, cursing the White Guard officers and their frightening stories.

"Saya?"

There was no response—only the wind rustling through the trees in the dark and the river, its low roar steady and relentless.

CHAPTER 53
THE BOUNDARIES IN DREAMS

Dreams dance on the edge of reality, blurring the lines between what is and what could be. In them, reality and illusion intertwine. In this space where the boundaries vanish, gods create tangible worlds. - Poliormos

Kharis glanced at Saya with a pang of envy.

Her sister had surrendered to the tug of dreams and softly snored in her bedroll, the rhythm of crickets keeping time. How could she always fall asleep so effortlessly the moment her head touched the pillow? It seemed unfair.

The Djinnshirukh heaved a weary breath and closed her eyes, hoping for the comforting pull of sleep. An unusual sound disrupted her journey. She scanned their encampment, columns of moonlight filtering through the trees. The darkness toyed with her imagination, and every wavering branch presented a lurking threat. Dangus and v'letas came to mind. Her fingers curled around the hilt of one of her daggers.

A flutter of leaves made her heart skip a beat. She poised herself to strike, but instead of a menacing foe, a fox leaped out from behind a thicket. Moonlight illuminated its furry form. Its silver eyes glowed with otherworldly intelligence, assessing her.

Startled, Kharis turned to her sister, still sound asleep. The fox crept closer, its paws gliding quietly above the ground as if the animal were made of mist.

Kharis rose slowly, her blanket slipping down her legs. The fox sat on its hind legs, its silver eyes shimmering with curiosity, waiting.

"Saya?" Kharis whispered, keeping her eyes on the animal. "I need you to wake."

When no reply came, she glanced back, only to find herself alone—the fog had swallowed her sister, the patrol, the campsite.

Kharis waited for the familiar shiver of magic to ripple across her skin, signaling danger. Instead, a delicate, wispy mist danced lazily around the trees, winding through the branches and curling around her ankles. Stars glimmered through the canopy, serene and indifferent to the world below. In the distance, the waters of the Ibaia Sea splashed and sloshed against the shore.

Before her, the fox waited.

"Fine," she grumbled. "I know I'll regret this." Gesturing to the fox, she said, "Lead the way."

Kharis moved cautiously over the uneven terrain, lifting low-hanging branches and weaving around thick bushes. With her focus fixed on the fox ahead, an exposed rock snagged her foot. She tumbled, a curse slipping from her lips when she hit the ground.

The fox yipped.

"Are you laughing at me?" Kharis muttered, brushing leaves and dirt from her clothes. "This better be worth it."

Unperturbed, the fox resumed its silent pace. At times, the mist curled around the creature's form, clinging to its silvery fur like a second skin before dissipating into the night air. The forest seemed to shift, with the trees stretching taller and their bark gleaming faintly in the moonlight. Shadows deepened and twisted. Kharis's skin prickled with unease, but the fox remained calm and steady.

When they reached the shore, the fox sat with quiet dignity. Angling its head, its silvery eyes met hers as if inviting her to join it. A fleeting sense of déjà vu swept over her. The creature's silver eyes were so achingly familiar. She sensed no malice from the animal, but its presence felt significant, as though it existed on a plane beyond her understanding.

The fox's gaze held steady, its luminous eyes hinting at patience.

Slowly, Kharis took a step closer.

To keep her boots dry, she stayed clear of the water's edge and gazed at the colossal volume of water surging past with a low, thunderous roar, the Ibaia Sea feeding the Isa River.

"This is my first time seeing the sea this close, not as a blue glimmer through trees or shrubs," she told the fox, apparently a good listener. "Considering my water prohibition, I'd never been this close to any body of water."

The Djinnshirukh waited for something monumental or terrifying to happen.

Nothing did.

"See?" She flashed a smug smile at the fox. "Not a thing has come to pass. So why all the fuss?"

The fox cocked its head, its curious eyes studying her. Perhaps it already knew nothing would happen, and was simply waiting for her to figure it out.

Even under the moonlight, the inland sea was a remarkable sight.

"Just look at it," she said with a hint of awe. "It flows smoothly as if made of melted glass." Without a visible far shore, she couldn't fathom how vast the sea was.

Temptation urged her to dip her hand into the waters and feel its power. Her fingers hovered above the surface when movement from the corner of her eye caught her attention. A tall, sinewy shape in a billowing black cloak loomed against the backdrop of a rising Sharan.

Kharis froze. Her thoughts raced toward v'letas and dangus.

She cursed.

The fox growled—fangs bared and hackles raised. It stepped closer to Kharis, its fur bristling in warning.

Kharis rose slowly, taking a step back. And then it happened—a blur of motion, a sharp whistle through the air.

The arrow zipped past her, so close she felt the rush of displaced air against her leg, and struck the fox. The impact was brutal, hurling the animal off its feet. A yelp of pain cut through the night before the fox's body hit the water.

"No!" Kharis screamed, lunging toward the water's edge. The fox's sleek form vanished beneath the churning surface. "What did you do?" she shouted, her fury rising as she turned toward the figure.

The black silhouette dropped the long bow. When their dagger came out, gleaming against Sharan's light, Kharis knew this wasn't a v'leta or a dangu but a dangerous mortal seeking revenge like Korshak had seven years ago.

The attacker lunged—a flicker of limbs and shadow. She twisted, narrowly avoiding the blade, but the collision knocked her off balance, and the ground slammed into her back. Kharis rolled out of the way, and the attacker's dagger plunged into the mud instead. Before they could strike again, she sprang to her feet and dodged him. Her fingers found her dagger, and the blade scored his arm as he swiped at her. A hiss erupted from him as he staggered back. Blood, black against the night, splattered onto the ground.

Kharis scrambled toward the campsite, but the assailant vaulted and seized her leg, a large hand curling around her ankle. Her dagger flew out of her hand as she stumbled forward.

Landing face first, her mouth filled with grit. The man quickly dragged her by the leg. Kharis dug her hands into the mud and kicked, her boot striking hard. The attacker groaned and slumped, but he kept his grip on her. Kharis kicked again, and when the grip loosened, she whirled to her feet.

His dagger emerged from the tangle of fabric. Kharis shielded herself from its arc, wincing as the blade slashed her palm. Pain shot up her arm, blood gushing from the wound, fingers twitching.

A fist struck her face, sending her reeling backward. She crashed into the cold water, half her body sinking beneath the surface. Sounds and sights blurred in the murky depths, darkness enveloping her senses.

Before the currents towed her away, his hand seized a fistful of her tunic, yanked her out of the water, and dragged her back onto the shore. Dripping wet, she coughed water out of her lungs.

Frost raced toward her, spreading rapidly, while a thin layer of ice formed on the shore. Her breath crystallized in the frigid air. Her clothes, caught in the icy spell, stiffened against her skin, the cold seeping through every layer. She crumbled to the ground, her limbs numb.

The stranger's dark chuckle hinted at victory.

He clamped a hand around Kharis's ankle again and dragged her through the dirt, her leg throbbing with every pull. Her skin scraped against the gravel, pain shooting through her limbs. Fear surged as she caught sight of the assailant's dagger, catching the moonlight in a sinister gleam.

Her survival instinct took over. Kharis thrashed wildly, her breath ragged as she flailed and kicked hard. The man yanked her leg harder, pulling it at an odd angle, and pain shot out from her hip socket. Determined, Kharis wouldn't give up. She screamed her lungs out and twisted her body, seeking to pry herself from his unrelenting grasp.

It worked.

But a large hand clutched her belt and yanked, and a wall of muscle pressed against her back. A hand grabbed her throat and squeezed.

Air stopped flowing.

The croaking of frogs dissipated. The sight of the glorious Sharan quickly faded as darkness encroached on the edges of her awareness. In that stillness, she heard the crackling of a small flame and a simple reminder: She was the Djinnshirukh.

She'd been taught to suppress his magic. The more she used it, she was told, the faster she would unravel, and the sooner resealment would become her fate. The irony didn't escape her.

She was dying now.

"*Not today,*" the Voice commanded. "*You shall not die today.*"

The words jolted her like a spark in the dark.

Unraveling be damned.

Kharis unleashed her magic—all of it.

Her vision shifted as a fiery red haze consumed it. The tiny flame within her surged to life, and its terrifying power unfurled. Scorching heat radiated from every pore of her body, turning the air around her into a searing inferno. The grip on her neck vanished. Air gusted into her lungs. Her attacker's harrowing shriek split the night, but it sounded as if coming from a different world.

It didn't matter.

This blaze exorcised the cold, infusing her with delectable warmth. Immersed in this wondrous heat, she wanted to burn and burn. To explode and envelop the world in this balmy, vibrant fire.

Crimson flames had engulfed her body.

Around her, the trees had caught fire, too.

Swarms of birds burst into the sky, their frantic chirping piercing the air. Tiny creatures scurried across the ground, squeaking and yelping. The ash from burning leaves whirled wildly while embers and sparks danced in the heated wind. Columns of fire raced through the woods, devouring everything in their path. The campsites in the distance lit up, tents going up in smoke. Explosions boomed in the night. Screams followed.

Her panic surged.

"How do I stop this?" Her throat burned with her scream. "Make it stop," she begged the Voice.

Something oily and slick coiled around her ankles and pulled. She yelped before hitting the ground and being hauled with brutal speed. Her body kicked up a whirlwind of plant debris and jagged stones that cut at her skin. She collided with the water, the liquid swiftly enveloping her body and snuffing out the flames. For a moment, the world was silent, save for the dull roar of the currents.

She sank into the cold, murky depths as the unseen vines

dragged her downward to where the currents churned. Amid the frantic chaos, she fought to break free from their grip and reach the surface.

Her lungs burned, the need for air clawing at her insides. Darkness pressed in around her, heavy and suffocating.

"*Kharasdir...*"

The haunting voice echoed as though carried by the current itself. It rippled through the water with clarity, belonging to an entity that had just awakened to her thrashing.

Her eyes darted through, searching for the source. Then she saw it: a vast, shadowy form glided through the depths. It grew, its immense presence darkening the water with unsettling grace as it swam toward her.

Panic ignited her every nerve. The vines around her legs tightened as the shadow loomed nearer, its form shifting in the watery gloom.

"*Kharasdir,*" the voice called again, this time closer.

Kharis kicked harder, panic overtaking her. When a giant maw appeared before her, she screamed, and the last air bubbles escaped her mouth.

CHAPTER 54
THE WEIGHT OF DREAMS

Dreams are whispers of a reality barely out of reach. - Poliormos

A violent force ripped her from the depths. Her stomach lurched. Her limbs flailed. She twisted and tumbled as she was dragged away, the world fracturing around her.

Then, impact.

A crushing weight slammed her down, pinning her to the ground. Kharis writhed against it, her breaths shallow and labored, her lungs needing air.

Her chest heaved to gulp it... when she felt a steady heartbeat pressed against her.

"Khiri!" a familiar voice shouted in her ear. "Khiri, please. Wake up."

The darkness faded.

The voices became sharper.

Kharis stopped struggling.

A quiet sob rang in her ear. She opened her eyes in slow blinks, and reality shimmered softly.

Saya was on top of her, her arms wrapped tightly around her. General Zhegur, on top of Saya, had pinned Kharis's wrists to the ground with force. A White Guard officer straddled her legs, holding her ankles with an iron grip.

"What's going on?" Kharis asked.

After releasing her, General Zhegur and the officer slowly got up. Saya didn't let go, her warm tears rolling down Kharis's neck.

"Saya?" A jumble of foggy thoughts swirled in her mind.

"She's awake now, Your Highness," a kind voice said to her right.

Kharis squinted, familiar with that voice. "Master Hillal?"

"You gave us a scare, Your Highness." Hillal's smile was warm, his face revealing nothing but relief.

Saya eased her grip, caressing Kharis's face as if she couldn't believe Kharis was finally awake. "You were dreaming."

Kharis slowly propped herself up on her elbows and shook her head to rid herself of the last of her daze. "Then why were three people holding me down?"

Saya's forehead creased, her eyes glistening with that too-familiar fear.

Kharis feared asking. "Night terrors?"

Saya nodded, the gold in her eyes intense.

A tremor passed through Kharis. She clenched her fists, then shut her eyes hard, fighting the urge to scream. After three years of silence, they'd returned—dragging her back into that realm where reality unraveled at the seams, she could no longer tell what was imagined and what was real.

With their return, her fragile peace had shattered like glass.

"How are you feeling?" Saya's voice was gentle, but the undercurrent of concern was strong.

Kharis sat, rubbing her face, unsettled and unsure. "Given I wasn't crushed to death," she said with a chuckle.

It died in her throat—no one laughed with her.

The campsite had stirred. Several officers had formed a loose circle, weapons at the ready, eyes sharp. Beyond them, a small crowd had gathered. And among the onlookers, she spotted a man, taller than the rest. Lean. His long silver hair was tied at the nape, and his silvery green eyes—impossibly familiar—locked onto hers.

"Khiri." Saya drew her attention. "Are you all right?"

"Yes. What about you?" she asked. "Did I hurt you?" Her voice was softer, guilt lingering. "I remember fighting someone... something."

Saya glanced at General Zhegur and Officer Dhan as if she were asking for their silence, and fear surged through Kharis. "No," Saya replied with a flicker of hesitation. "General Zhegur and Officer Dhan jumped in to help me." She smiled, but in the dim campfire light, now reduced to glowing embers, Kharis couldn't tell if it was genuine.

The officers began to disperse the crowd, but the tall man with the otherworldly eyes was already gone when Kharis turned.

"My little brother used to suffer from them," Officer Dhan said, pulling Kharis back. "We heard Her Highness's call for help, and once I saw what was happening, I knew what to do." Her smile was warm, candid. "General Zhegur here just likes to throw his weight around."

The general shot Dhan a sharp glare, but the laughter that followed eased the tension.

"Everyone, back to your stations," General Zhegur commanded, and the officers complied in a rustle of hasty movement. "How are you doing, Your Highness?" he asked Kharis.

"I'm fine." Kharis scratched her cheek. "I'm sorry I woke everyone up."

"Don't let it worry you. I'd rather handle a bad dream than an assailant."

"Here." Hillal handed her a warm mug. "A tea blend to calm your nerves. This long journey can be stressful, resulting in nightmares of all types, so please, don't let it get to you."

"Thank you." When she reached for the cup, a flash came unbidden—the glint of a blade under the moonlight, the roar of water in her ears, the voice calling that name again—*Kharasdir*. She shook it all off with a shudder and carefully set the cup beside her.

Saya accepted another from Hillal, and after taking a shuddering breath, she sipped it slowly. General Zhegur watched her in silence, worry still etched on his face.

Master Hillal got up with the help of his sangha. His knees protested, and a quiet groan escaped him as he braced his weight against steady hands. His spine straightened with a faint pop as old bones broke the hush. Still, he carried himself with dignity, nodding in quiet thanks as he steadied his footing.

"With the river crossing business over," he said, "we'll reach Zhegama in a few days. Rest on a good bed will help, but I'll gladly listen if you need to talk."

"Thank you, Master Hillal," Kharis said. "And please accept my apologies again."

"Nonsense, my child. I'm here to assist." He bowed to everyone. "Blessed be the earth and sun."

"May they sustain us," was everyone's reply.

General Zhegur turned to Saya. "Is there anything I can do to help?"

"There is. It's getting a little colder. Could you help me get some more blankets from the wagon? I don't know where they were packed."

Kharis found the request odd. All their blankets were in the covered wagon, and her perfectionist sister had packed them.

After helping Saya to her feet, General Zhegur guided her forward.

No longer the center of attention, Kharis reached for her cup. As she lifted it, painful heat flared in her palm—sharp, sudden—and she nearly dropped the cup. Wincing, she carefully set it down, her breath catching. She opened her hand—

A thin, pink line, crusted now in places, stretched across her right palm. The skin around it was tender, raw—a clean cut made by a sharp blade.

She gingerly curled her fingers as if hiding the wound would make it disappear. Saya had said it was night terrors. But... had it been a dream, or had the encounter been real? She reached for her holster, relieved that her two daggers were securely strapped. Then, a darker thought crept in. Was it the madness?

Fear clawed up her throat.

She couldn't tell Saya. There was no point in worrying her. Besides, by morning, there would be no trace of the wound.

CHAPTER 55
THE CURSE OF SHADOWS

Beware the shadows, for they are neither friend nor foe. They merely wait when hungry. - Poliormos

The fire sputtered weakly, its glow barely holding back the forest's darkness. Five men had crouched around it, their voices low but filled with excitement. Their greedy fingers brushed over the contents of a recently pilfered chest.

The rabbit they'd roasted earlier was reduced to scraps, its bones piled haphazardly near the fire. Their horses stood tethered a short distance away, their flanks still sweaty. The men had ridden hard, desperate to distance themselves from the cavalcade they'd just plundered.

Hedin, the leader, was pleased.

"Look at this," Davrin murmured, lifting a bolt of purple silk. He ran his calloused fingers over the fabric, his grin spreading. "This'll fetch a fine price in the market. Women love this kind of thing."

"Aye, but the jewels is where the coin's at," Tobias countered, holding up a delicate necklace set with tiny crystals. The firelight caught the stones, making them glint like distant stars. "Quick to pocket, quick to sell. No haggling over this."

"Don't forget these," Karrik added, plucking a lavish hair

comb from the chest. Gold inlay and flecks of turquoise adorned the polished red sandalwood base. "Some noble-woman will gush over this one." He cackled, tossing the comb into the pile.

"Don't be so loud, Karrik," Wrenn growled. "We got away, but we ain't in the clear." He spat on the ground. "One chest, though. Should've gone for more."

Karrik scoffed. "We lucky none of them convoy guards noticed us."

"Lucky?" Hedin's voice was a harsh rasp, heavy with deri-sion. "Luck had nothing to do with it. You think we made it this far because of luck?" He slammed the chest shut, Karrik yanking his fingers away just in time. "My planning kept us alive and fed, you idiots." Hedin's scarred face twisted into a grim smile, teeth missing.

"But boss—"

"Luck's for fools," Hedin cut Karrik off. "We sell it all fast. No delays. No mistakes."

The others grunted in agreement, but their celebration stilled when a sound broke the rhythm of the conversation—a soft shuffle, too deliberate to be the wind. Hedin's hand went to the hilt of his sword. Davrin, Tobias, and Karrik unsheathed theirs. Wrenn nocked an arrow and aimed.

"Quiet," Hedin hissed.

The men obeyed, falling still as their eyes flicked toward the dark woods.

A limping figure emerged from the shadows, pausing at the edge of their encampment. Beneath the woolen black cloak, the firelight caught on lavish black leather armor, its embossed surface oiled and gleaming, trimmed with a row of silver buttons gleaming like tiny moons.

Hedin's gaze lingered on them, already calculating their worth.

"I mean you no harm," a low, scratchy voice said. The hood obscured the face, but the accent marked him as nobility—each word clipped, precise, and laced with cold refinement. "I am cold, and I simply seek the warmth of your fire for the night."

Hedin's eyes narrowed, the old scar pulling his mouth into a cruel smirk. "Cold, eh?" he drawled, voice thick with mockery. "Then let us help death find you quicker."

The stranger tilted their head slightly. "So, no sharing of the fire?"

"No sharing of nothing," Hedin barked. His comrades cackled, weapons raised, their faces hard in the firelight.

The figure was silent for a moment before exhaling softly. "Too bad, then."

The hood fell back. One side of the face was raw and twisted, burned by fire, while the other was pristine—handsome, even.

"Five is a good number," the stranger said. His eyes gleamed black in the firelight with the faintest swirl of something unnatural. A smile tugged at the ruined lips that didn't reach those cold, void-like orbs.

The thieves faltered. The firelight dimmed—not due to the wind or the lack of wood, but as if the darkness had leaned in to smother it. The man's shadow crept closer, stealthily like a snake.

Karrik whispered a prayer.

Something moved in the dark—too soft to be footsteps, too wrong to be wind.

His voice came again, threaded with menace. "It's a pity you have nothing to share. So perhaps... I shall take what I need instead."

The fire guttered, and the dark swallowed them. For a moment, the night was still.

The horses shrieked.

A scream—wet and abrupt—split the air, then stopped.

Then, the killing began.

CHAPTER 56
THE SONG

Love is a truth that can't be concealed, yet remains unseen until it softly brushes against your cheek. - Poliormos

A little over two and a half months had passed.

Atop the pass, Kharis spotted the contours of Zhegama against the afternoon sun. Though blurred by dusty winds, the sight brought her relief. The journey was at its end. "How much further until we reach it?"

Mizha, the youngest Zherik-Umea guide at seventeen, cast her a knowing smile. His tousled brown hair framed his youthful face, lending him an air of untamed enthusiasm. "At this pace, we'll reach it tomorrow, possibly in the afternoon. We only have one more pass ahead of us."

"Rivers?" Kharis asked, still fuming over Saya pushing her into a cabin.

"None," Mizha said. "No more river crossings from now on."

"Good." Kharis straightened in her saddle, anticipation shaping her grin. "A large city means hot meals, warm beds," she closed her eyes, savoring the thought, "and long, hot baths."

"A bath and a bed sound great." Mizha stretched his back,

twisting slightly in the saddle, and glanced at the sun's location. "We'll be stopping for the night in a few hours."

Kharis groaned. That sounded like an eternity away. "Tell me a story, then."

Mizha cocked his head, surprised by her request.

"If the Forest Kin built the Zahar-Eliza," she asked, "do you have stories from when they lived in the Zahar-Katea region?"

"None, I'm afraid. Our stories are about the immortals that inhabited the mountains, magical beings with massive wings. Our Elders called them the Haize-Ibiltaria, Wind Walkers. They lived on high peaks and commandeered forests, traveling in the wind and summoning thunder and lightning. The Forest Kin may have built the Zahar-Eliza, but the Haize-Ibiltaria protected it. Lord Aditya and Lady Mathamurti blessed them with a long life to guard the Zahar-Eliza forever."

"Were they immortals, too?" Kharis asked.

"Not at all. Mathamurti was a sheepherder. Lord Aditya, the sun god, fell in love with her and, in his devotion, transformed her into an earth goddess."

Blessed be the earth. Blessed be the sun. The Zahari greeting took on a different meaning in the Zahar-Katea region—a deeper, more intimate meaning.

"Their love story sounds romantic." Kharis heaved a sorrowful sigh as her thoughts meandered toward a gardener in Urrun. "Tell me, how did they meet?" Her curiosity had been piqued.

"Lord Aditya hid in a cave," Mizha said, "taking the sun with him. The world was suddenly plunged into darkness. The gods, frantic, couldn't find him."

"Why did he hide?"

Mizha shrugged. "It depends on who tells the story, but the real cause is lost to the winds of time."

"What happened next?" Kharis leaned forward.

"Mathamurti, who had taken her flock to a nearby meadow, searched for a safe place to wait out the eerie gloom. She stumbled upon the cave where Lord Aditya hid, though she had no idea who he was. They spoke for a while, but he refused to leave the cave. She led her flock back to the village, but concern lingered, so she returned to speak with him again. Some say she brought him food. Others claim she sang to him.

"During those exchanges," Mizha continued, "they fell in love. She eventually coaxed him out of the cave. When he stepped out, he released the sun, returning it to the skies. Thankful for her actions, the gods granted Lord Aditya's request, making her an earth goddess." He gestured to the outline of the mountains. "She became the Zahar-Katea."

Her gaze traced the horizon. "To be loved like that," she murmured, not meaning to say it aloud. She caught herself, then cleared her throat. "It's a lovely story," she said. "Do you know of others?"

"Of course," he said. "Our lore abounds with them."

Kharis tightened her grip on the reins, listening with rapt attention as he recounted another.

❧

After dinner, the general guided the sisters to the summit of a nearby hill. The cool, crisp breeze greeted them at the top, dancing around the hair strands that tickled Kharis's face.

The city rested in a high valley three cliffmarks above sea level, so high that snow never fully melted in the summer.

"How many people live in the city?" Saya asked, noting its size.

"A little over seven hundred thousand as per the last time I visited," he said. "We have military camps north of it to train soldiers in mountain and winter campaigns, some created by His Majesty."

Kharis hummed. Before marrying the future queen, her father had once commandeered the Zahar-Katea region during the Unification Wars.

The three lingered, the cool air nipping at their faces. The city's faint glow created a magical dome of soft light against the night, while the faint silver glimmer outlining the mountains announced Sharan's moonrise.

"From afar," Kharis mused, "it's a place straight out of a

313

wondrous tale, shrouded in mystery and magic. A place inhabited by spirits—"

"You better not have nightmares," Saya interrupted. "Last night, you kicked me."

Kharis grimaced. "I kicked you because you were snoring."

"That was me, Your Highness," General Zhegur interjected with a swift, apologetic bow. "I am so sorry." And he descended the hill, his steps brisk.

"You and your big mouth." Saya glared at Kharis, flicking her forehead. "You better apologize." Without saying anything else, she stomped down the path, her footfalls mirroring her irritation.

Kharis rubbed her brow, grumbling. "How am I supposed to know?" Ever since the nightmare incident, both slept next to her. She faced the city again, smiling. "I still think it's a magical city."

"*So do I,*" said the silvery voice.

A smile parted her lips. "You've been quiet lately."

"*Have I?*" he asked, sounding curious. "*I prefer to watch and listen, but you already knew that. Besides,*" he paused, "*I sensed your need for space to let your emotions settle and find their course again.*"

She hesitated. "Noam?"

"*Yes.*" His voice softened to an almost mournful note. "*Your pain...*" He glided through her mind gracefully, offering a tender caress and brushing against the raw edges of her heart.

She closed her eyes, savoring his affection. "It was the right thing to do."

"*But this choice carved a deep wound,*" the Voice said gently.

"It did." Noam would always linger in her mind, her memories of him sweet. But so did the Voice, his presence woven into her as intimately as the heartache in her chest. "I've missed you." And this she meant. She'd missed the Voice as much as she missed air and sunlight. "Don't let it be so long."

There was a pause. "*I shall not.*"

Kharis imagined his cheeks flushed red—if only a face could confirm it. Would he be embarrassed and look away, or kiss her? That last thought sent her pulse racing. Noam would have done both: blush and kiss her.

"*How do you feel?*"

"When I think of him?" Kharis exhaled softly. "That there's a hole in my chest."

"*Yours was a hard decision.*"

"That it was." The sorrow was still there, wrapped around her heart. She'd thrown herself into training, combing through the Royal Archives and now the caravan—anything to dull the pain of loss. Her lips curved in a wry, bittersweet smile. "It seems farewell is a persistent thread in the tapestry of my life."

"*Then I promise never to leave you, so goodbye is never a word you shall utter to me.*" His gentle voice resonated in her mind, enveloped in such softness that she could almost reach out and touch it.

A warmth stirred in her chest. She pressed a hand over her heart, touched by his words. "You do?"

"*I wish never to see you cry.*"

A quiet conviction colored his tone. The words hummed through her like an unshakeable vow etched in starlight. But how he uttered his "never" echoed in her mind as if it meant more than a simple promise.

Her question slipped out. "Why are you so nice to me?"

"*Why would I not be?*"

Kharis hesitated, fingers tightening slightly. "People usually aren't, but when they are, they often want something." Her thoughts drifted to Hala.

The Voice hummed. "*I do not require anything.*"

"To need and want are different." She pulled on her jerkin, smoothing the tunic under. "You may not need anything, but I sense you want something."

"*My want is a simple one.*"

Her heart jerked. Of course, there would be one. She braced for it.

"*To never see you cry.*"

Kharis had opened her mouth, ready to argue, but his words stole her breath. Speechless, she let his answer sink into the spaces she often guarded. His kindness was always so unexpected.

She heaved a mournful sigh. "I'm the Djinnshirukh." Her voice was quieter now. "Tears have shaped my life from the moment I was born. There isn't much you can do about them."

"*Allow me to try.*"

Kharis stilled. His statement wasn't a command or a bold request. It was a plea as if the idea of seeing her cry affected him in some obscure fashion.

"Have I ever stopped you from trying?"

"*No, but permission should always be sought.*"

Permission. The word held weight. Noam had always given her the choice; now, the Voice offered the same.

Kharis let out a slow breath.

"Fate took Taika and Noam away from me. Perhaps I should fall in love with you—no one can take you away from me."

Was this hope? Desperation? The sign she'd gone mad at last?

The pause stretched. A silence that hummed with unspoken emotions.

"*Is that permission to court you? To make you fall in love with me?*"

Kharis tilted her face to the night sky, spreading her arms wide as the cool breeze curled around her. "Permission is granted."

This was her one chance at living while she still could. And when she finally surrendered to the madness, and the world faded into obscurity, she would cling to this voice—soft, silvery, resonant. It would be the last memory she would relish before everything slipped away.

Her exhale drew misty tendrils in the cold air. "If you're courting me, tell me something about yourself."

"*What do you wish to know?*"

Where to start? Kharis peeked over her shoulder. Saya and General Zhegur were deep in conversation at the bottom of the trail and didn't seem in a rush to leave. So Kharis clung to this moment with the Voice.

"Tell me your name."

"*We have had this conversation before.*"

"Yes, a long time ago, in a forest far, far away. I was hoping you'd reconsider."

"*No change of heart.*"

Kharis hummed. "What if I give you one?"

"*Would that require me to give you one as well?*"

She scratched her cheek. "I suppose a personal approach is called for."

"*Personal?*"

"Names imply a connection, sometimes intimate, especially when names result from affection. Wouldn't you wish to establish such intimacy if you claim to court me?"

"*Hmm.*" There was a long pause after that. "*This appears to be important to you, and you are important to me.*" Another pause. "*Thus... yes.*"

She couldn't contain her grin. "I'll come up with one, and you'll love it."

"*I already do.*"

Her heart skipped a beat. Fear, wonder, and a desperate wish to believe in hope came rushing like a storm battering a closed gate. She wasn't sure if she wanted to throw it open or bolt it shut. Kharis almost laughed at the absurdity. The Voice was perhaps a construct of her imagination, but she couldn't get enough of him. Long live this madness.

"Kharis!"

The Djinnshirukh turned at the shout, the spell interrupted.

Below, Saya waved. "Are you coming?"

It felt like waking from a pleasant dream. Her exhale left a fleeting cloud of warmth that unraveled and disappeared into the night, leaving only wispy tendrils in its wake.

"I must get going."

"*I am always with you,*" he said, unconcerned. "*I go where you go.*"

The sensation of having her face touched, as if ghostly fingers traced her features, sent a roll of goose bumps up her arms. How could madness be this enticing?

"Will we talk again?"

"*Why would we not?*"

Kharis took a deep breath and held it, willing her annoyance to ebb away. The Voice often answered her questions with questions.

"Tell me, what's your favorite color?"

"*Silver.*"

"And your favorite flower?"

"*Dandelions.*"

She laughed. "You're full of answers tonight."

"*And you brim with questions.*"

Her soft chuckle punctuated the mist curling in delicate tendrils around her words. "My sister would say the same."

"*Sing for me.*"

She flinched, startled by the unexpected request.

"*Would that be too personal?*" He'd knocked on the proverbial door and waited, curious yet hopeful about a favorable answer.

"No. Not at all," she said. "What would you enjoy listening to?"

"*Your voice.*"

Kharis's heart somersaulted. "If I didn't know better, I'd say you're flirting with me."

"*I am. You have permitted me to court you.*"

Kharis stared into the darkness, unsure how to respond. The Voice sounded so matter-of-fact and confident that it momentarily disoriented her. "You... weren't joking."

"*No.*"

"Khiri!" Saya's shout sliced through the moment.

Kharis sighed. "Coming!" she replied, scrubbing a hand over her face. "Now she's in a rush."

"*My song?*"

Kharis groaned. "Everyone's in a rush tonight." Her breath clouded in the chilly night air. "Would you sing with me?"

"*I have a terrible voice.*"

She arched an eyebrow. "And you're a terrible liar."

And yet, the heaviness in her chest had lifted. A song

always came to mind whenever she explored the night sky, so she sang it to her heart's content.

"Morning Star, oh Morning Star, guide us through the night.
  Rid us of this darkness, please, and lift our weary hearts.
  Shine your blessings, deary, and swiftly lead our paths.

  "Morning Star, oh Morning Star, shining o'er so clear,
    Whenever we are lost, you quickly draw us near.

  "Morning Star, oh Morning Star, so beautiful and bright.
    Rid us of this darkness, and lift our weary hearts.
  Shine your blessings, deary, and swiftly light our paths."

Kharis hiked down the trail, the gentle breeze carrying her song. Saya recognized it immediately. "That's a song about Queen Aghuti."

"Yes. The Morning Star. Our mavah." Kharis held onto Saya's hands. "Sing it with me, please?" She turned to General Zhegur. "Do you know the song?"

He offered a crisp nod. "Everyone in Zahar knows it, Your Highness."

"Perfect! Let's sing it together, then."

The three sang it on their way to camp. The Voice remained quiet, but Kharis knew he was listening. If he had a face, he would be smiling, too.

Above them, the stars became silent witnesses to their song, the last note lingering in the air like breath on frost, delicate and luminous.

CHAPTER 57
THE WEIGHT OF FATE

When the weight of fate settles, it reminds us of the threads that weave our life's tapestry. - Poliormos

The bugle blare pierced the camp's quiet before dawn. The first call jolted Kharis awake. She sat up, her instincts kicking in. Her eyes flew open, and the lingering fog of sleep vanished instantly.

"*Time to get started,*" said the Voice.

"I just fell asleep," she grumbled, her words muffled as she flopped back onto her bedroll.

He *fires-take-him* chuckled. "*We did talk until late.*"

"I'm blaming you." She rubbed her face and sighed. "It's still dark. Even the sun's sleeping." She gestured grandly to the pre-dawn gloom, settling the matter.

"*The sun is always punctual,*" he teased.

"Not another word." She turned over with an exaggerated huff, pulling the blanket over her head.

"*Your sister is ready.*"

"Good for her."

"Breakfast's ready," Saya called over the buzz of noisy camp activity.

Kharis burrowed deeper to escape the clatter. "Why is everyone in a rush?"

The Voice chimed in. *"Food tends to run out faster when you wake."*

She yanked the blanket off her head. "My appetite is perfectly reasonable." Rolling onto her side, she pulled the blanket tightly around herself. "I'm skipping breakfast to spite you. Consider yourself glared at."

His joyous laughter echoed in her mind. *"I have missed this —us."*

"Us?"

"Khiri!" Saya's voice rose over the morning clamor. Then she stomped over and yanked the blankets clean off her. "Get up this instant."

Kharis curled into a ball against the chill. "I'm awake! I'm awake! Fires take you all." She threw Saya a glare since she could.

People stirred to life and broke camp shortly after that, the sound of rustling tents and bustling activity filling the air. The trumpets resounded when the sun lazily climbed from behind the mountains, washing the valley in gold and rose.

The final stretch to Zhegama began.

§.

Atop the final pass, Kharis reined in her horse, letting her gaze sweep across the breathtaking expanse below.

The road unfurled before them, a wide ribbon of hard-packed earth flanked by two stark contrasts—the dense forest on her left and the shimmering blue of the Ibaia Sea on her right. In the distance, the Zahar-Katea peaks loomed, their jagged summits piercing the sky like the fangs of some slumbering beast. A veil of dust shrouded the city, softening its edges and casting it in a dream-like haze.

"Bless the earth and sun," said a voice beside her.

"May they sustain us," she answered, turning.

The man had appeared as if he'd been conjured from the landscape. She recognized him at once—the stranger she'd glimpsed on the night of her first night terrors episode. Now, he sat astride a dappled horse, his silver-streaked hair brushing the collar of a thick woolen riding cloak. A wide-brimmed felt hat was tied beneath his jaw, casting shade over his face. His seafoam green eyes shimmered with a knowing light. Curiously, his gambeson bore an embroidered silver fox.

Kharis narrowed her eyes. "Are you one of the riders?"

He snorted softly. "Blessed, no. A merchant."

She tilted her head, that silvery-green gaze all too familiar. "I feel I know you."

"And you do," he said. "Once, I sold kites at festivals."

Her eyes widened as the memory came to her. "You're... that man."

"Foághlam," he said, pressing a hand to his chest and bowing slightly. "At your service."

"What brings you here?"

He smiled, mysterious and wide. "A bit of this and that. I've left kites behind for something more valuable."

"And what is that?"

"Knowledge."

She arched a brow. "Would you have any to sell me? I'm searching for a spell."

He tilted his head to the sky, as if consulting the wind. Then, with a fox's grin and eyes glinting with mischief, he replied, "The spell you seek isn't here nor there. Head to Hegra, My Lady—"

"Hey!" Officer Dhan's voice cut through as the White Guard spotted the intruder.

With a wink and a tap of his heels, Foághlam's horse sprang forward, kicking up a cloud of dust as he disappeared down the trail.

Officer Xia Dhan rode up at once. "Are you all right, Your Highness?"

"Alive and well," Kharis replied, eyes following how the figure vanished with the wind. *Like seven years ago.* "Just a merchant in a hurry to reach Zhegama before the rest of us."

Xia exchanged hand signals with the nearby officers—a form of *hizkuntza* Kharis didn't recognize, though it wasn't hard to guess the meaning. Xia clearly didn't appreciate a tres-passer wandering this close to an imperial princess.

"I'll ride with you," she said, her almond-shaped eyes now scanning their surroundings with renewed focus.

"You sing?" Kharis asked. "I need a partner."

By the time the caravan wound its way down the pass, the sun had reached its zenith. Their lively contest of improvised verses faded into laughter as a halt was called for the midday meal.

With a weary sigh, Kharis dismounted, stretching her stiff limbs. Xia approached to take their horses toward the water's edge. Kharis, however, noticed how the Zherik-Umea guides whistled messages to each other and anxiously gestured to a place in the distance.

"Wait a moment," she told Xia and tapped on Saya's shoulder, who was fixing her boot laces.

"What is it?" Saya asked.

Kharis tilted her head toward the horizon. Saya and Xia turned, focusing on the growing cloud of fine sand.

"Something... Someone's coming," Kharis said.

At the same time, the caravan riders gripped their horns and broadcast the alarm: one prolonged blast followed by a series of short ones. The sound quickened everyone's steps.

"Get on your horses," General Zhegur belted at the sisters. "Now!" He scanned the surroundings, his eyes darting in every direction. "If it comes to it, we're breaking away and headed in that direction." His sword pointed toward a dense forest section. "We ride and don't stop, understood?"

Saya agreed with a crisp nod, but the order didn't settle with Kharis.

"We can't leave the people behind," she said.

"I'm sorry, Your Highness," he said. "Your safety is my priority."

Sporting a frown, Kharis turned to Saya for support, but the Sorukhipa shook her head.

Foot soldiers unsheathed swords and angled spears. The zenka mercenaries readied, some stringing their bows. Upon General Zhegur's command, ten White Guard officers took off on their horses to investigate. The remaining thirty drew their weapons and encircled the princesses.

Soldiers hoisted the royal flags, hopefully a deterrent, and tension spread across the convoy.

Saya drew her sword, and the Firegrazer hummed against the wind, the only sound in the eerie silence enveloping them.

With hands shielding her eyes, Kharis squinted. "What do you think it could be?"

"It's hard to say," Saya said. "Peace or not, it won't stop thieves."

"Well, it's reckless," Kharis said. "Our section alone is a hundred strong." She glanced over her shoulder. "Saya, there are children here. We... can't leave."

"Let's wait."

Kharis huffed, her heart racing, nearly exploding. "But the children—"

"Just. Wait." Saya wore a deep frown.

Zhegur shot them a questioning glance, but Saya shook her head at him.

Kharis clenched her jaw, furious at the thought of leaving anyone behind. Her fingertips heated, and a glow ignited. She gripped the reins tighter, eyes narrowing as she assessed the terrain—the road's incline, the sun's location, how the wind blew. Her mind moved swiftly, like a hand gliding over a xakea board. Her body awakened to its task: battle.

The air shimmered with heat.

Pendragham snorted and shifted. The glow crept higher, licking at her knuckles. Saya's Firegrazer hummed louder. She turned in her saddle, her gaze locking onto Kharis. "What's going on?"

Kharis ignored her.

The wind carried the blade's ominous whistle as Saya's knuckles strained under the effort. "Khiri, answer me."

Kharis focused on the roar of an approaching cavalry, every hoofbeat thrumming in her bones.

As if sensing Kharis's rising power, Saya's sword vibrated, its song clamoring to fulfill its purpose.

"Kharis." Saya lowered her voice an octave, her warning tone unmistakable. "I need you to stand down."

But magic surged from Kharis's core, branching to her

limbs. Her gaze locked onto the horizon as if she were traveling at high speed to meet the threat, rendering her sister's voice a distant echo.

"Kharis." Saya's voice cracked as if torn from her throat. "Look at me."

The Firegrazer howled as if requesting aid from the gods themselves.

A sharp bugle blow shattered the tense silence, its resonant notes jolting Kharis back. The world swiftly unfolded into familiar colors, shapes, and sounds. She blinked as if she'd just been shaken awake from a dream. A strange vertigo washed over her.

"What was that?"

"The sign that you're a reckless fool," Saya barked, her nostrils flaring.

"It's the all-clear," General Zhegur explained, giving both sisters a quizzical stare. The Firegrazer returned to its quiet state, with only a barely perceptible hum of its magic lingering.

The general refocused on the cloud of dust, wiping the sweat off his face as he grumbled a few flowery expressions. Emerging over the hill, two cavalry officers galloped at full speed.

"Stay with the princesses," he told his unit, spurring his mount to meet the approaching officers.

The world, still a moment ago, suddenly buzzed with motion. The low thrum in her chest dissipated, but the leather reins in her hands felt warm. A thin line of smoke lifted from them, the scent sharp and burnt. She let go, shaking out her fingers with a hiss.

A crease appeared between Saya's eyebrows. "Are you all right?"

Kharis cocked her head, covering it up. "Yes. Why wouldn't I be?"

Saya's lips thinned as she fought to suppress her annoyance. "Your power was awakening."

"Pfft." Kharis rolled her eyes. "Your sword hates me, Saya. That's what happened." A playful smile pulled at her lips, softening the tension. "Too bad it has to obey you."

Saya frowned. "Khiri, don't—"

"What do you think is happening out there?"

Ahead, General Zhegur was exchanging words with the two officers.

Saya shot her a sharp look, aware of her deflection. Turning toward the general, she muttered, "I don't know, but we'll find out soon enough."

The wind stirred, dragging a slow whirl of dust in its wake. In Kharis's mind, a different force stirred her thoughts.

"Don't do that again." The Voice held an edge she hadn't heard before—tight, shaken. *"I... I couldn't reach you."*

General Zhegur engaged the officers in a discussion with his sharp gestures and stiff posture, hinting at aggravation. The wind carried snippets of raised voices punctuated by curt nods and clenched fists.

"They're unhappy," Kharis muttered. General Zhegur. The Voice.

"So am I." Saya focused on Zhegur's gestures to glean something. "Do not test fate, Khiri. Never awaken the Fire-grazer. I was successful this time, but barely." Saya met her eyes. "I won't next time."

A few caravan riders joined the general, and after some discussion, they took off at his command, headed for their assigned lengths. "A Zhegami escort is coming," they shouted.

The tension turned to loud cheering, but General Zhegur rode back with a deep scowl.

"What happened?" Saya asked.

The general shook his head, vexed. "If they were coming, they should've sent a messenger yesterday." His voice was clipped, and his anger restrained. "This encounter could've ended badly." He clenched his jaw, swallowing the curse, and rode to the caravan's front.

The dust cloud grew.

White Guard officers cleared the hill, leading a large cavalry cantering behind them. Flag bearers held onto the royal banner, featuring a golden Zahari sun with seven radiant flares set against an ivory backdrop. The Zhegami pennons, adorned with a solitary pine tree on a field of gold, fluttered gracefully in the breeze.

The head of the Zhegami cavalry was a short, plump man wearing elegant finery. He met with General Zhegur, who waited to exchange information.

"I hope General Zhegur is telling him off," Kharis said.

"I doubt he will." Saya kept her eyes on him. "He's measured with his words and would never embarrass the Crown."

Kharis puckered her lips, her eyes narrowed at Saya. "You've come to know him well."

"So would you if you weren't running after Master Hillal's sangha to listen to their stories."

Kharis lifted a casual shoulder. "If Zhegur has stories to tell, I'll run after him, too."

Saya threw her sister a glare. Kharis flicked her eyes with an audible exhale.

"In any case," Saya said, "when General Zhegur puts this in his report to the Regia-Zenka, Ghan will howl like a wounded hyena—" She clamped her lips tight, suddenly aware of the implication behind what she'd said.

Kharis stiffened at the mention of his name. "He'll do more than that, Saya, sending his txakurri—"

"Do *not* curse," Saya admonished her. "Remember your place."

"Why? It doesn't stop others from using it on me."

"It speaks volumes of them." Saya tilted her head toward the group. "They're coming. Please mind your words."

"Fine." Kharis waved her hand, indifferent to the warning. "I'll use *princess-y* curses."

CHAPTER 58
THE CITY OF ZHEGAMA

To lead is to serve. - Poliormos

Kharis fiddled with the reins while General Zhegur led the mysterious rider to them.

"Blessed be the earth, and blessed be the sun," the man said, nasal, high-pitched, and louder than needed. "Welcome to Zhegama," he added before the sisters could reply. "I'm Azim Maharghan, governor of the city of Zhegama. I shall be at your service while you stay in our lovely city." His words came in a rapid, eager rush, the man barely pausing to breathe, his brown eyes blinking nonstop.

"We're extremely honored by your presence, Your Highnesses," he said. "It's a historic moment if I ever saw one. The whole city awaits your arrival."

He pulled out a scroll, his face hidden behind it.

"As per the Crown's itinerary, you'll spend seven days here and handle initial diplomatic duties," he lowered the scroll, "and I, of course, will assist you."

His face disappeared behind the blasted parchment again as he read aloud, each word carrying Hala's voice, dictating their every move and shaping their days with rigid precision. Kharis fought to suppress a groan. Had the cage simply shifted, invisible yet ever-present?

Azim's lips curled into an eager smile. "As governor, it will be my honor to ensure everything is done according to your requirements and conditions." He lifted a proud finger. "I shall meet every one of your expectations."

Kharis remained quiet. Hala was the one with endless requirements, conditions, and expectations. Azim grinned, a mouth full of teeth and clueless bliss, while her freedom slipped away with every word he read. Saya kept a neutral face, but her fingers impatiently curled and uncurled around the reins. General Zhegur sat stiffly on his horse, throwing Azim glare after glare.

The governor noticed none of it.

When done reading, Azim added, "Please, allow me to lead you into the city."

Saya turned to General Zhegur. With a frown, he said, "We have stopped for food and water. The animals need a break, too."

He made the proper introductions, and the governor and the sisters exchanged pleasantries, Azim chatting nonstop, cheerfully discussing lodging arrangements, plans, events, regional history, local lore, social gossip, and countless other details.

&

Kharis couldn't help the anticipation building inside her. After nearly three months on the road, she'd arrived.

"Zhegama." The name escaped her lips in a hushed murmur. "Our new home."

The Voice stirred, winding around her thoughts like a quiet brook. Curious, as if trying to peek over them to glimpse this place. And why wouldn't he? Being in a different region of the Empire, so far from the Senda, was a dream come true.

Small docks dotted the edges of the inland sea, each holding an array of colorful fishing boats. Their hulls glistened as anglers hauled proof of their hard day's work at the lake. The aroma of roasted fish wafted through the air, tempting Kharis with the promise of tantalizing meals.

Nearer to the Ibaia Sea's shores, the homes huddled tightly together, bracing against the unforgiving winters. These two- and three-story narrow dwellings, varied in size and shape, surged from the inland sea along the valley's edge like waves.

Beyond the clustered homes, a different kind of movement took hold of her senses. The city opened to a sprawling tapestry of life, colors, sounds, and restless energy.

The deep, resonant boom of drums rippled through the air as the royal convoy glided through the towering city gates. The drums were enormous—each as tall as the drummers and as wide as three people standing shoulder to shoulder. Atop the platform, the drummers moved with agility, their bodies bending and twisting with the rhythm. *Dancing.* The thought took hold, a quiet ember of curiosity. They leaped, spun, and swapped places mid-air, the heavy mallets in their hands blurring as they struck the taut drumheads perfectly.

As the procession ventured deeper into the city, blocky wooden structures with double-pitched roofs widened in size. These differed from the typical flat roofs in Zahar-Ghak, which became livable spaces during the hot summers of the central plain.

An ocean of eager onlookers had lined the streets, waving Zahari banners, but more voices rang out from windows and rooftops, their shouts a chorus of genuine hospitality. Jubilant cheers surged, weaving with the thunderous rhythm of drums that pulsed through the bustling streets, carrying the city's energy in every beat.

"The caravan will camp outside the city gates," Azim told the sisters as he waved at the crowds. "Tomorrow, the open-air markets will start the festivities planned around the royal visit. Lady Khostuna tasked me with arranging your lodging."

He sounded so proud of himself.

"Since Zhegama will be the site for the Mahazenka Court, an official royal residence is essential. The Regia-Zenka's demands and conditions were extensive," he said as if sharing a secret, "but I'm happy to say I more than delivered." He smiled smugly. "My wife, you see, would've yelled at me had I failed such a crucial task. Azim Maharghan," he lifted his finger most dramatically, "will not disappoint the Crown."

Kharis waggled her eyebrows, prompting Saya to suppress a chuckle. General Zhegur shot Azim a disapproving glance that conveyed his hope for Azim's wife to kill him.

The unannounced stop by the building that would house the Mahazenka Court intensified his scowl. Oblivious to General Zhegur's darkening mood, Azim introduced the princesses to giddy city officials, who offered them large flower bouquets.

After that, Azim led Kharis and Saya to the royal compound. The general followed closely behind, glaring at Azim whenever the opportunity arose. Kharis was amazed at how oblivious Azim appeared, encased in his bubble of joyful duty.

They soon came upon the royal residence. Thick stone walls surrounded it. Guards opened the heavy wooden gates, and Kharis's mouth fell open. The place was massive.

"The walled compound includes a large two-story royal residence," the governor said. "There's a lovely garden, quite sizable if you ask me. The stables are in the back, spacious enough for fifty horses. The secondary structures are the barracks for the officers and soldiers, including an expansive training patio. Crown Prince Hala was most insistent on this condition."

Kharis groaned quietly, resigned to her brother's demands.

"The upper floor offers sleeping chambers, guest rooms, and a comfortable sitting room for private gatherings. The lower floor features a grand dining room and a separate chamber for various functions, including meetings with dignitaries and entertainment. There's a full kitchen and rooms for your attendants."

"Attendants?" Kharis asked.

"Of course." He sounded most proud of this. "We can't have imperial princesses living here without them. They are here already. The remaining staff will come first thing tomorrow." Azim's smile was as bright as the sun itself. "I shall not impose on you any further today."

Saya and her general silently sighed their relief at the same time. Their faces softened, and the tension on their shoulders vanished. They exchanged discreet smiles, and that gesture between them warmed Kharis's heart.

"Besides," Azim added, "I fear my wife would yell at me if I did." He chuckled nervously.

Blessed be his wife.

"My carriage will pick you up in the morning so you may have breakfast with us."

"Thank you for your hospitality," Saya said. "We await your guidance."

Kharis cringed at the idea of Azim's endless blather.

"Blessed be the earth and sun," Azim said. "Have a relaxing evening. I shall see you early tomorrow."

Surrounded by his escort, Azim waved at them as he rode away. Kharis waved back.

General Zhegur helped the sisters dismount, taking his time with Saya.

"Thank you for your assistance," she said, smoothing her clothes as if that could keep Kharis from noticing the blush on her cheeks.

She narrowed her eyes, observing how the two chatted as if she weren't there.

The general motioned, and one of the White Guard officers took their horses. "I'll arrange tonight's security detail," General Zhegur said. "However, call on me if you need me." His gaze was intense whenever he faced Saya. "For anything."

"Thank you." Saya nodded with a smile. "I hope you get a much-deserved rest."

He lingered on Saya's face, a gesture Kharis caught. When the general realized she'd noticed, he cleared his throat, bowed to both, and walked away.

"Let's go in," Kharis said, snapping Saya out of her introspection. "Our new life is about to start."

CHAPTER 59
A NEW LIFE

All true beginnings are born of shattering. The soul fractures into
shards, each casting a wild reflection of who you might yet become.
Only then does the Blessed Mother gather what remains—and
pours it into a vessel vast enough to hold your becoming. - Poliormos

Three people waited for them by the mansion's
entrance. A middle-aged, heavy-set man of medium
height and kind eyes spoke first.

"Welcome to Zhegama, Your Highnesses." He bowed
deeply, his hands wringing the fabric of his uniform. "Please
accept our apologies for the lack of a formal reception. We had
expected you to arrive tomorrow and had prepared a proper
welcome."

A slight accent affected his Zahari in a way Kharis found
pleasant. "Good weather quickened our pace," she said. The
need for a bath didn't hurt either. "Besides, pomp isn't needed
when the welcoming is genuine."

The man smiled, and his nervousness eased. "I'm Abhiral,
master chef for the royal residence. Asha and Yalini," he
gestured to the two women beside him, "assist me in the
kitchens."

Asha, a rotund woman, and Yalini, tall and wiry, curtsied,
their faces alight with curiosity, their smiles hinting at enthu-

siasm. Kharis found it refreshing not to be greeted with the scowls or grimaces she expected at the Ghak.

"Please call on us if you need any assistance," Abhiral said. "Otherwise, with your leave, we return to the kitchens. Dinner will be served soon."

Kharis perked up.

"You must be starving," Abhiral said with a fatherly smile.

"That we are." Her stomach hopped with glee at the idea of food.

The three bowed again and opened the large doors. Asha and Yalini glanced over their shoulders, still grinning, eyes crinkled with excitement. Kharis liked them. Then she turned to Saya. "Shall we take a look?"

Saya gestured with a flourish. "Lead the way."

The entrance hall, paneled with dark wood, was spacious. Portraits and intricate tapestries hung from the walls, along with the expected Zahari and Zhegami pennons. Large flower vases with tasteful floral designs lined the walls. The broad, heavy rugs added to the stately decor.

A wide, grand staircase led them to the upper floor. The first room opened into a cozy library. "Books about Zhegama," Saya said. "A collection curated to the governor's liking."

"I'd rather read books about Zhegama than listen to his lectures," Kharis said.

Saya chortled at that.

The doors to their chambers opened to an anteroom with a fireplace and comfortable seating. There was a storage room, a large closet, a bathing chamber, and finally, their sizable bedroom.

Their chests were already in the room, a reminder that Kharis would have to act as a princess and wear uncomfortably stiff and complicated clothing. She undid the clasps on her vambraces, unfastened her pauldrons, and unbuckled her leather cuirass, taking them off with a satisfied moan. "I've been dying to get out of these for a while. Come. I'll help you with yours."

"General Zhegur had good reasons to insist we wear them always."

"Even when we slept?" Kharis gestured for Saya to lift her arms. "Nothing happened."

Saya raised an eyebrow. "Our safety is his priority. If nothing happened, it speaks volumes of his skills."

"I like him." Kharis unclipped the buckles. "He's been nice to us."

Saya smiled as she removed her cuirass. "I'm glad Hala chose him, not Uncle."

"May the Fires take him."

Saya frowned. "Please be careful with those comments. He has ears everywhere."

"No. No." Kharis waved a confident finger. "Jordha has ears everywhere, and our cousin hates his guts, too." Kharis walked over to the windows. "Does General Zhegur hate him?"

"He is measured and—"

"Yes, yes. Your general is perfect." Kharis batted her eyelashes to tease her sister. "So dreamy." She made kissing noises. "So scrumptious."

Saya wrinkled her nose at her. "You better watch it."

"Ooh! And what will the mighty Saya do?" Kharis parted the curtains and opened the windows.

"For starters, I could throw you out the window."

Kharis took a deep breath of the crisp air. "If I land in Zhegur's arms, I'm open to that."

Saya hissed.

Kharis laughed. General Zhegur clearly liked Saya; here was proof that Saya liked him back. And her sister deserved every ounce of happiness. Her smile wavered—just for a breath. Kharis was glad for Saya's light, but it made her think of Noam... and all the things that might've been. With an exhale to let the sorrow out, Kharis stuck her head out, resting her elbows on the windowsill.

Saya and Reza... Matchmaking, it is.

The scent of food wafted through. Her stomach's loud gurgling startled her. "Can you hear that?"

Saya arched a dark eyebrow. "All of Zhegama can hear your stomach."

They glanced at each other for a long moment and burst out laughing.

"Finally free!" Kharis shouted.

She ran to one bed and dove onto it, landing with a soft thud as the blankets lifted. "This one's mine." She stretched out and sighed contentedly. "What are we going to do? The Regia-Zenka scheduled every aspect of our lives. People came and left, leading us to whatever we were supposed to do."

Saya lay on the other bed with a satisfied groan, letting her body sink into it. "So, this is what a bed feels like." A smile parted her lips. "My immediate thought is to head down and eat with the officers. I want something other than dried meat and porridge. And from the sound of your stomach, you are, too."

He-he! She wanted to see her general. "We're royalty. Wouldn't they be uncomfortable having us eat with them?"

Saya shrugged the concern off. "No one's around to tell us what is right and wrong. We're not at the palace nor bound by its rules. Out here, we create our own, and if we want to eat with them, who's to stop us?"

"Our own rules." Saya had convinced her, and she lifted a proud fist. "Now, things are different and—"

Knocks on the door startled them.

Kharis narrowed her eyes. "General Zhegur?"

"Not likely."

"Housekeeper?"

Saya shook her head. "Coming tomorrow."

With a nod from Saya, Kharis pulled her daggers out and moved toward the door, her gut tensing in that strange, quiet way when the world subtly shifted. Another set of knocks, more insistent, followed the first. With lips puckered, Saya gripped the hilt of her sword and opened the door.

336

CHAPTER 60
THE ATTENDANT

In service, the self is not diminished—it is revealed. - Poliormos

"Good evening, Your Highness," the woman said, curtsying.

Unassuming, of average height, with brown hair and eyes, and likely in her thirties, she stood with her hands clasped before her to show she was unarmed.

"I'm Magda." She spoke with an accent that Kharis couldn't place, standing with an air of duty about her, her clothes impeccable and her hair short. Her sharp eyes would miss nothing.

Saya dipped her head. Kharis remained alert, daggers still in her hands. This woman had entered their residence, climbed the stairs, and knocked on their bedroom door, meeting no resistance.

Maybe the Zhegami guards knew her? A dark thought crossed her mind—that they hadn't seen her. Suddenly, Azim's insistence made more sense. Servants provided an initial layer of security. Sheathing her daggers, Kharis discreetly scanned for General Zhegur, who should've escorted Magda.

"Now, come with me," Magda said. "I'll ensure you have a bath and clean clothes before dinner is served."

Ah, yes. Kharis's body odor could scare dangus and v'letas.

The sisters followed Magda onto the front patio, where Zahari soldiers saluted them as if nothing unusual had happened. A second woman, slightly taller than Magda, crossed the yard to greet them.

"Lady Saya, it's an honor to assist you." This other woman, slightly taller than Magda, also had a slight accent. "My name's Zhandari."

Kharis spotted more women standing by the front gates, and Magda caught the gesture. "Given the lack of servants tonight, we'll head to a private bathhouse. The women will escort us. Zhegami soldiers and archers are stationed outside the compound's perimeter. Therefore, you won't lack in terms of security." When Magda clapped, the women marched over and settled into formation.

"Good evening." Zhegur's resonant bass drew everyone's attention. He eyed Magda with interest.

"General Zhegur." Magda bowed. "I'm taking Their Highnesses to a private bathhouse. Zhegami soldiers have been stationed—"

"I go where they go."

Magda lifted a dark brow. "And what exactly do you plan to do once we get there? Help them undress? Wash and rinse their backs? Perhaps soak your weary muscles with them?"

The general's frown intensified, but neither the gesture nor the dim evening light hid the color on his cheeks.

"An escort is already in place for these situations," Magda said, turning to the women. "The safety of our charges rests with us. Let's make Zahar proud."

The women took their daggers out in unison, holding one in each hand. They raised their right hands, pommels pressed against their chests, emulating the Zahari salute, and dropped to one knee with their heads down.

Kharis instantly recognized both the salute and the distinctive dagger design. Each was a double-edged blade, slightly curved, crafted to slip between ribs and strike the heart with lethal precision. The razor-sharp tip ensured a clean thrust, while one serrated edge promised to tear on the way out. These blades were meant to kill quietly and efficiently, with an unadorned pommel that could be used as a blunt weapon so that a surprise attack wouldn't last more than a few heart-beats. Considering their purpose, the elegant word etched on the metal—*zedek*, or justice—was almost profane.

Blessed Mother. They were Hitzalkea, the Sendatorsum's trained assassins.

Kharis swiftly scanned the roofs of nearby structures, searching for their usual companions, Shadow Walkers. Her initial cheeriness turned to dark apprehension. Despite the distance, the palace still had its eyes on them.

"So, General Zhegur, may we proceed?"

His lips twitched. He gave the Hitzalkea women a long, assessing look, then glared at Magda in silent warning. They stared at each other, sharp daggers flying between them until his nostrils flared. He gave her a curt nod and motioned the sentry to open a side gate. One of the Hitzalkea produced cloaks and covered the sisters.

"Lady Kharis, Lady Saya, walk with us," Magda said.

The women surrounded them and nudged the sisters out into the street. Kharis glanced over her shoulder. General Zhegur stood stiffly by the gate, arms crossed, watching them walk away with a narrowed gaze. He wasn't happy about this.

Soon enough, they came upon a sizable stone-walled building with no windows on the outside. The older woman opened the front door, and Kharis, Saya, and Magda entered the warm interior. The door closed behind them, leaving Zhandari to captain the group outside.

The woman handed them three baskets and led them to a small room.

"Place your clothes in these," Magda said. "The bathkeeper will wash your uniforms, clean and oil the leather, and return them tomorrow. I've taken the liberty of selecting clean clothing for you. I hope this meets with your approval."

Kharis lifted a shoulder. "I'm fine with it."

Saya nodded in agreement and sat to remove her boots. As she lifted her tunic over her head and undid her breast binding, Kharis spotted the peculiar blue mark adorning her sister's skin. It was an unexplained, permanent stain on the skin below her right armpit. She'd had it for as long as Kharis could remember.

Donning towels, the three entered a dimly lit room where steam rose from a pool. Small vents near the ceiling helped clear some of the steam.

Multiple scars etched Magda's lean, muscular body, sparking Kharis's curiosity about the woman's past assignments. Magda said, "Let me wash your back," and began scrubbing her with a soapy rag that smelled of lavender and oats.

"How long were you on the road, Your Highness?"

Kharis couldn't quite believe it herself. "Three months."

"It shows." Magda chuckled. "Let me know if the scrubbing hurts."

Her servants were never this nice. "What's that smell?" Kharis asked, making idle conversation. "Like rotten eggs."

"Ah, yes. This region is renowned for its numerous hot springs. Minerals in the water cause it, but those minerals also do wonders for one's skin. Hot spring water fills the pool before you. People say the waters of this region have medicinal properties, and many come to soak in the healing springs. The Ghak may sit on fresh river water. But here," she added with a warm smile, "we soak in hot springs."

Once Magda finished, she carefully poured a bucket of water over Kharis to rinse the soap off.

To Kharis's surprise, the water was pleasantly warm. "That was nice."

Magda hummed. "If you think this was nice, wait until you enter the pool." Wearing a satisfied grin, she jerked her chin toward Saya, already soaking.

Kharis carefully entered the pool, and the water swiftly became a warm embrace. She settled beside Saya, closed her eyes, and let go.

§

The group strolled back to the royal complex when Kharis felt a pair of eyes poke a hole in her back. She halted, glancing behind her.

"Is everything all right?" Magda asked.

"I'm unsure," Kharis said, anticipating a figure to emerge from a nearby shadowy alleyway. Her muscles tensed, every sinew ready for action, her body preparing for a fight. A rush of magic coursed through her veins, amplifying her senses to an even higher level of alertness.

"Your Highness?" Magda insisted.

Saya touched her arm. "Khiri?"

A musty, familiar scent hit Kharis's nose first, its dank staleness making her wince. Her body reacted before thoughts could catch up, her hands reaching for her daggers. Somewhere in the darkness, a pair of eyes intently assessed her every move.

Then, an all-too-familiar crawling sensation slithered over her skin.

It can't be. A shiver rushed down her spine. Shoving fear aside, she lifted her daggers, poised to strike.

"Khiri?" Saya's voice lowered, taut with unease. "What's wrong?"

"There's someone out there." Kharis tilted her head toward the back alley.

The Hitzalkea encircled the princesses, their daggers gleaming against the street's lanterns. They scrutinized their surroundings, eyes darting as if they couldn't pinpoint the source of danger the way Kharis could. One of the women whistled. A clear and distinct response echoed back, and the woman initiated a covert exchange of whistled messages with a few people on the rooftops.

A guttural yowl pierced the air, making the women flinch.

The next moment, a screeching hiss erupted, and a wild-eyed cat bolted into the street, its fur standing on end, tail puffed in terror. Another sleek and agile feline gave chase, its claws scratching the cobblestones as it weaved through the women, following a chaotic path.

Pots clattered to the ground, some shattering into shards, and a refuse basket tipped over, scattering rotten vegetables onto the street. The hissing and yowling faded as the chase disappeared into the shadows.

"Feral cats," Magda said, relieved. "That's all it was."

"*Fear not the cats,*" the Voice whispered, unnerved, his voice tight, "*but what startled them.*"

Kharis felt the gaze still locked on her. Her eyes stayed fixed on the shadowy alley, and goose bumps rippled along her skin.

"Come." Magda urged, nudging her out of the moment. "It's best if we return quickly." Her smile was practiced, thin— like someone trying to ease the tension. As if she knew it hadn't just been feral cats.

The group resumed their pace, no longer strolling. The Hitzalkea kept their daggers drawn, their formation tighter now.

But a lingering sense of disquiet haunted Kharis.

"*I felt it, too,*" murmured the Voice, as if knowing she needed to hear it. He moved through her mind, his indigo eyes glowing with feline alertness.

Kharis craned her neck every so often, wary of the shadows behind them, and silently begged the feeling on her skin to fade.

CHAPTER 61
THE DINNER

Love is a quiet feast—shared without request, savored without fear.
- Poliormos

"There you are," Saya said as Kharis entered the room. "What took you so long?"

Kharis sighed. "This place is a labyrinth." Hopefully, the answer would quell Saya's inquisition. She didn't want her surprise ruined.

Sitting on a cushioned floor chair beside Saya, Kharis served herself tea.

"Well, this evening was exciting," Saya said. "May catfights be all we handle."

Kharis forced a smile and sipped her mint tea.

"I'm glad to see this day over," Saya said. "Especially after a heart-rattling return from the bathhouse." She meowed, mimicking an angry feline while curling her fingers into cat claws, finally making Kharis laugh.

Singing and lively banter floated through an open window. "The last set of White Guard officers is returning from the bathhouse," Kharis said. "I bet they feel much better after a hot soak. I certainly do." Then she bit her lip. "How will bathing be handled at the Zahar-Eliza?"

Saya chuckled softly. "What if there's no bathing?"

343

Kharis furrowed her brow. If Saya was joking, she couldn't tell.

Just then, Magda and Zhandari walked into the room, balancing trays loaded with food. "Abhiral wanted you to try the regional cuisine." High-pitched excitement infused Zhandari's voice as she placed dish after dish on the low table.

Kharis's mouth fell open. The food array was a canvas of radiant reds, vibrant yellows, and fiery oranges, too beautiful to eat. A carnival of aromas teased her nose: cardamom's alluring sweetness, turmeric's earthiness, and coriander's enticing herbal notes. Ginger and spicy black pepper made her mouth water.

Magda pointed to each bowl, going clockwise. "This is mutton, and its sauce comes from red chilies. Be careful. It's quite spicy."

Heat. Fire. Kharis drooled.

"Here we have spinach and sheep's cheese cooked in an onion-based sauce. This dish is fried eggplant, and the other is Zhegami-style fried fish. This one is potatoes and cauliflower roasted with cumin and mustard seeds. This is lotus heart soup, and that is saffron rice."

"We can eat all of this," Saya said.

Zhandari chuckled. "Blame Abhiral, Your Highness. We didn't receive instructions on your diet. Thus, he made different dishes for you to choose from. He wants you to experience Zhegami food and hopes it becomes your favorite. If you would enjoy something else, please let me know, and I'll relay it to him. He'll cook whatever you desire."

"The people of Zhegama are excited about your visit," Magda added. "Abhiral is no exception. Your arrival is quite auspicious. The city will erupt in celebrations for the Harvest Moon Festival starting tomorrow. Zenkas will light bonfires throughout the city. People will sing and dance all night as they go from temple to temple to serenade Sharan, the moon goddess. Each zenka will carry elaborate floats along the streets. Therefore, sleep tonight, as you may not get much during the next two nights."

A soft set of knocks caught their attention. A playful smile danced on Kharis's lips, who got up before Magda or Zhandari.

"Welcome!" She ushered General Zhegur into the room. "I'm so glad you could join us." She pointed to a floor chair situated to Saya's left. "Please, sit there." Kharis took her seat to Saya's right, still wearing her mischievous smile. "Magda and Zhandari were telling us about the Harvest Moon Festival."

Magda said, "The governor has a full agenda for the princesses, including participation at the festival."

The general nodded. "His secretary already informed me. We were discussing details while you were gone."

With a quick bow, Magda said, "Enjoy the food," and the women closed the doors behind them.

Not one for formalities, Kharis grabbed a piece of flatbread, tore it apart, and scooped up a generous bite of mutton steeped in red sauce. She tasted it—cautiously at first.

Her eyes flew open.

The flavors burst across her tongue—bold spice, deep warmth, something primal, too. Heat. Nourishment. Life. Her whole body responded as if something within her had finally been fed.

"This is so good!" Kharis scooped more. "Here. Open your mouth."

Saya chewed slowly, and her face lit up. "Blessed Mother. Spicy and flavorful."

"Right?" Discreetly, she poked Saya with her knee. "Let's see if General Zhegur agrees." She waggled her eyebrows at Saya, urging her sister to feed him.

Saya hesitated but scooped up a portion. General Zhegur, his cheeks flushed, nervously opened his mouth. His face mirrored the crimson hue that now graced Saya's.

It was so adorable. Kharis smiled proudly. *I'm a match-making queen.*

"General Zhegur, what do you think?" Kharis asked.

He chewed slowly, his gaze on Saya. "It's divine."

Kharis didn't think he was talking about food. "Great. Let's eat!" She passed plates and served herself.

Sending protocol out the window, Kharis stuffed her mouth. After three months on the road eating dried meat, an occasional stew, and oat porridge, this feast redefined perfection for her. The spices added layers of decadent flavor, and the heat from the chilies tingled on her tongue.

"If Asurûn were here," she said, mouth half full, "Anela would be out of a job."

Saya burst out laughing.

"Ale would be nice with this meal." Kharis tapped the table with a confident fist.

"Ale?" Saya quirked an eyebrow. "When have you ever had it?"

Kharis shrugged, trying to cover up. "Just saying."

"I would have to agree, Your Highness," General Zhegur said. "Spicy food and ales go together."

"See?" Kharis glared at her sister. "I've been redeemed."

Saya shook her head. "I'll ask Zhandari about it."

"Perfect!" A broad grin stretched Kharis's mouth. "General Zhegur, you must join us for dinner every evening." She winked at the man. "Saya's getting us ale."

With playful enthusiasm, Kharis dug in, tasting dish after dish, unable to determine which she loved best. She eyed Saya and Zhegur, timidly eating beside each other amid a shower of furtive glances. The sight warmed her heart, and she almost squealed. They were so adorable together.

CHAPTER 62
WHEN THE STARS SIGH

When the stars sigh, the world forgets its weight, and in that awed hush, love dares to unfurl its truest form—unburdened, eternal, and whole. In that quiet exhale, two souls find the space to bloom. -
Poliormos

Saya and General Zhegur chatted (logistics, of course) while Kharis got lost in her thoughts and peppery ginger tea. A cool draft brushed against her, making her turn. The open balcony doors prompted her to rise.

"I'll be back." She stepped out and inhaled the night air.

A playful night breeze greeted her, rustling her hair and infusing the air with the scents of garden flowers, but the sight above stole her breath. The night sky unfolded, revealing a breathtaking expanse where scattered stars glittered across a rich velvet canvas.

The Silver River was magnificent, and more so tonight.

Sharan peeked over the mountains in the east. Round and bright, it would reach full moon status by tomorrow night, the start of the Harvest Moon Festival. But the Silver River felt so tantalizingly close that Kharis could almost touch it. She hopped onto the balcony rail and climbed the easy ascent to the roof, finding a cozy spot amidst the tiles.

"Saya will yell at me." That made her think of Azim's wife, and a chuckle rolled off her lips.

The world was alive with the whispers of unseen creatures. Crickets chirped, and an owl hooted its welcome from a tall tree. Not far away, the immense Ibaia Sea shimmered against Sharan.

Kharis inhaled, savoring the medley of fragrances in the alpine air as she gazed at the majestic moonrise. With its unhurried, regal ascent, the world seemed to slow. And at that moment, after the world seemed to exhale, time lost its urgency. All that remained was the breeze, the wet scent clinging to the city, and Sharan. Kharis sat quietly, letting this magic fill her soul.

"Are you there?" It was worth a try. "Can you see this?"

"*I can.*"

His voice brought a smile to her face.

"Even the sky is different at this altitude." She gazed at the sprawling, star-studded sky above. "I wonder if the sight would be the same near the ocean or the Koromai Desert. Would the same stars shine in Urrun or Kahurang?" The idea of visiting other places excited her. "Have you ever wondered what it feels like to be free?"

"*Do you not?*"

"I do," she said. "All the time." The enormity of the cosmos stretched endlessly above her, its brilliance pulling her in. "I want to break free from this curse, perhaps join the stars, and weave my own tapestry in the Loom."

The Voice listened quietly.

"If I were free of the curse, so would Saya, and with her freedom, she would chase after a certain general."

"*Freedom is a deceptively beautiful concept,*" he mused. "*But no one is ever truly free, least of all you.*"

She furrowed her brow. "Why?"

"*Mortals are bound by their emotions.*" Sadness crept into the Voice. "*You yearn for more, something you cannot define; often, that desire can imprison you.*"

Kharis kept her gaze on the North Star. "What about you? Don't you wish for more?"

"*Everyone does. Those who dream also wish for more.*"

"To dream. To envision a better outcome." It made her wonder. "Isn't there a way to find a new path and purpose in this life? To escape fate?"

"*No one can outrun fate,*" the Voice said.

"Then... maybe rewrite it?"

A deep hum caressed her mind. "*Spoken as the gem you are.*"

Kharis pouted, wondering if it was a compliment.

"*Freedom comes at a price. It means taking responsibility for your choices and facing consequences.*" His voice carried a subtle undertone of melancholy. "*Sometimes, it can be a lonely path. Freedom can be as much a burden as a gift.*"

"It sounds as though you speak from experience."

The Voice didn't reply.

"Do you... wish for freedom?"

"*Freedom, without you, is not freedom.*"

Her heart jumped a beat. "How come?"

The Voice kept his stoic silence. Was he pondering his fate? Or reminiscing about his past and what led him to this moment? And what was freedom, exactly, if she couldn't roam Zahar at will? And if no one could escape fate, was freedom an illusion?

"You wouldn't happen to know an unbinding spell, would you?"

A soft chuckle tickled her mind. "*No. But if I did, I would never use it.*"

"Why not?"

"*Sometimes, what binds us can also be a blessing.*"

Kharis tilted her head back, leaning her body against her hands. The stars shone so brightly. "To be imprisoned and lonely. It has defined my life, but shouldn't define my sister's. Saya deserves better."

"*The journey to find your freedom is as vast as the night, but it begins with you.*"

"My journey to a place called Hegra," Kharis breathed out slowly, letting the words wash over her. "As the Pharos of Hegra, couldn't you give me a clue—?"

"Khiri!" Saya's call pierced the stillness. "What are you doing up there? It's dangerous. Come down this instant!"

Kharis heaved a reluctant sigh. "Sister, being the Djinnshirukh is dangerous. This," she waved a casual hand, "not so much." Then, she hollered back, "Come and join me. The view is lovely."

She heard muffled arguing on the balcony, which she assumed was General Zhegur lecturing Saya not to climb.

"And bring the general," she shouted. "For our protection." She chuckled, wickedly amused. "Does he know what he signed up for?"

Saya managed her gradual ascent to the rooftop with General Zhegur. Both struggled in the thinning air, their breaths labored, yet his protective nature shone through, refusing to let Saya go alone. A smile graced Kharis's face.

"He truly watches after her." A pleasant warmth spread through her body. "If I were to die, he would take care of her. It's a nice thought, don't you think?"

"*Not if it means losing you.*" His tone had an edge.

Movement at the front gate caught her attention. Magda and Zhandari were leaving the compound.

"*Do you plan to stay here the entire night?*"

"Why not?" She gestured to the sky. "Do you have anywhere else to go that could compete with this gorgeous night?"

A ghostly touch—calm and reassuring—ghosted over her face. That was his answer.

"Welcome to my abode." Kharis grabbed Saya's hand and pulled her the rest of the way. "Isn't the view amazing?"

Saya settled beside Kharis. "It is," she said, breathless.

"I told you it was lovely," Kharis said as Zhegur settled beside Saya. "Sit and catch your breath. Then we can stare in awe."

Saya studied the fatal three-story drop instead. "How exactly do we go down?"

"Easy," Kharis said. "The same way a chimney sweeper would." Her finger pointed to the narrow door in a small alcove behind them.

Saya's eyebrows slammed together. "You mean to tell me we could've come that way?"

"Where's your sense of adventure?" Kharis flashed a roguish grin. "Besides, we should make General Zhegur sweat a little."

Zhegur laughed, amused. "It's a lovely night, Your Highness. I can't imagine a better way to enjoy it than sitting here."

"*I agree*," the Voice said.

And while Saya and General Zhegur chatted, pointing at constellations, Kharis kept her eyes on Magda and Zhandari, who leisurely strolled arm in arm down the street as the evening shadows gradually overtook them.

CHAPTER 63
THE SHADOWS ALWAYS FEAST

Shadows feast first on those who let their guard down. - Poliormos

Zhandari glanced over her shoulder, checking for prying eyes. When she spotted none, she clutched Magda's arm to stop her, fingers digging as a deep frown settled on her face.

"This isn't right."

Magda's glare dropped to Zhandari's hand, and she made a quiet, warning noise. Zhandari huffed and let go. "Why are you doing this?"

"I made her a promise," Magda said softly, something unreadable flickering through her eyes. "And I intend to keep it."

Zhandari grimaced, not amused by Magda's display of loyalty.

"I can't turn back now," Magda added. "Please, keep it up a little longer." She brushed her fingers against Zhandari's cheek, tender and pleading. "For me?"

Zhandari exhaled loudly. "I'm unhappy about the farce. This is dangerous, Magda—and you know it. We can't afford to become enemies of the Crown—"

"And we won't."

"If Prince Jordha finds out..." Zhandari huffed, her voice low. "I can't lose you. One more day. Then we're out."

"Thank you. One more day is all I ask."

Zhandari's eyes narrowed, and she glanced behind them. "Did you hear that?"

Magda shook her head. "Must've been another feral cat. The Zhegami keep them around to deal with the rats."

Zhandari's eyes flicked up to the rooftops before she turned away. Nothing moved—but an icy shiver crept down her spine.

Magda gave her a sidelong glance. "Everything all right, love?"

Zhandari shook her head and forced a smile. "Nothing. The shadows are just... heavy tonight. This job... It's getting to me."

Magda looped her arm through hers, smiling widely. "Ale and a warm bed will take care of that."

❦

Above them, a shadow waited, crouched in the narrow recess of a rooftop overlooking the royal compound. His cold, calculating eyes were fixed on the two unsuspecting women descending the sidewalk.

General Aghet Mendi watched them, intrigued by their tense exchange, while casually twirling a wicked-looking dagger in his bloodied hand.

"Would they tell me everything if I tortured them?" he asked the wide-eyed corpse behind him. "Hitzalkea are tough to break," he mused, pondering strategies. "But those two are familiar with the residence's layout. That will be useful information." He studied the deep slash on the man's neck and the blood pooling under him. "You didn't provide anything useful." He heaved a dramatic sigh. "I suppose Prince Jordha doesn't train Shadow Walkers as he used to."

A tendril of silver mist, coiled around his arm, fought Aghet's grip. "Oh, no. You aren't going anywhere," he uttered with grim satisfaction. "You're part of my collection now."

The soul strained against Aghet's hold, attempting to release itself. As it gradually turned black, its chilling shriek echoed down his arm. In an instant, it vanished, absorbed into Aghet's body.

He moaned, pleased. "That completes my healing." He patted his torso, pleased that the pain had subsided. "I can't believe she slashed my arm and kicked me that hard." He puckered his lips, unhappy with his next thought. "Her fire magic is a challenge, though." He turned his right hand over a few times, watching with relief as the burn scars gradually faded, disappearing bit by bit.

"I almost had her." He regretted not being fast enough to sink his dagger into her, but there would be more opportunities to capture her.

"Once the Akumi king's soul is in my prince's body, all will be as it should." For a moment, his hunger faded, and memories bled through the haze in his mind. The handsome king and his warm touch. His glorious smile—the one meant only for Aghet. How his voice always softened when speaking Aghet's name.

He closed his eyes and exhaled slowly. "Soon." He lifted his gaze to the night. "Soon, yours will be the lips I kiss."

Satisfied, his gaze returned to the street below.

The two women kept their pace, oblivious to his presence lurking above. He eyed the body behind him with boredom, his mind teeming with the darkness that usually enshrouded his heart. "Soon, the others will come looking for you. I must act fast."

He pondered his next step as he cleaned his dagger with the dead Shadow Walker's cloak.

"The festivities start tomorrow." He threw Sharan a glimpse and turned to the corpse. "I missed the Silver Moon Festival seven years ago. That stupid child burned me senseless in that tunnel, taking me too long to recover. I almost had her the other night, you know?" He studied his hand, clenching and unclenching it around an invisible object. "Her neck is so small." That thought excited him the most.

His dark chuckle melted into the night. "I had her—then she went up in flames. A cursed dragon wrapped in a rabbit's fur."

His disappointment flared for an instant.

"A night festival." An evil smile tugged at the corners of his lips. "It should make things interesting."

A thought popped into his head, bringing a broad grin. "You know what else would make things interesting?" He elbowed the corpse as if they were good friends. "A scar."

CHAPTER 64
THE RED SHAWL

I love you without condition. I give to you without reason. I care for you without expectation. Unwavering. Selfless. Genuine. With endless devotion. - Poliormos

The next morning, Magda and Zhandari assisted Kharis and Saya in preparing for the day's events. Just before they left, Magda gave Kharis a final once-over, smoothing her clothes and perfecting her hair. Stepping back, she nodded in approval. "There. All done. You look lovely, Your Highness."

Kharis begged to differ.

The form-fitting red-and-gold embroidered top was stiff and tight, and the corset boning dug into her waist. She could barely raise her arms, much less expand her chest to breathe. The long, flowing skirt was no better. Endless folds of silk tangled around her legs, hindering her movement if she needed to run or defend herself. The ornate headpiece clamped her head. The choker, an intricate cascade of gold and sparkling crystal, hung heavy around her neck. Each jingle from her gold and silver bangles grated on her nerves—a sound she associated with the staff Arjun Ghan used to maintain her rhythm during training. She wanted them off.

Worse still, Magda had taken her daggers away. "There's

no need for these, Your Highness. Your sizable White Guard escort is sufficient."

Kharis whimpered.

Used to simple, functional clothing (and her daggers), she felt at odds. But something else had added to her discomfort. Her mother had died the night of the Harvest Moon Festival twenty years ago. On this night, the Sendatorsum didn't celebrate—it mourned. Getting dressed this way was a betrayal.

"I can't move," she whined.

"You're not required to," Magda said. "These clothes signal your status as an imperial Zahari princess. Therefore, you don't move. We do."

"But these clothes yell, 'Look at me.'"

"Precisely the point—for people to look at you."

Kharis shuddered at the thought. It was going to be a long day. She groaned and complained nonstop. Magda, undeterred, moved to ensure absolute perfection.

Gently, she nudged Kharis to a full-length mirror, where they stared at a Zahari princess. Kohl framed her blue-gray eyes. Gold dust accented her cheeks. Merlot-colored rouge shaded her lips. Glossy crown braids adorned her black hair.

When Saya entered the room, wearing similar clothing, she halted mid-step. "You're so beautiful." Her eyes sparkled with affection. "I forget how arresting you are."

Kharis glanced away with a pout.

"You are lovely." Saya kissed her forehead. "A beautiful woman."

Kharis hummed, still pouting.

"The carriage is outside. Are you ready?"

"No." Kharis heaved a loud sigh. "But I don't have a choice."

Before they entered the carriage, Kharis caught sight of General Zhegur, who, spellbound, gazed at Saya in a not-so-discreet manner. Saya, as expected, was clueless about the attention she'd garnered from the general, making Kharis wonder. If the Voice had a face, would he gaze at her the same way?

"Doesn't she look exquisite?" Kharis asked the general as Saya got in the carriage with his help.

"Yes, she is." A pause. He then swallowed hard, wide eyes bouncing all over the place. "Both of you," he quickly added.

Saya threw her sister a glare, aware of what she'd done. Kharis bit back a wicked laugh. The general was about to get into position, flanking the carriage on foot, but Kharis had other ideas.

"General Zhegur, please join us."

The request confused the man.

"For our protection," she explained. "I'm sure our brother, the crown prince, will sleep better at night." She smiled all too innocently while gesturing to the space next to Saya. "Please, sit with us."

Zhegur pressed his lips, clearly torn between duty and desire. With a gentle nudge from Kharis, he climbed the carriage and sat beside Saya, his back so stiff Kharis could hardly contain her laughter. Her sister, equally rigid, blushed.

"Do you play xakea?" Kharis asked.

General Zhegur nodded, wearing a tight smile.

"My sister's an excellent player," Kharis said. "No one can compare. You should challenge her." She sighed in mock frustration. "I've been trying to beat her for a while, but I suspect she cheats."

"Khiri."

Kharis ignored Saya's warning. "Play with her, please. Keep an eye, then report your findings to me, will you?" She stared at the general, her eyelashes fluttering. "Promise me."

General Zhegur shifted slightly on the cushioned seat, quickly folding his hands in his lap—his attempt at composure.

"It would be an honor."

"Perfect. After dinner, then." Kharis leaned against the window, watching the world go by to give them a little time to steal glances from each other.

Kharis and Saya had breakfast with Governor Azim and his wife, Lady Farrazhin.

The sisters did their best to conceal their shock.

Farrazhin was a woman of common sense who possessed poise and sophistication. Her smile was warm, and her voice was soothing. Azim's worshipping eyes followed her everywhere.

Kharis couldn't help but gawk, wondering if the woman had ever raised her voice. There was no way she yelled at him. None.

The sisters toured a few city sites with the governor and his secretary and met with architects and hazenka leaders. After a few hours, all faces blurred. Excited, Azim took them to more places as more people showed up with flowers, boxed Zhegami candies, and other gifts. They were giddy to meet the royals—individuals not in any of the schedules the governor had shared with them during breakfast.

General Zhegur, never far from the sisters, threw Azim glare after glare.

The day would end with a visit to the main temple for the midnight ringing of the moonbell. Thus, by early afternoon, General Zhegur rescued the sisters and recited some obscure rule on Zahari protocol that Governor Azim had disregarded.

Embarrassed, the governor fumbled his words. "Yes," he scraped a hand through his hair. "Thank you for your assistance, General Zhegur. How clumsy of me." He giggled nervously. "One must not falter on royal etiquette. Yes, we shall see you this evening."

Kharis kept her mouth shut, aware no such rule existed, and swiftly climbed into the carriage, pulling Saya along. "You're deadly," she told General Zhegur, in awe of the man.

With a self-satisfied smile, he gave her a wink. Saya breathed a sigh of relief and sat back.

"These heeled slippers are killing me," Kharis grumbled. "Why can't I wear boots?"

Saya arched an eyebrow. "With that dress?"

Kharis sniffed.

The sisters savored their late lunch and tea, finding solace in the peaceful silence of the royal grounds. Kharis watched Saya and General Zhegur play a round of xakea until she eventually had to endure another change of clothes and hairdo. She complained. Magda ignored her.

"It'll get cool in the evening." Magda draped a luxurious shawl over Kharis's shoulders. Its rich red color perfectly complemented her garments. Gold embroidery adorned its edges, and the silk-threaded tassels in the corners sported tiny bells that chimed softly with her movements.

"Bells?" Kharis asked.

"They keep evil spirits away, Your Highness. A tradition among the Zhegami. Besides, this one will keep you warm this evening."

"It's so incredibly soft," Kharis exclaimed, running her fingers over the luxurious fabric.

"It's made from the finest wool in the region," Magda added with a hint of pride. "Do you approve, Your Highness?"

"I love it. The dress, not so much." Kharis could've sworn she saw Magda roll her eyes at her.

CHAPTER 65
THE HARVEST MOON
FESTIVAL

Beware the monster who toys with your senses, twisting what you see, hear, and feel—for their cruelty lies not in fangs or flames, but in the slow unraveling of your reality. - Poliormos

Soon, a horse-drawn carriage arrived, taking Kharis and Saya to the city's main temple. Their White Guard escort flanked them on foot. Under her lovely dress, Kharis wore... boots.

Zhegama's main temple rested on the city's highest point. The Zahar-Katea peaks, draped in a snowy mantle, provided a magnificent backdrop, reminding Kharis of the ascent still ahead.

A large crowd had gathered on the enormous terrace, which served as the viewing spot for the ancient ritual, and more continued to arrive. City dignitaries and notables sat closer to the bell structure in one of two reserved sections.

Governor Azim waved at them, and the sisters approached. Spotting Master Hillal two rows behind them, she waved at him. He waved back, his face always kind and fatherly. Then Kharis swiftly took her seat.

The moonbell loomed high within its towering wooden frame. The bell's sheer size commanded awe, with exquisite carvings and raised designs adorning the metal. Kharis's fingers tingled with the urge to trace every delicate etching and feel the history woven into its surface.

Noticing her interest, the governor's wife leaned in. "Our moonbell was cast three hundred years ago. Of all the moon-bells in the Empire, ours is the oldest."

"Even older than the one in the Ghak?" Kharis asked.

The woman nodded, filled with Zhegami pride. "Forged and cast here. Ours was the first. The one in Zahar-Ghak was our gift to the capital city."

"I didn't know that. I have much to learn, and your guidance would be most welcome."

Farrazhin patted Kharis's hand in a motherly gesture. "It would be my honor."

The farther Kharis was from the Ghak, the nicer people were. She smiled, drawing in a deep breath filled with incense, and adjusted the red shawl over her shoulders.

When the prayer chanting ended, a sacred silence enveloped the terrace. Several bhiksunim gathered and held onto the ends of ropes tethered to a large wooden beam, pulling in unison. The beam swung and struck the bell, and the resonant toll thundered through the cool air.

The sound slammed into Kharis, rippling through her chest, burrowing deep, shaking something loose. Her fingers clawed at her shawl, trying to still the ache blooming there.

Another toll.

The vibrations rattled through her bones, stirring ghosts of memory.

Had Noam reached Urrun? Was he settled by now? Was he safe? Was he blowing on the zenka whistle? Memories of his warm smile and kind eyes came to her.

With the seventh toll, Zhegama burst into life with music and fireworks. The streets flooded with people, their joyous clamor drifting into the temple grounds. Bonfires dotted the cityscape, and small, ivory-colored lights adorned the skies.

"Those are paper lanterns," Lady Farrazhin explained. "We write wishes on them and release them so Sharan can read them. With a little luck, some are granted."

"They are beautiful. Would we be able to light one?" Kharis asked.

"Of course." A smile graced Lady Farrazhin's face. "I'll ask Azim to procure some for us."

"Thank you." Kharis tilted her head, watching them drift, when a sharp, high-pitched screech pierced her ears. She flinched, but Lady Farrazhin didn't, as if she hadn't heard a thing.

The festival noise, from lively music to small fireworks, crested over Kharis, drowning out everything around her. Then, a crawling sensation assaulted her skin, stronger this time. She froze, trying to make sense of it. *It can't be him.* Kharis shook her head vehemently. *No. Impossible.* Ghan had sent him to Almarim.

Kharis swept her gaze across the crowd, but no matter where she turned, a shadowy figure lingered out of sight, yet watching her. The sudden chill made the hairs on the back of her neck stand on end.

The Voice growled like a feral beast. A ripple of protectiveness quickened inside her.

"Saya!" she shouted, but her sister, ahead, didn't seem to hear her over the firecrackers and excited shouts.

A dangerous hiss drifted toward her, and a frisson of fear coursed through her. She searched the sea of heads, but no one had shown signs of hearing it. Was it her? Was she going mad?

People in the reserved sections moved slowly, some stopping to chat, blocking the way out. The chill of that wicked stare intensified, and every muscle in her body tensed. The owner of those eyes was closing in, and the urge to shove people out of her way built up inside her.

Move it, people. She anxiously tapped her boots on the cobblestones.

Governor Azim had also stopped to greet a few attendees, and Kharis cursed him under her breath.

In this chaos, she didn't see their escort. Her gaze roamed the mass of humanity as she jumped over people's shoulders to search for them. People had flooded the temple, the plaza

A.S.R. GELPI

filled with bodies, an overwhelming mix of scents, and a cacophony of noise.

A second hiss resonated louder—closer. Desperate, Kharis searched for it.

Left? No.

Right? No.

"Behind you," came the Voice's strained whisper, edged in fear. *"He's here."*

"Who?"

She spun, frantic, scanning for a face that didn't belong. The crushing presence of people enveloped her, all inching their way out of the temple grounds. Then, amidst the throng, she saw it—and her eyes widened in shock.

The air rippled around a tall, black figure steadily closing in. She recognized the posture immediately—the attacker who had killed the fox. A hood concealed his face, but Kharis could feel the piercing glare and the sinister smile hinting at imminent victory beneath it.

"Spear me!"

Her breathing quickened. The threat from this attacker awakened her magic, and the air around her heated swiftly. Molten lava coursed through her veins, fueling the magic surging from her core and branching into her limbs. It swelled, threatening to burst into flames.

No. No. Not now. Not here. And not when so many people surrounded her.

Beads of sweat rolled down her back, and her muscles tensed as she battled for control. Desperate to tamp back the magical surge, Kharis clenched her hands tightly, nails biting into her palms. The sharp sting grounded her somewhat.

Behind her, the figure effortlessly weaved through the multitude, the air around him warping.

This had been his plan all along. To corner her here, among the crush of bodies, where any spark of her fire magic would unleash chaos. Where she wouldn't dare fight back without burning them all.

"Saya!" Kharis shouted over the noise.

364

Saya turned, one finger tapping her ear to signal she couldn't hear her. *"What is it?"* she signed, using hizkuntza.

Kharis's gaze darted back and forth, desperately searching for the intruder. The crowd had become a maze of lurking shadows and hidden threats.

"Khiri, what's going on?"

"I'm trapped," Kharis signed back. *"Help me."*

Her fear gushed through the bond. Saya sensed it immediately, her eyes widening in understanding, now aware that something was terribly wrong. Saya stumbled on her way to her while the throng jostled Kharis's body. Shoulders slammed into her, knocking her off balance. Elbows jabbed her sides, and someone's foot snagged the hem of her gown, nearly sending her to the ground.

A male chuckle echoed in her ears, sharp and unnervingly close. The attacker was closing in. And yet, no matter how hard she searched, she was alone in a sea of unfamiliar faces.

"Behind you!" The Voice's cry was ragged, panicked.

Unnaturally frigid fingers clamped around her arm, sending a jolt of icy pain through her body. Kharis doubled over from the shock.

A sharp yank followed—but instead of resisting, Kharis moved with the pull, twisting hard toward the pressure. The sudden shift threw her attacker off balance, just enough for her to wrench her arm free. Kharis started, but the cold grip returned, snagging her shawl this time—cinching it around her throat. She choked, panic flaring.

Instinct surged. She drove her heel backward, connecting with something solid—a shin, she hoped. As the pressure slackened, Kharis ducked low and spun out of the tangled fabric, slipping from his reach. She moved, shoving through the crush of bodies, jostling shoulders, drawing startled cries —until she collided with Saya.

"Khiri, what's happening?" Saya caught her, eyes still wide.

Before she could answer, another hand seized her—a warm, calloused hand. Startled, Kharis clung to Saya as someone yanked them into motion.

Behind them, the shadowy figure let out a piercing shriek that echoed painfully in Kharis's mind.

He held the red shawl aloft—a trophy, a warning—and vanished into the crowd.

CHAPTER 66
BITTER TEA AND
FIREWORKS

Deceit is the dark shadow that clouds the light of truth. It is a poison that damages the soul. - Poliormos

Magda moved, determined, shoving and jostling through a sea of bodies—her hand clamped around Kharis's arm.

Kharis stumbled, the crowd pressing from all sides, hot breath and incense thick in the air. Robes brushed her skin, sandals scraped stone, and the noise was a deafening blend of chants, shouts, footsteps, and clanging brass. A shoulder slammed into hers. Someone yelled, and a prayer bell rang too close to her ear.

Then a sudden turn. Stone walls rose on either side, and the press of people faded like a receding tide. Magda had yanked Kharis into a narrow alleyway, pulling the sisters free from the throng of the temple crowd.

She barely paused, her grip still firm on Kharis. "Inside," she urged them, shoving open the door of a teashop and ushering the sisters in. The shopkeeper barely spared them a glance, jerking his head toward the stairs. Magda didn't hesitate, nudging Kharis and Saya forward. "Quickly."

Kharis wavered. "Shouldn't we call on the White Guard?"

Magda ignored the question, pushing them into a private

tearoom on the second floor. Inside, a cloaked figure stood by a curtained window, silently watching the procession of people below. At the sound of their arrival, the woman lowered her hood.

"You made it," she said softly. Her eyes flicked to the window as if calculating how much time remained before the parade was below it. "You may approach."

Magda closed the door behind her.

"And who are you to command us?" Kharis asked, already unnerved by Magda's behavior.

The woman resembled Saya: wearing similar chestnut curls framing large eyes, a defined jaw, and a dimpled chin. It was the same face as in a palace portrait, showing a fifteen-year-old girl posing beside the queen and king of Zahar on her birthmark. All sorts of thoughts slammed into Kharis at once. This couldn't be happening.

"Please, join me." The woman gestured to the floor cushions. "I'm grateful you agreed to meet me."

"Agreed?" Kharis scoffed. "We haven't agreed to meet anyone, much less you."

The woman smiled ruefully at Kharis. "You too, Saya. Please, sit. Let me see your faces."

Neither Kharis nor Saya sat.

"Who are you?" Kharis asked without ceremony.

The woman heaved a long, sad sigh. "Please, sit," she insisted, well-mannered. "I mean you no harm. This situation isn't as ideal as I'd hoped, but I'm here to ensure your safety."

"Who. Are. You?" Kharis's voice turned harsher—threatening. She needed confirmation.

The woman gazed at her with glistening eyes. "Götrid, your sister." She clutched her hands nervously. "I can't blame you if you don't recognize me."

Resentment sharpened Kharis's tongue. There were portraits of her face everywhere in the imperial residence. "Regular visits or letters would've taken care of that." Her anger simmered. "Why now?"

"Magda can't hold off my escort for long, much less yours. Please, let me speak to you—"

"Why would I listen?" Kharis clenched her hands and turned toward the door. Questions battered her mind relentlessly, sharp as thorns, yet she was determined not to give Götrid a moment of her time.

Saya grabbed her elbow and pointed to a floor cushion. "Our sister doesn't present a risk." Her voice was firm. "This is a kindness we shouldn't refuse."

"A kindness?" Kharis huffed. "Surely, you speak in jest."

Saya shook her head. Kharis clamped her mouth, seething at Saya, then at Götrid. "Fine," she spat.

"Thank you," Götrid said, sadness shaping her smile. "I'm here to fulfill a promise I made to Mavah. I thought you would never leave the Sendatorsum, so I seized the opportunity when I learned of this trip from Khator."

Khator. Another name. Another log added to the fire blazing inside her.

"It's a substantial journey," Saya said, hoping to diffuse the tension. "If you came here from Almarim."

"Quite." Kharis brimmed with sarcasm. "Especially since Almarim's closer to the Ghak."

"Khiri, please."

Kharis scowled at Saya. "I'm repaying Götrid's kindness by giving in equal measure. Nothing for nothing."

Saya glared. "Sarcasm doesn't become you."

"Please," Götrid urged, palms up. "Don't argue, not now. Our time is short, and I must tell you about the night Mavah died."

"Why?" Kharis bared her teeth.

Götrid trembled, averting Kharis's intense gaze. "Jordha and I were in love. We wanted to discuss our desire to marry—"

"What does that have to do with my question?" Kharis demanded.

A pause. "When we entered Mavah's rooms, she and Athon were dead."

Kharis froze. The urge to argue left her body.

"That night," Götrid said, "fewer guards were stationed, and most servants were at the festival. Mavah, pregnant with

369

you, was too close to her due date, so she stayed, and Lord Athon refused to leave her side. Taking advantage of the lax security, an assassin entered her chambers. Lord Athon fought them off before succumbing to his wounds."

Kharis's body turned ice-cold.

"Mavah was stabbed," Götrid continued. "But the attacker didn't finish the job. When Jordha and I found their bodies, you were bundled between sheets in Mavah's arms."

Kharis felt as if the air had been sucked from the room and sank into a cushion. "S—She didn't die in childbirth?"

Götrid shook her head slowly. "She bled to death due to slash wounds in her lower abdomen."

Wounds. Plural.

"Someone cut you out of Mavah."

Breath fled Kharis. The aroma of fried foods and cheap tea wafting through the door assaulted her nose, and the pungent scent of black gunpowder burned her nostrils. Revolted, her insides churned, and her corset became tighter.

When she swayed on the cushion, Saya held her.

Götrid's hands shook so hard she couldn't sip tea from her cup. "Shock swept through the Sendatorsum. The Queen, The Morning Star, was gone. Grief-stricken, Tavah shut down— he'd lived for her. Her loss broke him.

"Hala, as heir, stepped in. Within days and under his regency, the Regia-Zenka enforced tighter security and ordered our removal. He claimed it was for our safety."

Götrid's chest swelled with her sharp inhale.

"Tavah shattered into tiny pieces and shut everyone out. Khator, Helena, and I didn't want to leave him when he was gone from us like this, lost in his anguish. We argued Hala's decision, but he forced us out anyway."

"Did Tavah know how she died?" Saya asked.

Dread etched deep lines on Götrid's ashen face, and she shook her head again. "Hala..." Her lips thinned as she clasped her hands to keep them from shaking. The scent of her fear was intense, like the flowers of the ash tree. "Hala forced us to lie to the Regia-Zenka."

Saya gasped.

Kharis's world stopped spinning.

"My assumption," Götrid continued, "is that he also lied to Tavah. That the official story was death on the birthing bed."

"Why?" Saya asked.

"I wish I knew. The servants—" Götrid squeezed her eyes shut. "The ones who witnessed the scene when we entered—our only proof of foul play—vanished without a trace."

Kharis let those words sink in like ink on parchment, staining her intensely.

Götrid continued, "Hala told the Regia-Zenka that Mavah had died in childbirth. Athon's death was attributed to her death, given their strong magical connection. Outside of Hala, only four others know what truly happened: Jordha, Khator, Helena, and I, and we're heavily monitored."

The outside noise filled the room and hammered Kharis's head. Her headpiece squeezed her temples like a tightening clamp. The hairpins dug into her scalp.

"Hala tried to push Nana out—but no one outfoxes her. As head royal physician, she insisted on examining the body herself. One look, and she knew Mavah had been murdered. But she hasn't been able to prove anything—Hala controls the narrative."

Kharis sat in shock. Not a muscle twitched; not a single thought surfaced.

"Hala...?" Saya uttered.

"He won't leave Tavah's side," Götrid said. "Helena and I are barred from the Ghak. I know my letters to the Senda-torsum are intercepted, so I hide my messages in the aljaicin wrappers I send Nana monthly."

"Only Khator visits, reporting to Tavah once a month—but never alone," Götrid said. "Hala's always there, finding reasons to stay. His Hasheret escorts Khator to and from the river barge."

"Why are you telling us this?" Saya asked.

Götrid hesitated, her gaze flicking to the door once, twice. "Because I fear for your safety."

Her fingers twisted her cloak.

"When Mavah was pregnant with her fifth child, she fell

mysteriously ill. The bhiksunim found no cause. Even Nana was baffled. She began slipping away, and in desperation, Tavah called on Athon, who brought her back from Anda-heimur—but it was too late for the child. Athon suspected poison but couldn't prove it. From that night on, he never left her side and insisted that her food be tasted first."

Götrid wiped her tears.

"Her illness faded, and she later became pregnant with you, but Athon feared the cycle would return—so he grew overprotective of Mavah."

Kharis pondered every piece of this intricate puzzle— Nana's dislike of Hala, Lord Athon's portrait hanging on some forgotten corridor, the lack of letters or visits from her siblings, and the peculiar friendship Hala had with Jordha, as if Jordha were forced to do Hala's bidding. And her brother's imposed rules and overwhelming control...? She thought it was broth-erly love, but now?

A different picture had emerged, and it sickened her.

"A few days before Mavah died," Götrid said, "she had a vision. She never shared it, but gave me these." She handed Kharis a small leather pouch. "Open it."

Kharis glanced at it, but Saya gently bumped her shoulder. Yielding to Saya, she unfastened it and took two leather bracelets, each holding a jade stone.

"Those are beacon stones. When these bracelets are sepa-rated, the gem in one will lead the wearer to the gem in the other." Götrid pulled them apart, but the power governing them drew them together like magnets.

"As a gift from the immortals," she continued, "the stones are imbued with magic and have been used between the Sorukhipa and the Djinnshirukh for centuries to find each other. Mavah instructed me to hold onto them, never revealing their existence. She also ordered me never to hand these to Hala, even if he became the Djinnshirukh."

That wistful smile returned to her face.

"They're yours now."

The world lost its sharpness.

"Khiri?" Saya asked, her fingers tenderly brushing Kharis's arm.

Kharis clutched the bracelets, her hand shaking as she struggled to rein in twenty years of resentment: siblings who knew the truth yet never came to take her away from Hala's clutches. Prohibitions that made no sense. Hala's shadow dominating every aspect of her life.

Secrets.

Omissions.

Deceit.

Outside, people had lined the street to watch a parade. Everyone sang and clapped, providing the rhythm to the slow-approaching float. Their music and noise filled the tearoom.

Saya tapped her arm, worried. "Khiri?"

Kharis pounded her fist on the table, rattling the teacups.

"What do you want, Götrid?" Her voice sharpened. "After twenty-one years, you want to serve me tea and chat about our family?" Anger and sarcasm burned her lips. "Now you come to tell me something that should've been disclosed years ago?" She shoved the bracelets into the pouch and gave it to Saya.

"I don't remember you attempting to write or visit, no matter how convoluted the circumstances might have been. You forgot about us. But now you play loving sister, deter-mined to protect me?" Her blood boiled. "What do you want? If you're here, you want something from me. Let's hear it and be done with this charade."

Outside, singers chanted as drums resounded louder and louder, making the walls vibrate. The singing was reaching a feverish crescendo.

Götrid's eyes teared up as she gulped, her throat bobbing up and down. "The children of a female Djinnshirukh may carry aspects of the Djinnshirukh's power. As a result, a female Djinnshirukh is discouraged from bearing children because their offspring lack the protection the Djinnshirukh possesses."

An icy dagger pierced Kharis's chest.

"Our mavah chose to risk it, refusing the idea of surrogates. The curse bypassed Hala, Khator, Helena, and me, but it hit my youngest daughter, Ananya. She's only twelve, Kharis. Twelve."

A shiver seized Kharis's body. She'd been told this, but no one had ever explained why.

"For two years, Ananya endured terrible visions," Götrid said. "We were powerless to help. The magic dragged her into Andaheimur, where she saw things no child should. Then it cast her out once it realized she wasn't the Djinnshirukh." Her hands trembled. "At first, she spoke of what she saw: a long, dark tunnel... a monster... the world in flames... a terrible hum in the distance."

Kharis's stomach turned to stone—those were her nightmares.

"The visions worsened," Götrid said. "Ananya couldn't sleep. She stopped eating. And two months ago, she succumbed to the last one. She's been unconscious ever since."

The parade was now in front of the teashop. The drums and trumpets rattled the walls and windows, sending tremors through the worn wooden floorboards and reverberating in Kharis's head.

Götrid got on all fours, her forehead touching the dirty rug. "Please help my child. Her soul's imprisoned in Andaheimur. Please bring her back to me."

Magda slid the door open. "We must go. Now."

Kharis didn't move, blankly staring at Götrid. The chaos in her head was overwhelming. The bruising blow of betrayal. A sister begging for help. Lies and more lies.

Somehow, Saya and Magda lifted her off the cushion because her body didn't obey her. She would've punched Götrid otherwise.

Götrid grabbed Kharis's ankles, unwilling to let go. "Kharis, please."

Saya pulled on Kharis while Magda unclasped Götrid's hands. "Please, Your Highness, you must let her go." She struggled with Götrid, who refused to release Kharis.

Götrid shouted over the resonant din rattling the room, "Bring my daughter back. Please, I beg you. Hate me if you must, but please save her. She's innocent in all of this."

Saya and Magda dragged Kharis away, or perhaps she was floating away, disconnected from her body. Kharis couldn't tell anymore. Her heart had shattered. The world around her seemed different—distorted. Sounds became distant echoes. Tears blurred her vision, and their salty taste lingered on her lips.

Götrid, with her forehead pressed against the tea-stained rug, bawled with desperation, repeating the same thing, "Please, save her. Please, save my sweet Ani."

Magda and Saya lugged Kharis down the stairs, the three women stepping into the narrow alleyway.

Kharis snatched her arms from Saya and clung to the rough wall to regain her balance. The world whirled around her in a disorienting blur, and the sensation of everything spinning out of control engulfed her senses.

The scent of fried food and bitter tea turned her stomach. The loud, raucous music assaulted her ears. The acrid stench of sulfur powder and vomit sickened her. In her nightmares, she sank into the murky depths of an icy lake, and her lungs burned with the lack of oxygen. She was sinking again.

Air. I need air.

She grabbed the top of her dress, so tight on her chest that she could barely breathe. Her fingers clawed at the fabric, her nails catching at the delicate threads. She yanked at the seams, tearing the organza sleeves, her heart beating erratically to the sound of the ripping fabric. She wrested the heavy necklace off, and hundreds of tiny gold beads and crystals cascaded to the sticky ground. Frantic, she snatched her headpiece off, pulling her hair out.

The sounds of drums bashed her head and made her insides shake to the unrelenting rhythm. Her throat burned with every scream, with every urge to tear, rip, break, and crush—to explode and burn this world.

She was about to when the night was ablaze with fireworks as if the universe had chosen to do it for her. Their strident explosions pierced the heavens, and the night bled, blooms of red splattering the sky. Their resounding booms punctuated each burst, and their vibrations rippled through the air, rattling the windows of nearby buildings. This sent the crowds into a feverish clamor while Kharis's world whirled nonstop, off balance.

She held onto the wall to make it stop—to make everything stop.

Frantic, Saya yelled at her, but Kharis no longer heard anything. The hammering rush of blood through her ears drowned everything.

Darkness crept at the edges of her vision, turning everything black as she plunged into a bottomless void.

CHAPTER 67
THE WEIGHT OF TRUTH

Cradled in silence, truth gains mass, becoming a steady anchor. It carries the weight of mountains, but it is also the quiet force that tips the scales of consciousness, its heaviness felt only by those willing to bear witness. - Poliormos

A chorus of shouts echoed in the distance—soldiers calling cadence as they marched past the window. Their rhythm was sharp and steady, a heartbeat of order far removed from the chaos in Kharis's mind. When she opened her eyes, morning light stabbed through the curtains, intensifying the pounding in her head. All she could remember was the dark alley, the stench, and the strident, *spear-me-forever* noise.

Her throat burned, and the taste of bile lingered on her tongue. Scratches lined her arms and chest—long pink tracks healing fast. The Akumi king, as always, ensured his vessel's speedy recovery.

He, however, did nothing to cure her sense of defeat.

Saya, asleep beside her, felt her move and stirred awake. "How are you doing?"

Kharis remained silent, unsure how to answer that question. There were so many ways to respond, and none felt quite right.

"My throat burns," was all she said.

Saya offered a wistful smile, opening her arms. "Come here." The safety of that hug stilled Kharis's anxious thoughts.

"Khiri?"

Kharis heard it in Saya's voice: the need to discuss whatever Kharis didn't want to discuss.

"We must consider Ananya's situation," Saya murmured. "She's innocent."

"I can't enter Andaheimur, remember?" Kharis snapped. "How exactly am I supposed to bring her back?" Tears stung her eyes. "You can do it. The Sorukhipa can save the day."

Saya heaved a long sigh. "As your Sorukhipa, I enter Andaheimur to rescue you. Unlike the Djinnshirukh, I lack the power to stay and search—"

An anguished wail pushed past Kharis's lips. "Why did everyone lie to us? Everyone, Saya. Even Nana."

"You don't know that."

A hot surge of anger crept under Kharis's skin. "Nana prepared Mavah's body for cremation. Nothing escapes her; you know that better than anyone. She knew our mavah was murdered." That knowledge hollowed her chest, cleaving her heart out of it. The heat behind her eyelids stung her eyes. "She knew."

Saya didn't utter a word.

"Why?" Kharis shook her head. "Why do this?"

Kharis exhaled in dismay, swallowing tears. "And now, Ananya, an innocent bystander, is caught in this mess." She heaved a long, low sigh. "I'd hoped for this to be a bad dream. Any moment now, I would wake up to the reality where Hala is a caring yet overprotective brother, and our siblings are simply selfish."

A bitter chuckle escaped her—twenty-one years of deceit now tainted every memory of her brother.

"Is this why we weren't allowed to leave the Senda?" she asked. "So we wouldn't learn the truth?" She curled away from her sister. "Khator, Helena, and Götrid left. They abandoned us in that place with Hala and Uncle. Had they come to fetch us, the massacre would've never happened." She pressed her fists against her temples. "But they. Did. Nothing."

"Khiri, please."

"No," Kharis shouted. "Let me be."

"I am not," Saya blurted out.

"I said—"

Saya wrapped her arms around Kharis again. "Do not ask me to leave you. Not when you're like this."

Kharis didn't fight her tears any longer. "I just don't care anymore."

She tried to pull away from Saya, but her sister only tightened her grip.

"I know, Khiri. *I know*." She pressed her sister against her chest. "Cry. Scream. Do whatever you need. But I'm not leaving you, for there's no world where you aren't with me."

The weight of everything she'd been holding inside came crashing down. She struggled to catch her breath between choked sobs and buried herself in Saya's embrace, moaning in anguish, desperate to purge the turmoil within her.

It didn't go away.

The curtains stirred in a gentle breeze, carrying Zhegama's crisp, alpine scent. It curled through the room like a quiet breath, a reminder that beyond this pain, the city still moved— that the world had not stopped.

CHAPTER 68
THE FUTILITY OF HOPE

Some truths strike like lightning—sudden, blinding. They live only a moment. But the thunder lingers, shaking the ground beneath your feet. - Poliormos

General Zhegur met with them for breakfast. Kharis sat quietly beside Saya, unable to touch her food. Nothing tasted right.

Nothing felt right.

Reliable to a fault and usually formal and collected, an unsettled Reza Zhegur provided his report. He looked exhausted, sporting dark circles under his hazel eyes. A dusting of stubble covered his jaw. He hadn't fastened all the buttons on the tunic under his leather jerkin, as if impressing Saya no longer mattered—as if he suspected he would soon be out of a job.

"We were posted in a poor location," he said. "By the time I realized it, the crowd had swept us away. I saw you heading in the other direction, but forcing through would've harmed others, especially children. When I saw Magda leading you out, I assumed she'd taken over for your protection. So, we went with the flow. I'm sorry, Your Highness. It was a grave misjudgment."

"General Zhegur." Saya's calm, modulated voice was the

epitome of common sense. "You found us in time, and we brought my sister back with your assistance. Thank you for your service last night."

He lowered his wrinkled brow to accept whatever fate awaited him. "I'm deeply sorry for what happened. I should've remained by your side at all times."

"There's nothing to apologize for," Saya insisted, offering a kind smile. "Unfortunately, it appears the confusion overtook us all."

Kharis didn't think so. Magda had betrayed them. That sting ran deeper than she'd expected.

"I'm still embarrassed that your safety was jeopardized under my command." General Zhegur rubbed his face and turned to Kharis. "How are you doing, Your Highness?"

"We're both exhausted," Saya quickly answered, "but glad the incident didn't escalate. It'll be best if you handle security logistics rather than Governor Maharghan. We must be better prepared for the remaining events."

The general lifted his head, disbelief flickering through his face. There was a beat of silence before the order settled with him. "Consider it done, Your Highness. I won't let this happen again."

"What about Magda?" Kharis asked.

He shook his head. "Magda and Zhandari were absent this morning. I've assigned officers to investigate their whereabouts."

A stir at the entrance drew their attention. Heavy footfalls echoed through the chamber, the royal guard's formation parting to reveal Governor Azim Maharghan and his secretary. The governor had arrived as summoned, with a haggard face and dark, swollen bags under his eyes. As he entered the room, he mumbled something about his wife.

He swiftly knelt, head meeting the rug. "Your Highnesses, I offer my deepest apologies. This was an egregious failure of leadership. The fault is mine alone."

Saya and General Zhegur shared a glance. "Governor Maharghan, lift your head."

Azim did, clearing his throat and awaiting his sentence.

Saya exhaled slowly. "Last night, a series of small decisions put together became problematic. My sister and I were kidnapped"—she threw Kharis a glance—"and while we were quickly released, it should've never happened."

The governor swallowed hard.

"While we appreciate the desire to have the White Guard enjoy the festivities," Saya said, "their task is to protect us, not watch ceremonies from the best spots possible. Therefore, General Zhegur must approve any decision connected to our safety to ensure these issues won't happen again." She turned to General Zhegur, and the man gazed at her as if staring at a goddess. "We can all learn from these mistakes."

Saya kept her voice steady, a diplomat to the end. But under the table, her fingers had curled into her skirts, restraining the urge to snap. It deepened Kharis's guilt.

Azim nodded, teary-eyed. "Princess Saya," he sniffled, his voice overly nasal. Zhegama will never forget your kindness." He bowed again—too low, too many times. He dried his nose with an expensive silk handkerchief.

"As for the attendants," Saya said, referring to Magda and Zhandari, "we can replace them. We would be most grateful if you could identify loyal and dependable ones."

Azim sat on his knees, enthusiastic once more. "I'll have two of my best, already vetted and properly trained, come this afternoon." He paused. "If they meet General Zhegur's security requirements, of course." Azim shot him a nervous glance, letting out a shaky laugh. "The daughters of His Serene Imperial Majesty, King Hröld, Son of the Sun, will not lack while I'm governor."

General Zhegur glared at Azim long and hard, and the governor shrank.

"I have one more request," Saya said. "Would you send a tailor over? Last night, my sister's dress was torn."

Azim gasped loudly, his face white as a sheet of paper. "S— Should I bring a healer?"

"It's nothing of that sort," Saya said. "Her dress was ripped and stained in the commotion."

Azim covered his mouth more in fear than surprise. "If my

wife finds out..." His eyes bulged. "Leave it to me. The best seamstress in Zhegama will be here this afternoon." With a hand wave, his secretary ran out the door.

"Thank you." Saya smiled, pleased.

Kharis didn't. She wanted that dress burned.

Breaking the awkward tension, Abhiral entered with Asha and Yanali in tow, trays in hand. "Pistachio nougat for Princess Saya," he announced with a wink. "And for our other princess —royal khir."

He handed Kharis a warm bowl of rice pudding drizzled with honey. "Extra cardamom and ginger. Good for the stomach," he whispered with a fatherly smile—a man who understood the importance of discretion.

Asha followed with a tower of pastel-hued nougat, and Yanali added trays of spiced nuts and dates. The scent of saffron and roasted sugar drifted through the room.

General Zhegur gulped his tea, thankful for the stimulant, and served himself more. Azim eyed all the nougat lustfully but settled for the carrot ones, timidly taking one.

"Abhiral's the best chef in the region," he said. "My wife personally selected him. She wouldn't settle for anyone else to serve you and would've yelled at me had I not followed her recommendations."

Kharis narrowed her eyes, wondering if Lady Farrazhin ran Zhegama.

Soon, Master Hillal arrived. He'd also heard of the incident and wanted to check on the sisters.

"I'll be leaving tomorrow, Your Highness," he said. "I had hoped to accompany you to the Eliza."

The sisters still had six more days before leaving Zhegama.

Hillal continued, "The trek will be on foot. At my age, that will be a challenge. Slowing you down is out of the question. However, a few of my bhiksunim will accompany you." He smiled warmly at Kharis. "Her Highness enjoys their stories."

"Please join us for dinner," Saya said. "Let us send you off."

Excited about the growing list of guests, Abhiral brought more sweets, savory pastries, and never-ending carafes of tea throughout the morning. Eventually, the discussion organically moved to the next phase of their journey to the Zahar-Eliza, debating whether to use an established pass or a shorter, more technical route on a map.

Kharis quietly sipped her tea as she listened to Azim and his secretary discuss departure details with Saya and General Zhegur.

She stared out the window, no longer listening—tired of thinking about everything ahead. The sunlight caught on rooftop tiles; it glinted too brightly as if daring her to move, to do something.

So she did.

She excused herself and headed upstairs.

CHAPTER 69
THE KINDNESS OF STRANGERS

One must brave the unknown to take the first step toward one's north. - Poliormos

Kharis had to break the Djinnshirukh curse before it broke her.

After the incident at the festival, she could feel it creeping closer—madness pressing in, warping her senses, bending the edges of reality. If she didn't act soon, it would unravel her mind completely.

She curled on the cushion by the window, her gaze drifting north. Was the answer waiting at the Zahar-Eliza? Would the Hatorisaita—a conduit of the gods—grant her even a kernel of knowledge? A clue? An answer?

Kharis could almost hear the Eliza calling. Like a single beam of sunlight slicing through storm-dark clouds, it beckoned, promising something miraculous—but only if she came.

After a while, Saya came in to check on her. "How are you doing?"

Kharis shrugged.

"The midday meal will be served soon. Why not come downstairs and join us?" Saya tried again. "You barely touched your morning meal."

"I'm not hungry." Kharis ran a hand through her braid as a

sigh left her, laced with frustration. How could she think about food? She wasn't close to breaking the curse and wasn't even sure if she could. Recognizing the edge in her voice, she tempered it. "My stomach hasn't settled yet."

Saya's eyebrows knitted, framing her concern. "Is there anything I can do?"

Kharis shook her head. "No, but I may go for a walk." A gentle smile graced her lips. "You and General Zhegur have plenty to plan for the journey. Please, don't let me interrupt your work."

"You aren't interrupting."

"Go." Kharis gave her sister a convincing expression. "I'll be fine."

"I'm worried about you."

"Don't." Kharis clenched her jaw. "I'm fine, Saya."

Saya made a grumbling noise. "You and your 'fine.'"

"But I am."

Saya glared at her.

"I swear," Kharis insisted, forcing a smile. "So go."

Resigned, Saya exhaled. "If you need to talk..." She let the silence settle between them.

Kharis saw her sister's eagerness, all the unspoken questions, and the silent plea to confide in her. But Kharis kept her silence behind a forced, reassuring smile.

Saya heaved a quiet sigh. "So be it." She kissed the top of Kharis's head and returned to the meeting downstairs.

All I ever do is make Saya worry. Guilt was a bitter companion.

At the Sendatorsum, each day was a blur of duties and demands, one task bleeding into the next until exhaustion clung to her bones. But here, she had much time to dwell on the things she'd rather ignore. Thinking had become a form of torment.

With a grunt, she exited the bedroom.

Downstairs, Saya, General Zhegur, the governor, and the rest debated routes, mountain passes, security, and a host of other matters. Groaning, Kharis walked away, choosing to stroll around the residence. She walked past the kitchen, its large exterior doors open to let the cool air in, and peeked in.

Abhiral and his helpers sang in Zherik, their joyful laughter floating in the air. Wearing broad smiles, a few stirred lentil pulses and mutton stews, their hips swaying to the catchy rhythm. One strummed a long spoon as if it were an oud. Another twirled with a bowl, whipping egg whites into stiff peaks.

The enticing aromas announced that dinner would be worth the wait. Governor Azim would surely jump at the opportunity.

The sound of sparring reached her ears, sparking an urge. She decided to join them, starting tomorrow.

Kharis found the garden and entered it through the ornate iron gate. The sweet scent of jasmine mingled with the perfume of rose bushes in full bloom, hedging the cobbled pathways. Flowering trees lined the garden, their vibrant blossoms spilling over in shades of purple and sunlit yellow. The wind chimes hanging from their branches clicked melodiously. No evil spirits would be lurking here.

Zhegama took their bells seriously.

A stone path wound its way through dense beds of greenery, where ferns and vines crept up trellises and statues, giving the whole place an air of forgotten enchantment. Birds chirped in the trees, their songs weaving through the rustling of leaves. A nearby fountain gurgled, its water glinting against the sunshine.

Not far, a pergola curved over a large sitting area. Climbing wisteria draped it, its sweet scent lingering in the air. It was a perfect place for reading.

She was about to sit when a leafy canopy arched over a narrow cobblestone pathway caught her attention. The path led to a much smaller, secluded garden. Slim trees with bushy tops lined the stone walls, and blooming shrubs added pops of color and a sense of the wild, intensifying the feeling of a secret garden.

An imposing oak tree, its bark weathered and gnarled, stood majestically in the middle of it. A swing, painted in vibrant shades of blue and green, dangled gracefully from one of its sturdy branches, swaying gently in the breeze.

A children's garden, she realized.

Kharis drew a sharp, uneven breath. Did Ananya have a place like this? A garden where she swung, legs kicking at the sky, her laughter bubbling as Götrid stood behind her, gently pushing her while laughing?

She lowered herself onto the seat, pressed her feet to the earth, and gave a slight push. The swing rocked gently, creaking beneath her weight, but the motion offered no comfort. Grief clung to her like a second skin, so she sang a melody as the swing rocked beneath her. The lyrics echoed her sorrow because her world was also broken.

"A thousand years ago, our world was broken.
A thousand years ago, they came.
They burned our forests. They razed our land.
A thousand years ago, our hope was stolen."

Her shoulders sagged, her gaze unfocused, and the song spilled as if someone else were singing. Her sense of betrayal roiled in her chest. Her brother's lies and her mavah's murder swirled like a storm wind, lifting everything and refusing to settle. Yet the words kept coming.

"But while our land recovered, and life was once rewoven,
The gods imprisoned the four.
And a thousand years ago, while we feasted and sang,
The lands of the four were frozen."

A few tears landed on her lap, where the fabric of her dress absorbed them instantly.

"*Are you well?*" he asked softly, hesitation threading through his voice.

She was unsure how to answer that question. "My mavah was murdered." She sucked in a breath, choking on a sob. "And the lying. That hurts the most. That everyone lied." She tilted her head, studying a wispy cloud. "So tell me, how would you feel if you were me?"

There was a beat of silence. Then, *"What I feel is irrelevant. Only you matter."*

It angered her that he didn't answer her question. "You aren't helping." She gripped the swing ropes. "Who should I trust now?"

"Your sister," the Voice answered, his words clipped.

Resentment, fear, and distrust had taken over her mind, painting every thought in black and gray.

"Why?"

"Because she knew not of this." A pause. *"Because she loves you."*

"So do Hala and Nana, and both have been lying to me." Anger gushed through her veins. "Hala hid the truth. Nana had known all along. For all I know, you could be lying to me, too."

"Then trust no one." His sharpness cut deep. *"Wallow in self-pity and thoughts of revenge, and let them embitter your soul."*

"Enough." She landed on her feet, halting the swing. "Arguing serves no purpose. I must find out the truth, except I'm moving away from the place where my answers lie."

"I thought you wanted to leave the Sendatorsum."

Kharis unleashed a heavy sigh, her heart torn between conflicting emotions. "Ironic, isn't it? If I can't break the curse, I won't ever find out the truth."

"Then become stronger. Head to the Zahar-Eliza and sharpen your mind and spirit. Stop obeying and following. Stop walking with your head down like a pitiful creature."

Her tone sharpened. "Is that what you think of me?"

"You are magnificent." A frustrated huff resounded in her mind. *"That is what I think of you."* It was the most emotion the Voice had ever revealed. *"But in believing their lies, you have accepted their definition of you and stopped fighting."*

Kharis felt him move in her mind, as if he were angrily pacing back and forth.

"Pitiful. Worthless. Useless," Kharis said. "And when angry, I destroy worlds. That makes me a monster."

"*You are not,*" the Voice boomed. "*This game does not become you.*"

"Easy for you to say. All you do is sit and watch."

A hiss slithered through her mind—sharp, grating, and sudden. It knocked her off balance, and she fell to the ground. The swing lurched forward, striking her back.

"*Did I sit and watch when you were at the Iluna? Or when your uncle pushed all those prisoners onto you?*"

Shame stabbed her in the heart. Kharis glanced away even though there was no face to avert.

"*I became the monster so that you would not.*"

Kharis shuttered her eyes, aware that the Voice spoke the truth. "I'm sorry." Embarrassed, she lowered her head. "I must sound like an ungrateful child. Why would anyone trust me?"

"*You are doing it again—not trusting yourself.*"

Trust. The word tasted sour now.

Trust and truth. How she needed these now.

Her forehead creased as worry twisted in her chest. Fragments of memory clawed their way forward. Endless arguments. Scuffles. Defiance. Untamed magic flaring in the hands of a wild, stubborn child. And now, a woman sat on the dirt, burdened by the wreckage of her power and many mistakes.

"Would you trust me?" she asked quietly.

"*Why would I not?*"

She swallowed hard, unsure whether to feel guilty or thankful.

His soft huff brought her back. "*Go to the Zahar-Eliza. Become stronger. Learn to trust yourself. And no one will ever lie to you again. Besides, you cannot save anyone if you lose yourself.*"

A heavy pause lingered between them.

"*Go,*" the silvery voice added. "*Because I trust you.*"

It was an earth-shattering revelation. Perhaps he was a sign of the madness, but he trusted her. Kharis couldn't say the same about Saya.

Her gaze dropped to her twitching fingers—a tremor born of the fear the massacre had etched into her bones. "My sister loves me," she said. "But does she trust me? She fears I'll trans-

390

form like I did seven years ago—losing myself to this dark magic and destroying the world."

She tilted her head, her gaze drawn to the goldcrests perched on the highest branches. Their vibrant yellow crests bobbed with their movement while their green plumage shimmered like fresh spring leaves.

"Saya is always trying to soothe me, but beneath it, there's an undercurrent of fear." Voicing this concern was like walking a tightrope stretched thin over a chasm. "She constantly reminds me to control myself, that I can't get angry... I don't doubt she loves me. But does she trust me?"

"*Her concern is an extension of the love she has for you. And as commendable as that is, you must stop living under its shade.*"

"She offers a soothing shade."

"*A tree, to grow, also needs sun.*"

Kharis blew a puff of air, conflicted.

"*The time has come to meet your fate, not run from it. Go to the Zahar-Eliza; only then will all the writings end.*"

"That was a verse in a prophecy kept at the Royal Archives," she said. "Let the world revel in fire. Let it be consumed again, so the spirits, once joined, transcend, and all the writings end." She slumped on the swing. "I don't even know what it means."

"*The answers shall come when you learn to trust your instinct. Then, you shall never regret your decisions.*"

Air rushed through her lips. "I've made so many terrible ones."

"*Let go of the burden of your past, and lighten your load. Only then shall your path forward be clear.*"

His words rang with clarity, like a bell calling to prayer. Gradually, Kharis felt her heart regain its calm. Her mind was no longer a storm of clashing thoughts. A renewed focus paved the road for her.

"Thank you for the lecture and the shoulder shaking." She chuckled at the image. "I probably needed that more than I realized."

She pushed herself off the ground, wiped her tears, and smoothed her dress.

"Here's what feels right to me." She raised a finger for each point. "Become stronger. Enter Andaheimur. Rescue Ananya. Break the curse." Her chest swelled with a sharp intake of breath. "What do you think?"

"*A good plan.*"

Would he nod his approval and smile? How she wished he had a face... and a name.

Kharis walked out of the garden. At least now she had a list to work with. Pondering her need to busy herself with something useful, she headed for the stables.

The stalls had been cleaned and the horses fed, so she wandered down the row, pausing at each stall.

"Pendry! There you are." The chestnut mare recognized Kharis, greeting her with a gentle neigh. Kharis grabbed a brush from a nearby peg and began working on the horse's mane as the cavalry officers had taught her. She hummed Abhiral's tune, the rhythm bringing a sense of calm to the task at hand.

She moved slowly, savoring the quiet, the softness of Pendragham's coat, and the way the mare leaned into her strokes.

The world faded to the simple act of grooming, stroke after patient stroke.

Pendragham's ears suddenly perked up, the mare releasing a low, questioning nicker as she shifted her weight. Kharis turned. A figure draped in a long cloak stood at the stall door.

"Your Highness?"

Kharis recognized the voice, and anger seized her. "Why are you here?"

Magda lowered her hood, revealing a weary expression. Shadows clung to her eyes, her skin pale beneath the light. "I couldn't leave yet." She hesitated, searching Kharis's face. "I'd hoped to find Zhandari here."

"Why?" Kharis's voice was sharp.

Magda exhaled a shaky breath. "She never made it to the appointed place." The words broke from her as though something had splintered inside her.

Kharis narrowed her eyes. "Is she truly your wife?" Or more deceit, she wanted to ask.

"The love of my life." A bright, eager, and genuine smile lit up her eyes. "Is Zhandari here?" Hope gleamed in Magda's expression.

"No," came the reply.

Magda's face fell, her shoulders sagging. "She has never disappeared. Not like this." Her watery gaze got lost in a thought.

Kharis wasn't sure whether to step closer and comfort her. All her sharp edges softened, watching Magda's honest pain. "I'm sorry," she said, her voice quiet. "I hope you find her."

Magda's eyes glistened, focused on a faraway place in her mind—a moment passed in loaded silence.

"General Zhegur is a man with a sharp mind," she suddenly said, lifting her chin to meet Kharis's gaze. "Trust his judgment. Your White Guard escort is also exceptional, unlike your Velathari. I can see Prince Jordha's hand in their selection. Law-abiding, reliable, trustworthy men and women who will remain loyal to you, not the crown prince."

Kharis's wrath slammed into her, clawing and biting. "Loyal, like you?"

Magda's expression turned wistful. "Loyal enough to open the door you're unwilling to."

Kharis opened her mouth, but voices drifted closer—soldiers. Magda pulled her hood over her head and glanced over her shoulder.

Kharis closed her eyes, forcing herself to breathe and calm the storm raging inside. When she opened her eyes, Magda was gone.

One hoof struck the ground hard. Pendragham's ears flicked back.

Fear clung to her ribs like frost. "I don't know what I'm doing," she whispered.

But she knew she had to face her doubts, even the ugly ones. And the only way forward was to go through the storm, bear its scars, and emerge on the other side.

She had to go north—*her* north.

"No more hiding," she told Pendragham. "No more being afraid."

She hung the brush on its peg and left the stables.

CHAPTER 70
A STORM IS COMING

*Truth does not meet you at the base; it waits for you at the peak,
demanding the climb. - Poliormos*

The days slipped past in a blur. For Kharis, time felt like
water through her fingers—impossible to hold or
stop. The peaks towered over Zhegama, the monsters
she would have to climb to reach the Zahar-Eliza.

Two days later, just before daybreak, the royal convoy
departed from Zhegama. Their destination? Herisvalen. In this
large town, all Zahar-Katea activity converged.

When they reached the top of the first pass, Kharis gazed
back at the city. In the pre-dawn darkness, it still seemed like a
magical place.

General Zhegur and Saya walked ahead, talking with
Mizha and his father, Barhan. White Guard officers, packed
animals, bhiksunim, porters, and pilgrims followed, their footsteps steady on the trail.

Kharis pressed on, keeping pace, though her thoughts grew
darker with every step. What if she couldn't enter Andaheimur? How would she rescue Ananya, then? And ending the
curse... Would she succeed or fail? Her nostrils flared with each
exhale, her frustration mounting. She knew peeling back one

layer of deception would only reveal more. Was she ready to face it all?

Her gaze locked on the peaks ahead, their jagged outlines bathed in the soft pink glow of sunrise.

Angry at herself and the world, she cursed under her breath.

CHAPTER 71
SILVER AND GOLD

Truth is a steep mountain. Its ascent is difficult, but your view will be boundless once you reach its summit. - Poliormos

On the third day of their journey toward Herisvalen, the view opened to a large, concave-shaped canyon. The remnants of a frozen river stretched endlessly. The jagged mountains towered over the group, reminding the convoy that they were deep in Zahar-Katea territory, traversing ranges that seemed to touch the heavens.

Saya was the first to reach the top of the pass. Wide-eyed and amazed, she opened her arms to take a deep breath of the frigid air and drink in the view.

"This landscape is spellbinding." Her breath misted as she turned to Kharis. "We must be at three and a half cliffmarks."

Kharis trudged through the snow, the steady crunch beneath her boots swallowing her curses, and settled beside her sister with a low mutter. The cold stung her face, making her eyes tear, but nothing could compare to the irritation building inside.

"Isn't it grand?" Saya asked, her eyes bright as they swept over the highlands. Forced cheerfulness colored her voice. There was a rehearsed cadence, chosen not for meaning but effect. Its scent was too sweet. Almost overripe.

397

The Djinnshirukh ignored it, letting the breathtaking expanse calm her frayed nerves. Saya's attempts to mask her worry with feigned brightness gnawed at her. Her gaze would linger a little too long on Kharis's face, searching for cracks. Everything about it set Kharis on edge.

She forced her smile in return—a thin, brittle thing meant to reassure the concern her sister tried so hard to conceal.

And then there was the unsettling sensation of being watched. An unseen presence lurked beyond the edge of her sight, hiding behind massive boulders, observing and assessing. Waiting. Her fingers curled instinctively, itching for her blades.

Enough already, she wanted to shout. *Come out and face me.*

The attack in Zhegama, Götrid's revelations, the impossible task of rescuing Ananya, and finding how to break the curse—all pressed down on her like the mountains looming over her.

Everything aggravated her.

The whistling of the wind, the uneven ground beneath her boots, the forced joy in Saya's tone. This journey had pulled her out of her complacency and into a world that demanded action, whether she was ready or not.

The rest of the group slowly climbed the steep zigzagging switchbacks. Some reached the top and halted to catch their breaths while others lagged, heavily panting on the way up the pass, one foot in front of the other with each hard breath.

"Are we ever going to make it?" Kharis thought not of this climb but of her destiny.

"Of course," Saya said. "We'll follow the river; the next pass is the last. Focus not on the destination and instead enjoy the company." She flashed a cheerful grin.

Kharis forced hers.

"Let's get to the bottom." Saya tugged on her pack in anticipation. "We can eat once we're there. It will be flat for a while, keeping everyone's spirits up. Soon, we'll set up camp." She patted Kharis's shoulder as if that gesture would make everything better. "Tomorrow, we reach Herisvalen."

Light as the mountain air, Saya headed down the trail.

Would she lie? Or hide the truth? Kharis's head whirled with a turmoil of conflicted emotions. Doubt, the leader, led the dance. Saya tried too hard, as if afraid of what Kharis would do. Jaded, she let out a bitter grunt.

Would she betray me? Hala had.

Kharis shook her head, hoping to erase this awful sensation festering inside her that her trust was fragile and already cracking.

She thought it ironic to feel this angry about lies and deceit because she'd lied, too. *Maybe I deserve this.* She'd lied, too—about the Voice and Noam. More than once, she'd smiled and shrugged off the truth. Those moments now flared through her memory, bright as fireflies.

Saya, who loved her more than anything, deserved the truth. Her kind, loyal, and dependable sister had earned Kharis's loyalty a thousand times over. So why was it so hard to come out and say it? How difficult could it be to admit it: "*Saya, I kissed someone,*" and let the rest follow?

Her heart hammered at the thought. It should've been easy, but losing her sister's approval...? She wouldn't survive that.

Her hands fisted tightly, the leather on her gloves almost ripping. Her simmering anger wanted out. It craved to burn everything.

"Where's the path?" Kharis grumbled loudly—the path to her freedom and a new life. The road to her answers. To the spell that ended the curse.

Officer Xia Dhan tapped her shoulder and gestured ahead, trying to be helpful. Talus and snow blanketed the slope, obscuring any trace of a path, much like the elusive spell she sought.

Kharis curled her hands around her mouth and hollered, "There's no path!"

Saya was too far down to hear her, and the wind blew Kharis's words away.

"Are you there?" Kharis asked the Voice. "Please, talk to me."

Where was he? His absence was frightening.

Kharis pressed a hand to her chest and drew her fur coat into a fistful of fabric. Mental and emotional fatigue was weakening her resolve. Could she do this...? No, she couldn't. She wasn't ready for any of it. *I'm nothing but a failure.* She turned, eyeing the trail back to Zhegama. Paused. Swallowed hard. Her feet moved—

A deep groan rolled through the air. The ground trembled beneath her boots, rippling through her legs.

The porters halted in unison, their cargo swaying as they steadied themselves.

Officer Dhan stumbled, her hand shooting out to catch her balance, eyes wide with alarm.

The tremor ceased as quickly as it had begun. For a heartbeat, everyone stood still. Kharis noted the uncertainty etched across the porters' faces, the questions in their eyes.

The ground shuddered again, more violently this time, as if the mountain were splitting open. Several boulders tore free from the cliffs above, tumbling toward the group. The air filled with alarmed shouts. Porters abandoned their loads. Everyone scrambled for safety.

Rocks thundered. Debris cascaded. The frigid air crackled with the sounds of crashing and splintering.

Kharis's gaze darted through the chaos, searching for Saya. A blur of bodies rushed in every direction. Then she found her, just as Saya slipped on a patch and tumbled, sliding helplessly down the icy slope. Her arms flailed, clawing at the ground to stop her descent.

A boulder hurtled down the same path; if Saya couldn't stop, it would crush her.

"Saya!"

Kharis's scream tore from her throat, from her heart, from her soul. She lunged forward, leaping over toppling rocks and loose debris, the world distorted by motion and chaos. Her desperation awakened her power, but rather than fire, shimmering silver light flared around her hands, burning through her gloves.

As if answering her command, the ground rippled under

Saya, fractured, and swallowed her before the boulder rolled over where she'd been a breath before.

Kharis jumped into this otherworldly hole, wrapping her arms tightly around Saya as the sisters plunged into this abyss. A sudden blast of golden light erupted, hurling them out as if they didn't belong in this other realm. Soaring through the air, they landed on a thick patch of snow, rolling to a stop in a heap.

Panting, Kharis clung to her sister, her fingers digging into Saya's coat. Her chest heaved, each breath ragged and sharp with the lingering taste of fear. The thought of losing her sister, of being a moment too late, left her shaking.

She tightened her grip and didn't let go of Saya.

The Voice's unsettling silence had curled in her chest like smoke. Where was he?

Large clouds of dust and snow lingered in the air. Coughs were heard around.

The mountain groaned with the aftermath. Rock shifted and settled, and an unnerving stillness descended upon them.

After moments of eerie silence, someone shouted, "Is everyone all right?"

Voices responded with quick affirmations.

"What about you?" Kharis managed to ask, releasing Saya from her hold.

Saya bobbed her head slowly. Wide-eyed and shaken, her gaze locked on the boulder resting at the bottom of the slope. "The ground... I—I don't understand. It was solid. Then I was falling."

Kharis wasn't even sure what to say. "Well," she bit her lip, "I'm just glad this earthquake didn't happen when we were climbing that ridiculously thin excuse for a trail. Whoever called that a path had a cruel sense of humor—"

"Your Highnesses!" General Zhegur shouted as he sprinted toward them, dropping to his knees beside them. "Are you all right? Are you injured?"

He checked Saya first, his hands moving methodically over her arms and legs. "I saw you take a nasty fall, and that boulder..." His words faltered, his face paling even more at the memory.

"Don't move," he instructed Saya. "I must ensure nothing is broken."

Unsettled, the general kept checking Saya, worry etched across his face. His touch was gentle, yet there was an underlying intensity. He genuinely cared for her, and the thought warmed Kharis's heart. If Lord Athon's bedroom had a revolving door... Why couldn't Saya take a lover? And who better than General Reza Zhegur, who worshiped the ground she walked on?

Nearby, everybody was gathering.

General Zhegur turned to Kharis. "What about you, Your Highness?"

Kharis half-chuckled, half-coughed her answer. "Only the Sorukhipa can kill me."

She got up with a groan, limbering her neck and dusting her uniform. Then, she landed a reassuring pat on his shoulder. "Everyone seems fine," she said, gesturing to the group. "Shaken but not showing signs of injury."

"Let's move," Mizha hollered from a few paces away.

"Fine by me," Kharis replied with an arm wave. "General Zhegur, help me lift Saya."

The general swallowed hard, the fear of what could've happened casting a shadow over his features. With a nod, he got up and banded his arm around Saya's waist. She leaned into him as he brought her to her feet.

Once collected, General Zhegur turned to everyone. "Let's head down to get our bearings." He scooped Saya in his arms and carried her down the slope.

The group stirred like a hive disrupted. The low hum of voices filled the air—murmured check-ins, the creak of straps being tightened, a few shaken jokes offered like offerings to calm frayed nerves. Soldiers helped bhiksunim to their feet. Mizha shook the dust from his satchel. Porters bent to check their loads, muttering about shifted weight and cracked jars. Someone's flask clinked against a rock.

Kharis faced the mountains, their presence a stark

reminder of the arduous journey ahead. Eight more days to reach the Zahar-Eliza. She glanced at her hands, peeling away the remnants of leather that clung to her skin. The Voice hadn't spoken after the quake, and his silence felt ominous now.

A different type of magic had come to her aid. It had made everything ripple and blur under Saya, opening a narrow void through which Saya had slipped to safety. Kharis was about to chew on her nails, but pulled her fingers away from her mouth, deciding never to chew on them again.

She watched General Zhegur gingerly descend the slope with Saya in his arms. In the blink of an eye, she could've lost her beloved sister.

I can't be useless anymore.

She couldn't depend on the Voice. And for the first time since the Voice had begun speaking, Kharis felt this was her journey. Hers alone. Tucking her hands under her armpits to keep them warm, she followed Saya and Zhegur.

CHAPTER 72
HERISVALEN

To endure the mountain's wrath is to be claimed by its grace. Only those who belong will weather the storm. - Poliormos

On the fourth day, the group arrived at Herisvalen. "The center of Zherik life," Mizha had explained.

The Zherik-Umea nation, as ancient as the soil beneath them, had made Herisvalen their heart. An accord with Zahar had folded them into the Commonwealth—sovereign but allied.

The town sprawled across the mountain peak, its heart centered around a wide, open square. At its forefront stood a grand building. From there, houses climbed the mountainside in layered terraces, their stone foundations carved into the rock. The curved ledges wrapped around the slope, giving the town an almost otherworldly silhouette while shielding it from the relentless gusts and sharp, sandy dust that battered the cliffs.

The weather had been on their side, but it shifted when the group reached the town. The clear, blue skies turned angry grey, and the freezing wind picked up. Wet and shivering, the group cleared the last pass to the town as low clouds enveloped the mountain, blanketing everything in a thick, icy fog.

Within the hour, the blizzard arrived.

CHAPTER 73
THE RELENTLESS TUG
OF FATE

Fate does not ask for permission; it grips your soul and steers you toward the unknown. - Poliormos

The storm's unrelenting howl clawed at the mountains, sending sheets of snow whipping against the rocky outcroppings. Aghet Mendi crouched deeper into the cave; his cloak pulled tightly around him to block the cold's insidious bite. The meager fire he'd coaxed to life offered little warmth, its flickering light barely pushing back the cold.

His hands were numb, the cold leeching feeling from his fingertips. He flexed them against the chill, jaw tightening as another blast of wind roared past the entrance, sending icy tendrils snaking toward him.

Aghet's lips twisted into a snarl.

Someone had aided her, he thought bitterly.

Not nature's unexpected chaos but otherworldly will. Some divine force had once again stepped between him and her. It wasn't a coincidence—it never was with her. Forces beyond his grasp had always intervened where the Djinnshirukh was concerned, tilting the scales in her favor.

The wind screamed, its wail whistling loud enough to prick his ears. His anger had coiled tightly in his chest, waiting for the right moment to strike. Now, when victory was within reach, he'd been trapped—like an insect beneath glass.

A faint hum lingered in the stormy air. A flicker of magic. Watching. Waiting.

"I'm wasting time," he hissed, venomous and unrelenting.

Aghet ground his molars hard. The moment he'd drawn near, the earth had shuddered—magic, unmistakably. Then came the blizzard, striking with unnatural ferocity, as if summoned to trap him.

"Coincidence?" he scoffed. "This reeks of divine obstruction." He knew the signs too well. He'd been so close, had nearly touched her, only to be cast away like dust on the wind.

With a snarl, Aghet grabbed a jagged rock from the cave floor, hurling it at the far wall with a roar. The stone struck hard and shattered, shards skittering across the ground. He laughed—short, sharp, and bitter.

"Mock me while you can," he spat into the storm's howling mouth. "But even the gods bleed."

A gust of wind howled through the cave entrance, carrying a flurry of snow that hissed as it hit the fire. The flames sputtered. Aghet stilled. For one breathless moment, it felt like the storm had answered.

His gaze drifted to the entrance, a jagged maw opening onto a world of white chaos. The blizzard was alive, its winds shrieking with fury and its snow falling in thick waves. It taunted him with the promise of death if he tried.

When the storm passed—and it would pass—he would find her... and him. That thought steadied him. To finally have him.

A smile tugged at his lips. The wind outside had barred his path for now, but storms did not last forever. And when the mountain ceased its howling tantrum, Aghet Mendi would emerge.

And he would not fail.

CHAPTER 74
THUNDER AND GALES

Love is the quiet conqueror, winning battles without striking its sword. - Poliormos

The blizzard pounded Herisvalen without mercy.

To pass the time, Saya recorded their journey, flipping the pages of her weathered journal as she penned observations or sketched. Sometimes, she would read passages out loud, and Kharis would share a comment. Otherwise, her sister did nothing but lie on the cot and stare at the walls, lost in her ruminations in a place far away from everyone.

Unreachable.

She glanced at Kharis's still form again, her pen pausing mid-sentence, tracing the same sentence twice in her journal before moving on.

The second day was no better than the first. Kharis hardly spoke, mentally adrift in her own world.

❦

"*Khiri?*"

That call glided into Kharis's mind but sounded distant, as if her sister's voice came from a different world.

"*She calls,*" the silvery voice said.

"So?"

"*What bothers you that you would ignore your sister?*"

"Everything, including that you won't let me into your void."

"*Are you in danger?*" he asked.

"Not now, but where were you when the mountain was breaking apart before our eyes?"

An uneasy quiet settled between them. "*I had to settle a score.*"

"With?"

"*A troublesome bug.*"

Kharis frowned, aware she wouldn't get much more. "I must think."

"*Then do. Nothing else is needed.*" His deep sigh rumbled through her mind.

She hated not knowing his name or who he was. It made her feel as unmoored as the rest of her life.

"Something happened," she shared, her voice softer now. "When I saw Saya in danger, I somehow summoned silver fire. It was cold—sharp and crystalline, like liquid moonlight pouring through my veins."

"*A lovely description. It defines you beautifully.*" He seemed amused, waiting for her to catch up to something he already knew.

"It wasn't my usual fire magic. It made the ground disappear under Saya. What does it mean?"

He chuckled, the pleasant sound reverberating through her mind. "*That you are extraordinary.*"

"I don't need flattery," she shot back.

His sigh attempted to infuse her thoughts with patience. "*You are a gem—rare and powerful.*"

She blinked, caught off guard by the compliment. "Are you calling me precious?"

"*Precious and dangerous, too,*" he corrected. "*A gem can withstand fire, pressure, and time.*"

"And the silver fire?" she asked. "Will I conjure it again?"

"*If you so wish,*" he said.

"How?"

"*When you wish it.*"

Kharis's hands fisted with her growl. "That's not an answer."

"*It belongs to you,*" he said cryptically. "*Yours to wield and name.*"

She didn't know whether to feel empowered or terrified. "And what happens if I can't control it?"

The Voice grew quieter. "*Then it shall consume everything, as fire always does.*"

"Great. Just *fires-take-me* great," she muttered, throwing up her hands in exasperation. "As if I needed more reasons to end this curse."

The Voice chuckled softly. "*Perhaps you should stop fearing your power and embrace it.*"

"Not happening," she grumbled.

He hummed, pondering something. "*Do you remember what you must do?*"

Kharis would ink it onto her skin if she could. "Become stronger. Enter Andaheimur. Rescue Ananya. Break the curse."

"*What holds you back?*"

An awkward hush settled over her. "I wonder whether I'm brave enough to face the truth."

The truth about Hala, her siblings' banishment, her mavah's death, and everything else that would peel off as she ripped the layers of deception apart. What if... she wasn't ready for any of it?

"*Speak to your sister,*" he insisted.

"I'd rather speak to you."

The huff resounding in her mind carried a note of annoyance. "*You are stubborn.*"

"Stubborn and weak and useless—"

"*Enough!*" His anger thundered in her mind, the force of it so intense as to be painful. "*You are neither weak nor useless, and your stubbornness is a trait I admire, for it conveys how you adhere to your values, regardless of the pressure imposed on you. You are lost, but rather than find your way again, you have chosen not to move.*"

The Voice exhaled, seeking to collect himself.

"*Stubborn*," he scoffed. "*Once, I asked you to reconsider your decision, but no argument would dissuade you. I want that same woman to stand before me.*"

Every single thought whirling in her head halted. From that silence, one emerged. "Why won't you tell me your name or who you are?"

He growled. "*Find your way, and I shall answer your question.*"

Her frustration flared. She needed answers. "That's cruel."

"*As cruel as ignoring your sister.*"

The comment stung her. Saya always came to her rescue. Her kind, loyal, and dependable sister, who would deny herself General Reza Zhegur's company to stay with Kharis through thick and thin.

He was right. She was being cruel.

Her anger melted and turned into guilt. She rolled on her side to face her, keeping her voice soft. "Would you like to play xakea with me?"

Saya stopped writing. When she lifted her head and met Kharis's gaze, her golden eyes were bright, and her smile was warm and eager. "I would love to."

Outside, the blizzard raged on. When Kharis got up from the cot, the lace-like frost across the small windowpane drew her gaze. The wind howled its warning to the world. And yet, it didn't whisper escape this time—it whispered forward.

CHAPTER 75
THE LETTERS

Little lies are drops of poison in a clear stream. They corrupt the willing and taint the unwilling, eroding the truth and unweaving the fabric of our integrity. - Poliormos

Marya Levandran protected her assigned section of the royal enclave with wit, street smarts, and sweat. She bent ears to her will, mastering the language of the underworld in a city that never slept.

The knocks on the door interrupted her train of thought.

"Enter," she said after a frustrated huff.

Sergeant Orlen Dëtka entered. He glanced at the room, shaking his head with a soft tsk-tsk at the chaos she called her study. Levandran did her best not to throw a sharp object at him.

Northerners, she grumbled silently.

Situated within a fortified structure on the outer Zahar-Regia ring, her quarters comprised a central chamber with adjoining rooms, some used for storage.

Marya sat on a high-backed leather chair that had seen better days. She refused to have it replaced. An oak desk dominated the room, covered with maps, documents, scrolls, a magnifying glass, daggers, inkwells, quills, and reed pens. Ordinance books filled her shelves. Cabinets overflowed with scrolls and more maps. Her weapons, armor, and tools lined the walls. The city's coat of arms hung on the wall behind her, reinforcing her status as a captain. It was, however, off-kilter.

She flicked her eyes at the wooden bench, and Dëtka sat. "Stop judging me," she warned.

"But the coat of arms—"

"I know, and I like it that way. What is it?"

Dëtka scratched his head, tongue poking the inside of his cheek. That gesture told her she wouldn't like the news. He extracted a letter from his jerkin and placed it on her desk. "This is a report about three bodies found in Zhegama."

She arched an eyebrow, stamping her signature on a document. "That's *waaay* out of our jurisdiction."

Dëtka frowned at her. "Don't you want to know the rest?"

She rolled her eyes, waving her quill at him. "Go on."

"Two bodies belonged to Shadow Walkers; the third was a Hitzalkea, a woman identified as Zhandari. She worked in the Zhegami royal compound, and some of the soldiers identified her body."

Marya narrowed her eyes, dipping her quill in the inkwell. "Get to the point."

"All three bodies shared a commonality: a slash on the left side of their faces with a missing left eye."

The captain stopped mid-motion, and her attention shifted to Dëtka. "Cause of death?"

"The Shadow Walkers sported slashed throats as if caught off-guard by their attacker."

"And the Hitzalkea?"

"I'm afraid that's a bit more difficult since the woman was tortured."

An uneasy silence hung in the air as she processed the news.

"Two Shadow Walkers and a Hitzalkea." Marya's fingers tapped her desk as she played with that information. "That must be our killer—the same precision and pattern," she mused. "Whoever they are, they are not improvising—they are following some ritual." She hummed, piecing everything together. "And the woman served in the royal compound?"

413

Dëtka nodded. "All three of them did, but the woman served Her Highness Princess Saya as her attendant."

The captain groaned, slamming a hand on her desk. "You should've started with that. Were similar bodies found on the way to Zhegama?"

Dëtka scratched his temple, deep in thought. "There was an incident—a band of five bandits. Wolves got to them first, so their exact cause of death is unclear. But a chest of valuables belonging to a zenka merchant traveling with the royal convoy was recovered." His gaze suddenly sharpened, a flicker of realization crossing his face. "Are you thinking...?"

Marya got up and paced the room. "I suspect the killer traveled with the royal caravan, hiding among the people headed for the Zahar-Katea. Our only clue, a silver button, hints at a White Guard officer. If I'm not mistaken, the palace assigned forty to guard the princesses. It means one of them could be our killer."

"About the button," Dëtka muttered. "How exactly did you recognize it?"

Marya shrugged. "I was once a White Guard officer."

Dëtka blinked. It implied a demotion.

She walked to a window, parting the curtains to observe the bustling street and the impressive West Wind Gate.

"Here, our killer targeted petty thieves and drunks. People nobody would miss. But now three individuals connected to the princesses are dead." She let the curtain fall.

"Captain, what should we do?"

The pressure behind Marya's eyes was intensifying. The headache wasn't far.

"Zhegama is out of our jurisdiction," she said. "If the killer is a White Guard officer, the investigation is also out of our hands. With these three deaths and the possibility that the princesses are being targeted, Prince Jordha and Lord Mehta will be involved." Her grunt was long and low, fisted hands trembling.

"Get my horse," she shouted at someone outside her study. "Dëtka, we're going to see the commander right now. If my hunch is right, the killer is after one of the princesses."

Dëtka scratched a bushy eyebrow. "The Djinnshirukh one?"

"Precisely."

&

Crown Prince Hala ruled the city with ink and silence, mastering a world of bureaucracy bent to his will. He worked through the city's tedious but necessary paperwork with his usual advisors and scribes. He read, asked questions, and signed and stamped documents as they were given to him.

The doors to his extensive study swung open unexpectedly, and Jordha entered in a rush. Usually calm and collected, his face was tight this time. "We have an issue."

Hala couldn't ignore the concern in Jordha's voice. "What is it?"

"I've been informed of the death of three—"

An imperial guard opened the doors, interrupting Jordha mid-sentence. Everyone turned as Hala tore his eyes from his cousin to acknowledge the guard.

"Your Highness," the guard said. "A royal messenger with a letter for you." He moved aside to allow the messenger entry.

Hala grimaced, unhappy with the disruption. "Just leave it." He gestured to a spot on his desk where he could drop it. "I'll take care of it later."

"My instructions are to place it in your hands." The messenger stepped forward, determined, holding the letter out. "It's from Her Highness Princess Götrid."

Jordha's eyebrows raised.

"Götrid?" Hala mused. When had she ever written to him? "Very well, hand it over."

He broke the wax seal and started reading silently until his eyes focused on a damning passage:

They're adults. The time is upon you now. Deliver on your promise as we have delivered on ours.

His fingers twitched. The parchment trembled. A memory flickered. Götrid had met Khator's eyes first, then Helena's, before her gaze had landed on him. "*As long as you keep them safe, we'll step aside. But know that our sacrifice is already tainted with blood.*"

Hala refocused on the letter and went from mild amusement to anger as he skimmed the rest.

"She did... what?"

He shot up, anger burning his stomach. His chair screeched across the polished marble floor before toppling backward.

His advisors stiffened, keeping their eyes down.

"We're done for today," was his terse command. "Everyone, leave!"

The advisors and scribes scampered out of the chamber. The messenger left, and the imperial guards closed the doors behind them. Hala fumed, pacing around the room, clutching the crumpled letter, and rubbing his sweaty forehead with a trembling hand.

"Hala...?"

Without uttering a word, he thrust the letter into Jordha's hands. As Jordha read it, his face drained of color. He dragged his gaze from it and stared at Hala, his eyes wide with terror. He dropped into a chair, his body shaking. "The past is coming for us."

Hala screamed, sweeping everything off his desk in a sudden rage. Objects crashed to the floor, a riot of noise and glass. Papers fluttered like a swarm of white vultures descending on carrion.

His body trembled with rage. His chest rose and fell in ragged bursts as he stared down at the wreckage. Everything lay broken, like his plans.

"Hala?" Jordha's voice was unusually soft.

Panting, Hala turned around, the rage still burning his insides. "What is it?"

"We have another issue."

"Another?" He didn't curb his sarcasm. "Worse than this?" He snatched the letter from Jordha's hands and waved it in his face.

Jordha didn't flinch. "An assassin is after your sisters, but not any assassin."

Hala's face blanched. "What do you mean?"

"It's Aghet Mendi."

Hala staggered back. "But he—"

"Is *not* in Almarim," Jordha said. "Never went there. My spies have confirmed it."

Somewhere in the storm-wrapped heights of the Zahar-Katea, a figure knelt by a dying fire. Snow hissed in the embers. The wind howled its fury.

Yet the man smiled.

PART FIVE
AT THE CROSSROADS
OF FATE

CHAPTER 76
LOVE AND MIRTH

Love is like a wild storm, fierce and intense, but it is also a gentle, nourishing shower that feeds the soul. - Poliormos

After two long, dark days, the storm finally cleared.

On the third day, Kharis rose before dawn and made her way to the mountain's summit to watch the sunrise. Her breath fogged the air with each step, boots sinking into the fresh blanket of snow. At the top, she lowered her hood and glanced at the world below. Ivory stretched in every direction, glittering beneath the pale light. The sight stirred a memory without context.

After brushing away the snow, she settled on a small boulder and drew in the dry, cool air. It was the first breath in days that felt truly soothing. A gentle wind whispered along the slopes, filling the silence with a serene quietness.

Heat unfurled from her chest, spreading into her limbs like a slow bloom. Soon, the sun would crest the peaks, and the wait to witness that burst of color would be worth it. Besides, she wasn't cold anymore.

"Are you there?"

The Voice stirred. A ripple of mirth skittered through her mind like wind over still water.

"I have questions," she said.

"*I may have answers.*"

A smile blossomed on her face. "Tell me a story."

There was a long, curious pause. "*Why?*"

She shrugged. "I'm curious about what you've seen. You must have a thousand years of stories to share."

"*I also had a life before that.*"

Shame heated her face. "Yes, right. Of course—a life before the One War." Kharis shifted on the boulder, anxious to smooth over her mistake. "What if this time you ask me questions?"

The Voice chuckled.

"I'll answer anything." Nervous giggles bubbled up from her. There was this gnawing little issue of talking to someone no one else could see or hear. Was this how the unraveling manifested? This couldn't be the madness. The madness was dark and frightening. The Voice was a bright joy.

She waited for his questions, but moments passed in silence.

"*Sing for me,*" he said.

How could someone who didn't exist sound so... beautiful? Madness couldn't be this deceiving, could it? She hugged her knees, an irrepressible grin spreading across her face. It was odd to wonder about him like this—like a man.

"*Hmm.*" His low-pitched hum made her heart skip a beat. "*My song?*"

She laughed. "You're feisty this morning. Any requests?"

"*Surprise me.*"

Kharis tapped her lips, thinking. "What about this one?" She parted her lips to sing, her tune light and whimsical.

"Sunlight in the morning, gold on my shoulders,
Dew on wildflowers, fragrant in the summer.
The wind blows forever, gurgling in the rivers.
Butterflies flutter, dancing on the heather.

In spring and summer, there's merry laughter.
And when the weather cools, my love,
The lacy veil of fall a'cometh.

Dance for me, my darling, before we slumber."

There was a pause, a savoring of music, before he spoke again. *"Lovely song."* Then, with warmth curling around his voice, he said, *"Sing me another."*

Kharis smiled, pressing her palm to her chest, the rhythm of the words already in her blood.

"A thousand years ago, our world was broken.
A thousand years ago, they came.
They burned our forests. They razed our land.
A thousand years ago, our hope was stolen.
But a thousand years ago,
Four warriors came with their armies.
They fought his darkness. They brought the sun.
Four warriors came with their armies,
And the battle was won.
We mourned our losses, and we gave them our son.
And from that turmoil, a weapon was born.
Our lands, we reclaimed, and life was golden.
We rose from our ashes like the phoenix of old.
And a thousand years ago, we feasted and sang,
Under a brilliant Zahari sun.
But while our land recovered, and life was once rewoven,
The gods imprisoned the four.
And a thousand years ago, while we feasted and sang,
The lands of the four were frozen."

Kharis exhaled slowly, allowing the aura of sadness to dissipate.

"Your song." His pause carried a melancholy sigh. *"It was lovely, but the songstress is far lovelier."*

The unexpected compliment drew a small smile to her lips. "You think so?"

"Why would I not?" His sorrowful tone softened, lifting slightly. *"Your voice fills my world."*

She wasn't sure if the warmth rising in her cheeks was due to bashfulness or excitement. "I'm glad you enjoyed it."

A quiet pause settled between them. In the distance, deep indigo softened into violet as dawn's fingers stretched across the sky in shades of crimson. A cool breeze brushed her cheeks, and she absently swept a few loose strands of hair from her face. When he spoke again, his voice was lower, subdued.

"*The song also resonates with me.*"

She tilted her head, studying how the wind feathered a cloud apart. "Do you have a name?"

"*You have asked this before. Why do you wish to know?*" he teased.

"A name would be nice, other than calling you 'the Voice' when I think of you."

"*You think of me?*"

His surprise was intriguing. "Of course. You don't?"

His silence was like a timid glance away. "*I do,*" he finally whispered.

If he were here, would he sit beside her, their thighs bashfully grazing, or sit behind her, cradling her between his legs while resting his chin on her shoulder?

"How much of the song is true?"

"*All of it.*"

Kharis cocked her head and let that knowledge sink in. "Why were the four warriors imprisoned if they came to our aid?"

"*As punishment.*"

"For helping us?" she asked.

"*For defying the gods.*"

She scoffed. "Then curse the gods."

The Voice laughed and laughed, a deep, honest sound that made Kharis grin. "Tell me, were their lands frozen?"

"*They still are.*" His quiet grief curled around the words, tugging at her heart. "*So much was lost.*"

She was about to ask when a soft exhale tickled her ear.

"*Sing it again,*" he whispered. "*Please.*"

That subtle hint of sadness—the veiled grief—had returned. She could not wrap her arms around him to comfort him, so she obliged and sang, not just for him, but for the frozen world that lived a little longer through song.

CHAPTER 77
THE PAST ALWAYS HUNTS

The past does not sleep—it lingers in the shadows, waiting for a careless step to call it forth. - Poliormos

Aghet Mendi emerged from the cave like a wraith unchained, his hunger a gnawing beast clawing at his insides.

An unforgiving expanse of endless ice and snow had swallowed the world. The white landscape stabbed at his vision like a thousand tiny needles. He hissed, his eyes watering from the searing glare. His breath curled in the freezing air like ghostly tendrils. The storm had buried all landmarks beneath drifts, transforming the terrain into a treacherous world of hidden crevasses and concealed ledges that could crumble under his weight.

The hunger, though, was unbearable.

It consumed every thought, every shred of patience.

He chose a direction and pressed on, sinking knee-deep into the powdery snow—the cold bit into his legs, the effort draining what little strength he had.

The relentless trek stretched on—an endless, torturous climb that only deepened his hunger. He had to reach Herisvalen. And this time, she wouldn't escape him.

Hours bled into days. The landscape remained unchanged —bleak, white, and merciless.

Then, a soft chime caught his attention.

His head snapped toward it, nostrils flaring.

Bells. Not one, but several, their peals carried on the wind. Then came the bleating of sheep. Aghet's grin widened. Where there were sheep, there would be sheepherders.

He climbed higher, the frigid air biting his exposed skin, until he reached a rocky outcrop overlooking a high meadow. Below, a shaggy dog barked at intervals, darting after stray sheep, its tail wagging as it worked. Not far, a boy no older than ten sat idly with his staff, carving its surface with absent-minded strokes.

Aghet's mouth watered. His fingers twitched.

Then, another voice.

From behind the tree line, an older adult emerged, fastening his trousers, his breath fogging in the cold.

Two, not one. Aghet's grin sharpened, satisfaction settling in his bones.

He stepped onto the trail, moving toward them with the unhurried ease of a traveler. He'd learned long ago that a smile, a pleasant word, a touch of charm could mean the difference between slim pickings and a feast.

The boy saw him first, his hand clutching the staff too tightly. He stiffened, eyes wide with fear, before scrambling behind his elder. The dog settled by his master, growling, its hackles raised and ready to pounce. The man turned slowly, his sharp gaze assessing, his expression giving nothing away.

Aghet prepared his pleasantries, his voice smooth, his manner inviting—

"You are not welcome here."

Aghet faltered, his practiced expression slipping, his steps slowing. That was... unexpected. Few resisted his charm. The elder stood firm, his staff crossed over his body in a deliberate stance. A faint glow emanated from the carvings along the wood, but it was the gleam in his saffron-colored eyes that gave Aghet pause. A color he'd seen before...

His smile vanished. The acrid stench of magic now tainted

426

the air, coiling around the sheepherder like an invisible shroud. A familiar revulsion churned in his gut.

"I thought your kind were dealt with," Aghet spat. "Once a backstabber, always a backstabber."

The sheepherder raised a bushy, gray eyebrow. "Backstabber?" He rolled the word on his tongue as if tasting its bitterness. "How ironic for you to use such a term. After all, your backstabbing brought our misfortune."

The sheepherder's eyes gleamed with mockery. A corner of his lips lifted as he casually tapped the ground with his staff. "You are far from your home." His smirk deepened, thick with sarcasm. "Oh, wait, you have no home."

That remark hit a nerve. Aghet stiffened, his anger igniting.

The sheepherder held Aghet's gaze with the quiet confidence of a man who had commanded armies. He didn't flinch. Didn't cower.

"You are not welcome here," he repeated, dangerously softer this time.

Out of the corner of his eye, Aghet saw the boy step back, as if clearing space for the elder. The dog settled by his side, resonant growls directed at Aghet. Its limbs stretched, spine lengthening, coat darkening from brown to ink-black. Canines sharpened. Gold bled into its eyes.

Aghet froze. Magic crackled like an avalanche about to break loose.

The wind shifted. The air pulsed, twisting and curling around him in unnatural currents as the ground beneath his boot trembled.

Aghet's instincts flared a moment too late.

The herder struck his staff against the frozen earth. The blow hit like a war hammer, and a howling force exploded outward.

The wind slammed into Aghet, ripping him from the trail and hurling him over the cliff's edge.

The world twisted. Snow, sky, and rock spun into a blur as he plummeted, his roar lost to the long, unforgiving fall.

CHAPTER 78
THE RIVER OF FATE FLOWS

Fate is a mighty river that leads the willing and drags along the reluctant. - Poliormos

Saya exited the cabin, and her gaze swept across the bustling town.

Originally a seven-day stop, they were now on their sixteenth. The blizzard had deposited enough snow to close all the passes to and from Herisvalen, engulfing the high world in ice and deep, treacherous snow.

The White Guard officers didn't mind, chatting with the locals and exploring the town. Saya didn't mind it either, appreciating Zhegur's company as they discussed a variety of subjects amid games of xakea. She found their conversations enchanting, peppered with friendly laughter. Over time, he'd become more than a Zahari general sworn to protect her—he became a trusted friend.

Standing in a sunny spot this morning, he basked in the warmth with his eyes closed. The wind gently caressed his hair, barely brushing it.

Saya wondered whether to exchange greetings and have breakfast with him or let him enjoy his moment of peace. He was always working, checking on the sisters often, providing Saya with updates, and requesting feedback.

She stared at her hands, chapped and red from the cold, her fingers already numbed. Yet, when her gaze landed on Reza Zhegur again, she wished the route would remain closed so they could stay in Herisvalen forever.

❧

After breakfast, Saya spotted a familiar scene: a small crowd of children clustered around Kharis. It had become a daily occurrence since their arrival. Kharis had always been drawn to children—and they, in turn, to her. This morning, two little ones clung to her hands as if she were their older sister, while the older children chattered excitedly around her. Kharis laughed at something they said, and her face lit up with a rare, unguarded joy.

Children didn't see a monster. Only adults did.

General Zhegur waved at her, his smile sparkling in the morning air. "Blessed be the earth and sun," he greeted her, his voice carrying a warmth that cut through the icy air.

Saya could hardly control her heart's wild drumming. "May they sustain us," she said, her voice softer than usual.

"I missed you at breakfast." His tone was gentle, almost intimate.

Saya hesitated. "I saw you earlier but didn't want to impose."

His eyes held hers with an intensity that made her breath catch. "You'd never be an imposition, Your Highness."

A flush of warmth spread through her. "What if I make it up to you with a good cup of tea?"

General Zhegur's smile grew. He was about to reply when blaring horns shattered the moment. She saw the shift in his expression, the impertinent tug on his shoulders. Duty had overshadowed the light in his eyes. "I'll see what that is about." Then, more softly, "Would you wait for me?"

She nodded, her smile small but genuine, hiding the flutter in her chest. He bowed, an inner glow brightening his eyes again, and headed for the trailhead to get a report.

The horns blew again, louder this time, prompting more

townsfolk to step outside their homes. Over the pass, the guides appeared, waving colorful flags as they made their way down the trail. The vibrant banners cut through the monotony of ivory snow, and the crowd greeted the good news with a joyful Zherik trill.

Saya couldn't hide her disappointment.

After sixteen days, the pass to Leruak was finally open.

CHAPTER 79
WE CELEBRATE

In every true feast, the world remakes itself. Joy sings in the bones of the earth, and even the stars lean closer to listen. - Poliormos

B y early afternoon, the town thrummed with life. People draped in thick furs streamed through the streets toward the trailhead, their breath puffing out in clouds of white. Laughter and conversation filled the town square, adding to the distant bleating of sheep. The scent of smoked meat and fish wafted through the crisp air. Children with rosy cheeks and wet noses darted between adults, their footprints crisscrossing the snow. The older ones collected snow in large wooden buckets to melt for water.

Saya breathed out, her misty breath blurring the world briefly.

"I'll be sad to see you go," said a voice.

Saya jumped out of her skin.

Olga, the leader of the Zherik Elders, stood beside her, but Saya hadn't heard or sensed the woman's approach.

"How do you do that?"

"Do what?" Olga's low, croaky voice held a pleasant timbre laced with mischief. The harsh mountain climate and long life had wrinkled her face. She was short and plump. Rather than a hairpin, a long feather collected her long white hair into a frazzled bun. Her sparkling brown eyes, sporting a trace of gold, stared with an impish glint.

"You're stealthy," Saya said. "You must teach me."

Olga chuckled, flicking her hand. "I walk with the wind."

Saya lifted a single eyebrow. Olga's innocent smile didn't strike Saya as that virtuous. "Good morning, Elder. How are you doing?"

"Ak! My back hurts. This weather. It isn't good for my bones."

"We can't help the weather, but I have a salve for achy muscles. I could massage—"

"No need, child," was Olga's clipped response, waving her hand dismissively. No matter how often Saya offered, Olga always refused it. The other Elders appeared to suffer from the same backache and had also declined her offers. It made the Sorukhipa wonder.

Unlike Zahar's monarchy, the Zherik-Umea nation was governed by councils—an elders' council handled local matters, and the High Council handled regional ones. Olga led the High Council, speaking directly with Zahari emissaries. She'd been instrumental in selecting the guides and arranging the royal convoy's journey from Zhegama to Herisvalen. Widely respected, a few in town had shared that Olga was a seer who could sense all sorts of storms approaching before anyone else. Weather storms. Human storms.

And now, this fascinating woman stared at Saya with eyes as ancient as the world itself—eyes that could see something Saya did not, as if unraveling truths Saya had yet to discover. As if Olga were merely a vessel through which the gods examined their chosen Sorukhipa child.

Slightly unnerved, Saya glanced away. "It'll be sad to go." She hoped her voice didn't sound as rattled as she was.

Olga shrugged. "Then don't go. Stay with us."

Saya chuckled. If only it were that simple.

She'd come to love the mountains and their people. She could now see why her father had always spoken highly of the highland tribes. The Zherik-Umea were straightforward folk. They meant what they said without hidden agendas. They paid little mind to Zahar's politics, ignoring it all as though the mountains sheltered them from the world below. Titles carried no meaning to them. Words like Djinnshirukh and Sorukhipa didn't exist in their language. Conversing with individuals who didn't see them as something other than regular people was refreshing.

"There will be a big celebration to send you off," Olga said.

"But you just asked me to stay." Saya teased her with a wink.

Olga hummed, glancing askance, her intensity radiating off her in waves. "Make sure to sit with me." The woman patted Saya's back and walked away.

Saya turned toward the sound of drums, her eyes lingering on the snowy trail. She watched Zhegur speak to the guides. The river of fate was flowing again.

❧

Sipping her tea, Olga stood before the *harrizkoetxea*—the communal dwelling at the heart of Zherik-Umea culture, where Elders oversaw everything from disputes to celebrations. Among the square's bustle, she spotted the tall Zahari general, the princess she liked, and the black-haired one who didn't belong.

"The weather shifts," Olga murmured, eyes on the raven-haired woman. "But not all storms ride the wind."

A gaggle of children rushed forward, encircling that princess, bouncing around her, arms up in gleeful anticipation. The older kids pointed toward a spot past all the houses. The princess waved at her companions before the children tugged her away and disappeared around a corner.

Good. And stay away.

With a satisfied huff, Olga spun around. "They're here," she told the other Elders as she entered. "Get ready."

Polite conversation and reports peppered their breakfast. The group sat on floor cushions, eating savory spinach and sheep's cheese pastries. Olga sipped her tea, the rising steam veiling her gaze as she watched Saya and the Zahari general with narrowed, calculating eyes. *Something flickers between them.*

"And now the pass is open," Mizha said.

That brought Olga back from her mental wandering.

"But is it safe?" General Zhegur asked.

Mizha replied, "If it weren't, we wouldn't advise travel." He seemed calm, accustomed to the annoying Zahari habit of asking the same questions repeatedly. "The need for the pass extends beyond yours. Our people use it regularly, and we must also consider the bhiksunim and pilgrims in our charge, all eager to reach the Zahar-Eliza."

"We could use your woolly oxen, your karanji," General Zhegur said.

"Although the pass is open," Agham, Olga's husband, interjected, "the snow is still high in certain sections, and thus, you can't bring karanji."

"We must get over the pass and reach the Garai Plateau quickly," Saya said. "Before another blizzard comes."

"Your climb must be paced," Agham said. "Even if you've been here long enough to adjust to the thin air, a fast trek is out of the question."

"Agham is right," Olga said. "Your safety is our promise to the Zahari Crown."

All the Elders agreed with nods and approving murmurs.

"Without packed animals, we'll need more people," General Zhegur countered.

Olga studied him, then Saya, with keen interest. "Pray tell, what will the princesses need once they get to the Zahar-Eliza? You'll need our karanji to return their belongings to Zhegama."

Saya exchanged a glance with her general that bordered on annoyance.

Olga huffed, her gaze fixed on Saya, wound tighter than the yarn on her loom. *Pull too hard, and she'll snap.*

Collecting herself, Olga said, "Princess Saya, General Zhegur, please forgive this old woman. My eyes have seen too much. You're no different from the pilgrims coming through our towns. Truly little is needed at the Zahar-Eliza besides an open heart and a willing spirit."

With a grunt, Olga rose to her feet, done with the discussion and not in the mood for more opinions. "Too many, and you'll be encumbered. Too few, and you'll be vulnerable." She hit her staff, a long piece of exquisitely carved red oak, against the floor. "Ten officers to accompany the princesses and no more."

"Ten?" The general's mouth slackened.

"Yes." Olga faced him with a defiant frown. "Ten."

"That number barely accounts for half my unit. I've trained every officer for this journey—how will I choose?"

Olga shrugged, uninterested.

His lips flattened.

Saya exchanged a glance with him, a flicker of concern dancing in her golden eyes. "We'd be outmatched—"

"Then choose wisely." Olga's voice held no sympathy. "How you select them matters not to us. We'll see to the porters."

The Elders agreed with Olga, leaving Princess Saya and General Zhegur glancing at each other in veiled irritation.

"And now," Olga said in a commanding voice, thumping her staff on the floor again, "we celebrate!"

CHAPTER 80
THE PRINCESS AND THE ELDER

*Listen to my whispers in the wind and surrender to me. -
Poliormos*

And celebrating is what the Zherik-Umea did.

That night.

The Zahari officers sat among the crowd, trading stories over endless glasses of *edan*—a rice-and-flower-based liquor. Locals urged them to join the dancing, and some gave it a try, stumbling through the steps to the sound of laughter and good-natured teasing.

The Elders sat on a dais overlooking the celebration, where Saya spotted Olga. She made her way through the crowd, exchanging greetings, and Olga waved at her.

Olga appraised Saya's clothing with a crisp nod: a traditional Zherik black tunic dress with lovely red and gold embroidery and a long woolen shawl in matching colors draped around her shoulders. "Are you enjoying yourself?"

"Yes." Standing beside Olga, Saya could see the entire floor: people dancing and clapping, those walking around to greet others, those eating, and those drinking and laughing. "The town has outdone itself. I wish we could've had more of these before leaving."

Olga laughed. "Young people are so greedy." She patted the

cushion beside her, signaling Saya to sit, and turned to the women behind her. "Everyone, this is Princess Saya."

"Oh. She has good hips," one said. "Has she met my Bahir?"

"Are you married?" asked another.

"I want grandchildren with those eyes."

"Olga, you've been keeping this one to yourself, haven't you?"

"Don't embarrass our guest," Olga chided with mock severity. "You're making her blush."

The women laughed harder, their cackles loud and infused with warmth and mischief.

"Ak! Ignore them," Olga said, loud enough to be heard, then leaned closer with a conspiratorial grin. "They're jealous you're sitting beside me."

Saya smiled softly. "It's fine. I enjoy their sincerity."

"Your father said the same thing."

Saya raised her eyebrows. "Did he?"

"We were young back then. And he wasn't the king—yet. He laughed when I told him that one day, he would sit on the Zahari throne. Because of him, we agreed to the treaty with Zahar." Olga gazed thoughtfully as if replaying the past in her mind. "I knew the day would come when I would ask Hröld, the king, not the general."

Saya's eyebrows lifted in surprise. "I'm impressed. That treaty was signed some forty years ago."

Olga let a sly laugh. "As I said, we were young. But you see," her eyes narrowed as if savoring a well-kept secret, "we agreed to sign the treaty on one condition."

Saya leaned in, her curiosity piqued. "What was it?"

Olga's demeanor suggested this was no ordinary agreement. "That when the time came, he would grant our request, no questions asked."

"And what was the request?"

Olga shook her head. "All in good time, child."

"I see. You're holding onto your good cards."

"He-he." Olga's eyes twinkled. "And good cards they are."

The musicians concluded the song. The rustle of fabric and the murmur of voices broke the hushed anticipation that had settled over the room. Women swiftly gathered at the heart of the chamber. As the music resumed, the women moved in perfect harmony. Their arms and legs flowed in unison, creating intricate patterns.

"They're so graceful," she said. "What is this dance?"

Olga's eyes darted between Saya and the dancers. "That's Mathamurti's dance. It tells the story of Mathamurti, who fell in love with the sun god, Lord Aditya. He loved her back and made her an Earth goddess in return. As they embraced, her body transformed into the Zahar-Katea. Every night, she longs for her husband. He comes out every morning to embrace her."

"It's a lovely story." The heat inside the structure made Saya wonder if that was how Mathamurti felt when Aditya held her in his arms.

Olga tapped her shoulder and jerked her chin toward the other end of the room. "It appears my kin are teaching your sister to dance."

"Dance? No, she shouldn't."

"And why is that? Another Zahari prohibition?" Sarcasm dripped from Olga's words as she dramatically rolled her eyes.

"She can't enter open bodies of water or dance."

"Ak!" Olga grunted her displeasure. "It's unnatural to keep the body from moving when it wants to. You should know this yourself."

Olga was right, but Saya grimaced anyway. "She shouldn't dance in public. I must stop her."

Olga pulled on Saya's arm with a stern tone. "Sit and watch."

"But—"

"*Watch!*"

She sat, compelled by Olga's voice.

At first, Kharis was uncertain, but she soon grasped the rhythm, memorized the steps the women taught her, and followed along, dancing with controlled, sensual steps.

It bewitched Saya. She'd never seen her sister dance with such abandon, gliding with the music as if nothing mattered.

More women joined the dance, moving as a single body. Their graceful arms swept through the air, hips swaying with precision, while their rhythmic foot stomps added layers of percussion to the music. A vibrant energy pulsed through the group, rising and falling in waves. The women spun, their arms lifting toward the sky, reaching out as if mirroring Mathamurti's fabled gesture toward Lord Aditya, embodying an ancient ritual of devotion and power.

Saya then felt it—the shift in the air.

An awakening of magic.

Goose bumps traveled the length of her body as this familiar power wrapped around her the way sunlight warmed a body in the early morning.

Her gaze fixed on Kharis. Was she doing this?

The music became richer, filled with complex layers of melody and harmony. The colors around her turned brighter, and the air felt light and sweet. A wave of joy inundated the place, and Saya's heart sang with it. Her worries and fears melted away, urging her to smile. The scent of citrus and sea salt filled the space, and Saya breathed it in. Time appeared to slow, and this moment of inner calm stretched endlessly.

Olga pulled on Saya's sleeve, waking her from her trance.

The music had ended.

"This next dance is where young women select their future husbands." Her eyebrows waggled suggestively. "The married ones leave the floor, but the unmarried ones stay and continue dancing. Like Mathamurti, they seek their Aditya." Olga pushed her, encouraging Saya. "Dance, child. Make yourself seen. Don't hide from your Aditya. Let him keep you warm."

The women sitting behind Olga trilled loudly, knowing fully what she meant.

"Me, dance?"

"Who else?" Annoyed, Olga pointed to the dance floor with her chin, daring her. Saya froze, speechless. Men weren't attracted to her. She was the Sorukhipa, a tall and imposing crimson warrior, the Djinnshirukh's guardian, and nothing more.

"Or would you rather dance with Mathamurti?" Olga tilted her head to the side with a curious glint.

Saya blinked. "No. I... It's not that."

Olga gave her a firm shove, snapping her out of her anxious thoughts. "Then make yourself seen," she said, vexed by Saya's inaction. "Step into the light and shine for Aditya or Mathamurti. Here, no one judges."

It was tempting to let herself be taken by the music's flow and forget her obligations for one night.

Olga pushed her again—a shove filled with frustration—and Saya finally moved, headed toward Kharis and the rest of the women. Her heart was racing so fast she thought it would explode. Her vision blurred, and the wall of people around her seemed to grow taller.

What am I doing?

Saya was about to turn around when someone lightly tapped on her shoulder.

CHAPTER 81

BLISS

To dance with another is to become a story—two flames weaving into one breathless legend. - Poliormos

"Would you dance with me?"

General Zhegur stood before her, and all of him filled her eyes with ecstatic warmth. His soft smile sent ripples through her. His hazel eyes melted her hesitation. A hot flush crept across her face, but Saya managed a nod, her whole body eager. She hoped he wouldn't notice how his presence awoke a hunger she didn't think she had.

He extended his hand to her. She glanced at it and took it just to stop her hands from shaking. His hand swallowed hers, and his calloused grip sparked cravings she'd long ignored.

The general led her to the dance floor, where they twirled around each other to the music as he gazed into her eyes, not once looking away from her. She smiled at him, bashfully welcoming the attention. Emulating what the other men did, Zhegur touched the small of her back and clumsily brought her to him, standing so close that his lips almost brushed hers. Her neck turned hot, and it surprised her to want his body pressed against hers forever.

When he pulled away to follow the dance steps, the space between them brought a dull ache to her chest. It made her heart pound so loudly she feared it could be heard over the vibrant music.

Zhegur made her heart jump up and down, demanding more of him. The fluttering muddled every rational thought, urging her to surrender. Her eyes focused on his mouth, and she savored the idea of kissing him, imagining the feel of his full lips against hers.

"Is everything all right?" Zhegur asked, leaning closer to her.

Saya gulped. She'd stopped dancing. "I—I don't know the steps," she heard herself say to cover up her moment of adoration.

Zhegur grinned, his eyes sparkling with such bliss. "Neither do I." That winsome smile melted any arguments she might have harbored. "We can stop if you wish."

"No." She glanced away, aware she'd blurted it out. "I don't mind dancing." *Not with you.* The thought surprised her. "I don't mind at all."

She wanted to dance through the universe in his arms.

Forever.

To enjoy an endless, pleasurable entanglement of arms and legs and intimate breaths.

He leaned in closer still, tipping her chin to him. His fingers burned with the searing heat of embers, and Saya wanted them branding every inch of her skin. She forgot to breathe, charmed by hazel eyes and luscious lips. She couldn't tell if the music had stopped or if the world had.

"Your eyes are spellbinding," he said.

Saya stopped thinking. Electric sparks flickered between them, and the sensation was divine.

His hand tightened around hers. Without letting go of her, he resumed their dancing, doing his best to keep up with the other men. He struggled to follow their spirited rhythm, facing the wrong way, missing steps, and making his own. It made her laugh, and he beamed as if he wanted more of her joyous laughter.

The couple swayed their hips, spinning and swinging their arms to the bright, resonant Zherik-Umea music. Saya, drunk on his attention, teased him with a sensual smile. He teased her back with touches that her entire body welcomed.

Mimicking the other men's dance moves, Reza wrapped his hands around Saya's waist and lifted her off the ground. A surprised squeal burst from her lips. Her eyes widened in delight as he spun her through the air. The world blurred around her, the rush of movement filling her senses until he gently brought her down, her body slowly rubbing his in a moment that stole her breath away.

Blessed Mother.

The way he gazed at her, with such intensity, jolted Saya. Heat flooded her entire being. She swallowed hard, unable to tear her eyes from him. The brown and green details in his irises were beautiful. His warm breath, infused with the enticing scent of edan, drew her closer still. His lips, slightly parted, were hers for the taking.

A kiss, her heart demanded.

A kiss, her soul urged.

Her mind shut down. Something feral inside her grew claws, ready to tear fabric and leather to get to his skin. This beast was drooling at the idea of skin against skin.

"Your Highness?"

Stunned by how quickly she'd lost control, Saya staggered back, breath catching in her throat. The familiar storm of thoughts and emotions crashed in. Duty. Responsibility.

"I—I need air," she said, her voice breaking. She ran, bumping into bodies to part the crowd until the sharp bite of icy air hit her face and quieted the chaos in her mind. She wrapped her arms around herself to steady her trembling body.

Why did I run out?

She pressed a shaky hand against her forehead. *I'm such a fool.* Her breath curled into wisps of mist. The intoxicating music floated in the air. The stars lit the clear night, twinkling in rhythm. Above, Sharan shone on the world, and Tung, crossing over its sister, gave the ivory moon its peculiar red eye.

"If I overstepped." Zhegur had followed her. "Or if I offended you, please accept my apologies."

Blessed Mother above. "No, you didn't. I never meant to worry you." She reached for a white lie. "I—I didn't realize how hot it could get with so many people inside. Please accept my apologies."

"It's cold." He draped his fur cloak over her shoulders.

Words failed her. His scent, a blend of leather and sandalwood, tugged at her senses.

"Would you like some water?" he asked.

Saya kept her head down, afraid he would see how much she wanted him to hold her as he did on the dance floor. "Some air will do."

He stepped closer, his shoulder touching hers. "Are you all right? Do you need to sit down?"

She shook her head. "No, no need. Just some air." *Liar.*

His eyebrows arched, framing insistent eyes.

"I'm fine, I swear," she said.

He studied her for a moment longer before giving a soft nod, his expression easing.

She glanced at the scar crossing his left eyebrow. His eyes softened the firmness of his jaw, hinting at quiet strength.

"Aren't you going back in?" she asked.

"As long as you're out here, I'll stay with you," he said, tilting his head as the crisp night breeze ruffled his hair. It was longer now, with strands dancing over his ears. In the moonlight, highlights shimmered through his brown curls.

"The cool air does feel nice," he added, closing his eyes to savor the moment.

He was a few fingers taller than she, with broad shoulders and an athletic constitution. He was reserved and collected, always in control, an innate leader who'd earned the respect and admiration of his unit. A man Saya could trust with her life.

The memory of him holding onto her waist and lifting her sent a pleasurable shudder down her back. A different side of him had emerged when they danced. A man who laughed with his entire being, honest and kind, with a hint of roguish charm.

She stood beside him, wrapped in his scent, and Saya surrendered to an ineffable feeling bigger than her. Soon, she would enter the Zahar-Eliza and spend a year away from the world, and so much could happen. Life was about seizing opportunities, as her Nana often told her. Her heart was beating fast again. Olga was right. It wasn't good to deny the body what it wanted—what it needed.

"Would you like to dance?" She gestured toward the *harrizkoetxea*.

"Yes," he said with a hunger in his eyes that spiked her pulse.

Saya's mind went blank. Her heart led the way for a change, and although she was so nervous her knees would buckle, she leaned in and awkwardly pressed her lips against his.

General Zhegur flinched, his eyebrows lifting in utter surprise.

Blessed Mother, what did I do?

"I... I'm so sorry." Burning with embarrassment, Saya stepped back, her hands cupping her mouth. Too shocked to look down, she stepped onto an ice patch and lost her balance. He swiftly caught her to prevent her from falling, but didn't release her once she was steady in his arms.

"Don't apologize," he whispered, warm lips brushing her ear. Pressed close to him, his heart hammered against her chest as wildly as hers. "I've wanted to kiss you from the moment I first saw you. I... I didn't think it was possible."

Saya remained in his arms, allowing his voice to echo through her. Her heart raced in circles. Her mind was half here, half gone, but her hunger was ever-present. Exploding.

He was an officer in the Zahari imperial army, and as an imperial princess, she was his superior. She became keenly aware of her status, the ethical conflict, the breach of conduct, and the potential consequences that could arise from it. And yet, she summoned her courage. "I... I want you to... to kiss me."

Reza stilled, then pulled away, clutching her arms. He studied her face, a frown on his, and scanned his surroundings.

"Come." He gently pulled her by the hand and led her to a quiet alleyway. Above, the stars twinkled with delight. The moons watched, approving of the couple below.

"Was that your first kiss?"

Embarrassed by her dismal effort, she held her breath and lowered her head. "Yes."

"Then I want mine to be even more beautiful. I'll make it an unforgettable memory." He lifted her chin, gazing at her. "Your eyes are truly mesmerizing, Your Highness."

"Saya, please," she whispered, almost breathless, words faltering. "Call me Saya."

He paused, savoring the moment without breaking eye contact. "Then you must call me Reza." His gaze intensified. "Saya." He uttered her name, admiring it as if it were a lovely rose, immersing himself in its heady scent.

Saya stood utterly still. How he uttered her name echoed through her like a stormy wind. She longed for him to whisper it in her ear, allowing those sounds to roll down her body and strike a light in her core.

Reza slid a few hair strands off her face and gently tucked them behind her ears as his eyes explored every detail of her face. He caressed her ear's fleshy outer rim, slowly moving his fingers to stroke her neck. Saya allowed his timid exploration.

His lips brushed against her ear first, and Saya swallowed her moan. She'd spent years mastering discipline, yet one touch from him, and she was unraveling.

He slowly traveled the length of her ear to her neck with his lips, pausing after each gentle kiss as if giving her a chance to change her mind. It made her quiver. It made her want more. Before she knew it, her hands moved on their own, resting on his waist until desire, hot and enticing, urged her to pull him closer.

The heat he exuded was overwhelming, exorcising the chilly air and seeping into her bones.

He leaned in, hands resting flat against the wall. She realized he'd promised to kiss her, not touch her. His body pressed against hers, trapping her not with force, but with the gravity of his want. Reza brushed his lips along her throat, then lingered at that tender hollow beneath her jaw. Her breathing quickened, and she got lost in everything that defined him.

Her muscles tensed in anticipation. When Reza's lips finally brushed hers, her mind burst into color. Her lungs seized with the pleasure of it. His tongue gently parted her lips and stroked hers, and her soul melted. She moaned his name, a breathless prayer for more. She felt him shudder at the sound she made, how she uttered his name, and his groan dragged through his breath. He pressed her against the wall, and his mouth devoured her as if a containment had been broken and water spilled freely.

He kissed her as if breathing weren't necessary.

With a hunger that knew no end.

As if she, and only she, existed in his world.

She closed her eyes and surrendered to him. No more order and discipline. No more rules or common sense. She let the wild, tempestuous Saya out of her cage and offered her to this man who teased her senses with lips made of honey and sin, and scorching kisses.

A wild pulse flooded her entire being with incredible warmth. The world dissolved, leaving her completely immersed in a state of pure, unshakable bliss.

The storm had swept through, washing away doubt and leaving only clarity. No longer timidly holding onto his waist, her hands moved possessively on his back, pressing him closer to her. Her fingers dug into his shoulder blades as Saya and Reza moved, enticed by the same passion.

Her soul vibrated with the rhythm of life itself.

I want this. I want all of it.

CHAPTER 82
JOY

Love is the unexpected tingle that sends ripples of joy through the soul. - Poliormos

When the music stopped, Kharis found herself in the middle of the dance floor. Around her, the energy had shifted—couples had begun to drift toward quiet corners, drawn together in soft conversation and shared laughter.

Mizha was already kissing a pretty Zherik girl in a shadowed alcove, his hands confidently at her waist. A handful of his friends turned their attention to Kharis, their gazes bathed with curiosity.

Her reckless actions had already put someone in danger. Avoiding their eyes, she slipped quietly out of the building.

Her sweat met the frigid night air, sending a shiver down her neck. Her eyes roamed toward their cabin, suspecting Saya had gone to sleep. Dancing had energized her, the thrill still coursing through her veins. Sleep was the last thing on her mind. She turned toward the *harrizkoetxea...* and her face twisted into a grimace. No, she had to stay away from men.

An idea sparked in her mind—the viewpoint.

Kharis wove through the winding streets, dodging passersby. The cliffside came into view past the apple orchards. Keeping a safe distance, she gazed into the canyon's abyss below. The sheer drop was dizzying, at least three cliff-marks deep.

Vibrant music soon floated with the cool breeze, and Kharis danced to it, letting joy guide her steps.

Millions of stars twinkled above. Sharan commandeered the heavens, competing with the Silver River in brightness. Tung had given its sister that peculiar red eye.

"*Why are you alone?*"

Her eyes widened in surprise, her heart leaping with a joyful jolt at his unexpected appearance. "My sister went to sleep."

"*Did she?*" The Voice sounded curious. "*The night is still young.*"

"Do you enjoy celebrations?"

"*I enjoy watching the stars.*"

A snort escaped her. "Then you're in good company."

"*You are always charming company.*"

Heat warmed her cheeks. "You sure know what to say."

"*Did I make you smile?*"

"Yes, you did." Kharis exhaled quietly and sat on a boulder, her gaze fixed on the stars. It was nice to speak to him again. "Tell me about your life before fate tied you to the Djinnshirukh."

His pause lasted a few breaths. "*As I have said, I am not the Akumi king.*"

The emphasis on his "not" intrigued her. "You could say that to fool me."

"*I could say anything to fool you, but I chose not to. Lying serves no one. You bound yourself to the Akumi king. I chose to bind myself to you.*"

"Hmm." To bind himself to her. "Are you the madness?"

"*Would you want me to be?*" he teased.

She shook her head, laughing. "No. I would rather you were real." To kiss. To hug. "Why did you bind yourself to me?"

The soft swoosh of wind wove through the canyon before he answered. "*That was my choice.*"

"But why choose that?"

"*Because that was my vow to you.*"

She groaned. "Circular arguments won't get us anywhere."

"*I never meant to anger you.*"

She exhaled loudly, this time mad at herself. "Don't mind me. I shouldn't press you when you wish to keep your privacy."

An owl hooted in the distance. Another replied.

She slid to the ground, leaning against the boulder, gaze lingering on Sharan and its red eye. "Did you love her? The Spirit Kin queen?"

"*I love her with every fiber of my being.*"

A tinge of jealousy squeezed her heart as Kharis hugged her knees. Noam had loved her like that. "Tell me about her. Please?"

"*She is the most powerful of us. One of the seven gems in the Infinite's Crown.*"

His use of the present tense caught her attention.

"Sounds poetic," she said. "To be someone's gem." Curiosity stirred. "What made you love her?"

"*Her sense of justice and compassion. Her smile. Her laugh.*" Pride and affection powered his voice. "*Her aggravating stubbornness.*"

Kharis pouted at that.

"*How she looks at me, and my entire being shudders under her gaze.*"

"You must've loved her deeply."

"*I still do.*"

"What happened to her?"

"*She bound herself to the Akumi king to end the One War.*"

Kharis exhaled softly, resignation curling on her breath. Everything—her fate, her life—had been shaped by that war. Its echoes still rippled a thousand years later.

The music started again, and multiple voices joined in. "I wish I knew what they were singing."

She gazed at the night sky to assess the constellations. One had always called to her. "Herensuge's my favorite." She pointed to a spot in the black vault.

"*The silver dragon,*" he said. "*It fits you.*"

"You can see it?"

"*I do.*" His voice softened. "*I sit atop my peak, watching the stars while your voice brushes through my mind.*" A quiet sigh followed. "*Perhaps I am the one going mad.*"

Kharis chuckled, then bit her lip. "Would you share your name with me tonight?"

"*We have talked about this—*"

"Yes, yes. You don't believe names are important."

"*I would never say that.*" A quiet moment passed between them. "*Names imply intimacy and connection.*" A profound exhale ruffled her mind. "*But they can also enslave you.*"

The slap stung. "I suppose they can."

"*A name should not define us, either.*"

Anger crawled under her skin. "There are diverse types of names. The ones given to you at birth and those hurled at you. Believe me, I know."

Memories flickered—sharp-edged words meant to bruise and shame, trailing her like hyenas waiting for her to fall. But stronger, brighter memories rose in defiance and scattered them.

"And then," she said, "there are the gifts of love and affection. Noam called me Hya. My sister calls me Khiri. My nana calls me Gutxi. Whenever I hear them use these, it warms my heart. It tells me there's a thread connecting us that no one can take away. It reminds me that despite everything I face, they love me."

"*I see.*" His pause was contemplative. "*I shall ponder this more carefully.*"

A soft breeze danced through Kharis's hair, and she combed it away from her face.

"*Do you still wish to give me a name?*" The Voice sounded like he was waving a white flag.

She lifted her eyebrows, her hand drying damp eyes. "Do you truly mean this?"

"*Yes. More so if...*" Hesitation rode on that quiet caesura. "*If it is a gift of love and affection.*"

The song ended, and a more vibrant piece of music began. "They're dancing again." It brought a smile to her face. "I wish you could dance with me."

"*Do you?*" His voice quivered. "*Do you wish this? To dance with you?*"

"Could you?" She grinned at the night.

"*For you, the world.*" A pause. "*Allow me to surprise you. Close your eyes.*"

She did, half intrigued, half afraid of what might come. The evening breeze blew softly, rustling the snow off the branches of nearby trees. A sweet scent she couldn't place tickled her nose.

"Open," he said.

A tall shape of curling black mist stood before her as if the night had taken shape. He studied her with a soft gaze as if he were smiling. Kharis couldn't tear her eyes away from his. The power of the stars and the moons at midnight resided in that gaze.

"Y—You are real?" Her hand tentatively brushed against his form, feeling the cool, glittering mist drift away.

"Teach me the steps," he said, determined.

"You... You are real." It wasn't a question anymore. She blinked, once, twice, then reached out, fingertips grazing her sleeve as if to test the miracle. She was awake, and he was real. Not solid, but present. Excitement surged through her chest, her thoughts drifting like dandelion seeds. Could he hug her? Kiss her? Whisper sweet nothings in her ear?

"The steps?" he asked again, gently prompting.

She steadied her breathing. "You are here," she whispered, still in awe. "But how?"

"Magic has allowed me a moment in my eternity to spend it with you. Soon it will wane, but for now, it suffices." His voice deepened. Commanding. "Now. Shall we dance?"

Kharis snapped out of her awe. "Right. Follow what I do."

"I shall follow you until my very last breath."

Kharis stilled, letting those words settle. "The things you say." Her cheeks burned fiercely hot. "Do you mean them?"

"Every single word," he said. "I already love you, but I want you to fall in love with me all over again."

"A—Again?"

His voice wrapped her in genuine affection. "I knew I would be yours from the moment I first saw you."

Kharis gazed at him, all her questions fleeing her mind. Well... Not all of them. One rose, a persistent little thing: who was he? He was the voice hiding in the dark corners of her mind, her protector, the Pharos of Hegra, a mass of midnight and stardust.

"Itzu..." Her voice trailed off as she pondered everything that he was to her.

"Itzu?" he asked, a playful spark flickering in his eyes.

Kharis blinked, the name startling her into stillness. She'd meant to give him a name, and there it was.

"I just gave you a name." Her fingers brushed nervously against the fabric of her woolen shawl. "Itzu, short for Itzalt-su." She tilted her head, the tiniest spark of daring glinting in her smile. "It means shadowy."

He laughed, indigo eyes gazing at her with amusement. Kharis swore that joy flickered in them. "Then I must give you one," he said. "A gift of my love and affection for you."

Kharis wanted to squeal and hug an unhuggable shape.

His form shifted and swayed like the murmuration of starlings as he pondered. "A name for you..." His breath created delicate curls of glimmering black mist around his face. He straightened as if an idea had come to him and leaned forward. "You are my lovely Dhordan."

"Dhordan?" That piqued her curiosity. "What does it mean?"

"Hummingbird."

The tiny birds had always flitted around her, their jewel-colored feathers bursts of joy. Had he noticed this?

"Why?"

"You are charming and agile like them," he said. "You are a glorious blur of elegant movement, hovering from flower to flower with determination. You move gracefully in the wind, making my heart soar with pride." He lowered his head to meet her gaze, his eyes warm and earnest. "You are my lovely crimson hummingbird. My Dhordan."

A flush of heat spread across her cheeks. "You're a poet."

"And you are my beautiful songstress."

His words jolted her heart—again.

"So?" he asked. "You were about to teach me the steps."

"Yes. Right." Her cheeks were still hot, the heat melting her tangled thoughts. He was standing before her, so close and so willing. So real.

"This is the first step." She somehow managed to tap her foot to the rhythm of the music and twirl. "There are a few movements, but this is the main one. Tap, tap, twirl. All else is variations on it."

Itzu hummed his approval. "Let us dance."

With those three words, her world shifted. He'd taken a risk she couldn't fully grasp—just for a dance. That quiet courage mended the broken parts in her. Heat rose behind her eyes, but instead of tears, she broke into a wide, unrestrained grin.

Her heart was whole again. "Thank you."

"What for?"

Her body buzzed in anticipation. "For coming. For dancing with me. For wanting to be with me."

His head shook, stardust rippling in the soft evening breeze. "I come willingly because you wish to be with me."

Wearing a smile that could rival Sharan's brightness, Kharis danced with Itzu to the rhythm of the music drifting from the *harrizkoetxea*. The wind joined them, rustling frosted leaves. Sharan lit their steps, as if watching them with silent approval.

CHAPTER 83
PARTING IS NEVER SWEET

Destiny's call entwined our souls, but fate's cruel hand demands our fall. Our cherished moments are now memories we keep. Oh, my love, parting is never sweet. - Poliormos

A few days after the festivity, Olga did her best to behave despite Kharis's aggravating questions. She'd avoided this princess several times, leaving Agham to deal with her while she gravitated toward Saya.

Today, it couldn't be helped. Saya came with her general and her annoying sister. This time, the sister didn't leave to play with the children.

"The start will begin before sunrise," Olga repeated, glaring at Kharis, who pouted unhappily. "That is not changing. This trek is long and physically demanding. Starting later implies tramping into the evening, and when tired, people make mistakes."

"But why can't we?" Kharis asked.

Olga's tone harshened. "Exhausted people die when surrounded by darkness in the mountain region. It's been explained multiple times. The climb to the plateau will challenge you," she said tersely. "The last storm closed the pass for sixteen days. The potential for an avalanche is always present, even days after the pass has opened. The trails are iced over and exposed, offering little protection. One misstep and the tumble will send you flying. Last I checked, you don't have wings, *printzesak*."

Olga's sarcasm oozed when uttering the Zherik term for "princess." Annoyed, she drank her tea, using the moment to collect herself. Kharis narrowed her eyes, studying her for a long moment. Olga waited for the imminent outburst, salivating at putting her in her place.

Aware of the tension, Agham turned to Olga, questions residing in his gaze, and flashed the princess a fatherly smile. "Getting you to Leruak in one day is best. Your safety is foremost in our minds."

Kharis got up, facing her sister. "I promised the children I'd play with them. I understand why you wanted me to participate in this discussion, but it's best to let you and General Zhegur attend to this." After a curt bow, she walked out.

"Please, excuse her." A pink flush crept across Saya's cheeks. "My sister has become attached to the children here. She means no disrespect."

Olga scoffed. "She's certainly not as level-headed as you."

"You think too highly of me, Elder."

"Child, have I not asked you to call me by name? You're not in Zahar-Ghak. Agham, tell her."

Agham put his hand up. "Pay no attention to my wife. She enjoys stirring up trouble."

Olga sniffed, offended.

"General Zhegur," Agham said. "Is your group settled?"

The general stiffened, uncrossing his legs and shifting his weight on the cushion as if he'd hoped to skip this part. "Yes." He threw Saya a nervous glance. "The high elevation has been a challenge, but I have selected the ten who'll manage the ascent."

"Good," Agham said. "We can't afford another delay. The Zahari Crown expects us to deliver on our promise. And so, you stay?"

"Yes." Zhegur rubbed the back of his neck, his throat bobbing up and down. "Officer Ortega will lead the expedition."

Olga pursed her lips, her eyes darting between Saya and her general. Her deep hum caught Agham's attention, and he gave her a warning frown.

"Then, it's settled," Agham said with a nod. "With this matter resolved, may everyone find favor with Mathamurti."

Zhegur bowed and walked out, limbering his neck and shoulders as if trying to push an invisible weight off them. Olga didn't like what she saw. "What's wrong with him?"

"No idea," Saya remarked, extending a helping hand to help Olga to her feet.

Olga gave Saya a narrowed stare, smelling the lie, and scratched her silvery bun, pondering what to do with this princess. Before joining a group of women, Olga patted Saya's back. "I must meet with them, but come see me later. I'll make you the tea you love, and we can chat."

❧

When Saya walked out, Reza was waiting for her.

Without a word, she settled beside him, her gaze fixed on the quaint houses lining the opposite side of the square. Saya broke the silence, struggling to contain her anger and frustration. "When did you decide not to come with us?"

Reza lowered his gaze and pinched his lips, clearly grappling with his decision. "If I allow this to go on too long, it would be difficult to say goodbye—to see you go. Perhaps..." He tilted his head, turning his attention to the ever-shifting clouds. "Perhaps we should end this before it hurts too much."

A sudden chill swept over Saya, and the vibrant hues surrounding her turned dull. "What are you saying?"

His hand twitched at his side, like he meant to reach for her, then stilled. He gazed at her, pain creasing his brow.

"I want more." He closed his eyes, his voice wavering as he spoke. "I want everything with you." A ragged breath escaped him. "A life that includes you at my side forever. A life where my children bear your eyes and smile."

His heartfelt confession hit her with the force of a lightning bolt.

457

"I want everything." His eyes returned to the wispy clouds. "But you're the daughter of the Imperial King of Zahar, Son of the Sun." His voice cracked. "And I'm the son of a humble orange farmer from Cecchio." His chest rose with a sharp inhale. "I must accept our roles. Our fates." He gazed at her with sadness, eyes filled with unshed tears and the guilt from letting it get this far. "I don't dare dream beyond my station, Your Highness."

That title had become a wall. Back to titles and formalities. Back to never hearing his mouth utter her name right before their lips met.

"All I do is dream," she said, eyes welling with tears. "Dream and hope."

"Saya." Her name tumbled from his lips—a whispered plea, one more attempt to hold onto her before parting.

She shook her head, not prepared for this. Not ready for anything. Saya wanted to scream, to kiss him, to forget everything—instead, a strangled breath caught in her throat. She swallowed her tears, and her heart sank to the bottom of a murky ocean.

They stood beside each other.

Neither spoke.

But neither moved away.

CHAPTER 84
THE SWEETEST OF HOPES

Love is the seed, and hope is its delicate bloom, unfurling in the quiet spaces where the darkest shadows yield to light. - Poliormos

Two days later, a knock on their cabin's door announced it was time to leave. Giddy, Kharis slung her pack over her shoulder. The crisp chill nipped at their noses as the sisters emerged into the dark, frosty air. The crunch of packed snow beneath their boots echoed in the stillness. Above them, the stars twinkled fiercely.

Saya stopped, hesitant.

Kharis, eager to get started, nudged her forward. "You've got to move, Saya, or we can't get started," she teased, chuckling as she stepped ahead.

Saya forced her smile.

❧

The porters stood around a bonfire, discussing how to split the cargo. The White Guard escort chatted, sharing a joke here and there, their laughter drifting in the air.

Reza Zhegur moved through the groups, providing the last set of instructions. The moment he saw Saya step out of her cabin, his heart slammed against his chest so forcefully it hurt.

He battled the urge to approach her, his mind whirling with everything he wanted to say. Yet, no excuse came to him except to wish her a safe journey and say goodbye.

That pained him the most.

Their first proper kiss, so sweet and indulgent, transformed into passion and longing for him. It became the source for secret encounters filled with timid explorations and blushing cheeks, fueling his desire to hold onto and love her for as long as he lived.

The first day he met her at the Academy, his heart was swept away. She was so beautiful, a spring goddess incarnate.

Never fazed by conflict or challenges and always disciplined and collected, Reza stammered when she was around, losing his train of thought. For months, he'd loved her in silence, knowing it was a love he could never claim until the night she asked for a kiss.

Reza knew it was preposterous to wish for more. She was a high princess of the Empire and would be married off to some royal, as was the custom. If the rumors he'd heard in Cecchio were accurate, Saya would never marry anyone. Fate, fickle and cruel, had placed her on his path, and he fell head over heels for this enticing woman. He decided to stay with his officers and let her go. But could he?

"Reza?"

Her voice startled him out of the whirling in his head, and he stiffened, chest out, shoulders squared, arms rigidly at his sides. "Your Highness?"

Saya quietly stared at the bonfire, her shoulder brushing his. His breath caught when her slender fingers wrapped around his—a timid, discreet gesture, hidden behind cloaks, that roused all the emotions he'd contained.

He wanted to yell that this woman was his and that no one was taking her away from him. Instead, his eyes etched every detail of her face into his memory: her long, glossy chestnut curls; her warm smile; the soft lips he craved to kiss again and again; and her astonishing golden-colored eyes, glittering in the firelight.

"You must go with her." Emotion choked his voice,

reminding himself of Saya's duty as the Sorukhipa. "My presence," he swallowed hard, "would only interfere with your training."

She faced him, her eyes intense. "What will you do?"

Reza's gaze lingered upon the woman he loved, and his resolve to walk away dissolved. "I'll go to Zhegama... and... if you wish it... I'll wait for you."

A gentle breeze rustled her curls.

"Please," she finally whispered. "Wait for me." Her glorious eyes glistened. "Don't give up on us."

Us. That word meant everything to him. A single syllable that held the weight of their shared dreams and promises.

"Others have planned my life," she said, "and I've never strayed from the path imposed on me." A tear rolled down her cheek, leaving a trail of liquid diamonds. "But you? You're what I want and need. I'm crossing a line, Reza. I don't know where it leads us, and the not-knowing scares me, but I won't be afraid as long as you're with me."

He focused on her lovely face and clutched her hand, wishing he would never have to release it.

"I am yours," he whispered. "I was always yours."

The world around them melted away. He wanted nothing more than to freeze time, to linger with this woman in the embrace of shared heartbeats, where their entwined hands spoke a language of their own.

His fingers curled tighter around hers. He wasn't ready to let go.

"Reza," she said tenderly, "I want to kiss you."

He glanced away, heartbroken. "If we kiss, I won't let go of you, and you must accompany your sister."

Another tear trailed down Saya's cheek, and his stomach clenched. Without a thought, his thumb gently wiped it away.

"Be safe and return to me." He stood tall, lingering on her face with a pain-filled gaze. "When you do, I promise to kiss you. Every day. Every night. For as long as I live and for as long as you'll have me."

Hope illuminated her gaze with a radiant glow. "You swear by it?"

The fire in his heart burned brightly. "On my honor and my life, Saya."

Her eyes gleamed, the gold in them bright and sparkling. The warmth in her gaze spoke of trust and affection, and Reza reciprocated with a genuine smile that spoke of his devotion to her.

"I love you," he said.

Saya smiled through her tears. "And I love you more."

CHAPTER 85
NAMES AND GIFTS

*True love knows no bounds. It is an eternal flame, an endless dance,
an everlasting promise, an unbroken bond. - Poliormos*

Olga walked out to see Saya off, yet the first face she
saw was Kharis. Whatever spirit resided inside that
princess waited for its chance to sting and poison
like a scorpion. It watched Olga with loathing—with eyes
hungry for revenge.

"Please, be nice to both women."

Agham's voice pushed her out of her dark thoughts. She
turned to him, expecting an explanation.

"A few have noticed," he said, "how you treat the princess
with black hair, myself included." He watched Olga blow her
cheeks, her sign of annoyance, and release the air in noisy
puffs.

Agham frowned with concern. "Why aren't you nice to
her?"

"Agham." Her voice sharpened in warning. "If everyone's
nice to her, she won't leave. And she must return. But Saya?"
Her breath misted in the chilly air. "She should stay with us."

Agham huffed in aggravation. "You've attached yourself to
her, haven't you?"

Olga's lips curled into a wistful smile. "Like a mother to a daughter."

He clicked his tongue, shooting her a disapproving glare. "Olga, you know better."

"Oh, Agham," she gushed. "She's special. I can feel it in my bones. She belongs with us."

"Olga." His voice carried a stern warning, and a tense silence hung between them, sharp as knives. "Treat both princesses well. Do not cause trouble for us."

Olga grimaced as a bitter memory came to her. Back then, she'd turned her back on a princess-turned-queen who begged for help. Olga had not listened, a decision that turned the world upside down. A thousand years later, she was still paying for her arrogance while her people had paid the price.

She met Agham's gaze, her sarcasm masking the guilt. "I'll do my best." Without another glance at Agham, she joined the crowd. "Good morning, *denek*."

"Thank you for your hospitality," Kharis said after a quick bow.

Olga half-smiled, trying to hide her dislike as Agham had asked her. "Thank you," she said, forcing her politeness, and turned toward Saya, who discreetly held hands with her general as if she wouldn't see it.

"Princess Saya, I want a word with you," she said.

Surprise widened Saya's eyes. Saya and her general exchanged a silent glance, an unspoken message passing between them before he released her hand and gently nudged her forward. She hesitated, reluctant to leave his side.

"*Go*," he mouthed, encouraging Saya to comply, and she unwillingly stepped forward.

Seeing them together softened Olga's heart. The way they gazed at each other... If they genuinely loved one another, why couldn't they be together? It made no sense to her.

"Princess Saya," the Elder said, "you've graced us with your presence." Olga meant it. "We've learned from you, and you've opened your heart to learn from us. Your medicinal knowledge improved ours, and we hope our humble wisdom aided yours.

After discussing with the Elders, we've agreed that you deserve more than a blessing from us."

The other Elders pounded their staffs on the ground in approval.

Olga gestured for Agham to hand her something. She held it, memorializing every detail of this chilly, dark morning. "From this day forth, you shall be known among us as Sayarragh of the Zherik."

Confused, Saya's eyes darted between Olga and Agham.

"We believe there's power behind a chosen name," Olga said. "Names shape a child's fate, and thus, we choose wisely. With yours, you shall be a princess among the Zherik. Please accept this humble gift as a token of our love and affection for you."

Olga unfurled her fingers to reveal a gold medallion the size of her palm, carved with intricate engravings of a mountain and its swirling patterns of perpetual wind.

"We're the Zherik-Umea, and the Zahar-Katea is our homeland. Take this medallion, our zintzikaroa, as proof that you've earned the protection of our gods and clan and entry into places others can't enter."

Olga put the necklace over Saya's head as the powerful resonance of the Zherik-Umea cry, a high-pitched succession of sounds reverberating vibrantly in the back of the throat, filled the night.

Olga stepped back, filled with pride and tears. "May the winds carry you far, *Zheriken Sayarragh*, and may they return you to these mountains every time."

She then addressed the porters.

"The time has come for you to begin." Summoning the ancient magic of the Zherik, she pounded her staff on the ground. The earth rumbled, responding to her call. "May Mathamurti share her strength with you, may Aditya keep you warm, and may the winds carry you forward."

One of the men blew a ram's horn. The porters bowed low, picked up their cargo and lanterns, and started their trek, moving confidently up the path.

Olga pounded her walking staff on the ground again, and

thunder infused the air. This time, the etchings on her staff glowed.

Addressing the princesses, she said, "Mathamurti brought you here and kept you safe, and she'll carry you forth to the Zahar-Eliza. May her power be yours. May her wisdom light your path forward." Her voice cracked with emotion as her gaze fixed on Saya. "With Mathamurti's blessing, may the winds return you to this mountain—to us." Her sobs choked the rest of her words.

❧

Long and loud, the ram's horn blew again. Mizha and his father bowed to the Elders, then motioned the group to pick up their packs and follow them.

Saya searched for Reza in the crowd. Their eyes met, and time stopped. Sorrow had etched the lines on his face. The crowd became a distant hum. Behind him, the bonfire crackled, wrapping his figure in gold and crimson. Reza smiled at her, uttering silent words.

"I will wait for you."

Like a phantom kiss wrapped in starlight, his silent promise brushed her heart to deliver his eternal vow.

"Saya?" Kharis tapped her shoulder, gesturing to the trailhead.

Everyone was already making their way up the slope, their lanterns flickering like fireflies. Kharis was eager to start, but Saya lingered, her eyes meeting Reza's one last time.

The memory of his gift, a beautiful and unforgettable first kiss, flooded her mind; the spark of that magical moment was etched into her soul. But now, there would be no more sweet kisses or stolen caresses in secret corners.

"Come," Kharis insisted, tugging on her sister's sleeve.

Saya followed, but a battle raged within her. Walking away from Reza tore her soul apart, the pain of it almost unbearable.

She told herself not to look back, to move forward instead, picking up her pace and focusing on the rhythm of her steps. But it didn't drown out the turmoil in her heart. Conflicted, she halted atop the pass and turned, her eyes locking onto the tall, solitary figure standing by a bonfire, the only one remaining when all others had retreated to their homes.

Standing at a crossroads, Saya wavered.

One road led to Kharis, the bond urging the Sorukhipa to keep walking and fulfill her destiny.

Her heart led her to Reza Zhegur, screaming at her to ignore the call of fate and run to him.

Why couldn't she have both?

Her feet stayed rooted to the ground, frozen in place by indecision. She tilted her head to the sky, searching the heavens for guidance, for a sign that could break this stalemate.

"Saya?" Kharis's voice was soft, her smile filled with hope for answers, for the end of their curse—for freedom.

Freedom.

That word echoed in her mind as though it were the push she needed to move. Above, Sharan hung full and bright in the sky, casting light on her path ahead.

Kharis's happy tune floated in the icy air as she descended the trail.

Saya gazed back at her general, still standing by the bonfire, and wayward tears trickled down her cheeks.

Why should she have to choose?

Once this journey was over, she wouldn't have to. She wiped her tears and, determined to find a way, followed Kharis down the trail.

CHAPTER 86
THE RECKONING

Fate is a sea without a shore; we're merely waves that abide. -
Poliormos

Agham waited for Olga, who watched the last of the lanterns drift up the mountainside and vanish. Darkness swallowed the slope again, but she didn't move from her spot.

He stepped closer. "Come. It's freezing out here."

She didn't turn.

"She doesn't belong with us," she uttered, her voice deep and otherworldly. "She must return."

Agham tensed. That voice wasn't entirely hers. He frowned, worried. Was she having another vision? Her eyes were distant, glazed with the eerie sheen of ancient magic. She wasn't blinking. She wasn't there.

"Olga?" he said carefully.

She swayed slightly.

"We must pay our debt." A wet, guttural sound rose from her throat—half moan, half growl.

He gently reached out, tapping her shoulder to pull her out of the spell. At his touch, she flinched, and the spell shattered. Patient and observant, Agham waited for his wife to regain her composure before compelling her.

"Come," he said, concerned. "Standing far from the fire's warmth isn't good for you."

Olga probed the darkness, pondering something.

"Is everything well?" he asked.

"I'm fine, husband."

His eyes narrowed, endlessly annoyed with his stubborn wife. "Did you tell the princess about the zintzikaroa beforehand?"

Olga stared into the unknown. "Sayarragh understands she's now a member of our clan." Her smile turned enigmatic, and she strolled to the nearest bonfire.

"No." He followed. "Did you explain what receiving it meant? Did you ever discuss *that* with her?"

"The Council recognized her as our own, and she accepted the honor. Isn't that enough? It will give her protection and passage to places others can't enter."

"Such as?" Agham asked, suspicion poking his ribs.

Olga didn't reply.

Agham sighed, vexed. "We've been married for so long I've lost count of the years, yet you still manage to shock me. Don't you see how serious this is?"

"Of course I do."

"We've done this backward." He rubbed his forehead. "Give first. Ask later." He shook his head, worried.

Olga ignored him, warming her hands and staring at the flames while deep in thought. "The future is always shrouded in fog, but there are things only I can see."

"You're a meddler," he said, slightly aggravated. But she was a seer, too, able to see what others couldn't, as if she had a second pair of eyes gazing into Andaheimur. "What is it that only you can see?"

"Saya will return to us," she said. "When she does, we must help her."

Agham was perplexed. "Why are you so attached to her? Why one and not the other?"

"The other one doesn't belong here." Her eyes turned harsh. "She's not of this world."

"What in a tangled wind are you talking about?"

"She's like us, Agham. She doesn't belong here—just as we don't." Olga paused, wetting her lips. "She's... *Adatari Haguru*."

Adatar. Agham's nostrils flared at the term, at the guilt, and his voice snapped like a whip. "That's ancient history." A cold dread twisted in his gut. "It is done with," he growled. "And forgotten."

"Is it?" she asked, lifting her chin in defiance. "Done with and forgotten? Or is she the reminder that we must pay our debt?"

Agham groaned at her. "Stop changing the subject. Saya should've been asked first, allowed to consider it, and agree."

"What if she belongs with us?"

He glared at her, baffled.

Her face softened. "Saya reminds me of Inaki when he was that age. Don't you think?"

Agham huffed emphatically. "Our son is dead, Olga. Our curse took him. Inaki's not coming back, so stop chasing ghosts."

"I know he's dead." Her voice was shrill, then turned low and complicit. "But what if Mathamurti gives us something in return for what the gods took?"

Agham tilted his head with a grunt. There was no point arguing with her.

Deep down, he recognized that the ways of the gods were mysterious. His people flew to the mountains a thousand years ago to avoid a war with the Akumi. Rather than join the fight, they'd fled. As punishment for their cowardice, the immortals clipped their wings. And yet, as if balancing a harsh penalty with kindness, some of these gods allowed them to live on these peaks to feel the wind on their faces—a reminder of a time when they could fly.

What if Mathamurti had finally lifted their curse?

What if all the writings of fate—like threads in a nearly finished tapestry—were nearing their end?

Their punishment would end with them.

Agham gazed at the towering mountains, the cold dawn brushing his face. He had no wings now, but he let the thought carry him home.

CHAPTER 87

THE MONK

Kindness is the air I breathe, and compassion is the water that sustains me. But love...? Love is the gravity that binds me to this earth so that I may offer you breath and life. - Poliormos

T he group reached Leruak without incident.
Determined to make it (and show Olga a thing or two), Kharis had set an intense pace and was the first to clear the pass into town.

When the villagers spotted them, they rushed with water and food. The moment became an impromptu celebration as they escorted the group to the *harrizkoetxea*. There, the Leruak Elders greeted them warmly.

A crowd quickly gathered, finding room wherever they could. Barhan, Mizha's father, addressed the crowd while Mizha translated for the sisters. Questions flew from every direction, leaving Kharis struggling to keep up. When there was a pause, the villagers exploded with questions and comments. One inquiry ignited an uproar that Kharis couldn't fully comprehend. Voices clashed, and everybody spoke over one another, arms gesticulating wildly in a chaotic dance of limbs and words.

In the middle of the villagers' back-and-forth, the Elders' leader stood with a hand up. The crowd immediately hushed.

"*Begira*," he said, pointing to the medallion hanging from Saya's neck. "*Zintzikaroa janzeten du.*"

The Elders exchanged glances. "*Egiten du*," they murmured among themselves.

The White Guard officers stiffened, their hands inching toward their weapons. Their stances shifted as they readied to spring into action to protect Saya.

"Mizha, what's going on?" Kharis yanked on his sleeve. "What are they saying?"

"It's the medallion, princess." His attention stayed on the scene unfolding before them.

Kharis's stomach tightened. "Have we offended them?"

"No, never, I assure you."

The Elders whispered among themselves. The villagers craned their necks, some rising on the balls of their feet, eager to catch a word. The Elders' leader straightened, his shoulders squared with authority.

"*Denek*," he announced, his gaze sweeping over every face. "*Neska gutako batda. Olgaren et Aghamen alaba.*"

The villagers erupted into loud trills and ululations.

Kharis tugged on Mizha's tunic. "What's going on?"

He grinned broadly. "Elders Olga and Agham have adopted Princess Saya as their daughter. She now carries their lineage forward."

Eventually, the excitement subsided. When the villagers left, Kharis pulled Saya aside. "Did you know?" she asked. "That Olga and Agham adopted you?"

A flicker of surprise crossed Saya's face. "Isn't that what the Zherik-Umea do with important visitors? Make them honorary members of the tribe?"

Kharis arched an eyebrow. "Then why wasn't I included?" She saw the uncertainty in Saya's eyes, how her sister hesitated, the minute shifting of her weight.

"Apparently," Kharis added, "you now carry their lineage forward."

"I do... what?" Saya's voice wavered.

"Hang on." Kharis spotted Mizha in a quiet corner, chatting with a group of young Zherikh. In a few swift strides, she reached him, grabbed his wrist, and dragged him away while ignoring his friends' teasing whistles.

"Tell her what you told me," Kharis demanded.

Mizha's eyes flicked between the two women, amusement dancing in his gaze. "Sayarragh is now Zherik-Umea," he said. "A clan member with all the rights and privileges. We will enter your children into our records as grandchildren of Olga and Agham—"

"—And Hröld," Kharis insisted. "Let's face it. His Majesty did all the work."

Mizha laughed. "It's a great honor, Your Highness. I assure you. Among the Zherik-Umea, Elders Olga and Agham are like your Zahari nobility." He gave Saya a warm smile. "We believe it's a good choice. Sayarragh was an orphan. Now has a mother and two fathers, and her children will walk between your and our worlds."

Kharis sighed. "When you put it that way..."

"That's the spirit," Saya said. "Besides, it's intriguing that I could walk in both worlds."

Shaking her head, Kharis dropped onto a bowl-shaped chair with a deep, round cushion, glad to finally think of nothing.

"How much longer until we reach the Zahar-Eliza?" Saya asked Mizha.

The young guide motioned her to a window. Kharis stretched her body, arching her back against the chair and twisting her neck to catch a glimpse—unwilling to abandon the comfort of her seat, but curious nonetheless.

"Do you see the mountain ahead?" Mizha asked. "The Eliza sits at the top."

"How long will it take to go up?"

"The climb should take about half the morning."

"Truly?" Saya's smile widened. Without warning, she grabbed Kharis and pulled her outside. The sharp, chilly air hit them instantly. "Look! The Garai Pass."

Against the fading sunlight, a narrow path snaked up the steep slope in a dizzying series of switchbacks.

"Ah," a voice said. "You must be the princesses."

Kharis spun around and came face-to-face with an elderly monk. The corners of his eyes crinkled with warmth, a universe of wrinkles etched deep with joy and quiet wisdom. He was small in stature and slightly stooped, leaning gently on a wooden walking cane for balance.

Bhiksunim wore robes according to their spiritual leanings. Healer monks donned blue, warrior monks wore dark purple, and those who trained the Sorukhipa wore black. This monk, however, was dressed in brown, a color she'd never seen among them.

"Allow me to introduce myself," the monk said. "My name is Nukha, and I welcome you to Leruak."

Kharis felt the corners of her lips lift involuntarily, drawn into a smile by the gentle warmth in his eyes. There was something quietly disarming about the man.

"I'll be guiding you to the Zahar-Eliza tomorrow," Nukha continued, his tone filled with quiet pride as if this simple task held great significance. He pressed his hands together at chest level and bowed deeply from the waist. "Blessed be the earth and the sun."

"May they sustain us," Kharis, Saya, and Mizha replied in unison, bowing respectfully.

"It's kind of you to come greet us." Saya's expression flickered with polite doubt over how this tiny monk could lead them up a mountain. "I'm Princess Saya, and this is my sister, Princess Kharis. We're grateful for your guidance tomorrow. Mizha," she gestured to the young man, "was telling us about the pass."

"Ah, yes!" Nukha straightened with surprising ease, considering his age. "It's best to begin the climb early—before the winds wake and turn unruly."

Soon, the three of them began discussing the climb for the next day.

Kharis struggled to follow the conversation. Her weariness was winning out.

Sudden movement caught her attention—a tiny hummingbird. Its golden wings were a luminous blur as it hovered. The air shimmered in its wake, delicate contrails of spun gold catching the light like strands of liquid sunlight. She followed the little creature as it darted into the forest and landed on a gnarled branch.

Then the branch moved.

What she'd thought was a tree was no tree at all.

The shadows rippled, revealing the outline of a tall figure cloaked in darkness. Vivid green eyes locked onto hers. Kharis flinched, startled by their brilliance. Yet the figure, half veiled behind trees and shadows, remained still, watching her.

Was this person the Hatorisaita?

An inquisitive tendril of power reached out, brushing against her face. It circled her as if testing the contours of her soul. Then, just as quietly, it withdrew.

She stood still, waiting for the figure to move or speak, perhaps wave an arm, but the forest remained quiet. Birds sang, preening in their hidden roosts, chirping softly and unbothered.

"Can I help you find anything, princess?"

"Um," Kharis wavered. "I think I'm exhausted." *Seeing things*.

The nearby chatter made them turn around.

The monk's grin stretched so wide it turned his eyes into cheerful slits. "Please excuse me while I greet Master Hillal. I'll return to assist you tomorrow." With that, the little monk shuffled off, his walking stick tapping a steady rhythm as he made his way toward Hillal and his group.

Kharis watched him leave. "Is *he* the one guiding us up the pass?"

Saya shrugged; the same question flickered across her expression.

Master Hillal bowed to Nukha with deep reverence. Kharis didn't think much of the gesture. Nukha was as old as the wind —perhaps even older—and the mountain tribes revered their elders.

Kharis waved Saya goodbye. Her thoughts drifted, but the memory of the cloaked figure remained. The curiosity it sparked tugged at the edges of her mind, and she wondered whether it had been a figment of her imagination. Had it been the Hatorisaita? Their power couldn't be denied. Noam had shared once that the power of the gods thrummed through their chosen one.

Once inside, she moved to her cot, sighing as she let her body sink into it. The bedding was a welcome relief, but even as she closed her eyes, the image of the stranger and the tiny golden hummingbird lingered.

Sleep soon claimed her.

CHAPTER 88
THE PATH BEFORE US

*Every journey ends at a door, and every door is a question. -
Poliormos*

Dawn peeked out from behind the mountains to greet the world.

As people woke up, the quiet gave way to the roosters greeting the sun with their usual crowing. Adults slowly filed out of their homes, tending to their daily duties. A flock of sheep bleated in the distance as sheepherder dogs gathered them. Children ran around, some eager to see the princesses, others merely interested in playing.

The officers were up, and after a good breakfast, they packed their belongings. Kharis sat by the fireplace, holding a cup of tea.

Saya packed and repacked their things, unable to control her excitement. "Going up the Garai Pass is the last stage of our journey," she said. "We'll reach the Zahar-Eliza by midday."

Kharis smiled. It was the fifth time Saya had mentioned the same thing this morning.

Soft cheering rolled through the crowd as the sisters emerged with their packs.

Yet Kharis's attention slipped away from the noise, drawn back to the woods. Sunlight dappled the snowy underbrush.

From deep within the trees, an aura pulsed, subtle yet unmistakable, and as ancient as the world itself.

She tilted her head, curious. *The Hatorisaita?*

"Good morning!"

The greeting jolted Kharis out of her reverie. Master Hillal had addressed her, the lines of his wrinkled face framing a kind, fatherly smile. "Blessed be the earth and the sun."

"May they sustain us," the sisters replied.

"I hope you're rested and ready to go," he said.

"We are," Saya said.

Kharis wasn't so sure. Against the morning light, she could better assess what lay ahead: steep, narrow switchbacks with little protection. One single misstep and the fall would be fatal. "Master Hillal, how many people—?"

"There you are!" Monk Nukha approached, the tick-tick of his walking staff punctuating his steps. "Let me carry something for you," he said, eyes darting around the group. He bounced slightly on his heels, scanning for anything he could lift. "What can I carry?"

He looked up at her, beaming—his expression wide-eyed and earnest, like a child eager to help with tasks too big for his hands.

Kharis wasn't convinced Nukha could be of much help. Given his slight figure, how could he carry anything, much less walk up the Garai Pass? The steep trail was daunting. Vertiginous. But Nukha stood there grinning, undeterred and waiting. With a resigned sigh, Kharis slipped the leather satchel from her shoulder and handed it over.

Saya shot her a questioning look. Kharis only shrugged, conceding defeat.

"Come." Nukha adjusted the satchel and gestured toward the trail. "It's time."

People were already climbing the path, moving in a single file—an endless line zigzagging on their way to the Zahar-Eliza. Kharis spotted Master Hillal at the bottom of the trail, his maroon robes swaying sideways as he began to ascend with his group.

"Khiri, move it." Saya had picked up her pace behind Nukha. "Everyone's going up."

"What about those in need of coming down the trail? It's a rather narrow trail." She caught up with Saya. "I wonder if those coming down must wait for everyone to come up. See—?"

A loud thud echoed from above. Gasps erupted all around.

A crate tumbled down the slope in a sickening spin, followed by a cascade of rocks and dust that made those waiting in line scramble away. The crate crashed and exploded against the rocks, spilling a cloud of grain into the wind. A startled pilgrim clung to the chains, his legs dangling off the edge.

With help, the poor soul scrambled back to his feet.

Kharis released the breath she'd been holding. The drop had been steep. The fall—fatal.

Itzu glided in her mind like a cloud on a clear, blue sky.

"Be careful, Dhordan."

She blinked rapidly, her hand tightening on the strap of her coat. The cold seemed to bite deeper now.

"How safe is it to—?"

"Khiri, let's get going," Saya bellowed. "The officers are waiting for us."

Kharis gestured to what remained of the crate, but Saya was already moving.

"Fine." Kharis blew the hair off her face and followed Saya and Nukha.

Around them, the mood had shifted.

Bhiksunim stepped forward, helping the shaken pilgrims brush off the dust while murmuring calming mantras. A few officers adjusted the straps on their packs, their faces drawn tight with focus. Further up the line, someone muttered a prayer, fingers clutching a charm tucked into their collar.

The trail had everyone's full attention now.

CHAPTER 89
HUMILITY

Humility is not the absence of power—it is the door through which it enters. - Poliormos

It was a frosty morning, so quiet that Kharis could hear every footfall and the shifting of belongings inside their packs. Everyone had focused, saving their breath for the strenuous climb.

Nukha led the princesses, but five White Guard officers marched ahead of them, and five more followed.

Kharis kept her eyes on Nukha, who walked ahead of her. To her surprise, he handled the switchbacks with little effort, using his walking pole to steady himself. She found him intriguing and given her boundless curiosity...

"Nukha, how long have you lived at the Zahar-Eliza?"

"Twenty years, princess."

"Twenty? Don't bhiksunim join early in their lives?"

"Yes," he said. "We usually do, but I joined after my wife died."

"You were married?"

Saya poked her in the back, a warning to curb her curiosity.

"Yes," Nukha said. "I took over the family business when I was young, a sizable pear orchard. I married a wonderful woman, my Sohmi, and we had several children. We worked hard and had a good life together."

"Did your children work with you?"

Nukha laughed. "Yes, some took to growing pears, but others did different things. The good thing about living in Zahar-Ghak is that there were many zenkas they could join."

"You lived in the Ghak?" She got another poke from Saya.

"Yes, we did. In the northern hills. Is it still a beautiful capital?"

"Yes," she said, reminiscing about her trips with Master Rawiri. "The views from atop the Zahar-Homa, the water canals, the quaint neighborhoods... Do you miss it?"

"I do. I spent two-thirds of my life there. It's where I met my wife and raised our children."

"Then why did you come here?"

Nukha chuckled. "Life's strange. I didn't come to the Eliza. It came to me."

She narrowed her eyes. "How so?"

"One night, I had a peculiar dream. I told my wife about it, and she said that the Zahar-Eliza had called me to serve."

"So... your wife encouraged you to come?"

"She did, but I wasn't interested. I had a family, a large orchard, and barrels of the best Zahari pear liquor ready to be shipped." He laughed. "There was no time for monastic callings. Besides, I was happy with my life, so why would I leave?"

"It makes sense," she said. "I wouldn't have left, either."

"Then, why are you here?"

The question stunned her, and Kharis halted in her tracks. Saya walked straight into her, bumping her head against Kharis's knapsack. Kharis lurched forward, nearly toppling— saved only by the chains. Saya shot her a glare, rubbing her forehead. Kharis glared back, then quickened her pace to catch up with Nukha, silently wondering how he was handling the climb better than she was.

"I didn't have a choice," she finally confessed.

"Why didn't you?"

She exhaled slowly, resignation riding on that breath. "I'm

here to gain control of the Akumi demon. My duty's to become a stronger vessel."

"Why didn't you have a choice?"

"I was happy to leave the Ghak," Kharis remarked, "but I didn't get a choice as to the destination. I simply followed orders." It was all she'd done. "I often wonder what would happen if I didn't follow them. If, one day, I could make my choices. I'm here to find the courage to do so."

"You're on the right path," Nukha said. "Self-realization is not possible without self-reflection."

A large blue-winged insect buzzed past Kharis's face, and she instinctively swatted it away. A moment passed in silence before Nukha spoke again.

"When my wife died, I was outraged. She became ill, and before I knew it, she was gone. Before she died, she reminded me of the Zahar-Eliza dream. She told me not to ignore the call of the gods, but how could I listen to them when they were taking my beloved Sohmi away?"

"How did you do it?" she asked. "Stop being angry?"

Nukha hummed. "I realized that deceitful attachments led to darkness."

A shiver ran down her spine. That was Saya's mantra.

"However," he added, "I don't believe that's always the case."

"What do you mean?" Saya asked.

Kharis glanced back, surprised Saya had joined the conversation.

"We mustn't assume all attachments are evil, but attaching ourselves to objects is what creates deception. As with everything in this universe, we must strive for balance." Nukha stomped the ground. "If we stare at our feet, we miss the heavens' beauty, and we could fall if we always gaze up."

The bhiksun chuckled.

Kharis studied the precipice. It wasn't a laughing matter.

"Balance is the key to everything we do," he said. "I loved my Sohmi dearly, and she loved me. That gave us the courage to become better people."

He faced the sisters with a beaming smile.

"If you attach yourself to something that can't respond in kind, then yes, that attachment will deceive and lead you to darkness. You will live unable to see the emptiness it engenders. Once deceived, nothing will ever fill the hole it leaves in your soul, sustaining a cycle of pain."

Kharis stumbled slightly on a jagged rock, her boot scraping against stone. She eyed the precipice again.

"My Sohmi and I," Nukha said after a quiet sigh. "We added to each other's light, lifting and comforting each other. But when she died, I couldn't let go. Devastated by my loss, I withdrew from everyone I loved."

Overhead, a hawk circled, its cry echoing the loneliness Nukha had described.

"I'm so sorry," she said, her voice infused with sincerity.

"Please don't. That was my path to spiritual growth. Remember, self-realization is only possible with self-reflection. At some point, I realized Sohmi wasn't gone. Her body was, but her spirit was still with us, and I had lost sight of that."

"How so?"

"I saw her in my children and grandchildren. Her gestures. Her words. The way she saw the world. I had failed to see that. I questioned my anger. And it turned out I had to face my selfishness. I was attached to my memories of Sohmi, when I should've kept her memories alive. I should've focused on her life, not my desolation.

"When I saw my error," Nukha said, "I refocused on what she'd achieved in this world and allowed my children to share their pain with me, for I had forgotten it was their loss, too. To keep her memories alive, we worked to make her dreams a reality, recognizing she was alive inside us."

A wave of unexpected emotion caught her off guard. Admiration had replaced the sorrow she'd felt. Nukha had overcome his anger and monumental loss, walking away from a painful cycle of resentment to become a man at peace with his life.

He stopped and faced her, his expression wrinkled with concern. "Princess, promise me you'll question why you didn't speak up and instead followed orders." He gazed at her with that fatherly gaze and resumed his pace.

Kharis opened her mouth, then closed it, stunned into silence.

Guilt and regret had shamed her into submission since the massacre. Worse, she'd forgotten who she was, allowing others to define her.

Useless.

Raven Spawn.

Monster.

At the Ghak, she smiled at everyone until her cheeks ached, her mask of perfect politeness firmly in place. She worked hard to prove she was Kharis of Zahar, not the Empire's terrifying weapon. Her every word and gesture was measured to counter the fear that clung to her name. And yet, in the end, that was all people saw—the monster.

"I've been angry and resentful for a long time," she confessed. After a lengthy silence filled with footsteps, panting, and rolling pebbles, she asked, "When did you let go of yours?"

"It was gradual. A series of small steps gradually placed me on the right path. I discovered that deceptive attachments fed my sense of loss, which incited the fear that fueled my anger. That was my mistake."

Kharis cocked her head. "How so?"

His gaze, shining bronze, fixed on her. "Because nothing is ever lost, only transformed."

Those words echoed in her mind like the distant beat of drums at the start of a festival parade, swelling with intensity until they reverberated through her thoughts, triumphant and unshakable.

She considered the people in her life. Prince Taika had gushed at the potential bride. Noam had kissed a lovely lass. Her nana had embraced a capable young woman. Saya loved her clever sister. What did her father see? What about Itzu? She feared losing those she loved. And the one who could take them all away had a name.

"Is it possible to erase my fear of the Akumi king?" she asked.

"Are you scared of him?"

Kharis cringed. "Terrified."

"Why?"

Kharis missed a step, and her knapsack bit into her shoulders. Didn't he know? "Well, everyone fears him."

"No, princess. We can't control others. But you control your thoughts and feelings. Therefore, why are you terrified of him?"

She bit her lower lip. "He can destroy others."

"Has he?"

Kharis opened her mouth to respond but closed it. Her boots crunched the gravel on the path as she pondered the question.

"He did a thousand years ago." Then, he slumbered quietly until the massacre seven years ago. "He hasn't done anything since the immortals sealed him." She meant it. The massacre was all hers. Her anger. Her hatred. Her need for retribution. And there they were—the three monsters she had to face: Anger, Hatred, and Revenge.

"What scares you about the king of the Akumi?" Nukha asked.

She exhaled shakily. "I fear losing control—that he'll possess me completely. What if the Akumi king wants to destroy the world again and uses me to achieve it?"

A faint warmth bloomed in her chest—Itzu was listening.

Nukha hummed thoughtfully, the clack on his walking staff a soothing rhythm. "The Ancient Writings don't provide much. So let me ask you this. What does he say?"

Kharis stopped. "Ask... him?"

"If you enter Andaheimur, you certainly can. You possess the key to his prison."

Saya nudged her from behind to keep walking. Kharis resumed. If she could enter Andaheimur, she could rescue Ananya. But enter his prison...? That sounded more challenging. Dangerous, too. "What do you know about the Akumi king?"

Nukha hummed as if he'd been hoping for this question. "Why don't we start with what you know? I can fill in gaps."

Kharis shrugged. "The Akumi king wanted to destroy the world and led his army toward the Ghak, but the Forest and

Spirit Kin clans defeated him. Since he was an immortal, his brethren imprisoned him via a sealing ritual we replicate."

He looked over his shoulder. "That sounds ominous, doesn't it?"

"It's downright sinister."

"It's no wonder you're scared," Nukha said. "I would. However, let me share this with you. The Ancient Writings don't tell us who the Akumi were, where they came from, or why they followed their king. The Writings only speak of this war but never its cause. I find these omissions interesting."

Kharis glanced at her sister, who listened quietly to the conversation.

"The term 'Akumi king' appears once in the texts," he continued. "It's the one time we see the words *akumi erregia.* Since there was a king, we assume there was an army. But was there? It's an interesting puzzle."

The sprightly monk kept his energetic pace.

A quiet enveloped the hikers as they climbed, at times gripping the rusted chains bolted onto the rock walls. The skies were clear, and the sound of wind rushing through the mountainous terrain carried an earthy scent.

"Why seal someone so dangerous in a mortal body?" Kharis asked.

Nukha took a deep breath. "Yours is a good question. King Owain desired a powerful weapon, but why did the immortals tackle his request in this fashion? As you can see, the Ancient Writings leave us with various quandaries we must explore." He glanced back with a smile. "The puzzle lies in exploring why they exist."

"Forgive me if what I say offends you," Saya suddenly said. "You seem to challenge the Ancient Writings."

"If I can't question ancient texts," he said, "I can't question my ancient life."

He laughed joyfully, his head tipping back as his shoulders shuddered. Kharis felt like holding onto him lest he fall. That precipice...

"If I can't examine my purpose in this universe, I have stopped the process of self-reflection that leads to enlightenment. To me, it's contradictory to allow one and not the other. So yes, I'm happy challenging the Ancient Writings."

Nukha then turned to Kharis. "Princess, you must ask why more often. Why are you scared? Why remain silent? Why follow and not lead? Let go of the discomfort 'why' brings you." He grinned at her with a reassuring glint in his eyes.

Kharis smiled back.

Her breath was steady, her steps more confident. She looked up, and for the first time, the trail ahead didn't seem quite so daunting.

CHAPTER 90
VOICE

There is no healing without sound—grief must cry, love must name.
- Poliormos

The roar of alphorns resounded, startling Kharis out.

"Ah!" Nukha exclaimed. "We've been spotted."

Blown a second time, the alphorns' deep timbre echoed as a call to action. Suddenly, Kharis wanted to scream into the void she was leaving behind. She stopped, startling those behind her, and faced the midday sun. Gulping in as much air as possible, she released a loud, sustained cry, releasing the anger that had been building inside her for a long time.

Following orders.

Tolerating Ghan's abuse.

Allowing the Regia-Zenka to wield power over her.

Twisting herself to fit a mold rather than forging her own.

Kharis screamed and screamed. When she finally stopped, her throat burned. She panted, her breathing ragged. But the release...? It was joyful. Utter bliss. Wiping her sleeve across her face, she felt lighter—ready.

"Now I can get to work."

A hand reached out and held hers. Kharis didn't need to look; she would know that touch anywhere.

"Let's do it again," Saya murmured. "Together?"

Kharis gave a sharp nod. Hand in hand, the sisters tilted their heads back and screamed—an unrestrained release of frustration, grief, and everything that had been caged inside them.

The White Guard officers joined in, whether out of solidarity or their buried anguish. Then, one by one, the pilgrims followed. Their voices rose in a chorus, tearing through the wind as if to sever the chains that bound them.

When silence finally fell, it came with a deep, collective exhale. Everyone paused, gathering themselves.

A breeze stirred, cool against their flushed cheeks. Above, a hawk soared, its wings brushing the clouds. A few pilgrims sank to the ground on the trail, their shoulders trembling with quiet sobs. The world had exhaled with them.

The tension that had clung to Kharis lifted, leaving something sweeter and filling her hollow with optimism. Hope had slipped in—quiet, unannounced. Humility had been the door. Itzu moved through her thoughts, gentle and steady like a calm river. She hadn't screamed alone.

As they resumed their hike, the quiet wasn't heavy anymore. It was full of promise.

"Did it help, princess?" Nukha asked, always gentle and kind.

Kharis sniffled. "I killed twenty-seven people. Maimed more. All because of my anger." Her voice cracked. "It's a debt I'll carry forever."

Nukha smiled softly. "Then, to pay your debt, start by saving the lives of twenty-seven people."

Her tears blurred the world. Her thoughts fluttered to Ananya—trapped in Andaheimur. Saving her would be the beginning.

"I have a lot of work ahead of me," Kharis said. "And I don't know where to start. Please, light my path."

Nukha's gaze held hers, a fatherly expression on his wrinkled face. "I'll do everything I can to help you. The light within you is already bright. With time and effort, it will compete with the sun, and you'll be the one lighting my path." He smiled again, a gesture so light and honest that she couldn't help but smile back.

"Come," he said. "We're very close."

Kharis dragged her sleeve across her face, dashing away the tears. Once they cleared the pass, the entrance to the Zahar-Eliza emerged.

Kharis gasped.

But it wasn't the sight that stole her breath away.

CHAPTER 91
THE FIRST NAME

Love's power is revealed not in grand gestures but in the small,
humble acts of kindness that shape our world. - Poliormos

A formidable power seized Kharis's soul, thrusting it into a realm where it vibrated in rhythm with the universe. In this space, the force of creation pulsed wildly. Black voids met endless radiance, and time stood still, preventing itself from exploding. Constellations danced, their celestial bodies colliding with one another in a breathtaking cascade of stardust reshaping the bones of the universe.

In this fantastical place, a colossal tree rose, exuding steady waves of formidable magic that rippled the air with its power.

Kharis's jaw dropped in shock. She stood before the sacred Mahabhal.

The air hummed, thick with magic and the honeyed scent of its sap. A mesmerizing network of veins, ascending the bark like tiny rivers of gold-colored sap adorned the tree's gnarled trunk. Thick branches radiated outward and upward, cradling this infinite space. Luminous globules—like ripened fruit born of light—sparkled before detaching from the canopy and drifting.

The Mahabhal's intense power embraced her. Yet, beyond

its sheer force, the overwhelming sense of belonging struck her deeply.

Kharis had finally come home.

A woman stood not far from her, donning finery woven with glimmering stardust and moonbeams. She was pale, but her hair, as black as a moonless night, floated around her face, releasing glorious indigo glimmers. A lavish circlet encrusted with seven diamonds adorned her forehead. As she walked, the sands of time shifted under her feet while golden dandelions bloomed with each step. Her magic thrummed as if she were the source of power in this endless space—as if every universe began with her.

Kharis hardly blinked.

The woman's glowing silver gaze locked on Kharis. "You finally came," she said, delighted. "Our wait is over."

Kharis stared at her, initially confused, but then a long-buried memory surfaced from a quiet corner of her mind. "I... I know you."

The woman laughed, and that sound was soft and sweet, like a cool breeze on a sweltering day, lazily swaying fragrant jasmine flowers. The joy in her eyes was indescribable. Her smile could coax the sun to rise again and again.

"I see you no longer need to skulk at night."

"The Archives!" Kharis sucked in a breath as the memory came to her. "You were that woman. The ghost."

"Indeed," the woman replied, a nostalgic expression on her face. "It appears fate has brought us together once more." Her smile shimmered with an alluring, magical aura. "Do you remember my name?"

That question stumped Kharis. She remembered the endless stacks of ancient tomes and the woman's figure emerging from the midnight gloom bathed in moonlight. But the name had escaped her.

The woman's radiant gaze, a source of endless wonder, softened. "With you, all the writings will end."

Kharis's heart fluttered. "I've heard that before."

"It's an important reminder." Her voice sounded like the

rustle of branches after a playful autumn gust, making leaves flutter and dance on their way to the ground. "It brings me joy to see you here, for you will rectify all that was wrong. As for the writings, you will end them all."

Kharis's mind filled with questions. "How do I do all of that?"

The woman's smile remained unwavering, a playful glint dancing in her argent gaze. "When the time comes, you will know."

Kharis angled her head, mostly in frustration. "You remind me of someone who's also rather vague with his answers."

"Farrádh can certainly be." The woman's laughter bubbled up softly.

Huh?

Guilt creased Kharis's brow. "I'm sorry, I don't remember your name."

"You were quite young then," she said, her gaze filled with divine understanding. "A spirited little thing." A warm smile spread across her face. "I've had many names, each marking a chapter in an endless saga. But the first one is the one that matters most, for it gave birth to all the others. And now, with you here, I end my journey and return to the beginning—to my first name."

Kharis stilled, awe crashing over her as she stared at the woman. It felt like she was looking into a mirror, catching glimpses of her soul gazing back at her. The baffling sensation stirred something profound inside her.

"And which was your first name?" she asked.

The hint of a smile appeared on the woman's lips, a flicker of amusement sparking in her eyes. "You already know it, for it is your own."

The magic in this other world thrummed before Kharis could ask any more questions. Invisible strings played, unleashing an explosive concerto. The massive wave hurled her out of this endless space.

A distant memory stirred as her soul eased back into her body, softly and without pain. Then came a name—soft at first, then resounding—echoing through her mind like a bell tolling through the fog.

Poliormos...

CHAPTER 92
THE JOURNEY BEGINS

The journey to seek the truth begins when one questions everything
one already knows. - Poliormos

Kharis blinked, adjusting to this peculiar sensation of returning to her body as though she now wore an unbearably tight garment. With a deep inhale, crisp mountain air filled her lungs, and Kharis felt like herself again.

"Are you all right?" Saya's voice anchored her to this world.

The landscape slowly emerged, and a vast alpine expanse stretched before her. Jagged peaks pierced the sky, their snowy tips glinting in the midday sunlight.

"What happened?" Kharis asked.

Saya laughed, wrapping an arm around her shoulders. "The Zahar-Eliza left you speechless."

"I guess it did." The hum of ghostly music still lingered in her mind.

Awe sang in Saya's voice as she gestured to the Zahar-Eliza. "It's breathtaking," she said. "We stand before the most spectacular of the immortals' gifts."

The temple's entry was hewn from the mountainside, and its facade towered three stories high. Ancient artists had chiseled it with carvings depicting mythical creatures, intricate geometric patterns, and celestial events.

"The Forest Kin immortals left their mark and legacy in every stone," Saya added with quiet reverence. "They wove their magic into its foundation."

"I can feel its power." A tingling sensation rippled through Kharis like feathers caressing her skin. "I can't wait, Saya. I'm leaving everything behind. I'm starting anew."

Saya grinned from ear to ear, giving Kharis a crisp nod.

Bhiksunim, grouped by robe color, populated the front plaza. Pilgrims flanked the patio, their excitement electrifying. And amid the anticipation, a towering figure stood in the back. Their power radiated toward her, pulsing with a deliberate rhythm. Invisible tendrils tugged at her as if singling her out.

Could that be the Hatorisaita? The one chosen by the gods had to be powerful beyond measure.

Though cloak and shadows obscured their face, Kharis could feel them observing her, leaving her with a haunting sense that this person would change her fate. A sudden urgency gripped her, and she tapped her sister's arm.

"What is it?" Saya asked.

"The person standing in the back." Kharis gestured toward the congregation.

Saya scanned the sea of faces. "Who?"

"They are much taller than everyone. You can't miss them."

Saya surveyed the crowd again but shook her head. "I don't see anyone fitting your description."

"The Hatorisaita is here." Kharis couldn't contain her excitement. "Such power. I can still feel it humming beneath my skin, like charged air during a thunderstorm. Can't you feel it?" she asked. "It purrs in my ears, swelling in waves."

Saya was about to answer when the air shifted. Conversations waned, and footsteps stalled. The murmuring withered into an expectant silence.

Kharis and Saya turned, instincts sharpening.

A profound hush had fallen over the assembly. Nukha waved at the sisters, urging them to come as the soft rustle of fabric and movement rippled through the assembly. In unison, the crowd knelt, their heads bowing low until their foreheads brushed the stone. The wind's whispers curled around the mountain's carved entrance.

Kharis's eyes widened, her pulse roaring through her veins. She attempted to voice her surprise, but her words fizzled out, never reaching her lips, except for one.

"Nukha...?"

"Welcome to the Zahar-Eliza," he said with a shining smile.

The rich timbre of his voice vibrated with the wisdom of ages. It was an endless thread of sound connecting Kharis to the dawn of creation when only the gods resided in the Blessed Mother's primordial ether—back to a time when the worlds were a whisper in the void, waiting to be spoken into existence by the dreams of gods.

The elderly monk bowed before Kharis, his grin stretching from ear to ear, brighter than the sun, filling the plaza with a warmth that could thaw even the coldest of hearts.

"With you, all the writings will end," Nukha said, radiating joy. "Now your true journey begins."

Kharis stood still, speechless and in awe.

Nukha... was the Hatorisaita—the one chosen by the gods.

WANT MORE?

A Curse to Break. A Fate to Unravel. A Soul on the Edge of Ruin.

Kharis is haunted by a thousand-year-old curse, the fire demon bound to her, and her sister's tragic fate. Her mind teeters on the edge of madness, and her body carries the echoes of a destructive power she can barely contain. To break her curse and free her sister, she must brave the treacherous world of the ancient immortals, outwit the scheming Aghet Mendi, and face the truth Itzu—her fiercest guardian—has long kept from her. When she finally stands before the powerful Akumi king, will he offer salvation—or obliteration?

As fate draws near, Kharis must choose whether to preserve her soul... or sacrifice it all to end the cycle of ruin.

Darkly lyrical and emotionally fierce, The Dandelion Tree, Part Two is a literary epic fantasy that blends slow-burn romantic tension with mythic resonance and soul-deep intro-spection. This is a story for readers who prefer character to combat, consequence to spectacle, and prose that lingers long after the page is turned.

Kharis's journey unfolds like poetry—layered, deliberate, and full of aching humanity. In this third installment of The Dandelion Chronicles, every choice draws Kharis closer to a fate that may have been written before time began.

For fans of:

- The Books of Ambha by Tasha Suri
- The Realm of the Elderlings by Robin Hobb
- The Poppy War by R.F. Kuang (in tone more than theme)
- The Winternight Trilogy by Katherine Arden
- Tigana and Under Heaven by Guy Gavriel Kay
- The Goblin Emperor by Katherine Addison
- Readers of The Bear and the Nightingale, She Who Became the Sun, and The Jasmine Throne will also find resonance here.

Note: This is Book Three in an ongoing series. Prior reading is recommended for full impact. *The Dandelion Tree, Part Two*, is scheduled for release in October 2025.

Learn more at www.asrgelpi.com

Sign up for my **newsletter** and be the first to learn about special offers, including promotional offers, bonus content, sneak peeks, new releases, giveaways, cover reveals, and more.

Follow me on Instagram and TikTok. My handle on all plat-forms is @asrgelpi_author

Curious? Scan the QR code to browse the series and grab your free samplers!

Glossary

This glossary provides a pronunciation guide and a definition of each term. Don't let these words slow you down. How you sound the letters in your head will be close enough, so don't sweat it. Go forth and confidently read *The Dandelion Tree, Part One*. Welcome to Zahar.

A – pronounced like the "a" in apple
E – pronounced like the first "e" in elegant
EE – pronounced like the first "e" in eve
O – pronounced like the first "o" in honor
OO – pronounced like the "u" in utensil
G – pronounced like the "g" in general
GH – pronounced like the hard "g" in get
H – pronounced like the hard "h" in hot

The syllable in ALL CAPS reflects where to place the stress for the word.

List:

Adatari Haguru	a-da-TA-ree ha-goo-ROO	A title meaning sparkling fire.
Aditya	a-DEE-tee-a	The sun god in Zherikh-Umea mythology.
Agham	A-gam	Olga's husband, an Elder, and member of the Zherikh-Umea mountain tribes.
Aghet Mendi	A-get MEN-dee	A Zahari general, and Arjun Ghan's lover.
Akumi	A-koo-mee	A race of fallen immortals that attacked Zahar a thousand years ago. The word is both plural and singular, referring to an army or an individual.
aljaicin	al-ha-ee-SEEN	Hard candies from the southern region of Zahar.
Almarim	al-ma-REEM	Southern city in the Zahari empire.
Anaia Bibiak	a-na-EE-a bee-BEE-ak	The Twins constellation.
Andaheimur	An-HAEE-moor	A realm behind a veil only immortals can inhabit; also known as the spirit realm or world.
Aravani	a-ra-BA-nee	Kharis's tutor at the Zahar-Eliza.
Arjun Ghan	AR-joon GHAN	Retired High General of the Zahari armed forces.
Azim Maharghan	a-SEEM MA-har-ghan	Governor of the city of Zhegama.
Barhan	BAR-han	A Zherikh-Umea mountain guide; Mizha's father.
bhiksun	BEEK-soon	A monk or nun; a singular genderless term.
bhiksunim	BEEK-soo-neem	Plural for bhiksun.
birthmark		Similar to a birthday, it marks someone's birth date.
Cecchio	CHE-kee-o	Capital city of the Zahari Westernlands
Chul	chool	Bhiksun in Master Hillal's sangha

Term	Pronunciation	Definition
cliffmark		A measure of altitude, based on the height of one peak.
dangu	Dan-GHOO	A monster in Zahari mythology that drags people into a watery grave with their long fingers
denek	DE-nek	Zherik-Umea term used to reger to a groun of people
Djinnshirukh	GEEN-shee-rook	The human vessel to a fire demon; also known as the Keeper of the South Wind
Dulaä	DOO-la	A city to the north, twin city to Tulaä
Duri	DOO-ree	Bhiksun in Master Hillal's sangha
edan	e-DAN	An alcoholic drink from the mountain region made from rice and flowers.
Forest Kin		A race of immortals that lived in what is now Zahar prior to the One War. Legend claims they tended to the forests when magic flowed freely.
Garai	gha-ra-EE	The name for a plateau and pass in the mountains that leads to the Zahar-Eliza
ghak	gak	Suffix that means "city"
Ghetu	GHE-too	The name for a river east of the Zahari capital (Zahar-Ghak) and the plains in which it flows.
Götrid	GHO-treed	One of Kharis's siblings
Gutxi	GHOOT-chee	A Zahari term of endearment that Monk Yuna uses with Kharis. It means "little butterfly"
Haize-Ibiltaria	Ha-EE-se ee-beel-ta-ree-a	A race of immortals that lived in the Zahar-Katea region.
Hala	HA-la	Crown Prince of Zahar
harrizkoetxea	ha-rees-ko-et-CHE-a	A communal house in the mountain regions, often used for town gatherings.
Hatorisaita	ha-to-ree-SAEE-ta	Zahari term for "The Enlightened One."
Hazenka	ha-SEN-ka	An assembly of guilds, usually between 5-10 zenkas of the same trade.
Helena	HE-le-na	One of Kharis's siblings
Herensuge	he-ren-SOO-he	The silver dragon constellation
Heriskan	he-REES-kan	Large town in the Zaharkatea mountains; the stronghold of the Zherikh-Umea homeland.
hitzalkea	heet-zal-KE-a	Trained empire assassins. Selected ones also provide protection to the royal family, acting as bodyguards.
hizkuntza	heez-KOON-za	A signed language used in Zahar
Hröld	rold	Imperial King of Zahar, Son of the Sun
Ibaia	ee-BA-ee-a	A river west of the Zahari capital but also the name of the freshwater inland sea
Ifran	ee-FRAN	A mythical location where the Fires of Creation reside.
Itzaltsu	eet-SAL-tsoo	Zahari term for "shadowy"
Itzu	EET-soo	Term of endearment. Short for Itzalsu, shadowy.
Jordha	JOR-da	A Zahari prince, cousin to Hala and a member of the Regiazenka
Kahurang	ka-hoo-RAN	An island continent to the south of Zahar
Kahurangi	ka-hoo-RAN-ghee	That which pertains to Kahurang

kashaya	ka-sha-EEA	A large, rectangular shawl wrapped around the body seven times that is part of a bhiksun's wardrobe; The last fold goes over one shoulder.
Kharis	ka-REES	The current Djinnshirukh, human vessel to the Akumi King
Khator	HA-tor	One of Kharis's siblings
Khona	KO-na	A female bhiksun at the Zahar-Eliza
leagh	LE-ach	A mythical water horse that appears during foggy weather.
Leruak	le-roo-AK	Village at the foot of the Zahareliza temple
Mahabhal	ma-ha-BAL	Also known as the Great Tree, the Tree of Legends, and the Tree of Life. It was a symbol of Forest Kin pride.
Mahazenka	ma-ha-SEN-ka	A governing body of leaders that represents and addresses issues of a commercial nature through an established court system. It handles product pricing and zenka disputes.
Mara	MA-ra	A monk at the Zahar-Eliza
Mark/marks		A measument of length or height based on the width of a finger.
Marya Levandran	MA-ree-a le-BAN-dran	Hazenka captain in charge of zenka patrols on the west end side of the Zahar-Regia
Mathamurti	ma-ta-MOOR-tee	A mountain goddess in Zherikh-Umea mythology
Mizha	MEE-sa	A Zherikh-Umea mountain guide
Müs	MOOS	Zahari word for mouse; used in the northernlands.
Müsi	MOOS-see	Aravani's protégé
orea	o-re-A	Fried balls of orange-flavored dough covered in powdered sugar
Pharos	FA-ros	A title (the Pharos of Hegra); it means guardian.
Rawiri	ra-WEE-ree	Kahurangi Prince, and Kharis's and Saya's tutor
Raysänen	ra-ee-sa-A-nen	The name of an archipelago in the Northeast
Regia-Zenka	re-jee-a-SEN-ka	A parliamentary body that balances the power of the Imperial King. They have sway over the Djinnshirukh and the Sorukhipa.
Resealment		A ritual by which the Sorukhipa removes the two souls residing in the Djinnshirukh and places them in a new vessel. This process kills the former vessel. With resealment, the Sorukhipa binds themselves to a new vessel/Djinnshirukh.
Reza Zhegur	RE-za SE-ghoor	A Zahari general; leads the royal cavalry to the Zahar-Eliza
sangha	SAN-gha	A group or community of Zahari bhiksunim
Saya	SA-eea	The current Sorukhipa; Kharis's guardian and sister; a high princess of the realm
Sharan	sha-RAN	The large ivory moon. Zahar boasts two moons.
Sohmi	SO-mee	Nukha's deceased wife.
Sorukhipa	so-roo-KEE-pa	The Djinnshirukh's Protector or Guardian

Spirit Kin		A race of immortals that lived in what is now Zahar prior to the One War. Legend claims they created Andaheimur as a sanctuary for the immortal races. They were also responsible for the creation of the first Djinnshirukh and Sorukhipa.
Taika	ta-EE-ka	Son of King Kiwa and Queen Ataahua; almost bethroted to Kharis.
Teppe	TEP-pe	Nickname for Kharis. It means little badger.
Tetxikia	tet-SEE-kee-a	A town in the Southernlands.
The Ghak	ghak	The term capitalinos/locals use to refer to the capital, Zahar-Ghak. For example: "I am from The Ghak."
toirmeasgh	tor-me-ACH	An abomination created by defying a magical prohibition.
Tulaä	TOO-la	A city to the north, twin city to Dulaä.
Tung	toon	The small red moon. Zahar boasts two moons.
txakurra	cha-KOOR-ra	A pejorative term that means "filthy bitch." Used for women.
txakurri	cha-KOOR-ree	A pejorative term that means "filthy dog." Used for men.
Urrun	oor-ROON	The easternmost city in the Zahari Empire.
v'leta	BLE-ta	Blood-drinking creatures luring people by taking the shape of whatever they desired most.
Vaghri	BA-gree	A bhiksun at the Zahar-Eliza, a member of The Four.
Välissa	BA-lees-sa	An in-between realm between the physical and the spiritual realms; also knows as the One Bridge.
vessel		Another term used to the refer to the Djinnshirukh.
xakea	cha-KE-a	A popular strategy board game in Zahar.
Xia Dhan	CHEE-a dan	A White Guard officer under General Zhegur's command.
Yuna	YOO-na	Former crown princess of Zahar; sister to Aghuti and Arjun; Aunt to Kharis and Saya; Royal head physician.
Zahar	SA-har	An empire kingdom in the Commonwealth; it encompasses 2/3 thirds of the known landmass.
Zahar-Eliza	sa-har E-lee-sa	The Grand Temple of Zahar, located in the Zahar-Katea mountains.
Zahar-Ghak	sa-har GHAK	Capital of the Zahari empire; also known as the Ghak.
Zahar-Homa	sa-har HO-ma	An ancient wall encircling the imperial city/enclave.
Zahar-Katea	sa-har ka-TE-a	An imposing mountain range east of Zahar-Ghak.
Zahar-Kayo	sa-har KA-eeo	The southern ocean.
Zahar-Regia	sa-har RE-jee-a	The royal/imperial city located within the capital of Zahar-Ghak. An ancient wall, the Zahar-Homa, separates it from the Ghak.
Zahari	sa-HA-ree	That which pertains to Zahar.
zaldun	sal-DOON	A knight-like officer of the Zahari army, selected based on noble status and lineage.
zaldunak		Plural of zaldun.

zenka	SEN-ka	A single trade guild. Six zenkas form a hazenka. Six hazenkas form a mahazenka.
Zhegama	SE-gha-ma	City and trading center in the Zahar-Katea region; it will become the site of the Zahar-Katea Mahazenka Court.
Zhegami	SE-gha-mee	That which pertains to Zhegama
Zherik-Umea	se-RIK oo-ME-a	The name for the independent tribes living in the Zaharkatea region. Legend states that they existed before the Empire of Zahar was created.
zintzikaroa	seent-see-ka-RO-a	A gold medallion identifying someone as a member of the Zherikh-Umea tribe.

Kharis

Saya **Reza Zhegur**

Noam

PUBLISHER'S NOTE

Dear Reader,

Thank you for choosing to read this book. We're excited to share this story with you and truly appreciate your enthusiasm and support!

If you enjoyed the book, we would appreciate it if you could take a moment to leave a review. If you're reading an e-book, click here. If reading in print (paperback or hardback), go to www.asrgelpi.com.

Your review matters, and here's why:

- **Support for Authors:** Your review helps others discover new stories, giving authors the visibility they need to keep creating.
- **Guidance for Fellow Readers:** Your thoughts guide others toward stories they'll love, creating a ripple of discovery and joy.
- **Inspiration for Writers:** Honest feedback helps authors grow and refine their craft for future books.
- **Community Building:** Your review sparks conversations, connecting readers and authors in a shared love of storytelling.

We'd love it if you could share your thoughts on any of your favorite platforms, such as Goodreads or Amazon. Your feedback will help this series reach more readers who might cherish it as much as you do.

Thank you for sharing this journey with us. We hope this story captivates you as much as it did us.

Happy reading,
The Silver River Publishing Team

ACKNOWLEDGMENTS

Although writing is technically a solitary endeavor, it rarely happens in a vacuum. I am forever indebted to my parents, Ana and Carlos, who instilled a love for reading from a very young age and nurtured my endless curiosity—mischief and all.

Then, there's my family, who suffered through endless book talk. When frustration flared, my daughter offered me chocolate. The cats waited their turn to take over my chair, and our beloved Chihuahua simply slept by my feet.

I am deeply grateful for Michelle, my chosen sister, who walked this path with me. A dear friend, lunch provider, coffee-bringer, and the one who kept me on the straight and narrow when I felt like giving up on the idea of being a published author.

I also want to thank Alice Creswell, Ana, Deborah, Noelle, Nick, Margaret, and Robin, who beta-read the series and provided invaluable feedback that improved the story. I am grateful to Rebecca Scharpf from Scroll Work Edits, Poppy Kuroki from Kuroki Books, and Sophie Huhn from Silver River Publishing for their thorough editing and proofreading.

To everyone who reviewed *The Dandelion Tree, Part One*, you've made my world shine brighter.

We write to share our stories with the world; you discovered mine. I am forever grateful for your support and encouragement.

A.S.R. Gelpi

PRAISE FOR A.S.R. GELPI

An extraordinary hero energizes a measured but absorbing fantasy.

— KIRKUS REVIEWS

"The Dandelion Tree: Part One" is a spellbinding meditation on power, grief, and the quiet defiance of a cursed soul. Kharis's journey unfolds like poetry etched in shadow—layered, deliberate, and full of aching humanity. With every choice, the stakes deepen, not just for the world she inhabits, but for the woman she's struggling to become. Darkly lyrical and emotionally fierce, this is fantasy for those who crave soul-deep stakes over spectacle, and strength that looks like survival.

— NEWINBOOKS.COM

"Destiny rarely asks for permission; it arrives dressed as duty and leaves with your heart." The Dandelion Tree, Part One, by A.S.R. Gelpi, is a fantastic novel that harnesses its fantasy elements to the truly complicated emotions of guilt, grief, and love. Kharis is and has always been portrayed authentically, but her reconciling of trauma and the desire for redemption feels so much more strikingly real here.

— READERS' FAVORITE

Once again, ASR Gelpi has woven a mesmerizing tale of magic, adventure, political intrigue, forbidden love, and powerful heroines. From the very first page, I was completely enthralled, and I cannot wait for the next installment!

— ERIKA SAPPIA, NETGALLEY ARC REVIEWER
@ERIKAREADSNOVELS

Find your cozy reading spot and immerse yourself in this story.

— ALICE CRESWELL, AUTHOR, THE TIME MERCHANT

I just want to say WOW! This one, so far, is by far my favorite. Quite literally, blew me out of the water. Intriguing and well-written... this one SUCKED ME IN!

— ROBIN DEGAN, AUTHOR

The story is engaging, the characters are defined excellently, the worldbuilding is explained naturally without breaking the story's pace, and the way the story is presented leaves little for confusion.

— A. CASTON, BETA READER

A beautifully crafted fantasy that weaves together magic, destiny, and an unbreakable sisterly bond.

— R. VRÁBELOVÁ, NETGALLEY REVIEWER

Spectacular world-building and wonderful character development.

— AMANDA ROCHELLE, NET GALLEY REVIEWER

A beautifully depicted world with exceptionally well-done characters and rich storytelling that is so immersive.

— ABBIE RIDDLE, NETGALLEY REVIEWER

ABOUT THE AUTHOR

A.S.R. Gelpi began penning fantastical tales to entertain classmates (and scare teachers... OK, not all of them, right, Mr. Cumbie?). While her dreams of fictional realms took a backseat to her academic pursuits, which included earning her a Ph.D., the magic never truly faded. Instead, it simmered, waiting for its moment to burst forth.

After a few years of scholarly endeavors, A.S.R. Gelpi embraced her inner storyteller again, weaving her academic prowess with her boundless imagination to pen "The Dandelion Chronicles" series. Each page is a testament to her unwavering love for the fantastical, brimming with intricate characters, richly detailed worlds, and mythical lore that captivates the reader. These aren't just books—they're a culmination of years of passion, dedication, and dream-chasing.

When A.S.R. Gelpi is not engrossed in her literary worlds, you'll find her devouring books, jotting down her next imaginative concept, indulging in anime, videogaming with her kids, exploring hiking trails, pedaling through mountain bike routes, battling an occasional dragon, or soaking in the breathtaking vistas of Yosemite National Park.

Join her on this enchanting journey, where every moment invites you to dream.

ALSO BY A.S.R. GELPI

A Land of Shadows and Moss

The Dandelion Tree, Part One

Kharis's journey is just beginning—stay tuned for upcoming books!

The Dandelion Tree, Part Two (October 2025)

A Land of Mist and Loss (February 2026)

www.ingramcontent.com/pod-product-compliance
Lightning Source LLC
Chambersburg PA
CBHW031023030726
47497CB00004B/972